JASON STRIKER
MARTIAL ARTS
SERIES VOLUME I

28-ANTH

JASON STRIKER

MARTIAL ARTS

SERIES VOLUME I

Kiai! and Mistress of Death

Piers Anthony and Roberto Fuentes

28-ANTH

To order additional copies of this book, contact:
Xlibris Corporation
1-888-7-XLIBRIS
www.Xlibris.com
Orders@Xlibris.com

CONTENTS

MISTRESS OF DEATH

CHAPTER 1

KIAI!

I was afraid. I saw him from the edge of my eye, and it was as though the *kiai* yell had exploded around me. My muscles trembled, my heart beat rapidly, and I felt the thin smear of cold sweat. My strength deserted me, and I wanted to hide.

But my class was before me, standing barefoot in a great half-circle on the *tatami*, the judo practice mat. The preliminary calisthenics and limbering exercises were over and my students were ready for the formal instruction. They were young, mostly; some were only fifteen years old, and most were under twenty. But many were apt; several were brown belts already, and more showed promise. Next month I meant to take my top three candidates to the examinations for *shodan,* the first-degree black belt, and I expected two of them to make it with points to spare.

I fought for control, and in an instant I had it, superficially.

"Pair off!" I cried, forcing volume from my tight throat. "Alternate on the sweeping ankle throw. And yell when you hit the mat! *Saaaa!* I want noise!"

Noise to cover my own confusion, to conceal the horrible weakness I felt. I needed time to recover, to work it out. But not in front of my judo class.

They paired, they took hold, they threw, they landed, they yelled. This was routine for the experienced students, who were showing the clumsy beginners how. The sweeping ankle throw is easy to grasp in theory, but difficult to perfect. Timing is vital. But it absorbed their attention and gave me an essential respite.

It would not have been good to have the class become aware that Jason Striker, their fifth-degree black belt instructor and one-time U.S. judo grand-champion was quaking with something very like terror.

I watched them, but my mind was years away.

Diago. Diago had been a flaming meteorite fifteen years ago. A small man, even for a Japanese—though he was only half Japanese—but quick and strong and determined and amazingly skilled. He had skipped several of the beginning *kyus*, the student grades, then moved up the black belt ladder with phenomenal rapidity, winning most matches in bare seconds. He was rough, leaving many injuries in his wake, but there was no evidence that he broke bones deliberately. He struck with such devastating effectiveness that mortal substance seemed unable to withstand the punishment. Soon he was *godan*, fifth degree, one of the leading judokas in the world—and he was only twenty-three.

Then his career slowed. His ability remained, but few men cared to meet him in contest. This was common sense, not cowardice. Injury can destroy the career of a judoka, and the conventions that militated against physical damage did not seem to be operative with Diago.

Still, in four more years he made *rokudan*, the sixth degree, and assumed the coveted red and white striped belt. No other non-Japanese held that rank at that time, yet it did not appear to be his limit. Diago's only liability was that roughness—-but that was enough to make him unwelcome around the world, despite universal acclaim for his prowess.

Generally when a man achieves such distinction he eases up, growing old gracefully while the younger judokas contest for points. Degrees higher than sixth *dan* normally go to those who have done genuine and continuing service to the art, rather than for victories on the mat. But there was one *rokudan* who was not content to rest. At forty-two Masaki Tanaka was still contending, though age was beginning to tell. Perhaps he was resentful of Diago's progress and reputation, and determined to show the world that fifteen years did not make a difference. Or that Diago was overrated.

At any rate, the two sixth-degree belts met in a highly publicized contest—and it was Tanaka who got a *kansetsu-waza,* a standing arm bar, on Diago's left elbow. Diago tried to escape by making an immediate forward somersault, but it was already too late; he succeeded only in wrenching his own shoulder. They fell together—and Diago's joint popped out just as both men landed crushingly on that arm.

The mischief was about as devastating as was possible in the few seconds the accident took. Diago's wrist, elbow and shoulder were dislocated and the tendons wrenched.

Diago had been served as he had served others. Some said old Tanaka could have let up in time, had he wanted to; others pointed out that his reactions were bound to be slower at that age, and that Diago was a dangerous opponent who could be afforded no leeway. The very speed of Diago's countermove, that violent somersault in place, had been stunning; instinct would have governed Tanaka's decision, nothing else.

The referees called no foul, and that was the verdict, officially. Diago was finished. He healed, but his magic was gone. He could still compete against lesser *dans,* but lacked the power to go higher. He dropped out of sight.

Masaki Tanaka, too, retired. It was as if he were ashamed of what he had done, but could not admit it. He had broken the code in spirit if not in letter, and that was a shameful thing for such a highly ranked *sensei,* a judo instructor. He never fought again. And he never boasted of his victory.

Five years later Diago reappeared—with a new weapon. He had perfected a *kiai* yell that was devastating. When he stood up to a man and screamed that scream, that man was stunned even though braced against it. For only a second, of course—but an instant of immobility was all Diago ever needed. He had his hold, and with it his victory.

Where had Diago been? Where had he learned that *kiai* yell? He could not have developed such a unique weapon himself. A local trainer who ran a *dojo* not far from mine, Dato, claimed *he* had taught Diago the yell. But Dato couldn't do the yell himself, and nobody credited his story. Dato was past his prime, quarrelsome, and always alert for notoriety—hardly a credit to judo, though in his youth he had been an outstanding player. He had been the first to set up shop in this region, and seemed to resent those of us who had come more recently, calling us squatters on his territory. Maybe if he'd been willing to teach all he knew, he'd have less concern about the competition. But many old-time Japanese *senseis* always held their finest arts back, lest their students become more proficient than they and beat them. In the centuries when students might indeed kill their instructors and take over, this was a necessary precaution, but today it could only hurt judo. No, Dato, even if he knew how to teach that yell, would not have given it away to Diago.

Another suggestion was that Diago had gone to Japan, to the island of Hokkaido, to study under one of the deranged ninjitsu mystics, Fu Antos. (Dato, of course, claimed to have studied under Fu Antos himself. But this, too, was the stuff of dreams. If Fu Antos existed at all, he was a harmless ancient, unable to impart any of the ninja techniques along with ninja's fabulous lore.)

Whether Diago remained the judoka he had been, no one could say. But his *kiai* was more than sufficient. He was now more careful of the welfare of others, and was able to compete in more matches. In the ensuing three years he earned the seventh degree: *shichidan.*

Then his fortune took another fall. Though born in Japan of a Japanese mother, Diago was in essence American. His father, a waiter in the American embassy, had U.S. citizenship, and Diago evidently felt a strong inclination toward this country. Between matches he roamed alone. There was an incident in a ghetto, and two men died. Diago said it was self-defense against an attempted mugging, but the prosecutor claimed it was murder. Diego was tried, and the evidence seemed inconclusive, but he was convicted. It was whispered that he would have gotten off if he had not been half-black. Or if he had been tried in Japan, where his martial skills had a following. But it had happened in America, a nation backward in the martial arts.

He escaped. The police guards had thought guns and hand-cuffs sufficient but had not reckoned with his terrible yell. They transferred him from one van to another, and one of them shoved him contemptuously, and Diago stunned them with his voice and knocked them down with the metal chain that manacled his wrists. He used his handcuffs to break the skull of one and crush the cheekbone of the other. Now there were more counts against him, but he was gone.

For two years Diago had stayed lost, and it was generally thought that he was out of the country. But I had heard other rumors. America might have treated him shabbily, but his heart remained here. Some of the leading black belts in large cities had turned up mysteriously injured. They claimed these were mere training accidents, but I had watched Diago fight in the old days, before his *kiai,* and I recognized the pattern.

Now he had entered my club, and I knew.

*

There is a camaraderie among black belts that goes beyond mere courtesy. Any *sensei* can enter any judo club anywhere in the world and be granted the hospitality of the premises. If he needs help, he will have it. If he wants to work out, he will be accommo-dated. If the club happens to be short-handed, he will assist. He does not attempt to embarrass his host, and it is always friendly. This is the nature of this truly international society of the martial elite.

But Diago was no ordinary judoka. He had killed, and he stood convicted for murder. He was a criminal. To help him was to become an accessory. I believed in my country and in the law; I knew my duty.

Yet there were so many questions about that conviction. People do get mugged in ghettos, and the law there is scant; people do sometimes have to kill in self defense. If two armed men jumped me in a dark alley, I'd react violently. I'd lay them out any way I could, because any weapon is dangerous, and most particularly a gun. If I ever killed a man, this would be how. And Diago had a violent disposition.

Half yellow, half black, and the law, unfortunately, not always color-blind. Perhaps the white jury had been unfairly predisposed. Diago *had* stood still for justice; in fact, he had originally turned himself in. But what he had received had not necessarily been justice.

Oh, he should not have broken and run, and he certainly should not have bashed a policeman in the process. He should have appealed his case to a higher court. Our legal system has its strengths, and the appeals system is one of them. Still, he had been raised in the Orient; it was hard to blame him completely.

Now he was here. I had to choose between three: help him, turn him in, or ignore him. The law denied the first, and I had never before broken the law. I'd never even gotten a parking violation. The very thought of it shocked me. Yet my own conscience forbade the second alternative. And I suspected he would not let me get away with the third. Those injured judokas . . .

This was my real fear, I saw now as I worked it out objectively: not the man himself, but the ugly choice his presence forced on me. Even if I pretended not to know him, I would be shading both the ethics of my patriotism and the courtesy of my profession. Traitor, either way or neither.

So I quaked while my class drifted, hung on the horns of an ethical dilemma. I saw my honor inevitably compromised, and my career damaged, for I could not continue in judo without self respect.

I glanced about——and he caught my eye. Then I knew I could not temporize. Diago had come to me, and he knew that I knew him. He would not let me pass him by.

I had to act. But still I could not.

Jim, my bull-necked young assistant, realized something was wrong. I was letting the class practice the same movement too long. Practice is imperative in judo, but these students needed variety too, or their attention flagged. None of this three months drilling on the horse stance to the exclusion of all else, the way an apprentice to the martial art of kung-fu might start. I'd lose half my class if I drilled them for three *hours* on one position!

Jim was a good boy, a *shodan* at nineteen who would soon make the second degree black belt. He was one of my most promising students, and he worked hard with weight-lifting on the side to strengthen himself, but he was still impetuous. You have to act quickly, in judo—but you have to know when to wait, too, and that was where he sometimes slipped. I didn't want him getting involved with Diago.

Now Jim approached as if summoned. "Want me to spell you for a bit, *Sensei?*" he asked eagerly.

"Yes!" I said, relieved. I glanced again at Diago, unable to help myself, and Jim followed that look.

"Who's that fellow?" he asked. "Seems to me I've seen him before somewhere."

"Never mind!" I snapped. "It's a——a private matter."

He nodded dubiously, comprehending my attitude if not its root. I had told him this was not his business, and professional courtesy required him to stay out of it. That was part of the discipline of judo, a discipline I had tried to impress on him, and on all my students, many times.

Jim faced the class. "Stop!" he barked, and they stopped. "Now gather round for a demonstration!" He really liked being *sensei*, and actually he wasn't bad at it.

They came, sweating from their exertions, and in the confusion I slipped away. Jim would keep them occupied for the duration, probably on hand throws, his current favorite. As with the ankle throws, timing was essential, so the novice seldom succeeded; but at Jim's level the challenge was irresistible. He thought every level should perfect these techniques.

I walked to my private office. I knew Diago followed.

I turned to face him. Suddenly. I saw a fourth alternative. Honorable—but dangerous. The only one for me.

"I greet you, Diago," I said.

"And I you, Jason Striker," he replied with perfect courtesy. One of the things that outsiders seldom appreciate about judo, or any martial art, is that respect and courtesy increase with proficiency. A man capable of killing another with a single blow will take extreme precautions to avoid the necessity of doing so, being most considerate of the feelings of others. A bully is normally an ignoramus about combat.

"You need help? Go to Dato," I suggested, though that was not my real notion. "He claims to have taught you."

"Dato!" he barked with rich contempt. "He went to Hokkaido, and came away empty-handed."

So I had shot down one rumor, but I still didn't know where Diago had learned his *kiai*. Well, it was none of my business.

But this was: "Why didn't you use your *kiai* to stun those muggers? You didn't have to kill them."

"I had a cold. Laryngitis. I could not even warn them off. They thought I was tongue-tied with fright."

There it was: the last bastion of my doubt about his guilt. How could he have reasoned with criminals intent on mayhem when he couldn't even talk? So I was justified in giving him an even break. "Let's do *shiai*," I said.

He only nodded. Master judokas do not deceive one another. We would meet on the *tatami* in a practice match. If he beat me, I would provide what he needed and keep silent, regardless of the law. If I beat him, I could report him to the police with a clear conscience, having earned the right. It was not necessary to voice these terms; they were inherent in the situation. In fact, it was important that there be no specific commitment, for who else would understand? Certainly not the law.

I gave him a *judogi*, a judo kimono, jacket and trousers. He stripped immediately, setting his worn suit neatly aside. He was small and dark, with a flat Japanese face and somewhat frizzy Negro hair. And he was less muscular than I had expected. He looked hungry; probably he had gone without many meals before being driven to this alternative. That left my feelings mixed. I was in the peak of condition, having worked out daily for many years and participated in regular *shiais*, or meets, apart from my erstwhile championship days. Thirty is not old for a judoka, and I was larger than he. If he were physically debilitated, I might beat him, for there is no substitute for conditioning. But that would be a cheap victory, unworthy of me.

Still, it was his voice that made him what he was. And his experience. He was seven years older than I, and held one of the highest degrees in the world today. That skill and that experience could not be discounted. In fact, I was doomed—unless I could withstand his terrible cry. I had never actually heard it myself, for we had not met during his later period, but I had no reason to believe I would be immune. Diago did not need to be in top shape, if he retained his *kiai.*

He was ready: naked under the baggy *judogi,* as was I. Any clothing at all is a hindrance in judo, and even more so in karate and other disciplines. It can get in the way in case of injury, and it restrains free motion and offers purchase for the opponent's grips. But men do not fight naked in America.

Diago lifted a student's white belt from my shelf and knotted it about his waist. This was a necessary artifice; his own belt would have given his identity away immediately. White is also the color of nonregistered judokas of any skill: those who have the physical ability to compete, but have not acquired the proper formal credits for black belt degrees.

We walked to the large training room. The instruction had progressed to hip throws, and the paired-off students were going at it with vigor.

"*Ma-te!*" I bawled from the sideline, and they all halted and fell back while Diago and I marched to the center of the great mat.

Jim looked at us curiously, suspecting that Diago was no rank amateur. "Announce a *shiai,*" I told him. "Myself and this anonymous challenger, who is of equivalent grade."

Jim shook his head in surprise, for no such demonstration had been scheduled tonight. But he knew the camaraderie of the black belt. If for some reason a skilled visitor wished to match the instructor before his class, and the instructor was amenable, no one else could complain.

Jim explained the situation as he understood it to the class, and cautioned them to watch carefully in case techniques new to them were employed. "Don't be deceived by the challenger's white belt," he said with a finishing flourish. "He is not a student, as you will see when the match begins." As though he knew all about it. Then he turned to us, inquiring with his eyes whether we wished him to serve as referee, and Diago nodded.

We commenced with the full ceremonial bow, the *zarei.* I faced Diago, about six feet away, and both of us kneeled, placing our hands on the mat before our knees and inclining our bodies forward until the tops of our heads pointed toward each other. Then we stood.

"*Hajime!*" Jim cried, signifying the start of the match.

I approached Diago cautiously. *Now it comes!* I thought. The *kiai* yell, the sound that stunned. The scream no other man had been able to duplicate or resist. In this confined space there could be no escape from it. If I covered my ears I would lay myself open for any of a hundred devastating attacks, and, strangely, the ears were not necessarily the prime vulnerability. One man had plugged his ears, and had still been stunned. There seemed to be nonauditory waves, perhaps subsonics that chilled the flesh and brought terror without reason.

But I was hardly going to wait for him. I tried for a conventional hand grip, my right holding Diago's lapel, my left grasping for his right sleeve. Normally several grips were tried before either party attempted a throw, grappling for some advantage. But Diago moved with surprising swiftness, bringing up his right arm and throwing his right shoulder into me. It was the *seoi-nage,* the shoulder throw, very well executed. But he had tried too soon; I retained my balance, and I was heavier than he.

Even so, he almost threw me, despite the years I had drilled my students in this very motion and the mode of countering it. My left foot lifted from the mat momentarily; then I threw myself to the rear, hauling him back over me. As we fell I whipped my right hand under Diago's chin, putting pressure on his windpipe with the edge of my wrist. He struggled to right himself, but I got my left arm around to assist the pull of my right, and at the same time wrapped my legs around his waist and squeezed.

Diago was caught. Now he could not use his shout, because of the pressure I was applying to his throat. But he supported his weight on his right leg, arching his body back in a bridge, easing the pressure. He had a bull neck, like Jim's; most men would have been unconscious by this time, and that put me off my guard. I have never been one to hurt a man gratuitously, and the choke hold is deadly.

Diago passed his left leg above my two, then threaded his right through to brace against it, applying pressure to mine. The pain was sudden and awful; this was a semi-legal submission hold, and in order to win free I had to release my stranglehold and stand up.

First contact had been a draw. My class applauded, though they could not have comprehended the key aspects.

"Hajime!" Jim called. I knew that he, at least, had been watching very closely, noting how Diago's neck had served him. Jim believed in strong necks.

We grappled again, trying for good hand-holds, contesting for the initial advantage. I was certain that this time he would use the shout, for my weight and strength were far beyond his. The first exercise had demonstrated that. He had to get an early advantage, and his voice was his one certain means. But again I gave him no time to set up for it. I went for my favorite move, *uchimata*, the inner thigh throw. My right leg went deep between his legs, and I lifted him into the air. He went easily-—too easily, I realized too late.

For Diago, catlike, had maneuvered to fall on his side in a sacrifice throw, and now he had hold of me, using my momentum to counter me to the front. He led me into the *uki-waza*, or floating throw. It was a beautiful move, and I heard my students exclaiming in amazement. They had never seen a man recover from my *uchimata* like that.

Small wonder! Neither had I.

Meanwhile, Diago's left leg was blocking mine. I was hauled off balance and thrown over his head as he lay on the mat. My elbow struck his face, accidentally; the blow was hard enough to send a shock up my forearm and momentarily paralyze the hand. I struck the wall and fell outside the contest area, so the fall did not count.

I sat up. Pain lanced through my neck and shoulder and chest. It felt like a heart attack. But it could not be, I told myself. Not at my age! It was an injury of some sort, sustained in the fall.

I should have stopped, then. But I'm ornery when hurt, and I didn't want my students to know how much in trouble I was. I felt the sweat dripping from me-—not just exertion sweat.

"Hajime!" Jim called a third time, signaling the continuation of the match. There was real excitement in his voice; he was agog as any novice, witnessing a performance he could only begin to hope to equal some year. He would have been less impressed if he knew how my chest pained me.

Then I saw Diago's face. There was blood streaming from a cut over the eye, and the eye itself was bloodshot and already swelling shut. My elbow-—I had smashed him in the eye!

I would have called it off, but realized that Diago was like me:

he would not quit in adversity. Evidently Jim had not seen the injury; Diago's face was away from him.

A third time we closed, and this time I *knew*. I could afford neither to wait nor to close precipitously. Diago was consumately skilled, ready for anything I could do. But my strength and endurance were bound to bring him down soon if he did not act. Already his reactions were slowing, and he was panting. Judo is no sport for the out-of-condition; even a month of idleness hurts, and I knew now that Diago had been slack for at least a year, as far as really disciplined physical practice went. He knew his moves, but he was weak, weak. He had no choice.

Unless he had recognized my own incapacity. My shoulder was hurting worse; what had that fall done to me?

His mouth opened. I flinched—and shamed myself for my cowardice. He was on me then with another sacrifice, a *tomoe-nage* stomach throw. He went down on his back, his foot in my belly, ready to flip me over his head. But voiding such a move was almost instinctive with me. I shoved his foot to one side while dropping down on my stomach to lower my center of gravity. He lacked the force and leverage to throw me that way. I slipped down on top of him, seizing his lapel and punching my fist against his throat. This time I was sure I had him.

But I had underestimated him again. Diago was a master of groundwork. He slipped his leg in front of my arm and grabbed my wrists with both his hands. It was the *jujigatame,* an armlock against my elbow. The pressure was tremendous. I felt my arm giving, and I knew I would have to slap the mat in surrender or suffer a broken arm. This was the way so many had gone before, holding out a moment too long against this inflexible adversary. I had lost; better to admit it, than to throw away my career.

But that weakness of his gave me that tiny leeway I needed, and I managed to grab his lapel with my other arm. Immediately I shifted my weight, ignoring the agony this brought to my locked elbow, and got my bare feet on the *tatami*. I stood. Onehanded I brought him up with me so that his back lifted free of the mat. He had to let go, otherwise I would bring him all the way up and slam him down hard, and he was in no condition to absorb that punishment.

So the third bout also ended in a draw. I was breathing hard, but I was ready for more despite the agony in my chest.

"*Hajime!*" Jim shouted, breathless himself. My students were straining forward raptly. They had seen how close I had come to defeat, and they could not know what the end would be. Neither could I.

I approached, but Diago smiled and shook his head in negation, drops of blood flying from his face and staining the *tatami*. We had tried three falls, and drawn three, and he had had enough.

"*Soremade, Hiki-wake!*" Jim yelled. "End of match. Draw!" Then he did a double-take, as he saw Diago's eye. "What happened?"

Diago and I bowed formally, terminating *shiai*, and the audience applauded. He walked back to the office to change. I knew he would not see a doctor about the eye. How could he, with a price on his head? But I was under no such restriction. I gestured to Dr. Cue, an M.D. who was taking the course without charge in return for his availability. He had helped me with injured students many times.

Jim was already recapitulating the fine points of the encounter for the benefit of the students. They had seen real judo today.

"You have a broken collar-bone," Dr. Cue said, after he examined me. "You'll have to rest up for a couple of weeks."

"I will!" I said, relieved that I was not going to drop from a heart attack. I had been lucky to finish the match. "But don't spread it around; it would look bad to my students."

He nodded wisely, not commenting on my vanity. "Should I also take a look at your friend?"

"You could try. He may not let you. But that eye——"

A few minutes later we had the students lining up for joint exercises when Diago reappeared in his street clothes. The eye had been cleaned up somewhat, but was now swollen completely shut. I was sorry about that; I had not meant to hurt him. "I gave him a shot to relieve the pain," Dr. Cue murmured in my ear. "The eye will be all right."

"Thanks," I said. Dr. Cue could keep his mouth shut.

I left Diago alone, deliberately. But Jim took another look, and something clicked. "Hey! Isn't that—"

"Forget it!" I rapped. "He's going away. We don't know him."

"Like hell we don't!" Then Jim looked at me, comprehending. "So that was why you had the match! He wanted you to—-"

"What other way was there?" I demanded brusquely.

"Why didn't he shout?" Then he answered his own question. "He's weak! He must have lost it. He had no weapon against you."

"None but his seventh degree skill," I said with some irony. "Do you think I could have matched him in his prime? Anyway, we don't know that his voice is gone. He can talk well enough." But I wasn't satisfied myself with that, and had to work it out further. "I met him with honor; maybe he respected that. He's seen little enough fair treatment the past couple years, especially from white men. Must be very important to him, that camaraderie of the elite. It is to *me,* and just the thought of losing it terrifies me." Jim. would take that as an overstatement, but I had just experienced that terror. "One thing I know: he's no coward and no quitter. And he's still good."

"I can't accept that! I could beat him myself, the way he is now!"

Big ambitions! "Maybe so. It's still a draw where it counts. Let's get the class moving again."

But I saw Diago making his way toward the exit, looking tired, and already I regretted my professed indifference. I had shown him respect, and he had responded in kind. He could not be the criminal others claimed. Perhaps it is illusion, but when I know a man on the mat, I feel I *know* him.

I almost called to Diago, then, wanting to extend my hospitality and damn the consequence.

I glanced about, startled. In my moment of preoccupation Jim had run after Diago, catching him at the door and whirling him about before he could make his escape. "I know you!" Jim cried. "You can't just walk out! You're wanted for——"

Then it blasted out like a strike of lightning: that eerie, appalling, devastating sound. I stood transfixed as it echoed from the walls, pressing against my ear-drums, tingling my skin, hurting my teeth, constricting my throat. Like the maddened roar of a pouncing tiger, like the hiss of a striking python, like the wail of a banshee, like the nearby burst of a concussion grenade——no! Like none of these cliches, like nothing I could imagine, that awful scream resounded through flesh and brain and spirit, freezing me in place. *KIAI!*

I blinked, catching my balance. Jim had fallen to the floor. The lines of students were in disarray, the youngsters shaking their heads, dazed and frightened. My heart was pounding madly. And Diago was gone.

CHAPTER 2

THERA

The phone rang. Right away I recognized the atrocious English: Dato, my rival judo instructor.

"Thief!" he screamed in a high voice, almost a falsetto. "You steal my pupils! You suffer!"

"I don't know what you're talking about," I told him as calmly as I could. But it is hard to be hit with a screaming accusation like that without bristling some, and this was not the first time Dato had accused me of some devious crime. For the sake of the good name of judo I tried to keep the peace, but sometimes I was privately tempted to give him a good old-fashioned unscientific rap in the chops. "None of my students are—"

"Smith! Smith! Smith!" he cried. "Smith Charles! You bribe him away!"

I untangled the name. In Japan, the surname comes first, and Dato had never fully acclimatized to the American system despite his decades in this country. Perhaps he considered it barbaric; more likely he simply didn't care. "Charles Smith? I have no student by that name."

"And on top of your thievery, you lie to me!" he cried. "You will pay for this, Striker Jason! You can not fool me. You—-"

I cut him off. I had trouble just making ends meet without quarreling over imaginary issues with my associates.

The phone rang back immediately. I snatched it up. "Listen, Dato, bother me again and I'll swear out a complaint!"

"Do you want my business or don't you?" a strange voice interjected.

Abashed, I apologized. "I thought you were someone else. Uh, who *are* you?"

"I am Johnson Drummond, of Drummond Industries," he said. "Nobody else, ever. And you'd better be Jason Striker."

Drummond, the multi-millionaire. Hastily I admitted my identity. It was well that I did, for he came bearing money. Maybe my luck had turned.

*

A pretty girl in tight faded jeans answered the bell. "I'm Jason Striker," I said. "Judo instructor. Mr. Drummond arranged——"

"Sure!" she said brightly around her quid of gum. "Come on in."

I trailed her flexing derriere through the foyer and down a richly carpeted hall. It was not news to me that Johnson Drummond had money. Everything from the elaborate hedgework in the palisaded grounds to the art originals on the walls strengthened the suggestion of pelf. Everything except this extraordinarily informal maid.

She opened a door with a nonchalant sideways thrust and faced me, standing within the arch. "This is the rumpus room. Okay?"

I peered beyond her perky young bosom to inspect the chamber. It was palatial. "Needs a mat," I said. "I explained to Mr. Drummond that——"

"So we'll fetch a mat!" she said, and beckoned me with a familiar twitch of four fingers as she moved out.

This time her winking bottom was nose-level as I followed her up steep, narrow winding stairs. I was tempted to slap it.

We emerged into an upstairs hallway and entered a plush master bedroom with a custom round bed. She began ripping off the sheets.

What kind of help did Drummond hire? "I said mat, not mattress," I said. "The *tatami*: oblong, not round. Three feet by six feet. Several are put together for practice."

"Cool it, baby. The order hasn't come yet." She tugged at the great circle of padding. "Come on, big boy. I can't get it downstairs all by myself."

"I think I'd better talk to Miss Drummond," I said.

She stared at me a moment with that strange feminine wide-eyed mock-innocence. Then her cheeks puffed out as though she were sick, or laughing. She flopped indecorously on the bed with her head in my direction and lay looking up at me.

"Oh, I see," I said heavily. "Well, we'll dispense with the mat this time. Do you have a *judogi—-a* practice uniform?"

"That's on order too," she said, her breasts heaving with half-suppressed mirth.

"Then this will have to be a lecture session. Let's go on down to the practice room."

"Lecture!" she exclaimed, making a wry face. "You're supposed to teach me self-defense." But she came.

I faced her. "Now, Miss Drummond, the first thing to understand about judo—-"

"Call me Thera. That's my name, you know. It's from the Greek, meaning 'untamed.'"

"All right, Thera. Now you may think of judo as purely a defensive technique, but in fact—-"

"Thera is an island in the Aegean. It blew up in 1450 B.C., destroying the civilization of—-"

"But in fact judo is also an art and a sport of international repute, as well as a way of life. It is well worth doing well, even if your interest is only—-"

"Oh, let's go for a cheeseburger and shake."

"Miss Drummond," I said firmly. "Your father is paying fifty dollars an hour for these lessons."

She turned abruptly. "Because I'm going to college this fall and he's afraid I'll get raped. He's not sure I can handle men."

"You're not interested in learning judo?"

"I just don't think it's necessary. I mean, this is supposed to be the twentieth century."

I sighed silently. I had taken this tutoring assignment because it represented a handy chunk of cash at a time I was short. A six-week crash course in self-defense, fifteen hundred dollars, paid in advance. If I dropped it now, I would have to make a refund, and part of it had already been sunk in the rent.

But more than that, my pride was suffering. This girl knew nothing about judo and wasn't interested in learning. My fifth degree black belt meant nothing to her.

"If you don't like me, there are other judo instructors, all competent," I said somewhat stiffly.

"You utter dope!" she said. "Don't you know why Daddy hired you?"

"I presume he found my credentials satisfactory."

"We have a black sheep branch of the family. Second cousins, I think. We don't even know they exist, officially, and we never interact socially. But on this one thing Daddy wanted pro advice, so he asked Diago."

"Diago!"

"That's right," she said. "It's diluted, but we're blood relations. Same great-grandfather on the Caucasian side. He likes to claim he's half Japanese and half black, but the black's half white."

"He came to my *dojo*," I said, things falling into place.

She shrugged indifferently. "Is that your judo shop, you mean? He must've been checking out the local scene, after Daddy paid his way here. It had to be quiet, 'cause Diago's in some kind of trouble with the law, but what he knows, he *knows,* Daddy says. I guess you passed."

I didn't know whether to be relieved or furious. Sending a man like Diago just to check me out.

"All right," I said. "Cheeseburger and shake."

"Ninety seconds," she said as she disappeared.

Out of curiosity, I checked my watch, setting the bezel. Thera was very nearly as good as her word. In just under two minutes she returned, fetchingly dressed in blouse, jumper and bobbie-soxer shoes. A yellow ribbon held back her brown hair. How she had done it all in that time I didn't know, but I had to admit that she had really brought out her distaff assets. I had forgotten how pretty seventeen could be.

"I'll drive," she said.

I shrugged. It was her show, at fifty-dollars-an-hour. All I wanted was a chance to get her offstage and relaxed so that I could get through to her about judo. Because I could see that I did have things to teach her. If anybody was going to need the womanly art of self-defense in college or in life, she was the one. She was a rich vamp who thought male-female was no more than a game.

She had a high-powered sport car, of course, with an inverted silver Y circled on the hood. I hung on as she tooled it through midmorning traffic, and I felt insecure even in the shoulder harness.

It was no hamburger shop she parked beside. The lighted sign said **CALVIN'S BAR.**

"Not here!" I said. But she had already jumped out of the open car while I fumbled with the unfamiliar harness. She was pushing through the door, and I had to follow.

It was dark inside, and I didn't spot her immediately. The decor was red, the bartender big and black. Now I knew the game Thera was playing, but there was no polite way out of it.

I tapped on the counter. Two miniskirted B-girls, blonde and redhead, glanced my way, but I fixed my stare on the man. "The girl is underage," I said.

Bartenders are wary of such statements. "Who are you?" he demanded.

I laid down my card. Now I could see well enough in the twilight.

He squinted at the paper, then at me, appraisingly. I knew he didn't want trouble; no bartender does, however tough he looks. Particularly not age trouble.

"Her?" he asked.

"Thera Drummond. Daughter of the founder of Drummond Industries." That was identification enough; Drummond was by far the largest local employer. "I'm supposed to be teaching her self-defense. Once I get her attention."

He decided I was legitimate. He glanced nervously into the back where there were several small tables and chairs. Thera was there, talking with a pair of husky college types. No wonder she had gotten herself up like a coed.

"Can you get her out quietly?" the bartender asked.

I shook my head dubiously. "She wants a scene."

"No rough stuff," he cautioned. "I don't want to blow the whistle, but——"

"I'll try." I walked to the corner.

Thera was watching me covertly, waiting to see what I'd do. I could guess what she had been telling the boys.

"My card," I said, setting one down on the table. "This girl is with me and she's underage."

Both boys stood aggressively. "That ain't the way we heard it!" the one on the left said.

I didn't fool with him. I put out my left hand and applied the *Shi atsu* grip, pinching his upper trapezius muscle between my thumb and fingers. I put pressure on the nerve center halfway between shoulder and neck, producing extreme pain. The Japanese name for the grip, loosely translated, means "pain hold."

"I'm sure you didn't mean to question my integrity," I said quietly, bearing down just enough to paralyze him. "Come to my club this afternoon for a free lesson, and no hard feelings. Okay?" I was giving him an out.

"S—sure!" the youth whispered, sweating.

I let him go. If there is one thing tough punks respect, it is superior force, and they know it when they experience it. I spoke to Thera: "More trouble from you, child, and I'll haul you out of here bottoms up!"

"Nice bluff," she said, seeming unconcerned. But I had gotten to her too, for she came out. If there is one thing the spoiled children of millionaire recluses dislike it is being made to look ridiculous in public. I had, in effect, put a pain hold on her pride.

*

Jim had to fill in for me in the morning class two days a week, because of the tutoring conflict. Mostly this was just a matter of warm-up and *uchi-komi* set throws, and I would make it back in time for the real instruction. I don't like to delegate that part of it, because they are in the end *my* students, nobody else's.

Jim also took care of the roll-call and much of the paperwork: registering new students, selling *judogi* uniforms, listing lesson payments and paying our bills. He taught the new students the basics, the first two or three lessons, saving my effort for the serious techniques. All part of learning how to run a successful judo club, which of course was his long-range ambition.

"New student, looks promising," he announced as I entered.

"Good! We need that kind! What's his name?"

"Charles Smith. He's had some prior training."

Something nagged me. "Where?"

"Dato's. He was there several months, but just didn't like the method. So he——"

"So that's the student I'm supposed to have stolen."

"Stolen?" Jim looked at me quizzically.

"Dato called me a few days ago, accusing me of——never mind. Dato's crazy." I paused. "But maybe I'd better have a talk with Charles Smith, just to get things straight."

"I'll point him out to your tomorrow," Jim said.

*

The next morning the mat was there, and so was Thera, in her *judogi* uniform. But her attitude had not improved.

"This is pointless," she said. "College isn't the jungle Daddy thinks. He never went himself."

"Maybe not," I said carefully. "I went only a couple of years. But you won't spend your whole life there. It's smart to know how to take care of yourself."

"I know as much as I need! Only stupid girls get raped."

"Any woman can run into trouble," I said. "If her car breaks down in a bad neighborhood, or if she's alone."

"Pooh!" she said, tossing her head. "All she has to do is lock her legs together and scream. And bite, if necessary."

I shook my head. "A man can overcome a woman, if he has the time and the privacy and the nerve." Not strictly true; it depended on the particular man and woman. But her foolish certainties annoyed me.

"That's a lie! *You* couldn't rape *me!*"

So that was her game today. Set me up for a demonstration, then scream rape.

"You teenagers have funny ideas," I said, emphasizing her youth again. "Do you really want a demonstration?"

"Sure," she said, eyeing me sidelong. "Try it."

I applied the *shi atsu* pain hold to her shoulder. "Try to scream," I suggested.

Thera opened her mouth and took a breath. I increased the pressure. Her lungs deflated, but she did not scream.

"Bite," I said.

She tried to turn her head to find flesh, but couldn't.

"Spread your legs," I said.

She resisted. This time I wasn't inhibiting her response, I was forcing her active cooperation, and that is much harder. But I pinched more firmly, giving her a real taste of what pain could be.

Tears beaded in her eyes, but still she held out. Slowly I tightened the grip yet more, centering directly on the nerve complex. She was in agony, I knew, but it was a necessary cruelty. "Spread," I repeated softly.

And slowly she spread.

I let her go. Thera fell away with a little anguished cry. She rubbed her shoulder and looked at me, smoldering.

"Would you like to learn the countermove?" I inquired innocently.

*

"So you're Charles Smith," I said. "Why did you leave Dato?"

The young man——a tousle-headed blond, not large but strong and graceful——shook his head. "If it's all the same to you, sir, I'd rather not talk about it."

"If it's all the same to *you*, don't call me 'sir,'" I said, smiling. "Okay, I know Dato, so you don't have to say anything there. But you ought to understand that he was most upset about your departure."

He looked at me sharply. "That's not true!"

"Uh-huh. Then why did he call me up and cuss me out about it?"

Smith shook his head in bewilderment. "That doesn't make sense! I *thought* he'd be mad when I told him it was my last day, but he wasn't. He was very calm about it. Wished me well and everything. So you must be wrong."

"He certainly *seemed* upset," I said. "Maybe he cooled off before you actually parted."

"Sir, I only talked with him the last day, at the end of the session. Couldn't bring myself to do it earlier. But I needn't have worried. And he didn't get mad later, either, because he asked me to come in the next day, no charge."

"What for? Dato gives nothing away free."

"He did this time, sir. He showed me several important blows, some deathblows too. Way beyond my present level. He really knows his stuff!" He paused. "I know what you're thinking. That he roughed me up. But he didn't. He was extremely nice. He explained each move and demonstrated it, not hard at all. Only one time he forgot and really hit me, and he apologized immediately. Said he was getting old, and had misjudged. And those blows are important, too. I'll be able to use them for self-defense, once I reach that proficiency. Now does that sound like anger or poor sportsmanship?"

I shook my head. "No, it doesn't. I must have misjudged Dato." But I wondered about that abusive call, that must have been made between the time Dato learned his prize student was leaving and his demonstration of those select judo blows. What did it mean?

I could imagine only one consistent pattern—and that was so ugly it was paranoid. I put it out of my mind, ashamed to harbor such a suspicion.

*

Thera's lessons went well enough thereafter. She was a healthy girl and well coordinated. She had gone the physical sports route, of course: horse riding, tennis, swimming and so on. She liked to excel, and that's a good attitude, when not pushed too hard.

But I suspected I had a price to pay for my early victories over her unruly will. Thera had seldom been curbed before, and it was possible she was merely biding her time before making some more effective move.

I didn't like the empty house. Not when I had an attractive seventeen-year-old girl to train. Judo entails considerable handling, necessarily; you can't throw anyone to the mat without physical contact. Certainly you can't initiate a complete novice without intimate demonstration.

No problem in itself, of course. That's my business: training people to be judokas, and to defend themselves. I have trained women and children. But always in the club. Always in the semi-public atmosphere of the class, where parents may freely enter and watch. There is no such thing as sexual temptation in such a situation. More importantly, there is no question of propriety, for there are many witnesses to every act of instruction. I have pinned beautiful women and felt their soft bosoms heaving under my body as they struggled to nullify my advantage; I have had their rounded resilient buttocks against my masculinity; I have been subjected to *kami-shiho-gatame,* my head locked between feminine thighs so that I smelled the odors of passion or of struggle while feeling her panting breath upon my private parts. What tales I might tell, if I were a tale-teller! But on the mat I am like a doctor: I observe without arousal.

Until this tutoring sequence.

"We'll start with *o-soto-gari,*" I said, taking my stance before her. "In English, that's 'major outer reaping.' It is an elementary judo throw."

I grasped her lapels, and with my right foot I swept her right leg out from under. She had to fall, but I let her down gently.

She landed and rolled. Her belt had gotten loose, and her jacket fell open. She wore no halter underneath. She lay for a moment on her back, one breast exposed.

I didn't comment. Dishabille happens, in judo. I've seen jackets torn off in the throes of matwork, and trousers yanked down, male and female. All one needs to do is get on one knee, dress again, retie the belt, and proceed as if nothing has happened. That way, nothing *has* happened.

But I had to admit, privately, that Thera had a fine figure. She was not voluptuous, and she was a bit scant in the bosom, as teenagers tend to be, but she was lithe and slim and strong and as nicely formed overall as I had seen. Ah, youth! No other age could match the splendid physical tone that came naturally to the newly mature. If only her temperament could be as pleasant.

"That was not a good landing," I said. "You hung onto me instead of striking the *tatami* with your hand. That way can make me lose my balance so that I fall on top of you, perhaps breaking your rib."

She nodded thoughtfully.

"Now I'll show you how to take a fall. Try o-soto-gari on me."

She got up and I showed her how to make the push and sweep, and I took a couple of dramatic spills for her, showing her how to break the fall without dislocating the elbow.

The next time she did it perfectly. She learned quickly.

It is possible to progress quite rapidly in judo, if the student is apt and industrious and if the instructor is competent. This is especially true in tutoring, for the instructor's whole attention is given to the one student. Thera worked hard, much harder than her original attitude had promised. When I told her to practice a particular motion, she *practiced* it, and next day she had it down pat. I gave her more difficult assignments, and she mastered these too. But she was not slavish about it; she asked intelligent questions, trying to grasp the purpose as well as the mechanics.

"Why is it so stylized?" she asked when I drilled her on the *katas*. "For self-defense, wouldn't it be better to get right into it and not give the guy a chance to counter?"

"For pure self-defense, yes," I admitted. "But this is not self-defense, now. This is training. Your object is to learn without being hurt, or hurting another. This formal drill will fix in your mind the proper response to any attack, so that you do it automatically in an emergency. And don't forget the sport aspect of judo. As with any other sport, the purpose is to demonstrate superiority without actually injuring your opponent or being injured by him. So it must be stylized to a certain extent, so that the moves can be exploited without danger. Attack and counter are done in set ways, and the man who performs best wins without damage. In a real fight, the superior man will still have the advantage of this skill, so nothing is lost."

"Hey, I see!" she exclaimed. "It's like fencing with caps on your foils!"

So she had fenced, too. "Pretty much," I agreed. It was becoming a real pleasure to work with her. But I remained alert for trouble, not trusting her moods.

In the fifth week of training I arrived to find her sitting in the middle of the *tatami*, her legs crossed in the yoga position, her hair hanging loose. She was nude.

"Meditation is good," I observed. "But this is practice time."

She pouted. "Don't you ever think about anything but judo?"

"Sure," I said lightly. "Karate, aikido, kung-fu, ninjitsu." But looking at her, I had urgent other thoughts. The muscle she had put on in the course of this training had filled out her thighs, cinched her waist, and lifted her breasts, forming her into a splendid figure of a woman. It is not true that muscle defeminizes; *flab* does. A truly healthy girl has more sex appeal than any bedroom-soft cow. Seventeen . . .

"Really?"

Of course she had me there. "I'm thinking about how much you'll need judo if you pull that stunt in the college gym."

"That must be a compliment," she said, her eyes serenely closed. "Thanks, I suppose. I knew I could get one if I worked at it for two years or less."

"Wisest not to shop too hard for sexual compliments," I warned. "Many a girl gets in trouble because of unwitting come-ons."

"Unwitting!" she exclaimed. "Do you need bi-focals?"

"I'm here to do a job."

Her eyes opened. "You've *done* it, Jason. Who could rape me now?" She paused, giving me a level gaze. "Except you, when you get the nerve." She touched her shoulder where I had demonstrated the pain hold, and smiled.

Fair enough. I had prepared her well to defend herself against that kind of attack, and soon she would be virtually——I smiled at my mental pun——impregnable. That was the point of this tutoring.

"And *you* wouldn't *have* to," she added, casting down her eyes.

I felt a reaction coming on, and I knew I couldn't afford body contact with her at this moment. In these weeks she had shown me some of what she could do when she really tried, and it was impressive, and I did like her. More than I ought to. I was hardly blind to the thirteen years between us, but now I perceived in the girl the woman she would become, and it was a heart-throbbing, groin-tightening vision. In sex appeal Thera was already major-league, and I envied that someone who would one year marry her.

I turned about and left the room. The phone was down the hall. I dialed the number I had memorized in case of emergency.

"Johnson Drummond," the voice rapped immediately. There was no intermediary on the industrialist's hot line.

"Jason Striker. I want a chaperone for the lessons."

I thought he would laugh, but he didn't bother. "Striker," he barked, "this is no damned school prom! I hired a man I could trust to do the job, so I wouldn't need to fool with—-"

Nobody interrupts Johnson Drummond. But I did. "Sir, you *can't* trust me anymore. Your daughter is a woman."

He wasn't fazed. "Don't waste my time with the obvious! Now you shut up and do what I hired you for."

"Why not have Diago finish her training? He—-"

It was as though he hadn't heard me, though I knew he had. "Do what needs to be done! I'll double the fee. Just don't bother me about trifles again."

I held the dead phone, bemused. To Drummond money was always the answer, yet he wouldn't pay any out to his black-sheep relative. The old man was shrewd, maybe too shrewd.

Slowly I returned to the practice room, thinking hard. I had used the pain hold to bring Thera into line, the first two days. Now she had it on me, figuratively. She understood her father, as I had not.

Do what needs to be done . . .

Not necessarily judo. Diago could have done that.

Jason Striker, sex education instructor?

Thera remained as she had been: statuesque, inviting. She looked up at me impishly. "Scream," she murmured. "Bite. Spread."

I paused, assessing her. Then I gave her the *kiai* yell, the judo attack scream that heightens strength and unnerves the opposition.

She was so surprised she fell over, her legs flying.

I found her *judogi* outfit on a shelf and threw it at her. The trousers wrapped nicely about her head, blinding her for an instant. "You're right," I said. "You're just about ready——for college. I see no reason why we can't wrap this up this week."

"This week?" she inquired, prettily perplexed. "But it's a six week course!"

"Why waste a week? The job is done and I've got a club to run."

She shook her head as if she had misheard. Then, slowly, she donned the *judogi*. She looked so forlorn that I longed to comfort her, and knew I would be lost if I did.

"Okay," I said when she was ready. "I'm a rapist coming at you." I charged.

She used the *harai-gosbi* sweeping hip throw. I cooperated, flipping over and landing resoundingly on the *tatami*.

"Beautiful!" I exclaimed. "Even my wife couldn't have done it better."

She froze, as girls do. "Wife?"

"She's a first degree black belt," I said innocently. "We still work out regularly. You really must meet her some day." I had broken Thera's pain hold; now I was applying a finishing choke on her casual romantic aspirations.

"Yes, I must," she said faintly.

We reviewed routine moves and holds, and she was competent, but the glow was off. On that day and the days that followed (I went the full six weeks, despite my baiting words) Thera behaved. There were no more studied exposures of anatomy, no more suggestive wriggles in the midst of matwork.

On the last day she confronted me, eyes blazing. I had a vision of an erupting volcano. "You're not married!" she cried. "I put a tracer on your social life. You don't even have a girlfriend!"

Oh-oh.

"I've had plenty of girls," I began lamely.

"And I can name them!" she flared. "Do you want them alphabetically or chronologically? Or only your actual affairs——all four of them?"

She had the dope, all right. "No need." That was the risk in countering a submission hold as I had done: sometimes the counterhold slipped, and then vulnerability was doubled. Why had I lied, anyway? That was a poor example of judo ethics.

"Why did you do it?" she demanded furiously. I would have felt safer if she had been coming at me with a machete. "I'd have given you just as good a time as any——"

I put my hand over her mouth, not hard. "One," I said. "Your father hired me to teach you what you needed to know. So I tried to convince you not to sell your body cheaply." But that sounded stuffy, even to me.

She nodded reluctantly. I shifted to the pain hold, without pressure. "Two: I am not looking for 'a good time.' When I settle down, it will be with a woman worthy of the name, not an easy mark." But that was wrong too, for Thera hadn't said a thing about "settling down," and I hadn't raised that objection with my prior girls.

She clapped her right hand over my right, brought her left around to apply pressure to my elbow, and twisted clockwise, capturing my arm in a submission grip of her own. No one would ever again use the *shi atsu* pain hold on her without regretting it. But then she gazed at me, her anger subsiding as she realized the broader implications. What a man chooses to leave may be more important than what he takes.

"Three," I continued, learning as much about my own motives as I was teaching her. "Give yourself a couple years of college. Apply yourself intellectually as you have these weeks physically. Show yourself what you can do with your mind when you're serious. Then, if you're still interested, look me up again."

"You really know the score," she said with mixed contrition and bitterness as she let go my arm. "I guess you knew it all the time." She tapped the wall with one finger, and looked at me meaningfully.

"I knew your first day's performance was a setup," I agreed. "One of those boys at the bar did come in to the club later, and—-" Then her signal registered.

A tap on the wall. The walls had ears.

No wonder her father hadn't been concerned about my behavior. He knew first hand everything that happened in this house. There must be audio and visual pickups all over.

"You didn't know?" she asked, surprised.

"Sorry. It just didn't occur to me," I admitted sheepishly. And I had been lecturing *her* about education!

It was her chance to crow. But she didn't. She stared at me long and thoughtfully. I was struck afresh by her beauty, for this expression became her.

"So everything you said to me," she murmured at last, "you really meant it. You weren't just protecting your fee."

Now I was angry. "Didn't anything I have told you about the ethics of judo sink in?" Ironic, for I had hardly been scrupulous myself. "Of *course* I meant it! I always mean it."

This time she put her own finger to my lips. "I always thought honest was square," she murmured. "And I guess it is. But it grows on you."

"No," I said with difficulty. "I lied about being married."

"You didn't lie," she said. "You just gave away your real desire."

I waited, not knowing what to expect, from either of us. Thera fascinated me.

"Two years," she breathed. "Two years of real education and real accomplishment. And a first-degree black belt."

I almost missed her irony. First degree belt—-the level I had given my fictitious wife.

Thera was going for broke, the way volcanoes do. She thought I had slipped her a veiled message, and perhaps I had. I had the feeling that she knew what she was doing: making an honest man of me.

I hoped so.

*

The *dojo* was in disarray when I returned. Something had happened.

Jim saw me and gave it to me in one stiff dose: "Charles Smith—
-he's dead!"

I was too stunned to make intelligent comment. From the incipient promise of a pretty girl a few minutes ago, to this. "How?"

"Right here in the practice hall! He was doing the *uchikomis*, and when it was his turn to throw, he collapsed. We couldn't revive him!"

"Ridiculous!" I snapped. "He was in excellent health. Who hit him?"

"Nobody!" Jim protested. "The whole class saw it."

I shook my head, feeling ill. "The autopsy will tell the story. He must have been on drugs secretly——steroids or amphetamines, or one of the dangerous new ones."

"I don't think so," Jim said. "I only knew him six weeks, but he was a straight guy. Good potential, clean living, shaping up to be a real asset to the *dojo*."

Those were my own sentiments. Charles Smith had obviously left Dato because he was an honest, cleancut judoka, quite capable of recognizing the un-*budo* attitude of his first teacher. Dato's actual knowledge was not in question, but he had lost the real spirit of judo, as his angry call to me had shown. One day his temper would bring him down; until then I would leave him alone and let bright students like Smith come to their own conclusions.

Had Dato known about Charles Smith's health problem? Was that why he had been so gracious about his student's departure? If so, he had not been bluffing about the grief it would bring to me.

*

But the autopsy brought no comfort. Charles Smith had died of a heart attack, apparently an embolism, yet he had no prior history of any such condition.

I thought again of Dato's threatening call. And I couldn't help remembering the wild, ugly notion I had fought off before. I had absolutely no evidence, and nobody would believe such a thing anyway.

What could I do but go on? At least I was in the clear. Smith had died before witnesses, in my absence, and no one had touched him. A hard blow on the chest can indeed injure the heart—but the autopsy showed that no one had struck him there recently. Whatever had attacked his heart had not originated at my *dojo*. But for the luck of my tutoring commitment that had kept me absent, he might have died while practicing with me, and possibly he *would* have been struck on the chest.

I regretted his death strongly, and it certainly did no good to my business, but it could have been worse. If I had thought *I* had done it . . .

CHAPTER 3

JIM

Jim Blake was shorter than I, but weighed more, and all of it was muscle. He was a collegiate wrestling champion who also lifted weights, and he had the drive and the health of youth in abundant measure. All of these were excellent assets for a judoka, and had led to his recent college-level judo championship. Contrary to popular opinion, muscle *does* help.

We were doing *randori*, practice competition before my judo class. We grabbed for coat-holds in the usual fashion, and Jim's hands fastened on my lapels while I took hold of his mid-outer sleeves. I pushed him lightly to the rear; he reacted by pushing back. I stepped away and pulled his left hand with my right, bending my knees. He thought I would continue back, but I put my left foot deep between his legs, dropped down, set my right foot gently into his abdomen, fell straight back and hauled him over me. It was the *Tomoe-nage,* round throw.

Unfortunately, he was ready for it. As I made the attack, he resisted by lowering his hips, bending his knees, and thrusting his lower abdomen forward. My grasp on his sleeves ripped free, and he retained his feet as I landed on my back. I thought he would fall on top of me, following up his advantage and seeking to utilize his wrestling skill, but he declined.

Jim was a good judoka, and getting better. He was the best of my students. I had qualified him through *shodan,* the first-degree black belt, and later sent him to the promotional evaluation for qualification as *nidan,* the second degree. This was more than mere physical competition; a judoka's basic knowledge and attitude is verified too, and these become more important as he climbs the black belt ladder. Jim had succeeded beautifully. Now he was working on *sandan,* the third degree, and already had five tournament points, though it would be a year-and-a-half before he could qualify officially.

I had trained him, and now he was making me look inept before the class. He had learned well. Go to it, Jim; see if you can take the old man down!

I got up quickly and went into one of my favorite movements, a standing arm bar. I grasped his right arm with both my hands, one at the wrist and the other at mid-forearm; I passed my leg in front of this arm, twisted my body, and fell on my side as my other leg pushed against his knee to bring him down. But Jim was ready for this too, knowing my ways too well. He kept his strong arm slightly bent, foiling the hold. I landed on my side while he stood over me, again having the advantage—but still not deigning to follow it up. If this had been a *shiai,* a competition match, Jim would certainly be ahead now.

But old judokas have many tricks. I couldn't really let a student beat me in my own club, before my own class. Not even one as talented as Jim. When all was said and done, he was a new *nidan* and I an old *godan,* a fifth degree black belt, and at thirty I was not yet over the hill.

I'm proud of you, Jim, but I have self-pride too. You would not have come to me if you hadn't been ambitious to train with the best in this area, and you would be disappointed if you could dump me already! I am no Dato.

God! Why did I have to think of that now. Dato, and the

death of Charles Smith. Why couldn't I have thought of something nice, like Thera and her nude yoga position? Now a pall fell on the exercise.

We sparred for handholds a third time. I could not get the grip I wanted. Jim was in a deep defensive position, almost bent in half, his upper torso parallel to the floor. He was giving away nothing, and I became frustrated. Was the instructor unable after all to take down the student?

I tried a *sumi-gaeshi-sutemi* corner reversal throw, but he stooped and stepped aside, forcing me off balance and breaking it up. It was as if he were the instructor, foiling every game effort of the student, and I found myself acutely embarrassed. It seemed that young judokas had tricks of their own.

Desperate to bring him to the mat where I might have better success despite his wrestling prowess, I stood there, letting him attempt whatever he would. And suddenly Jim made his move. He pulled hard at me, dropped to his right knee, and rolled me over his back in an imperfect *morote-seoi-nage.* No ippon, or contest point, but he had taken me down. This time, to my surprise, he seized me in a *yoko-shiho-gatame,* the side four quarter hold.

Good going, Jim! I'm glad to see this stuff, even though I didn't teach you that particular combination. Even if you are showing me up in my own *dojo,* my own judo exercise hall, and before my own students. Because you are going to need it all in that incredible tournament you're training for.

The tournament: a recluse multimillionaire, richer than Johnson Drummond, had recently taken it into his head to discover once and for all which of the world's martial arts was the strongest of them all. Usually boxers fight only boxers, and wrestlers wrestlers, and not only do the twain never meet, amateur never meets professional and grade never meets another grade. So a world champion boxer was only a fraction of a champion of one portion of his martial art. How would he do in a genuine combat situation, no holds barred?

So this anonymous fight fan had sunk a chunk of his fortune

into one gala tournament: the Martial Open. The only conditions for entry were that each representative be typical of his art, not a freak. That he have no gross physical deformities that might affect the outcome. No four hundred pound wrestlers, no seven foot boxers, no rock-fisted karate killers, no feeble-minded suicide fighters. Just good normal, healthy, skilled youths from all over the world.

And so it was that the finger of fate had fallen on young Jim, for he met the requirements precisely. Just twenty years old this month, handsome, and typical of the finest ideals of rising judokas. Already winner of several judo meets, and a college champion. They had wanted an American, for without some regional requirements Japan and the Orient would have dominated overwhelmingly, perhaps prejudicing the prospective television audience. America is said contemptuously to be a fifth-rate judo nation, but it is a *first*-rate television nation. Cynical motive.

Thus I was training Jim for the big event, and I hoped he would do well. Still, he had things to learn and techniques to perfect. His hold on me was flawed, as I was about to demonstrate.

I lay on my back, with Jim straddling me at right angles. His right arm passed between my legs to grip the back of my jacket; his chest weighted my torso. His left arm should have passed around my left shoulder, his hand grasping my jacket as far down as it could reach. Instead, he had hold of my sleeve at the shoulder, and his forearm lay across my throat. He should have known better; now his hold was not tight.

His arm moved. His forearm chopped down on my throat, bruising my larynx. There was a dull throbbing pain.

Then I realized that his position was *not* an error. He was trying to strangle me with his forearm!

I was furious. It wasn't the mere fact of the strangle, as that is a legitimate weapon in the arsenal of judo. It was the contempt Jim seemed to be showing for my skill as a judoka. Such a tactic might work against a brown belt, but hardly against a black belt. And never against an instructor.

I hunched my neck, blocking off his arm and abating the strangle. I passed my right hand under his body, where there was a space between it and the mat at my right side, and seized his belt at the waist. I ground my knuckles against his lower ribs, giving him back some of the pain I still felt in my throat.

With my left hand I took hold of his left arm, pushing it toward him as if I were trying to turn that way. Then suddenly I reversed the motion, pushing him the other way with my right arm. This elevated his body, bridging it across me. I used my leverage to throw him off my left side, then rolled over and jumped on his back before he recovered, and clamped a *kata-ha-jime* one-wing strangle on him. If he wanted to know how to apply an effective choke, I would show him, and in the process redeem my image as an instructor.

It was experience, nothing else. My own years of imperfections and mistakes had cost me matches until I had learned the hard way to make certain of every technical nuance. Jim simply had not had *time* to iron out every error. But I was teaching him, as I myself had been taught. He had just sacrificed a likely victory because of his seemingly minor lapse in technique, and I would explain it to him in detail later. Not to gloat, but to make sure he never again threw away his best opportunity like that. The next time might not be an inconsequential practice session, but the decisive match of a tournament.

I tightened up, waiting for him to slap the mat twice in surrender. I was behind him, my left knee on the *tatami*. My left arm trapped his left arm, pinning it over his head and pushing on the back of his neck; this was the "broken wing." My right hand passed under his chin and gripped his left lapel, giving me leverage for the choke. The bony edge of my wrist pressed against the front of his neck.

I had put strangles on Jim many times before in practice. But he had a bull neck of which he was proud—perhaps *too* proud, and he developed it constantly with exercises. I liked him, and had not wanted to humiliate him by demonstrating just how vulnerable that neck might be. So I had never applied force beyond a certain point, even when he did not yield. But I realized now that Jim was getting too cocky and thought he was better than he was. In a *shiai* contest, in a match with a less soft-hearted antagonist, he would quickly be rendered unconscious. So this time I meant to make him submit. As when I had applied the pain hold to the girl Thera: it was a necessary lesson.

But Jim refused to quit. He tried to resist by pulling down my right hand, alleviating the strangle. He bridged his body to minimize the remaining pressure on his neck, and pushed back while trying to close his chin against his chest.

I had only one recourse to prevent these measures from breaking the hold. I shifted to put a scissors hold about his waist with my legs and intensified the pressure on his throat, forcing him to the verge of unconsciousness. But still he fought stubbornly——far too stubbornly. He simply could not accept the fact of loss, and that was why he *had* to lose, this time.

Jim held his breath. He was good at that, too; he could swim for almost three minutes underwater. I was behind him in this position, so I could not see his face to judge how close he was to passing out.

There are four types of strangle: respiratory, in which the air is cut off; sanguineous, in which the carotid arteries——not the jugular vein——on either side of the neck are pressured, stopping the flow of blood to the brain; nerve, where the two nerve centers at the sides of the neck are attacked; and combination respiratory and blood.

All have their advantages and liabilities, and the experienced judokas keep these points in mind when applying any strangle. The respiratory is slow, sometimes taking several minutes for full effect, minutes in which anything can happen. The sanguineous strangles, properly done, can work in just three seconds, but require deep penetration by the hands to both sides of the neck, difficult with a muscular one like Jim's. The nerve strangles are forbidden in judo, being too dangerous. So I was using the combination air and blood——and Jim's continuing resistance told me it wasn't working well. I hung on.

Students suddenly stood up, walked toward us. In the midst of the match?

Then I realized that Jim had gone limp. He was out. I should have released him before this! When a choke is released at the moment of unconsciousness, the subject normally regains consciousness spontaneously in ten to twenty seconds, and there are no harmful side effects. It is another matter if the hold is maintained beyond unconsciousness. How long had I done so?

I let go immediately and turned Jim over. He was blue in the face and not breathing. The students had seen his face, and realized before I had. But the difference could only have been seconds.

I put him on the mat face down and applied *kwatsu,* the judo healing technique. I pressed with both hands against his kidneys while giving the *kiai* yell. "HAAAA!" My students stepped back, surprised——but Jim resumed breathing, shallowly.

I pried open his eyes, and only the whites showed. One was bloodshot, as if a small vein had burst inside. His lips were still blue, cyanotic. He had fought the strangle much too long and hard.

"Call an ambulance," I said, keeping my voice calm so as not to alarm anyone. I was not actually too worried, for these things do happen and are not normally serious, but I was taking no chances. With one student recently dead . . . And an injury at this point, with the Martial Open only two weeks away, would be very bad for Jim's chances.

The ambulance arrived with its sounding sirens, and somehow I heard Dato's voice in them: *You suffer!* The medics came with oxygen, but even that had no apparent effect. "Training accident," I explained tersely. I was worried now.

I ran through the remaining class session in a preoccupied daze. The choke hold is dangerous, of course, but it is a standard one in judo that I had demonstrated on students a thousand times without ill effect, and Jim certainly was familiar with its aspects.

Why had he pushed me, knowing he couldn't safely break the hold?

But something else was bothering me profoundly, and only slowly did I bring it to the surface. It wasn't Dato's threat; I knew he had nothing to do with this particular mess, whatever he might like me to think. I was the instructor, Jim the student; but he had been extending me vigorously in front of the class. Had I been so anxious to prevail that I had deliberately injured him? Getting even for my previous failures to make him surrender?

"No!" I cried aloud. At once, I was aware of my surroundings. The class was over, and I was in my car driving home. Alone, fortunately.

Yet my private denial lacked force. It was hard for a man to admit he might be slipping, especially one in my position. I had just sustained a couple of shocks: near-seduction by a teenage girl, and the abrupt death of a good student. I was bound to over-react to any new threat.

Jim was twenty, I thirty, and that decade had to tell at least marginally in his favor. I liked Jim, I had trained him, I wanted him to succeed——yet surely there was that in me that resented his powerful youth, that wanted to put him down. Every instructor, every *sensei,* fears that his pupil will surpass and defeat him. Had the green arm of jealousy circled Jim's throat, rather than that of his friend?

"No!" I cried again in anguish. But it was a fainter exclamation.

*

The mail awaited me at home, and there was a letter from Bill Bender, an old friend who had retired to a judo column for several newspapers. He was generally first with the inside information, though he was not free to publish much of it, and periodically he forwarded news and gossip of interest to me.

"Thought you'd better know," his letter said, "we were given a bum steer on the Martial Open. Only actual restriction is that each entrant be a 'legitimate and accredited' representative of his particular martial art. That can mean almost anything, considering how loose some karate clubs are, not to mention the inscrutable ways of Oriental kung-fu and aikido. The word is that some of the real pros of other disciplines are going to participate for that quarter-million grand prize. No real regulation, either; sponsor turns out to be a rich Latin American with a plantation down in Nicaragua, and he is the law in that region. If I were you, I'd get your boy *out* of that mess on one pretext or another."

Jim was going into a nest of vipers—and I had injured him just before the tournament began. How was he going to survive now, against the murder specialists of those other disciplines? Kung-fu, for example, had no organized contests and rankings, because it had no sport aspect; it was strictly for self-defense in an extremely offensive manner, and it was one of the most brutal martial sciences known to man. I'd hate to fight a kung-fu expert myself without very strict refereeing, let alone send Jim against him. Even without a recent injury.

But what could I do? I had not made the assignment, and I could not tell Jim to withdraw. He would feel his stubborn college-age masculinity questioned if I even suggested he quit because of the danger. He never did know when to quit, as this recent injury demonstrated.

I hadn't even looked at the newspaper yet. I picked it up and plopped into my chair. The lead off item struck me like a kick in the solar plexus.

JUDO CHAMP RAIDS RIVAL

Police arrested a leading local judo instructor for disrupting a class session of his chief competitor. Dato, of "Dato's Dojo," was released on bond after assaulting Andrei Kolychkine of "City Kung-

Fu." The two exchanged several blows in front of the astounded students before Dato abruptly stopped and left.

It was conjectured that Dato had been enraged by Kolychkine's recent acquisition of several promising students from a section of the city Dato regarded as his own "territory."

Kolychkine was unhurt except for bruises. "Dato is an old man," he said. "I don't think he'll try this again."

The article was inaccurate, the usual newspaper sensationalism. Kolychkine was not Dato's leading rival, *I* was. Students looking for better judo instruction would hardly go to a kung-fu parlor, as kung-fu was an entirely distinct discipline.

But Dato *was* lucky, at that. Kolychkine was a good-natured sort, not given to grudges; he would probably drop the charges. And of course he hadn't been hurt; as a kung-fu *sifu* he was well able to take care of himself. He was not a top-ranking practitioner; kung-fu is a Chinese martial art, and few non-Orientals are privy to its ultimate techniques. He wouldn't admit it if he *were* hurt; that would damage his projected image of invulnerability. Probably this episode would do his business good, for he had repelled the invader with honor and was receiving much free publicity.

But the whole thing gave judo a bad name. Something had to be done about Dato before he ruined us all. But what? *I* was in no position to talk. Here I had had one student die, and had put another in the hospital.

I don't like drugs in any form; that's why I don't smoke or drink or take coffee that isn't decaffeinated. But I finally took an aspirin (and some vitamin C against side-effects) so I could get to sleep.

*

Jim was no better next morning. He lay in the hospital, still unconscious, and visitors were barred. My guilt expanded with every hour that passed.

My phone rang and I leaped to answer it, hoping for news of Jim's recovery. But it was a strange voice.

"Mr. Jason Striker? I am Roger Wimble, attorney for the family of Jim Blake. If you will give me the name of your own attorney, I'm sure we can work this out."

I had had a bad night, and this did not improve my disposition. "Work *what* out?"

"Well, there's no point in going to court, is there, Mr. Striker? If you will agree to cover all medical expenses plus a reasonable—"

"You're holding *me* responsible for Jim's condition?"

"Who else? *You* strangled him." His voice was losing even the phony friendliness it had started with.

The view from outside! "Look, Wimble—-I'm as sorry about what happened as anyone, and I'll help Jim any way I can, but it's not a *legal* obligation! It was a training accident, and exempted from—-"

"We are familiar with your release form, Mr. Kane. But we contend that it does not apply in this case. Now if your attorney will—-"

I did not want to argue, for the moment. I gave the man the name of my attorney. I knew I was under no legal obligation, and certainly I was in a poor position to absorb the kind of medical bill Jim was running up. I did have some cash, thanks to the generosity of Johnson Drummond, who had meant it about doubling my tutoring fee. But one week at the hospital would gobble that up and leave me broke again. I was ready to contribute as a friend; what got to me was this instant assumption that any judo instructor had to be guilty of foul play, and should be docked like a criminal. The legacy of operators like Dato, already.

Yet that insidious voice inside me whispered that I *was* guilty. I had wanted to put down my rival for martial glory. Because *he* had been selected for the honor of representing judo, not I. I had risen to the rank of *godan* the hard way, and eased off because it was necessary to earn a living and a man can't eat trophies. Was a wet-behind-the-ears *nidan* to pass me by?

No, no! I cried silently, feeling a pang as though struck over the heart. I was not that type of man. I was no rival to my students; I was not like Dato, hoarding my skills. I wanted the youngsters I trained to succeed. If Jim could do well at the Martial Open, the glory would reflect on all judo, and especially on me, his trainer.

But then, maybe I was being protective toward him. I feared he lacked the ability to survive against killer karatekas and kickboxers in such a free-for-all, and I wanted him out of danger. So had I—?

But the letter informing me of the changed nature of the tournament had arrived *after* the injury. And I would hardly have saved him from injury by injuring him myself.

All the arguments rang hollowly in my mind. I *had* hurt him.

*

My attorney called. "It looks bad, Jason," he said. "They are trying to set aside the release form on the grounds that you failed to exercise proper caution when applying the stranglehold, a potentially fatal tactic. They're summoning expert witnesses, doctors—-"

"Ridiculous!" I snapped. "Why don't they check with any judo *sensei*—"

"Just the same, we're not in the clear by a long shot," he said. "It isn't just the possibility of a lawsuit. We could summon expert testimony of our own—-doctors who are knowledgeable in the martial arts, for example. But the man on the street has an exaggerated fear of strangulation. Your business could suffer severely. If that boy should die—-"

You suffer! Dato had vowed. And I was suffering.

I hung up, stricken. Jim couldn't die! He had such a promising future. And a simple choke wouldn't kill him—not hours or days later. There must have been a neck injury. But he was my friend, accident or no.

But my lawyer's words gnawed at me. My reputation was now at stake, and thus my livelihood. Surely a *godan* should know when to release a stranglehold on a student! How could I have done this to Jim—-unless it were deliberate? Consciously, never; but subconsciously. . . ?

The phone rang again, and I jumped guiltily. I tried to let it go, certain that only bad news was there, but it rang and rang. Finally I had to answer.

"Jason, this is Bill Bender," my columnist-friend's voice said. "Got another scoop that just broke. It'll hit the papers tomorrow, but I had this feeling you'd need to know now. Your boy is not going to the Martial Open."

"They withdrew him?" I asked. "Thank God!"

"Don't thank God, Jason. There's more."

"Uh-oh. You mean they did it because of his injury?"

"Uh-uh. He never *was* the choice. That was just a front while they watched what the other martial arts were doing. The real choice is a fifth degree *sensei* with plenty of experience. Former U.S.A. champ, placed third in Salt Lake—a real man."

"Nobody should send a boy to do a man's job," I agreed, almost sick with relief for Jim's sake. "Who is it, Bill?"

"A former Green Beret hero and silver medal winner. He recently fought Diago to a draw, despite the stun-yell. I think that was the decisive factor."

"Stop kidding, Bill. Nobody ever withstood Diago's *kiai!* He—-" Then, slowly, I realized. Some garbled account of my encounter with Diago must have leaked out, providing me with an obscure and undeserved notoriety. "Bill, I've been out of world competition for two-three years! I'm not in shape for—-"

"I guess somebody feels otherwise," he said cheerfully. "I heard you had mighty strong local sponsorship." He hung up.

"*What* local sponsorship?" I asked myself futilely. "I never asked for—-" Then I thought of something else.

I crashed out the door and drove to the hospital. Only sheer luck saved me from a traffic citation for reckless driving. I knew I wasn't going to any tournament, but I had to explain to Jim that he was out, before he heard it from someone else and felt betrayed. If he got the idea that I had put him out so *I* could go . . .

Disheveled, I marched into the lobby. "Jason Striker to see Jim Blake," I told the desk.

The nurse checked her book. "Jim Blake is not permitted visitors at this time," she said.

"I'm the man who put him here," I said. "I have to see him!" I saw the room number opposite Jim's name on the roster, and headed for the stairs. I always use the stairs, not the elevator. Better exercise, better release of tension.

It can take hours to find a doctor in a hospital when you're sick, but two doctors and another nurse met me at the third floor landing. "Mr. Striker, please leave at once, or we shall have to report you."

I brushed by them and strode toward Jim's room. A tall man with a briefcase came out as I got there, almost colliding with me. "No visitors, eh?" I said over my shoulder to the hospital personnel. "What is this—a mirage?"

The man stared at me contemptuously. "I am Roger Wimble. You must be Jason Striker. Exactly the sort of roughneck I expected."

The lawyer Jim's family had hired. I had walked into even more trouble, for my presence here surely did not look good. They would construe it as an attempt to make sure Jim was dead or dying.

"Listen, Wimble. All I want to do is talk to Jim. I don't care what you think."

"Striker . . ."

The call was so faint I almost missed it. "Jim!"

Wimble and the doctors turned, and the nurse stepped quickly into the room. The figure on the stark white bed was moving.

In a moment we were all inside, staring down. Jim was in

some kind of metal neck brace that immobilized his head, but his eyes could move. "Striker!" he whispered. "Why didn't you come before? Are you still mad about—"

"No!" I cried. "The idiots wouldn't let me in! They said you were in a coma."

"I guess I was in a coma, outside," he said more strongly. "Not inside. Not inside my head. It seems like a thousand years! I wanted to see you, to tell you—"

"You don't have to say a thing, Blake!" Wimble snapped. "We are suing this man Striker for what he did to you."

"Suing?" Jim asked, his eyes flicking over to Wimble. "I don't know who the hell you are, but *I* was the one at fault. I wouldn't yield to his stranglehold, so he thought it wasn't on tight. He's told me a hundred times not to fight that hold! I was a crazy fool, and I just wanted to apologize. For not knowing when to quit. For being a stubborn fool."

"It's okay," I said. "I should have realized—"

"For not being a true judoka," he finished. "It's been tearing me up, Striker. Nightmares, and I didn't really want to come out of it, until I could tell you. I don't have the proper judo spirit, and—"

"You'll get it!" I cried. "I was the same, when I was your age."

Wimble looked at the doctors. "It was the sound of Striker's voice that woke him, wasn't it," he said, and they nodded.

"Striker—" Jim said.

"Don't be so damned formal, Jim!" I said.

He smiled. "Jason. *Sensei*—I can't go to that tournament now. Even if this hadn't happened—I know I'm not ready. I—will you take my place? You could do what I never could. For judo. You have the experience."

Why did he ask that? Jim was never a quitter; duress only made him more bull-headed. Had he suffered some degree of paralysis, and knew it? He had been unconscious a long time; there could be anoxia, a lack of oxygen to the brain. If that were so, Jim's career as a judoka could be finished, and it was my fault. But I could not say it to him. I might have crippled him for life.

"Sure, sure," I said. And wondered whether he had suspected all along that he was not the real choice for the tournament. That, too, could have accounted for his desperation measures in our contest. "Now you rest easy, and when you're back on your feet we'll do more *randori*, okay?"

"Okay!" he agreed happily. Then his eyes closed, and he slept. It was a normal sleep, not a coma. Even I could tell that.

Wimble drew himself up, very dignified. "Mr. Striker, it seems we owe an apology."

"Forget it!" I said. "I'm just so glad he's going to be okay, I don't care about the rest, and I'll help all I can with the expenses." *If he is going to be okay,* I thought. Now that the attorneys were no longer bugging me, my own doubts were mushrooming. If only Dr. Cue, the M.D. in my judo class, had been on hand. But he was away on vacation. Jim was a long way from complete recovery, and the expenses could be phenomenal, and I could not live with myself if I didn't raise the money. Yet that was plainly beyond my means.

Only then did I realize what I'd told Jim, and understand my own private motivation. There was a great deal of money to be had at that tournament. Enough to cover any likely medical expenses. And Jim wanted me to go.

Now I was committed to take his place—and it was better that he never know the truth about my selection.

How was I going to do in the Martial Open?

CHAPTER 4

MARTIAL OPEN

I faced Makato. The Korean was not large, but his arms were enormous. His knuckles were one continuous band of scar tissue from his decades of intensive karate training. A blow from his fist could fell a bull, literally; he had done it many times. Often he would cut off the horns first, with short chopping motions with the sides of his hands. Then he would stun the bull with a direct punch, and finally kill it by twisting its neck.

Now those hands were lifted against *me*.

I went for a quick throw, certain I could handle him more safely on the mat. I lifted him with a *harai goshi,* the hip sweep. I pulled him toward me and turned, using my right leg to sweep his right leg to the rear, and I threw him over my back.

Makato went down, but his iron fist punched my kidney as he fell. It felt as if he had stuck a hot knife in my lower back. There was a hard burning pain, and the shock made my breath short. "Ahhhh!" I groaned involuntarily, to minimize the agony.

I reeled for a fatal instant, failing to drop on top of him for an effective judo hold when I had the opportunity. Makato kicked me from the floor, aiming for a crippling knee blow, but I saw it coming and flexed my legs slightly. The calloused, horn-hard ball of his foot struck my thigh numbingly. An expert never hits with his bare toes, but lifts them out of the way to let the more solid part of the foot take the brunt.

I stepped back, but he had hooked his other foot above my heel, and I stumbled and fell to the rear. I might have recovered my balance despite the double force of the blow and hook, but it was safer to take the fall and somersault back to my feet, than to remain open to another kick. Makato could instantly shatter my knee and my career.

I rolled back on my shoulders, still smarting from the kidney blow. I tried to stand up, but just as I got my feet under me I was smashed by a kick to my temple. This was worse than either of the other blows; it was like being hit by a hurled stone. I was dazed. I saw double. I had trouble coordinating, and when I moved it was like pushing through water. My head seemed to swell until it was ready to explode.

I had to get a lock on him before he could bring those terrible hands into play again. But Makato feinted to the right, jumped into the air, turned while aloft and made a terrific back kick. His heel connected with my chin . . .

*

It was about five hours by jeep, on a dirt road through almost untouched savannah. Low hills were covered by sparse grass and a few pine trees. I could see that there had once been larger forests, for there were many lumber cuttings: stands of stumps, like grave markers. A line of metal towers paralleled our route, perhaps used for carrying electric power to the primitive interior.

This was Nicaragua: the northeast corner near the Honduras frontier. I had arrived by plane at the Managua airport, where I soon tired of waiting in the red-dust covered terminal for the local flight across the country. There was no other way to do it; even in the dry season the road was said to take two weeks.

Meanwhile, I toured the city in my amateurish way, trotting along the narrow cobblestoned streets despite the heat. The natives stared, and I knew they thought me crazy, but it was good exercise. Traffic was my worst hazard, for nobody obeyed the rules. I saw crosses erected, one at each place there had been a fatal accident in the past; there must have been more than a hundred of them all told.

North of the city I encountered Lago de Managua, and I jogged along the walk beside it. I learned later that this was the only place in the world where freshwater sharks lived. Good thing I hadn't decided to swim. I rested under one of the shade trees of the park, looking at the large statues of Central America's foremost poet—and felt ignorant as hell for never having heard of the man.

I was admiring the beautiful cathedral of Managua when I looked at my watch and realized the time. Puffing like an old steam engine, I made it back to the airport and boarded a Nicaraguan Airline Lanica. Ahead of me sat a nun; beside me was an Indian woman suckling her baby. It was a far cry from my *dojo*.

I had the window seat and looked out to see the fringe of Lago de Nicaragua, the great interior lake. I wondered irrelevantly just who my strong local sponsor had been, and whether he had really intended to send me to a foreign country. If I had balled Johnson Drummond's daughter, he might have been glad to send me into the fight-for-life that the Martial Open promised to be; but I *hadn't*, and he knew it. Dato would have been happy to get rid of me, but I couldn't believe he had such influence with the judo associations. So it remained a nagging mystery.

About a hundred miles beyond the lake we set down at Bluefields, on the Atlantic coast, where I transferred to the flight to Puerto Cabezas, a hundred and fifty miles north. There a private car met me. The driver was a stolid Indian who could have had a cut tongue, for all the conversation he made along the way.

We crossed the Ulana River, forged into steeper country, and came abruptly to a checkpoint. Armed guards stood by a barricade across the road, rifles ready. The jeep jammed to a stop.

I didn't like it. I slumped in the seat and closed my eyes as if sleepy. I don't fool with firearms if I can help it, but I had no inclination to be locked up in some wilderness cell, ignorant of language and custom.

But the driver made a signal, and the guards nodded. They recognized him. They hauled aside the barricade, and we ground on through.

This, then, was the huge estate of Vicente Pedro, said to be one of the real owners of this Latin American nation. Fabulously wealthy, but with resources that went beyond money: fisheries, lumber, gold mines, sugar, cattle, and manpower. Educated in Europe, but specializing in good American graft and influence. I could not claim to have respect for my host's nature.

But this was evidently the kind of man it took to bring about a tournament of this nature: a fight-to-the-finish matching of the top representatives of the world's leading martial arts. No such meeting could occur in the United States, for there were laws about manslaughter, as there were in most developed countries. But here Vicente Pedro was the law.

The jeep slowed, coursing through elegant gardens. The contrast with the barren landscape outside was striking. This was an oasis in the wasteland; I gazed amazed at what seemed to be millions of beautiful flowers. Red, white, yellow roses; bougainvillaea bushes covered with purple blossoms; flowering trees, yellow, blue and white. Orchid vines hung from trees and trellises. Ferns ranged from a few inches long to tree size. Stately royal palms lined the curving road.

There were statues, too. One was of Neptune, king of the sea, holding his traditional trident. Mermaids and fish surrounded him, each well-shaped in its mammalian or piscine torso. Another statue was a small naked boy, a fountain, with the stream of water jetting from the obvious place. I had never seen much of that sort of humor in America. Other statues verged on the pornographic. Was our host given to revels of this kind, or was such display standard regional art?

Then we passed a twice-life size, bronze statue of Vicente Pedro himself, on a black marble pedestal. It dominated everything, that huge handsome man seated before the mansion.

The house itself was, unsurprisingly, Spanish style, and very large. The walls were bright white stucco, the tiles red. There were grandiose columns, and a *portal* surrounded the whole, with chairs in the shade.

A mulatto girl waited at the entrance to guide me inside. The interior was even more impressive than the outside. The wood-work was of black mahogany and fragrant teak; the floor consisted of mosaics in beautiful patterns. I saw a big interior courtyard with a scenic fountain; all the rooms on each floor opened onto it, probably for coolness at night.

On the ground floor there were a number of huge rooms with tall ceilings, too high for effective cleaning, it seemed, for there were swallows nesting on the beams.

At first I thought the maid was giving me a tour of the upstairs, for the room she showed me was like a gallery in a museum. Ivory statuettes sat in alcoves, alternating with ancient Greek or Roman vases and Chinese Ming Dynasty porcelain, and there were screens of lacquered hide and inlaid ivory. A balcony was outside, overlooking the central fountain. The giant canopied beds were protected by mosquito netting, a necessary precaution here in the tropics, where the biting insects could transmit malaria. The furniture was massive, being of old, hand-carved wood and hide. Costly carpets and rugs were scattered around the floor. Paintings hung on the walls, and I knew without recognizing the artists that they were semi-classics.

I found out that this was to be my room for the duration. As soon as the girl left, I stepped into the ornate lavatory to clean off the grime of travel. I hardly had time to assimilate the black marble bathtub, silver faucets and bidet before one of my roommates appeared.

He was Japanese, in his mid-fifties, about five-feet eight-inches tall and weighing perhaps two-hundred-and-forty pounds. Obviously not a contestant. But he looked familiar, and in a moment I placed him.

"Takao Kawaguchi!" I exclaimed, smiling, though actually I was not certain I liked his presence here.

"You must be Jason Striker, the American," he said with passable inflection, affecting a brief bow. "I regret having intruded on you."

"By no means!" I said, chagrined to have him pick up my private reservations so easily. "I am merely surprised to meet you in this context."

"No need to hide your feelings from me," he said, making a little gesture of conciliation. "It is well known that I am barred from competition, because I practiced special death blows on Chinese prisoners during the war." He meant World War Two. He had been a Japanese bomber pilot, shot down over China, and later an official in an internment camp. When Japan lost the war, his reputed atrocities were enough to rule him out of further judo competition, though he was in fact an eighth degree black belt and one of the all time judo greats, never beaten in tournament competition. How much of his one-time skill derived from that illicit practice against prisoners of war was problematical, but it *was* a severe personal liability, in my view. I had heard nothing of him for a number of years, and had assumed that he was no longer active in judo.

"I do not hide it," Takao continued. "I do not apologize. I only point out that I was younger then, and war had a brutalizing effect. They were the enemy. Even so I gave them a fair chance. I always chose strong and trained men, and they were permitted to fight, and any of them could have killed me, thus recovering honor. I thought I was doing valuable research, rediscovering lost techniques. Those prisoners were dead already, according to their military code, because of their defeat and capture. The Imperial Authority intended to allow none of them to survive Japan's defeat, and very few did. Those that I killed died cleanly, almost without pain, and were given honorable burial. It was a better death than the alternative."

I did not attempt to argue against his viewpoint. Mitigating factors such as these had been brought out at his trial, resulting in a nominal sentence. The judgement had been rendered, the legal price paid. I had no right to hold the past against him.

"I can't say anything," I said. "My own record is not clean."

His eyebrows lifted. He did not inquire, but now I had to match his confession with my own.

"I was in the Green Berets, Vietnam. Captured—-there was a girl who died. I escaped—but there was no honor in it."

"There is little honor in war," he said.

So we had come to a sort of accord, but still I could not *like* him, any more than I liked my own bad memories. And I knew he was too old to enter this tournament, even if the proscription against his competition did not apply here. The days of his physical greatness were long behind him.

"I am here as a judo judge," he said. "I need the money to bring my wife and three children from Japan to Brazil, where I am settled now. Our host desired knowledgeable officials."

Just as I needed the money for Jim's probable medical expenses. Were all the participants of this tournament justifying themselves similarly?

But one concern had been eased. So he was not to be a combatant. Now it made sense. Whatever his age and whatever his ethical reputation, there was no doubt that he knew more about judo than almost any man living, and this was exactly the kind of knowledge required for a tournament like this.

Seven major martial arts were to be represented, with two participating and one judge for each. Every art would meet every other art twice, for a total of forty-two matches, or six by each participant. The best won—lost record would determine the tournament winner—-and, by implication, the leading martial art of the world. For the Martial Open was the dream tournament: the one in which boxer met wrestler, karateka met judoka, and kung-fu *sifu* met aikido *sensei,* in fights to the finish. The debates of centuries were about to be settled here, and the matches would be broadcast on worldwide television.

There were virtually no rules of combat. A match would end when one man surrendered or was obviously unfit to continue. No fouls called, no techniques forbidden, no repercussions if men should die. The judges were merely to ascertain the situation, in the event it was not obvious, and to minimize injuries when the outcome was inevitable. (There would be no deliberate maiming after a combatant was helpless, for example.) Certainly I would feel easier with a man like Takao watching while I fought, alert for my interest and that of judo. I knew there would be some very tough men here, and I knew my chances of coming through the tournament uninjured were slight. Judo was not well represented, unfortunately; my own presence was something of a fluke, as I would hardly be ranked among the top hundred judokas of the world today. If I had a strong partner, judo might still do well enough, but I didn't even know who my partner was.

There was a master chart of scheduled matches in the main hall, and I studied them carefully. My judo partner had not yet arrived, so I could not be certain which days I would fight, and had to be prepared for them all. I guessed that the first judo match was mine.

I whistled. Some famous men were here, all right—and some infamous. I was going to have to watch my step, particularly since Judo's first match was against Karate, and the man scheduled to meet me was Makato Kubota: probably the top practicing karateka in the world today.

*

Something cold slapped against my face, bringing me out of my melange of dream and memory. "You're lucky!" the doctor was saying. "If he'd taken time to set up properly, your jawbone would have been plastered against the inside of your skull. Where did you learn to fight?"

I sat up angrily, and regretted it, feeling nauseous. It is not fun to be kicked into unconsciousness. I felt incipient convulsions in my stomach, and a splitting headache came in pulses, and I still had trouble focusing. For the moment I could not recall what had happened to me, or even who I was. I had this picture of a young man lying in a hospital bed, and I heard an accented voice crying "You suffer!"

"As I said, you're lucky," the doctor repeated. "No real damage done. But if you're the best judo can produce, it is not much of an art. You lost."

I knew it. It was coming back now. Makato had put me away as if I were a white-belt novice. I had always thought judo was basically superior to karate, but I certainly hadn't been superior to the Korean. Was this a taste of what I faced in the next two weeks?

I waved the doctor off and stood up unsteadily. My legs felt rubbery, and I suffered another siege of disorientation. I had taken a pounding. I walked with what grace I could muster to my room.

Takao was there. "You total fool!" he said as he cleaned up my face. There was blood on the cloth, and I discovered I had bitten my tongue sometime during the, debacle. "What were you trying to do—-dance him to death?"

For an instant a pure kill-rage suffused me. This killer of prisoners was trying to lecture *me!* But I controlled myself. I *had* lost, ignominiously, and I could lose again. Less luckily, if I did not improve my technique in a hurry. "You tell me," I said, hating him.

"You tried to play it by *sport* rules," Takao snorted. "Against Makato, the deadliest karateka extant! You actually threw the bull with *Harai goshi,* and of course you blew it! You had only to hold him and fall on top of him, breaking his ribs, or just kick him in the face, and the match would have been yours. Even a simple knee-drop on his skull—what did you think he was, a *Bakayaro* student, a dilettante?"

Bakayaro: a Japanese swear word. I didn't know Japanese, but expletives are readily picked up. I think the human brain has a special affinity for them. It was really me he was swearing at, not Makato.

I clenched my hurting jaw, knowing he was right. He had been there watching the match, in an excellent position to tell. For so many years in sport competition and in judo instruction, I had made every effort to avoid giving injury—and even then had not been careful enough with Jim. It was a conditioned reflex. So I was at a disadvantage facing a brute like Makato, who could shatter concrete tiles with his bare hands and had not pulled his punches in the match.

It was an important lesson for me. I could have gotten killed, literally.

"I'm here because I injured the young man originally assigned to this tournament," I said lamely. "The idea of deliberately hurting someone-—"

Takao rolled his eyes expressively, condemning my naivete. Then he smiled, not nicely. "It was the opposite with me. We all have good reasons for what we do, eh? But sometimes we are mistaken, and we have to adjust to the contemporary situation."

So now my disastrous gentleness was being equated with his murders. Yet perhaps there was justice in the parallel. "Yes," I said. "Are there films of the match? I'd like to-—"

"I have ordered a print. I want you to see exactly how you-—"

The intercom came to life, startling me because I hadn't realized it was there. "Judo representatives: a complication," an unfamiliar voice announced.

"Yes?" Takao snapped, evidently recognizing the speaker and not liking him.

"Your European combat representative has reneged, as I might have known. He will not report for the tournament."

Takao struck his head with the heel of his hand. "The East German? I know that man. He fears nothing!"

"The official report listed him as indisposed. Isn't that a synonym for cold feet?"

"The Communists must have stopped him, afraid he would defect. Why did they wait until the last moment?"

"I see Judo is good at making excuses," the voice said arrogantly.

Takao let out an amazing stream of Japanese profanity. "What do you expect us to do? The American sport-player just got wiped out by the Korean!"

No consolation for losers, I thought bitterly. If that was the East German I thought it might be, we would have had a winning team, regardless of his politics.

"If you can't field a fighting team, you'll forfeit," the voice said, sounding cynically pleased. "I have no patience with cowards or weaklings." There was a click of dismissal.

"Who was that?" I demanded, as resentful as Takao.

"Vicente Pedro, our esteemed host and sponsor."

Ouch! "He doesn't much like judo, does he!"

"He was crippled while practicing judo," Takao said seriously. *"Kata guruma."*

The *kata guruma,* or shoulder wheel: a throw in which one man lifts the other on his shoulders and throws him over his head. The result is a very hard fall, particularly if an incorrect landing is made. Pedro must have twisted in the air, trying to fall on his side so that there would not be an *ippon,* a point scored against him, and twisted on his side as he landed, injuring his spinal cord. I had heard he was confined to a wheelchair, but hadn't realized that he had once practiced judo. "But that's no reason to hate the art itself," I objected.

Takao shrugged. "The man is mad. But he'll be fair. He'll award the prizes to the victors, and reap ten times as much from the television royalties, but he'll not be sorry to see judo wiped out."

"I'll see if I can win a few matches," I said.

"You can't do it alone. You would get killed, trying to fight every day."

A fair statement. In sport judo, a man can participate in many matches in a few hours. But the Martial Open was no sport arena. A single throw for an *ippon* did not end the match here. "I'm not much for forfeiting," I said grimly.

"How are you for getting your skull kicked in?"

He was baiting me, and I didn't like it. But I wanted to fathom his motive, so I reined my temper, which wasn't easy with the headache I had. "There will be another match with the bull-stunner."

"You are not afraid?"

"I am a judoka."

"Well spoken!" he exclaimed, surprising me. "Still you need a partner, or Pedro will not let Judo compete at all."

Then I understood his drift. "Takao, you have given me honest criticism. Do you want it back?"

He stared hard at me. "Yes."

"You are old and fat and out of condition. Look *at* your beer belly! Your mind may retain its skill, but your body has deserted you. You would be a clown."

A deadly insult to an eighth *Dan* Japanese *sensei*. But Takao only laughed. "Strike the clown in his fat belly," he suggested, thrusting it out.

I did not like to do it, but it was best that he know the truth before he undertook a suicidally foolish mission. I got slowly to my feet, hefting my right fist, then struck him hard, in the gut with a left-handed reverse punch: knuckles down, palm up.

It was like smashing a wall. My hand, lacking the callus of the karateka, stung and went numb. Only the layer of fat on him had cushioned the blow; underneath was an incredible mass of rock-like muscle.

"Strangle the clown by his flabby neck," he offered.

Once this man had allowed two others to straddle a pole set across his neck, and against their combined strength bearing him down he had slowly risen up, suffering no apparent distress from all that weight on such a vulnerable part. But that had been a quarter century ago. Now he was in his fifties. I applied a two-hand strangle, *ryote-jime,* a reliable combination type.

He laughed, not bothering to resist. I tightened, using my leverage to stop both his breath and the supply of blood to his brain. He stood there breathing easily, fully conscious. I exerted my full force, feeling like a fool. Only then did his breath begin to rasp, but I was unable to cut it off entirely, or to make him pass out from pressure on his carotid arteries. I could strain until I grew tired, but I could not strangle him. No man could.

Takao might not be the judoka he used to be, but I had to admit he was still a lot of man. He had kept himself in shape, after all. And I did need a partner.

Judo was back in business.

*

I took another look at the big tournament board in the main lounge. Now there were cumulative rankings.

Karate, Kung-fu and Aikido were tied for first place, each with a won-lost record of 1-0. Wrestling was fourth with 1-1, followed by Boxing with 0-0. Judo was sixth, 0-1, and Thai Kick-Boxing was last, 0-2.

Sixth place! I couldn't blame Takao for being angry. He might have won the match I had lost, for the Korean's punches and kicks would have had less effect of Takao's gristle. But this was only the first round of a total of twelve.

Now that I had come to terms with my humiliation, I studied the board with interest. I was surprised that Thai Kick-Boxing had done so poorly, for the feet were said to be the strongest part of the body, and the kick-specialists were remarkably proficient at bringing that strongest part into hard contact with the opponent's weakest part: his head. I checked the other chart and saw that one loss had been to Aikido, which wasn't really surprising, and the other to Wrestling. No doubt the wrestler had gotten hold of the kick-boxer, after taking some punishment, and not let go. Hitting and kicking are only effective so long as one's limbs are free to hit and kick. Had I gotten a proper hold on the karateka——but that was futile speculation. I could not win retroactively.

Interesting that Boxing should have had no matches yet, while Thai Kick-Boxing and Wrestling already had two each. I understood why not every art could participate every day, since seven was an odd number. On any given day there should be three matches, with one art sitting out. But for some reason the Wrestling-Kick match had been scheduled a day before the main tournament began.

I studied the chart, and discovered how complex it was to fit in every match without duplication. No doubt there was a way to keep it even throughout, but that simply hadn't been worth the effort. Probably the television audience had appreciated the warmup, watching Grapple meet Kick. Then, today, Kung-fu had taken Wrestling, Aikido had beaten Kick—and Karate had tromped Judo. Tomorrow it would be Karate-Kung-fu, Aikido-Wrestling— and my new partner Takao would meet a boxer.

I returned to my room, where my evening meal was catered. Ordinarily I would have been eager to get out and meet the other tournament participants, but the ignominy of my first loss was still fresh and I preferred to be alone. What would Jim be thinking now, after witnessing the horror of my introduction to the Martial Open? Had Thera seen it? Was Dato laughing? And my mysterious sponsor: he had to be sorry now.

I watched the television news, hoping to take my mind off such unpleasant speculations. I now knew that Nicaragua had little TV, with broadcasts from Managua just six hours a day, and no doubt brought to this outpost by the relay towers I had seen on the way in.

Small consolation. There was only one channel, and the broadcast was in Spanish, but the subject was plain. It was a rerun of the day's tournament matches with animated commentary. It included my own humiliation at the hands and feet of Makato. I wanted to turn it off, but was morbidly fascinated.

Takao was right: I had gone into it like a rank amateur, and Makato had clubbed me down like a professional. From the first kidney-shot I had never been in the fight at all. All the time I had thought I was taking evasive action, I had actually been cowering; when I thought I was regaining my feet, I was staggering into the karateka's perfectly timed strikes. I had not been lucky to escape uninjured; Makato had spared me because he was toying with me and had no need of stronger measures.

The announcer chuckled as I sprawled unconscious on the *tatami*. A chuckle in Spanish carries all the meaning of a chuckle in English. I knew that the local audience enjoyed seeing an American bite the dust, almost literally.

Yet perhaps I had something to gain from this experience. Now I understood, all the way down into the unconscious, that hesitancy or gentleness was folly here, even though the actual meaning of the word "judo" is "gentle way." I would not again make a gift of a match to anyone. And if I met Makato again, I would show him another face of judo.

CHAPTER 5

MATCHES

The boxer was a tall black American stylist, the leading heavyweight contender. He was a former world champion who had been unjustly stripped of his title because of his involvement with the Black Panther movement, and now was denied a match by the current champion, a man he could certainly beat. I had never understood why politics was allowed to interfere with American ring success, but that was the way it seemed to be. Perhaps that was one reason America was not more highly regarded in the martial arts.

This boxer had taken the name of Mustapha, and was loudly anti-white, as well he might be. In recent years Mustapha had assumed a very high style of living, preferring white women for the humiliation to which he could subject them. A black Adonis, but of unquestioned boxing talent, and probably the actual, if not official, best in the world.

But even the finest boxer is mismatched against a hardened judoka. Mustapha had yet to learn this, and he was so arrogant it was hard to feel sorry for him. I watched because I had to, but I knew it would be cruel. Another Oriental was about to give another American another licking, and the world would cheer.

Mustapha pranced out, proud of his constantly moving legs, proud of his manly carriage. His hands were bare, of course; it would be ridiculous to use the voluminously padded boxing gloves against horn-handed bare-knuckles specialists. I was sure both boxers had been soaking their fists in brine for weeks to harden them. Mustapha wore standard boxing trunks and soft sneakers, and looked ready to knock someone out in fifteen seconds.

Takao, in contrast, was short and stout. His *judogi* uniform with its floppy sleeves and trouser cuffs and loosely tied red and white belt only accentuated the effect. He hardly looked like a fighter, let alone a master.

There was something very like a sneer of Mustapha's handsome face. That was his trademark, his confidence—builder—-yet it was not really an act. Mustapha believed in himself, as every fighter must; he was confident that no one could touch him, let alone hurt him.

Mustapha feinted with his left in classic form, then let go with his right. It scored: a solid hook to the ear. A painful blow, because of the bare knuckles. But at the same time Takao whipped his own right hand around for a *shuto, a* blow with the edge of the hand to the kidney. Such a shot was illegal in pure boxing, but perfectly in order here.

Before Mustapha, smarting as I had smarted, could draw away, Takao slung one arm around his neck and kicked his knee from behind, forcing the boxer to the floor. In that position Takao finished the fight with a chop directly to the nose. Mustapha's well-formed beak was smashed, the handsome face ruined. One more blow to the head, Takao's middle knuckle striking midway between the temple and the ear, and Mustapha was mercifully asleep.

I shook my head. I had lost because I had lacked the gumption to do what was necessary at the outset. Takao had demonstrated how to win. I didn't like it but I knew I would complete the tournament Takao's way.

＊

Everything a man could want was provided to the rooms, including beautiful, healthy, tractable girls of any race and shape specified. A number of the contestants were happy to take advantage of these services, but it wasn't to my taste. I was here as a representative of judo, and I intended to uphold its standards in all regards. Takao evidently felt the same way.

Now the tournament ladder showed Karate and Aikido tied for the lead, each 2-0. Judo had moved up to tie for third with Kung-fu, 1-1. That looked better than sixth.

It was late afternoon. I still did not wish to socialize, and certainly did not want another dose of TV recapping. I walked down the marble staircase, out of the hail, and into the sparkling gardens. It was hard to believe that such beauty could exist within such a barren region of the continent. Vicente Pedro, however eccentric he might be in other respects, had fine botanic and esthetic taste.

The garden was made with paths traveling around the floral and statuary displays. The paths themselves were formed of crushed colored stones set in patterns, with some sections of beautiful speckled granite. Small trees were clipped to resemble human figures. Marble benches were conveniently spaced, and there were arbors of vine-covered lattices with suspended orchids, grapes and hanging parasitic flowers.

I meandered through a garden maze, the hedge formed into devious configurations. A man could easily get lost in here. But I focused on a nearby fountain with colored lights and picked my way out. At night, dogs were loosed to patrol these grounds, German shepherds that sounded vicious. Was it because they were impatient with these winding byways?

Now there was a cactus enclave: dozens of weird prickly shapes, some with bright red flowers. I hadn't realized the cactus was a flowering plant before.

No one was about. I stopped before a remarkable statue whose plaque said "Dialogue of Priapus." No man could possibly be endowed in quite the way this representation was.

"Hell with it!" I said, and stripped off my clothes, tossing them behind the statue. I ran naked down a pebbled path, past red bougainvillaeas, yellow roses, assorted tulips and spurting fountains. It felt so good to be free even though I *wasn't* free. Even if the estate were not guarded by riflemen and dogs, the arid terrain would destroy a man on foot. I would remain for the full tournament, perhaps killing or being killed before it was over.

I drew up to a clear pool. A natural stream led up to it, the waters falling in a scenic cascade into a deep hollow. The crystal green liquid looked supremely inviting, and the banks of the pool were lined with stones that would make good footing for climbing out.

I dived in, cutting the water as cleanly as I could. The shock of entry was wonderful. The pool was much colder than I had anticipated.

I came up and flopped over, back stroking lazily. What joy to drift forever, at peace with all the world.

My eye caught an interesting movement on the opposite bank. I blinked. It was a woman, a girl, a young Indian maiden, perhaps fifteen. Evidently she had not observed me, for she was undressing.

And here I was, naked, with my clothing lost far back in the gardens. I treaded water, submerged except for my face, watching her. *Now* the transparency of the water was embarrassing. Yet why should it be, I chided myself, here where everything pertaining to any appetite was free?

The girl had long black hair and rather fair features. Not a full-blooded Indian, then. Her legs were well formed, and so was her bosom as it came into unfettered view. Yes, she was young, but girls evidently matured early in the tropics.

Then, with delightful innocence, she dived into the pool.

Well, why not? I swam across while she was under. "Señiorita," I said as her head appeared.

She showed no surprise. Her large dark eyes looked into mine for a moment, appraising me. Then she stroked unhurriedly away.

That was all. I finished my swim and climbed out, letting her see whatever she cared to see. It hardly matched the Priapus statue. Then I walked back to recover my clothing, feeling better.

*

My next match was with a Thai kick-boxer. Actually my opponent was not from Thailand, but was a young Filipino, not large at all: about 145-pounds, five feet two inches tall. He had very black hair, a big mouth, deep eyebrows, and a wispy beard. He was about twenty-two years old and his name was Filo Domingo. He was not a champion, but I knew he would not have been selected for the Martial Open if he were not near the top.

I was taller and heavier and more developed, but I took nothing for granted. Kick-boxing was deadly, because a man can put more power into his feet than into his hands, and this man would know how to score quickly. I was not deceived by the Thai team's two prior losses; *I* had not yet won.

I let him make the first move, wanting to see him committed before I acted. He tried a flashing head kick, and I ducked back; his foot missed contact by a good inch and a half. But immediately he came back with a hard gut kick. He knew I could finish him the same way the wrestler had, if I once got hold of him, so he was out for a fast win. His foot-reach was longer than my arm-reach, so he could strike first, and his balance was phenomenal. But I turned, taking the second kick on the thigh, absorbing its considerable impact.

I kept turning, converting my motion into a reverse kick that struck Filo's thigh. I had hoped to surprise him, but I failed; he bounced away, unhurt, ready for my followup. But I stayed clear now, knowing his counter would be more deadly than his initiative. I could not hope to outkick him.

In my first match I had not been aware of the TV cameras.

This time I saw them, and the three judges, and a fair scattering of other contestants there to study technique. One judge was Kick, another neutral—-actually the wrestling specialist—-and the third should have been Takao for Judo. But no contestant was allowed to judge, so the third was a substitute, the Aikido judge, representing Judo for this one match. He would argue our case if a question of procedure or decision came up. We were at a disadvantage without a proper Judo judge, but not a great one, because the officials were all well qualified and fair minded.

Filo whirled and came at me, trying to dazzle me with superfluous motions. But I watched his legs and the thrust of his body, and when his next kick came I was ready. It was another roundhouse to my side. I scooped up the foot with one hand while simultaneously sweeping at his other foot, throwing him backwards. He wriggled like a snake and tried to score with his free foot, but I would not let go. We fell together, and I landed on top. I had him immobilized with one arm behind his neck. Then I used my own legs to pry his open, twisting mine around his, so that I could apply a leg-lock on both his knees.

It was a submission hold, and I saw the judges nodding even as Filo yielded. The Aikido judge was probably familiar with this grip. If Aikido can be said to specialize, it is in arm and wrist locks, finger holds and arm throws, but the man surely recognized a good leg-lock too.

I let go. Filo got up, smiled, bowed, and shook hands. He was a pleasant person and a good loser, but had one of his business kicks scored, he would have been just as good a winner.

At least I had vindicated myself with a victory. Takao, watching, only nodded, as though it were the least I could have done.

My next match, according to the chart, would be in two days against Kung-fu. I made it a point to attend the Aikido-Kung-fu match scheduled the same afternoon. These two martial arts are not well known in the United States, apart from recent and somewhat distorted motion pictures and television exposure. But they are well established worldwide as ranking disciplines.

Kung-fu wu-su—the full name meaning "disciplined technique, Chinese martial arts"—was the ancient Chinese art of self-defense, going back longer than any other martial art. It might have been practiced as long ago as 2,000 B.C., and a number of other disciplines, notably karate, were said to have been derived from it. Originally secret, it had in the past twenty years expanded broadly, now being practiced by people of Mongoloid descent around the world. But only very recently had it been taught to other races.

Kung-fu was a very effective discipline, but dangerous. No sport exhibitions were held, because its practitioners did not consider it a sport. Rankings were not established, and little was known about comparative skills. But I knew that there was no more deadly a man than a competent kung-fu boxer. It stressed circular motions, in contrast to karate's linear ones, using the points of the fingers together rather than the side of the hand. Those fingers could strike like knives, cutting through a sack of rice—and sometimes human flesh—seemingly without resistance. The hand was not open as the motion started; only at the last instant before contact did the fist spring into the stiff-finger tool. A very neat gesture, and disquieting.

There were said to be five major forms of kung-fu, deriving from the motions of five fighting animals: the leopard's paw knuckle strike, the two-fingered thrust of the snake's fangs, the hand techniques of the thrashing tail of the dragon, the clenched fingers of the crane's beak, and the raking stroke of the tiger's claws. The motions were, ideally, shadowless: the victim never saw the hand until it struck.

The kung-fu *sifu*—equivalent to the judo *sensei,* or instructor—was Wang Hsu, a rotund middle-aged Chinese from Singapore. He was about five-and-a-half feet tall, weighing perhaps two hundred pounds, and had a deceptively jolly expression. But I looked at his hands and saw the extremely long, sharp fingernails, surely soaked and hardened. Tiger claws.

His Aikido opponent was Sato Shinomakii, a young Japanese

of about the same height but fifty pounds lighter. I had heard he
came from a martial family and had learned both ninja and jiujitsu
tactics from his father. There was a lot of potential in him, but I
had the feeling the *sifu,* twice his age, had tricks that would bring
him down. The man counts more than the art, when it comes to
the finish.

Yet Aikido was not without its points. Much more recent, and
known for its arm and wrist locks, it also encompassed both body
throws and the striking palm and fist. Many practitioners were
known for their *ki,* a special kind of force that made them much
more effective in combat than rational analysis would suggest. I
regarded aikido as a gentler discipline than karate or kung-fu, and
one more likely to prevail without breaking bones.

I was right about this match. The fight was brief and not pretty.
The smiling old Chinese Wang Hsu moved about with astonishing agility, kicking and leaping and even somersaulting with dazzling speed and precision. Like my partner Takao, he was all muscle
under that seeming corpulence. The young Aikido player took
evasive action, watching for his chance; but most of the *sifu's* motions were only feints. As Sato tried to close, Wang gave him the
tiger's claws to the forehead. Those razor-sharp fingernails ripped
open the younger man's eyelids, blinding him with blood. Sato
did not give up; he was ready to continue the fight by feel. But all
three judges were on their feet, calling an end before the hapless
man was permanently mutilated.

Wang Hsu, kung-fu *sifu:* this was the man I would meet in
two days. I would be a blind fool—perhaps literally—to play gentle
with him, or ever give those devastating claws an opening to my
face. The forked fingers of the snake's fangs were no less dangerous,
for they could poke out my eyeballs.

The crane's beak was devastating wherever it struck, like a knife.
Yes, my harsh lesson from the Korean karateka might well have
prepared me to save more valuable assets than my pride. What if
my opening match had been against kung-fu?

As usual, I checked the tournament ladder. Karate had now

assumed first place, 3-0. Judo was in a three way tie for second with Kung-fu and Aikido, all 2-1. Yes, I would have to watch myself with kung-fu, and with all the other martial arts.

I was now ready to mix with the other contestants—but was distracted by another possibility. I went for another swim in the crystal pond, half hoping to see the pretty maiden again. She was not there, but after I had swum for a few minutes she appeared, undressing and entering the water with exactly the innocence of the prior day.

I swam across and gave her a token splash "Do you speak English?" I inquired.

She looked at me for a long moment, and I feared I had my answer already. "No, I do not," she replied, almost without accent. Then, with a perfectly serious face, she stroked away, her smooth bare legs scissoring delightfully.

*

Takao's next bout was with the American wrestler. The man was monstrous in his tights: a good three hundred and twenty-five pounds, six-feet seven-inches tall, the largest man in the tournament. He was the "Whale"—but under the blubber was a powerful athlete. Whale had a reputation as a clown, a villain in the ring; but such a reputation was common to many professional American wrestlers, because of the showmanship demands of the unsophisticated television audience. But he could forget the slapstick and fight seriously when the money was attractive, and he was one of the current three world champions. Wrestling was like that; each major circuit had its own world champion.

Each tournament contestant received five thousand dollars per victory, and only one thousand per loss, so Whale was here on business. This might not seem like a great amount of money, considering the very real risk to life and health, especially when compared to the million dollar guarantees one heard about in prize boxing. But the fact was that all these men were accustomed to physical risk, and normally did not earn more than five or six thousand dollars a year from their martial abilities. Here they could earn that much in a single match—and considerably more in the course of the tournament, for there were team-placement prizes in addition to the match-awards that became quite fat. Anyone who did halfway decently here would depart with a very nice nest egg. Besides, few were doing this purely for the money.

Takao selected the Karate judge to represent him, and I hoped that wasn't giving away his strategy. I knew Whale was conversant with "dirty" wrestling—actually standard practice for the more serious arts—and would not hesitate to use it here. The neutral judge was from Boxing this time.

Whale charged Takao with a bull roar—and was met by a blood-curdling *kiai* yell that set him back. Whale shook his head as though struck and began laughing, and even the judges had to join in. The television audience would really go for this. The battle of the screaming beasts!

They closed again, and Takao threw the wrestler to the mat with a *uki goshi* rising hip throw. Whale landed hard, slapping the *tatami* with his hands to make it sound louder, reverting automatically to his showman ways. Then he groaned and lay there a moment as if stunned—but Takao was not deceived by that ploy. The wrestler's most effective technique was on the mat, where his extra hundredweight of mass could work for him. Once he got a lock on Takao, Whale would be able to last until age told. Perhaps.

Whale got up and charged again, this time omitting the roar. Takao threw him again with *sukui-nage,* the sweep throw, putting one arm between his legs, the other across his chest, making it look easy. Again the loud landing, the stunned-gambit, declined.

Three more times they repeated this playlet. Takao used the *o-goshi* hip roll, the *ippon-seoi nage* shoulder throw, and the *ushire-goshi* back lift throw. Whale seemed ready continue indefinitely, forcing the judoka to come to him after the throw. Takao was becoming annoyed—which was exactly what Whale wanted. I did not like the look of it, for the wrestler was obviously no dummy, but I kept my mouth shut. This was the old man's match.

On the sixth throw Takao put more into it, using a *kubi-nage* on head and arm, hurling the man farther than before. This was an unnecessary expenditure of energy, as Whale obviously knew how to take any fall harmlessly despite his mass. I saw Takao stiffen after that—only momentarily, but it electrified me unpleasantly. He had just suffered a partial black-out, and that probably meant irregular heart action. He was in trouble.

The seventh time Takao used the *o-uchi-gari*, or big inside clip, putting his right leg between the legs of the wrestler while sweeping with his left leg at the right leg of Whale and pushing to the rear. This was a dangerous throw, because it was possible to injure the other man severely by falling on top of him. It was also easy to injure yourself, trying not to hurt him. Takao had to strain to make Whale go down, and might not have succeeded if the man hadn't been expecting another forward throw. Or saw his opportunity to grapple on the mat, at last. Was Takao weakening?

Down they went—and suddenly I knew Whale had observed Takao's blackout, and was going to keep the pressure on. But Takao, deliberately, fell on top. His knee landed in Whale's crotch, backed by the full weight of his body. All contestants wore protective padding there, but this was too much.

Judo had won another match. But Karate still led, 4-0. More and more, I regretted my inept loss to Makato.

*

Wang Hsu, the kung-fu *sifu*, faced me with his pleasant smile. But I remembered the tiger's claw. This was no cliche Chinaman laundryman, and this was one match where I meant to go all out to win in a hurry, if I could. But if I lost, I wanted it to be by a clean knockout blow, not by eyeball gouging.

We fenced for a moment, circling each other without contact. I was on guard against those hands, not forgetting the other acrobatics Wang was capable of, but determined to stop his hands even at the cost of a leaping foot smash. The acrobatics I could handle, win or lose.

It came suddenly: what looked like a straight punch, unusual for circular kung-fu, but what could be converted into tiger or snake. Primed for this, I caught the arm and spun into a *soto-maki-komi,* a winding sacrifice throw that wrapped my body about his arm. I extended my right leg to the rear, as his whole body went over my leg. I dared not let go, even as we both fell to the floor. I went on to apply the *kesa-gatame hishigi* scarf hold neck lock, with one arm about his head and the other firmly gripping his left arm under my left armpit. Without pause I executed a neck hold ordinarily forbidden in judo, gripping the back of his neck with both arms and bending the head forward and to the right.

The judges interceded then, before I snapped his neck. I had played rough—but I had learned the necessity right here in the Martial Open, when I fought Makato. This time I had been lucky: I had conquered the dangerous one without a wound.

Wang Hsu got up and bowed formally to me. There was no sign of ire on his part, and possibly he felt none, for he had complete control. But I did not want to meet him again, for all his equanimity. The plain fact was that I was afraid of his weapons. I could not depend on my timing to trap him a second time.

"Congratulations!" Takao cried with warmth as we returned to our room. "You handled him like a real judoka!"

Was he trying to flatter me? He must have seen how shaky my victory had really been, however rapidly accomplished. "I trapped the snake because I had to," I said. "His fang was coming at me. Any other time I'd run from him."

"So would I!" he admitted, surprisingly. "I don't have much callus on my eyeballs. Do you realize you are the first man ever to beat Wang Hsu in competition? He is the kung-fu master!" Now I was certain he had something on his mind, though Wang's status was news to me, making me shaky.

We mounted the stair. "Aikido took Karate!" Takao exclaimed.

"Do you know what that means?"

Aikido took Karate! That *was* a surprise, for I knew it had been the turn of the young Japanese Sato, the man I had seen lose to the tiger's claw. The senior Aikido *sensei* was said to be a most remarkable man, possessed of *ki* and the leading figure of his discipline—but his pupil Sato, though promising, was not of that caliber. I'd have to take a look at the films on that one.

Then I realized. "It means we're tied for first place!" I said, gratified. "We've done it!"

Takao sobered, though he obviously had caught the victory fever. "Not yet. It is three way—Judo, Karate, Aikido. And there is a problem."

"No problem you can't solve!" I said. "You meet Aikido tomorrow."

"I must talk to you, Jason," he said. It was the first time he had used my first name. Now I knew he was going to confess his heart weakness. Yet it was better that we have the truth out, before something serious happened.

We entered our room and sat down in the pair of easy chairs there. "I did not come here expecting to fight," Takao said, after checking to make sure the intercom was off: a simple matter of disconnecting one of its wires. "You know I fear no man. But there is a complication. At my trial, after the war, I thought I was immune to punishment, because no one would testify against me, a *Hachidan,* eighth degree. But one did—and his stature in the martial arts was such that that alone was enough to convict me. I lost my right to compete, and I lost much face; that was the hardest thing to bear. Only one thing prevented me from following the *Bushido* code and committing *seppuku—hara kiri* to you Occidentals—as they expected me to do. That was my determination to achieve vengeance. Twenty-five years ago I swore to kill the man who had betrayed me, and it was for that I kept myself in combat shape."

This was not at all what I had anticipated. The *bushido* code—

literally, the way of the warrior—was an extremely strong force in the Orient. I did not know how to respond.

"But I have long since realized that my sentence was just," Takao said with difficulty. "The man who testified so eloquently about my atrocities was not a traitor to the martial arts, but a man of such great integrity that he did what he knew was right, irrespective of national or martial loyalties. He was right and I wrong, and now I am glad he did what he did, and I repent my vow of vengeance. All I crave is that man's forgiveness. But I have lacked the courage to approach him."

"Because he would reject you?" I asked.

"No. He rejects no one."

"Because he might think you came to kill him!" I said, thinking I had it now.

"No. He never feared my vengeance. It is because I wronged him by my oath, and caused him also to lose face, and now I lack the means to make appropriate apology."

I did not fully understand this, but chalked it up to my ignorance of the nuances of Japanese etiquette. "I am not certain how this relates to our present situation?"

"The man is Hiroshi: the Aikido *o-sensei* I must meet tomorrow."

At last it fell into place. Hiroshi, the senior aikidoist, who was also from Japan. With a history like that, Takao would be in trouble the moment he touched Hiroshi. If he fought to win, he risked injuring or killing the *sensei,* and people would think he had made good on his long-standing vow of vengeance. If he lost, it could be said that he threw the match in a craven effort to find favor with his long-time enemy. If he refused to fight, he would be judged a coward, and would never obtain the forgiveness he so desired.

"It occurs to me," I said carefully, "that my next turn will be against Karate, at the start of the second sequence. I lost to Karate before; but possibly you would have won. Do you think our chances would improve if we exchanged matches? It's a tactical decision, in the interest of team success."

"A tactical decision!" Takao agreed, and there was something almost pitiful about his relief. I was no expert in Japanese protocol, but I had the impression I had done the appropriate thing.

I had thought I would go swimming again, perhaps exchanging another word with the nymph of the pool, but this development forced a change in plan. I always tried to learn as much about the man and the martial art I was to meet as possible, so as to be prepared. I was very glad to have done so in the case of kung-fu; now it was necessary to bone up on Aikido.

I ordered films of all the Aikido matches and settled down for a long evening of play, replay, and assessment. I started with today's match, in which Aikido had beaten Karate, because I was curious about that for more than one reason.

Neither Makato nor Hiroshi were in this one. Instead it was the young Puerto Rican karateka, Jesus Granda, against the young Japanese, Sato Shinomakii. Jesus was perhaps the top karate fighter in America and Europe, the man who might one year replace Makato for world honors. Sato wore light bandages over his eyes that seemed to hamper his vision. He had real fighting spirit and was there to win, but I did not see how he could be a match for the karateka. Not at this time.

The actual bout did not have much overt drama. Jesus attempted to pound Sato into submission with punches and kicks, but the aikidoist dodged with remarkable finesse, considering his condition. It began to look as though Wang the kung-fu *sifu* had had a lucky break, scoring early on this young man, for he was certainly hard to hit today. How many of these matches, including my own, were decided more by the breaks than by genuine superiority of technique?

The karateka missed a major punch, and Sato seized his arm. Jesus tried to hit him with his free hand, but Sato turned, falling on the locked elbow, dislocating it.

Jesus had his arm reset immediately, so that he could continue in the tournament, perhaps with the aid of pain-killing drugs. But Karate had lost its first match. And I made a note: do not attempt many karate-type punches against aikido: Jesus had been lucky that the dislocation had been minor.

Then I turned to Hiroshi's two matches. The first had been against wrestling, and tiny Hiroshi, the smallest man in the tournament, faced Whale, the largest.

Hiroshi stood there in the traditional aikido costume, the *hakama*, a kind of pleated skirt extending to the ankles. Dresses seem effeminate only to those who do not know their martial history. Yet perhaps the suggestion of gentleness was appropriate, for Hiroshi was a kind man. That showed up even in the film: there was an aura about him that suggested no one need hesitate to ask a favor. Surely Takao was already forgiven, could he but bring himself to stand in this man's presence.

The match was fast and clean. Whale rushed at Hiroshi, thinking to crush him in a huge and fatty embrace. The tiny man waited calmly. Whale, surprised but hardly dismayed by this easy capture, seized him and started squeezing, ready to settle for submission in lieu of broken ribs.

Hiroshi calmly put one hand on the small of the wrestler's back, at his spine, and pressed there with his fingers. With just one finger of the other hand, he pushed under Whale's nose. It looked futile, but I knew that such pressure on the two nerve locations, spinal and facial, could be excruciating. A man of any stature can be brought up short by one finger held sidewise under his nose. Anyone can verify this by simple trial. Whale was trapped, and he had to surrender.

Then Boxing: and Mustapha made the same mistake of trying to finish the frail-seeming old man quickly. He started punching hard, and as the agile *sensei* moved aside, Mustapha rushed him, thinking to clinch with one arm while punishing him with short jabs to the kidneys and perhaps a rabbit punch to the back of the neck to finish him off.

Hiroshi stepped to the front and with his two hands tumbled Mustapha to the left and back. It was a perfect *sumi-otoshi*, or corner drop, a very difficult throw to execute. Then he seized

Mustapha's hand and used both his own hands to splay the fingers apart, applying pressure with his thumbs to the back of the hand. It was a submission hold, and the boxer submitted rapidly.

Yes, little Hiroshi was a remarkable man. But it seemed to me I could take him, if I were careful to stay clear of his arm-bar. I was intrigued by the care he took to prevent injury; apparently gentleness was not incompatible with victory.

*

Hiroshi in person was even more remarkable than on film. Not only was he the lightest man in the tournament, he was the oldest: sixty-two. He was five-feet two-inches tall and weighed 105 pounds. He was as graceful as a dancer; equilibrium was his keynote.

Gentle? Yes, but he was proud, too, and the two were linked. I had wondered, when considering him, why he had entered this brutal tournament. It was not that he needed the money. He was poor, certainly, but he lived austerely by choice. It was not that he craved notoriety, for he had little use for personal reputation.

Hiroshi was the leading *sensei* in his martial art, so he was called the *O-Sensei*. He could have sent anyone to represent Aikido. He had come himself because he did not wish to bear the responsibility for the possible injury or death of another man.

Some of the greatest pacifists are leaders in the martial arts, and this is no paradox. Hiroshi was the perfect example.

We closed, and despite my preparation and caution I was too slow. Hiroshi's hands were a blur as he caught mine, and then he had the *kote-gaishi,* the reverse hand, and I was in agony. He was turning my hand outward, putting pressure on my wrist, and I knew he could break it easily. I had seen him apply such submission holds in the films, yet I had fallen into this one anyway.

I rolled forward and wrenched myself free. But this was a blundering tactic against such a master, and I felt something break. It was my own fault; he had not been pressing really hard, assuming that I would yield—and perhaps I should have. But I was only half his age, and lacked his mature discretion in the heat of battle. If I had only somersaulted backward . . .

Now I was on the floor. I put both feet on his stomach and grasped his ankles with my hands despite the pain in my right. I shoved him down that way; even Whale could not have held his footing against that leverage. Immediately I was on him, turning my body to the side, catching his neck in a strangle scissors hold, choking him with my legs. Now he had to yield.

Afterwards, he checked my hand, expressing sincere regret. There was little I could say, for we both knew I had been responsible for my injury, and had accepted it as the price of victory. My wrist appeared to be sprained, and one finger was broken.

So I had won, but now I had a liability that could cost me dearly in the second half of the tournament.

CHAPTER 6

DANCE

It was time for the halftime show. We were to have three days of relaxation during which the rigors of training could be eased and battle animosities set aside. A small army of girls of every nationality arrived by truck to reinforce the regulars, and exotic aromas wafted from the kitchen complex. Vicente Pedro evidently planned to entertain royally.

There were motion pictures showing in three separate rooms: one conventional American romance with subtitles in Chinese/Japanese symbols, one Japanese martial arts sequence that I watched with interest, and one pornography that required no translations. Each had few attendees at any given hour of the day; most of the men preferred to skip the vicarious offerings in favor of the real ones. A number, however, eschewed sexual contact as debilitating during physical training, a myth that many athletes believed.

"The dance tonight is formal," Takao told me gloomily. "Full regalia, including women."

"Our host provides both clothing and distaff," I said. "Excellent selection, both. No problem at all."

He shook his head. "If my wife ever found out—"

I laughed, but stopped when I realized he was serious. My

tough roommate was turning out to be a man of many hesitations, when not in combat. He really did not want to date a local girl, or even a Japanese offering. "Your wife—good looking?" I inquired awkwardly.

"Fat like a Sumo wrestler!" he said, grimacing. "But for thirty years she has believed in me, when not many did, and there is not her like in all the world."

I was surprised to discover this particular loyalty in so callously practical a man. But the business with Hiroshi should have given me a clue. It was never possible to judge character on an incomplete basis. "Then decline the honor of company," I suggested. "If I were married—" To a girl like Thera Drummond? Foolish thought!

"Pedro insists," he said. I already knew enough of our crippled host to realize that his foibles had to be obliged if one cared to remain on the premises. He wanted his formal dance, each man dressed and with a pretty girl, and so it would be. "And I must have the money," Takao finished.

To get that wife over to Brazil, I remembered. "Then you'll just have to explain to her that you had no choice."

He shook his head lugubriously. "This one thing she would not believe."

Jealous wife! "Maybe if someone else explained?"

"No. She would believe only a Japanese *sensei* of high standing—and which of those would speak for me?"

I let it drop. It seemed like such a trivial problem, yet obviously it was a matter of great concern to him.

At least I was in the clear. I had no wife and no serious attachments. Probably I would never see Thera again, for she would meet boys in college. I could attend this function with one of the provided girls. Perhaps the pond-maiden. She was young, but old enough to appreciate the extravaganza.

But she wasn't in the lineup. I asked the *mayordomo,* the Spanish head butler—a genuine Spaniard from Spain, no doubt a status symbol—describing her. The man's eyes widened momentarily, and he took me aside. "Señor, that girl is not available! Do not inquire of her again!" he whispered.

I bowed to necessity. It was not important, really. The glimpses I had had of the nymph's bare torso did not give me any special claim upon her. I accepted instead a fine buxom Latin girl who spoke no English, thus solving the problem of inane conversation.

The banquet room was at one side of the main ballroom, and the whole complex was huge. The entire floor was of polished white marble, and there were myriad full-length mirrors on the walls alternating with costly hangings. Around the top was a carved and painted frieze illustrating mythological scenes similar to the motifs of the outdoor statuary: cupids, centaurs, and a great many well-formed nymphs.

At one end was a full orchestra in formal attire, playing soft music indefatigably. Also a battalion of *camareros,* or waiters, and a well-equipped *cantinero:* the bartender.

Every man was garbed in his national costume, making for a splendid and diverse array. I wore a black tuxedo, but Whale sported a very nice green suit with modern wide tie and ruffled purple shirt. Mustapha, however, was resplendent in a golden lamé suit with cerise pants, a shocking pink shirt, a mink hat and genuine alligator shoes. He had gold and ruby earrings, a big diamond ring, and a pendant on his chest: golden lion with diamond eyes. He must have done some fast talking to convince our host that this was his national attire.

The girls were all dressed almost alike in pastel-hued floor-length gowns of white, pink, or blue. Each had fluffy sleeves and decolletage showing their deep bosoms to advantage. My own date, Lufita, was in yellow, and I reined my gaze from her impressive and quivering cleavage with difficulty. It was all a rather neat counterpoint, though there was also a somewhat cynical symbolism: the implication that men were complete and distinct individuals, while women were interchangeable. Pedro had a fine regard for the martial arts and the men who practiced them, but it seemed that to him women were mere accessories.

I glanced at him, at the head table, seated in his wheelchair. He was almost concealed by the fare loading the table and I could not actually make out more than his right shoulder and part of his head. I did not know the precise nature of his handicap, but suspected it was similar to paraplegia: an injury of the spinal nerve that numbed and incapacitated the lower extremities. If Pedro actually had no sensation from the waist down, he would be unable to derive sexual pleasure, except, possibly, for a thin orgasm when his genitals were competently massaged. An almost intolerable situation for a rich, handsome (if the statue were to be believed), influential, and not too old a man who would normally have had his pick of the most desirable women of the world. Unless he constructed a formidable defensive psychological shield.

We sat at a tremendous carved mahogany table, with high chairs of leather and mahogany, real works of art. The service plates and vases were of beaten gold.

The *camareros* circulated with trays of drinks, and they would take orders for practically anything a man could want. Others pushed buffet serving carts bearing hot and cold delicacies, shrimp, lobster, oysters, button mushrooms, crab meat, snails and garnishes of raw vegetables carved into elegant shapes: radish roses, turnip daisies, parsnip petals, onions cut into chrysanthemum flowers, and carrot curls set off by ripe olive halves and parsley foliage.

Then the first main course: whole suckling pig, roasted over charcoal in a hole in the ground. It was accompanied by heart of palms salad, and a whole group of boiled and fried dishes like *yuca frita*—potato-like tubers, fried-plantains, guava omelette, rice, black beans, assorted fish, squid, and so many exotic soups I could not hope to keep track.

Dazed by the variety, and uncomfortable amid such opulence, I was daunted by the gustatorial array until Lufita helped me. She spoke only Spanish, but she made clear by gesture and example what was expected, and I appreciated it. She gave me a small fork for tasting the snails—which were not bad, actually—and indicated that I should taste a little bit of salt and lemon juice in my hand before attempting the potent tequila. Even so, it was more than I liked, and I reached for a rich red drink I supposed was tomato juice to cool my gullet.

Lufita cautioned me with a gesture, and I paused to take stock of that other beverage before actually sipping, despite the alcohol burning in my throat. It was warm and thick and not actually the hue of tomato, and the odor *"El toro,"* she murmured, and nodded at the cup, barely smiling as she sipped her own. I lifted mine to match the toast, then realized that it wasn't a toast, but a point of information. *Toro*—that was Spanish for—I stared into the rich warm fluid, but could not bring myself to imbibe. It was fresh blood from a slaughtered bull.

After that I confined myself to the mild Spanish cider, preferring to avoid the extremes of alcohol and *el toro*. Even so, my head soon grew pleasantly dizzy, and my bladder urgent. Later I learned that that innocent-seeming cider had more than twice the alcohol content of beer.

My gut was bursting by the time dessert came, and I could only pick at the fancy tropical fruit dessert, not even wondering what it might be. This high living was too rich for me.

At last the table was cleared, and I waddled to the ballroom proper, excusing myself *en route* for an imperative stop at the men's room. I discovered I had lots of company; the facility was crowded with unhappy warriors of the table. Whale was breaking wind gustily as he waited in line for a toilet. Mustapha the boxer was puking into a sink, and several others looked as though they wished they could do the same.

Mustapha raised his head and spied me. For the moment we were not Black and White, but two sick Americans trapped far south of the border. "I don't know if it was the pickled quail eggs or the fried caterpillars," he gasped, wiping the spume from his lips. "Or maybe that damned black doll laughing when she told me. Bitch!"

I had noted his date. "I thought she was original African."

"She *is*. Her folks were never slave. To her, I'm a honkey. Over one-sixteenth white, you know. God, my stomach!"

"You should have stuck to regular fare, as I did."

He raised an eyebrow. His nose remained in bad shape, but he appeared to have avoided facial damage after Takao's smash. "You mean those fritters you were stowing away? Those were made of calves' brains. I checked everything out after I ate one of those chocolate-covered ants. Or do you mean that roasted spider monkey meat?"

My stomach spoke. "Move over!" I yelped, putting my face to the stinking sink.

In due course I found my way back to Lufita, who was sitting demurely at the fringe of the dancing area. I dropped into the seat she had saved for me, hoping no spatters of vomit showed on my tuxedo. Chocolate-covered ants!

The music played. Lufita nudged me unobtrusively, signaling that the men were expected to dance and not sit out. All around the ballroom I saw men rising, some very uncomfortably, in response to similar hints from their partners. I almost laughed out loud; it was so like a junior high school prom, with the girls willing but the boys slicked down and hating it. Had Pedro set this up deliberately to humiliate the men who retained their physical prowess?

I moved out and danced with her, feeling like a puppet on strings. She was very good, which was fortunate, as I was not. I had never been much for this sort of thing.

The movements of the dance brought out the diverse costumes of the men. The Japanese were wearing formal black silk kimonos with trousers and wooden sandals. Makato the Korean had white trousers and a black hat and sandals. Wang Hsu, the Chinese kung-fu *sifu*, wore a luxurious silk robe with a golden dragon embroidered on the back; I knew without asking that the thread was genuine gold. But the younger kung-fu disciple, Pung Lii, was austere in contrast, in a simple Mao suit. The Russian wrestler, Oleg Usk, had the traditional baggy peasant trousers and blouse with voluminous sleeves, plus a fur hat. The Thai kick-boxer wore a saffron robe down to his ankles, tied by a black sash. The Argentinian boxer was in a gaucho outfit, with riding boots, leather pants, a wide colored shirt, black hat and even a whip.

And more—but I was receiving warning nudges from Lufita for rubbernecking. Yet it was a dazzling spectacle.

After a few minutes of mixed pleasure and agony—because I hated trying to dance, but liked holding a woman of her shape and grace—we sat down, and I began to regret my inability to converse with her. I had assumed that all the girls were hired prostitutes, but now it seemed that geishas might be the more appropriate term. Talented entertainers deserving of respect.

"How do you do, sir." I turned to the voice to find Hiroshi, the little aikido *sensei,* on my other side. He was, in his black pleated skirt, the epitome of the Japanese elder.

"Glad to see you," I said, somewhat at a loss. My broken finger gave a twinge, and I had a faint notion how Takao felt. It was embarrassing to receive an injury at the hands of this man, because only grievous blunder by the other party could put even that stigma upon him. But how did one apologize for *receiving* injury?

"I trust your hand is better?" he said. "I regret that my inexcusable carelessness—"

"Much better," I said quickly, though it wasn't.

"I would not presume to interfere with another man's business," he said obliquely.

I caught the hint. Was it about Takao? "Please feel free to speak without concern for offense," I said.

"Our host, while generous and effective, is a peculiar man. Perhaps he might be considered unreasonable by some, in certain respects. Yet he has a consistent rationale."

Hiroshi, old and discreet as he was, was not the type to gossip idly. What was he driving at? "He certainly has been strict about the festivities," I said. "But it is a nice enough dance, with no expense spared. Good experience for us all, I'm sure."

"It would seem advantageous not to express surprise at what

might develop," he said. "Even a slight reaction, a mere raising of the brow, might not go unobserved."

"Sensible advice," I agreed, mystified. Apparently I would have to find out for myself, after having been warned to expect something unusual from Pedro.

Then another matter occurred to me. *"Sensei,* is it permissible for an occidental to ask a favor?"

"It is," he said gravely, as I had known he would.

"I understand that you and Takao are not close."

"This is true, yet we are not so far apart as it may once have appeared. Takao has had an unfortunate life."

"Is the distance little enough so that you might be willing to write a letter on his behalf?"

He looked regretful. "I can not undo the past."

"No, no," I said quickly. "This does not concern his professional status. It is a private matter, and I speak without his knowledge." (I was, if I stripped away the euphemism, interfering, but I hoped I was doing right.) "It seems his wife is a good woman, but jealous, and she may misconstrue tonight's arrangements. All these young girls . . . Only a completely reputable *sensei* conversant with the situation can reassure her, and—"

Hiroshi smiled. "I shall call upon her personally."

The music began again and it was necessary to dance. I thanked Hiroshi hastily and got up with Lufita. I was half-pleased to note that a majority of the men were as uncomfortable as I. Makato the Korean had a partner taller than he was, and he looked about ready to lay her out with a karate punch. Whale was too big for his suit, and was literally bursting out. In addition he had a tiny girl perhaps a third his mass. But, surprisingly, he was dancing very well, swinging the girl off her feet with perfect aplomb, and they both seemed to be having fun. I did not see Takao, and presumed he was hiding in the hope that the jealous spirit of his wife would not spy him.

Meanwhile the copious alcohol was enlivening the party. I heard a commotion and looked over to the great marble staircase that ascended from one side of the ballroom. A man was at the head of it—a Japanese, I thought, but I couldn't be sure—urinating copiously in full view.

Oh-oh. If that was Takao—!

Someone went up to haul him away, getting spattered in the process, and there was an embarrassed chuckle below. But I knew no obscenity had been intended. Orientals are much freer about natural functions, and the copious liquors of a party like this could make them forget. Surely Occidental customs were just as indiscreet in Japan, on occasion.

"I hope our host did not witness that," a familiar voice murmured beside me.

"Takao!" I exclaimed, jumping. Then I felt foolish. Of *course* he wouldn't have . . .

"A natural error," he continued. If he had a date, I didn't see her, and perhaps that was just as well. "But a cripple who must use a catheter could take such a display as a very personal affront."

I hadn't thought of that. How would *I* feel, in Pedro's position?

Then, appropriately, it was my turn to go through the receiving line, for I had not yet met my host.

Vicente Pedro sat in a wheelchair. He was indeed a handsome man, despite his infirmity, and his arms looked very strong. I knew now that he had a third degree black belt in judo and a fifth degree in karate; possibly he still practiced the latter, breaking boards and striking dummies. He was about forty-five years old, with a dark skin and black wavy hair. He wore a white linen suit with a silk shirt bearing a diamond stickpin and pearl cufflinks. His hands bore large ruby and emerald rings.

The *mayordomo* introduced us: "Don Pedro, may I pressent Jason Striker of America. Judo."

Pedro studied me, frowning. I remembered that he did not like judo, because of his injury, and wanted it to lose. "You had a bit of trouble getting started," he said.

He must have enjoyed that! "Yes."

He paused a moment more, then decided I would do. "Striker, my niece, Amalita."

I turned with a polite smile to acknowledge the girl beside him. I had been so absorbed by Pedro himself that I hadn't noticed her before.

It was the nymph of the pool.

"You have met my niece?" Pedro inquired with an edge.

This was what Hiroshi had tried to warn me about. "I believe I have seen her in your beautiful gardens."

Now Pedro's gaze was ugly. "My niece does not socialize in the gardens, judoka!"

"Of course not," I agreed.

Amalita herself remained demure and silent. She was quite fetching in her formal dress, though it was of a more conservative cut than the standard for the other girls.

"Come," Pedro said, abruptly wheeling himself forward. He indicated Amalita and me, waving back the others in the receiving line including my own date.

Amalita walked gracefully beside him while I followed. We traversed the breadth of the ballroom, which was now silent, and entered a side gallery leading to a closed series of rooms. Armed guards saluted Pedro as we entered, then blocked the doorway behind us. That claustrophobic feeling crept up on me again.

The walls were covered with weapons on display. Not conventional ones, like swords and firearms, but oddities of Oriental martial arts. I had to read the plaques to identify most of them, and couldn't get a proper look because Pedro kept moving along. There is nothing clumsy or slow about a well-managed wheelchair.

There were *nunchakus*, like two billy-clubs connected by about nine inches of rope. I saw two little knobbed sticks, about five inches long; the plaque said *yawara-jutsu*. Apparently they were used to strike at nerve centers. There were several long bows and quarterstaffs, marked respectively *kyudo* and *ho jitsu*; also *nanriki gusari*, a pole with a chain; and several *shuriken*, which were starlike little throwing missiles with sharp points that, according to the legend, the ninjas of Japan threw with unnerving accuracy through the holes in enemy helmets such as eye-slits. But the main weapon I noticed was also one of the smallest: *shukos*, or metal tiger claws: barbed bands that fit across the palms, to scratch the victim cruelly or even aid in scaling walls. They could also be used as handguards, making it possible to foil or grip the blade of a striking sword. What a macabre preoccupation our host had!

We entered another chamber and stopped. This time I did not need to read the plaques. "Japanese *katanas*!" I exclaimed, amazed.

"Ah, judoka—you are a collector?" Pedro inquired with alert interest.

"Hardly! I could not afford the least of these fine swords," I admitted. "But I admire weapons from a distance." And indeed this display of blades was superlative. Many were embossed with jewels or gold and were precious works of art. The hilt of one thirty-inch curved sword was of carved wood in the shape of a wolf's head, the guard inlaid with silver, and a panel of engraved brass just below the guard. All the swords appeared to be genuine, not replicas—which meant they had been stolen from Japanese temples in the period after Japan's defeat in World War Two, when so many treasures had been looted. There was also a remarkable *katana-kake*, or sword stand, made in the shape of a giant dragon-fly, gold lacquer throughout except for green lacquered eyes. It must have been a very wealthy or royal samurai warrior who had originally owned this.

"And do you by chance know how the best *katanas* were made?" Pedro inquired.

"I have only a general notion," I said, wondering why he chose to question me along this line. "In the old days, methods of purifying iron and making steel were at best imperfect. Some pretty bizarre techniques were employed, but apparently they worked, because the steel in such swords is said to be as good as any modern steel, and their cutting edges have never been excelled."

"How could one tell?" Pedro asked, his eyes bright. I felt nervous, but answered him steadily.

"They were said to have been tested by allowing a silk hand-kerchief to fall upon the blade, to see whether the cloth would be cut in half by its own slight weight. It was claimed some swords never grew dull. And they were strong: the true *katana* had to be capable of cutting off the head of a man at a single stroke. Or to cut a human body in half. Sometimes two or more bodies were piled on top of a mound of sand, and cut across. I have heard that as many as seven bodies have been severed by one cut."

Amalita stood silently, showing no interest in either the collection or the discussion; but Pedro's eye had a fanatic gleam. "You are well educated, Striker," he said, leaning forward. "But the cooling—do you know about that?"

"Some were cooled in blood," I said, repelled by his morbidity. He *was* leading up to something unpleasant.

"This sword," Pedro said, wheeling up to take a *katana* in its scabbard from the wall. He drew the blade out slowly, and it was incomplete, snapped off a few inches below the guard. "See, it is broken. Can you imagine its history?"

So he had a story to tell. "Sir, I can not."

He held the imperfect weapon and gazed on it as he talked, as though fascinated. "This sword was to be cooled in the living body of the metalworker's worst enemy," he said, glancing sidelong at me. "But the proposed victim comprehended the plot the moment he was captured, and managed to scoop up and swallow a number of large rocks that littered his cell. When the heated blade was plunged into his body, it struck the rocks and broke. It was said that man died laughing!"

I merely nodded, uncertain how to respond to such a twisted joke.

Pedro slid the broken sword back into its scabbard and held it out to me. "A gift," he said. "For your prowess and discretion. Draw no blood with it in this household."

Astonished, I accepted.

Pedro spun about and wheeled, back toward the dance, Amalita keeping pace. I followed, carrying the precious but awful gift. Was it genuine? Was the story true? Why had he so honored me?

Or *was* it an honor?

*

The remaining half-time activities seemed routine. The dance ended promptly at eleven, so the relieved contestants could retire at a suitable hour. Next morning Vicente Pedro personally awarded the cash prizes to the members of the martial arts teams in direct proportion to their rankings, though the real payoff would come at the conclusion of the tournament. Judo received twenty-six thousand dollars for its five wins and one loss, as did Karate; Kung-fu and Aikido, with 4-2 records, had twenty-two thousand apiece; Wrestling at 2-4 got fourteen thousand; Thai Kick-Boxing, *1-5,* ten thousand; and Boxing got just the consolation money, six thousand dollars.

Mustapha, the American boxer, brooded alone, drinking heavily. I tried to talk to him, thinking he might prefer American company, but he would have none of it. "Just you watch that fuckin' sword, cousin!" he snapped, though I had left the gift *katana* in my room.

In the afternoon Pedro staged a jaguar hunt. We all had to wear elaborate hunting costumes: baggy khaki pants, black leather boots, khaki hat, white short-sleeved shirt, and a silk kerchief around the neck to inhibit the dust. Each man also had a canteen of water, for we were warned that although the streams looked clear, some were infected with river flukes—parasites of the liver—so that no natural water could be presumed to be safe for the unaware. Another reminder how difficult it would be to escape this place on foot. We also carried hunting guns of assorted makes, not the single-shot pieces I had supposed true sportsmen employed. Mine was a Belgian semi-automatic rifle, specifically, an FAL semi-auto 7.62 mm. I had only a vague notion how to operate it, and no intention of making the attempt.

And of course we rode sleek steeds, even those of us who had
never been near a horse before. I wondered how Pedro himself
managed to ride: did he have a special harness, or did he just sit in
his wheelchair and laugh at the rest of us? I saw poor Filo Domingo,
the Filipino kick-boxer, clutching the swaying saddle-horn and
looking seasick. Whale rode beside him, equally miserable, for no
boots fit him and he was in heavy socks and low shoes instead, and
his horse was none too comfortable, either. I made a gesture signifying a saddle being shoved into a pornographic aperture, and
both smiled wistfully.

But a number were expert horsemen. Pibe Rosario, the brawl-
ing Argentine slugger, seemed oafish in combat despite his strength
and stamina. But on horseback he was poetry in motion. He must
have ridden bareback since early childhood on some great ranch,
cowpunching, before departing for the greener pastures of American boxing. Oleg, the Russian sambo champion who had defected
to the West during the Olympics (probably explaining why my
original East German judo partner had been balked) and was the
second wrestler in this tournament, now demonstrated his Kipchak
heritage by doing some fine exhibition riding.

Again I was reminded: it was foolish to judge anyone by parts.
The complete man may be a very different person than the part.

Meanwhile, I would be exceedingly happy to get off this ga-
lumphing brute with my posterior intact. It felt as if the saddle
really *was* being rammed where I had suggested earlier. Every motion of the rein aggravated my bandaged hand, and I was not keen
on killing a jaguar anyway, even though I understood it was larger
than a lion and far more dangerous. *I* certainly wouldn't appreciate running barefoot through the forest while a pack of jaguars on
horseback chased me with guns.

As it happened, we did not flush a jaguar. We fanned around
the heavy woods along the river bottom and in due course routed
out a tapir, and that was deemed sufficient. I lagged back, avoiding participation in the kill; this pointless slaughter was simply
not my style.

Not that I was in shape to kill anything, or even to put up a decent fight. The swaying of the horse brought a headache, with waves of pain reminiscent of my karate knockout going across my head. My clothes were so drenched with sweat it looked as if I had ridden through a shower.

But better a match with Makato in a cold shower, than this. I began to chuckle involuntarily, and people glanced surreptitiously at me. I couldn't even care.

Even so, I had a bad moment when I dismounted, for I almost stepped on a snake. Wang Hsu, next to me, saw it before I did. His hand was a blur as he seized it by the tail and snapped it violently in the air, breaking its spine. Yes, it was a poisonous specimen; possibly he had saved my life. Such was my weariness that I hardly cared.

Attendants led the horses away, while we weary riders walked off some of our stiffness. It was a few minutes' walk through the brush to the cultivated grounds, and we moved along the narrow paths in small bunches.

Suddenly there was a commotion ahead. A large, hairy, hoofed creature appeared, snorting as it spied us.

"A peccary!" Makato shouted, grinning. At least that was what I understood; he had not said it in English. Certainly it was a wild pig, and a massive one, with ugly tusks and stiff bristles on its snout. It might have weighed as much as three hundred pounds, though of course I was no judge of hogflesh.

Someone raised his rifle, but Makato cried him off. Then he stepped forward.

The pig seemed to recognize the challenge. Perhaps it was one of the wild animals Pedro seeded on his premises, encouraged to attack men. At any rate, it charged.

As it came at him, Makato stepped aside and tried to finish it with one blow of his fist. But he was not fast enough; the boar caught his leg with a tusk, ripping the pants and drawing blood.

Makato backed up to a large mahogany tree, grinning again.

He seemed to live for the challenge, the death-combat, in whatever form it offered. He gestured to the peccary obscenely.

As the pig charged again, Makato raised his hands linked and brought them down savagely on its back, breaking its spine. The animal thrashed on the ground. Makato delivered a stomping blow that crushed in its skull.

He had done it all for sport.

Fortunately nothing big was scheduled on the third day, and we were permitted to recuperate from both the matches and the half-time activities. I slept until almost noon, ate, and meandered about the premises, chatting with people. I was surprised to find several contestants playing musical instruments with considerable skill. Takao and Makato, relaxing Japanese-style in underwear to abate the heat, were playing a bamboo flute and a zither, respectively. Wang Hsu the deadly kung-fu *sifu*—as deadly to snakes as to men—tapped his metallic nails on a small painted ox-hide drum in intricate counterpoint. Mustapha the boxer was rendering what sounded like Beethoven on a violin. It was a strange orchestra, but oddly evocative, with wind and strings and drum-beat. Three Orientals, all verging on the status of professional killers, and a black American—and as a group they could have performed at a swank night club for more pay than they were earning in prize money here. Strange that they didn't do just that. But then I remembered my own dedication to judo and knew that all else was dross. Money was nothing compared to the lure of true martial art.

I would have listened longer, but feared I would stare. In another room the second kung-fu disciple, a young and extremely tough Chinese named Pung Lii, was playing the complex Oriental game of Go with Hiroshi. I watched for a time, but could not make head or tail of the large cross-hatched board or the meaning of the black and white stones they set down in a pattern I couldn't understand. Both were intent and seemed to find deep satisfaction in the game.

In the courtyard Pedro himself was supervising entertainment of another nature: cock fighting. I had seen the cockpit before and had not recognized it for what it was. Now I saw the men gathered around, and the two aggressive cocks facing each other, iron spurs attached to their feet. Bets were made, and each bird had its coterie of fans. Busman's holiday, I thought: the martial artists relaxing by watching martial art.

I returned to the board-game section; cockfighting was not for me. The boxer Pibe was playing chess with the wrestler Oleg. It appeared to be an involved match, with neither man sure of victory, and I was unable to follow its strategies. These two men seemed to be developing a friendship, perhaps based on their common interests in riding and chess.

I saw Filo the kick-boxer contemplating another set. "Do you play?" I inquired.

He smiled comprehending though he did not speak much English. We set up the pieces, which were ornate hand-carved ivory. The rook was not the standard castle-shape I was accustomed to, but a complete elephant with a castle-like howdah on top, from the original India game. The pawns were foot soldiers, the bishops real priests, the kings and queens genuine royalty, and the knights armored men on horseback. My sore thighs tensed, and I was almost too bemused to play properly.

Filo took a pawn of each color, shook both in his closed joined hands, and proffered his fists. I chose the right, and got White, so the opening was mine.

This was fun! In college I had enjoyed chess, and had once finished third in a tournament. I did not know what to expect of Filo, so I opened more or less conventionally with the Evans Gambit. He declined, and I knew already that he was an experienced player. The proof was not long in coming; he checkmated me twice within the hour. I saw that I could not offer him meaningful competition and quit. But by then several others had set up boards, and the Wrestling judge took my place against Filo with somewhat better success.

I drifted on to the movie room, but found that dull. Music

continued; now someone was playing a *samisen,* the Oriental gui-
tar. Then I heard *kiais* and zeroed in on that activity.

The musicians had put away their instruments. Makato was
breaking tiles with his fist. This was a standard karate demonstration, but he was good at it. Not content to smash one or two at a
time, he piled up ten. They were heavy concrete, intended for
construction and not for punching practice, but he cracked them
all with a single blow. There was appalling power in that fist!

Then he had two of the house servants hold up a stout wooden
plank, and he broke it with a kick. Another servant held a smaller,
thicker piece before him. Makato gestured for him to prop it up
somewhere, but the man would not; he wanted to see whether the
karateka could break it when there was no possible fakery, and
obviously thought he couldn't.

I didn't like that, for I knew it was dangerous. But the man
had asked for it, and I didn't interfere. Makato's punch not only
splintered the board, it sent the servant flying. The man could not
get up; he had a cracked sternum. But now he was a believer.

By this time a considerable crowd had formed. Makato, perhaps chastened by the accident—we had to assume it *was* an accident—set up a different kind of exhibition. He placed a glass bottle
on the table and cut off the top with the edge of his hand. He
asked for a candle, lit it, dripped wax on the table and set the base
in the solidifying drop so that the candle would stand upright.
Then he aimed a savage punch at it, as if to sever the lighted end.
But his hand stopped just short of the flame, extinguishing it without a touch.

There was applause for that. It was a harmless yet effective
demonstration of control. But Takao laughed, breaking the spell.
He called for more tiles, piled up ten, and smashed his own fist
down on them. About half broke. Seemingly unperturbed, he set
up ten new ones, and with a terrific effort broke them all this time.
Then he kicked a plank, breaking it as Makato had done. He inquired whether anyone cared to hold up a board, but no one was
interested. He re-lit Makato's candle and struck at it with a pulled

punch. The flame flickered but did not quite go out, but again he succeeded on the second try. Finally he tried to cut a bottle, but it broke, not cleanly. He tried again and failed again, sending shatters of glass across the room. "A trick," he muttered. "I would master it, if I had the time for a little practice. But there is no practical value."

Nevertheless, he had made his point. He had done almost everything the karateka had. Less efficiently, true, but he *had* done it. There was nothing unique about the Korean's skills, and less distinction between judo and karate at the higher levels than most people believed. Probably the same applied for all the major martial arts; an expert at one was a man of many powers. I had heard of kung-fu demonstrations involving beds of nails.

I headed outdoors for a swim, but caught myself and returned to my room instead. Takao was there already, admiring the broken sword without touching it. "Check it over, by all means!" I said. "You must know much more about these weapons than I do."

"Perhaps so," he said. "For one thing, that is not samurai etiquette. May I illustrate?"

"Of course," I said.

He picked up the sword and scabbard, holding it very carefully. "Shall we assume this is my *katana*," he said, "and I have come to visit you? I should normally deliver it to your servant at the door, who receives it on a piece of silk, never on the bare hand. No samurai sword is ever exhibited except by special request, and such request is never made unless the blade is a rare one."

"This *is* a rare one," I said, playing along. "I should very much like to see it."

"By no means," he said gravely. "It is unworthy, and I would not bore so honored a host."

I caught on to the ritual. "Oh no, I insist! Seldom do I have opportunity to see so rare a blade."

We exchanged further apologies, and at length he consented to exhibit it. He held it with its back toward me and drew it slowly out of its scabbard, only an inch. I noticed that his hand was bruised and bleeding, from the demonstration. "This is *Iado,* the art of the naked blade. It is never drawn all the way free," he explained, "unless particularly requested." He drew it our another inch, just shy of the break, then put it away. "Turning the scabbard in the girdle is equivalent to a challenge. As it would be to lay the sword on the floor and kick the hilt towards anyone. Every motion of the *katana* is fraught with significance, and extreme care must be taken."

He was trying to tell me something. After my experience with Hiroshi, I was quite sensitive to these subtle Oriental hints. But I realized I could nor inquire directly. Obviously the sword carried important symbolism, and if I could fathom it, I might save myself a lot of grief.

"I shall certainly try not to give offense with this sword, even inadvertently," I said.

"One is less likely to give offense with a broken weapon," he said, absently mopping his hand.

Obviously! But was that all?

The discussion went no farther, and we went on to routine matters. Tomorrow the tournament would resume, and I suspected that the second half would be rougher than the first. I hadn't done anything notable in the course of these three days, but I had learned a few things, and that was good.

CHAPTER 7

AMALITA

I had seen the second karateka on film when reviewing the Aikido-Karate match. He was Jesus Granda, a young Puerto Rican, a fifth degree black belt who had won several American championships and even a "world" title. He had taken up karate to get out of the ghetto, but after seven years admitted to being disappointed. He had an impressive collection of trophies, but had found that the only way he could make money was to be a *sensei*. Unfortunately he lacked the personality to be an effective teacher. He was virtually illiterate, being a grade school dropout, and spoke English poorly. I understood via the grapevine that be had been taking pep pills for competitions. He was very dark, with wavy black hair slicked down with a perfumed hair pomade, strong and wiry and very fast.

Everyone knew why he was here: for the prize money. "You can't eat medals," he had said tersely in Spanish. He was a vicious competitor, though not as brutal as his senior partner Makato. Karate had a very strong team, and it seemed likely that Karate would take the grand prize, despite Judo's current contention. I was injured, which made a difference, and Takao seemed to have a weak heart.

Takao faced Jesus with an open sneer. I knew it was an act, but Jesus reacted immediately, displaying a quick temper that was apt to be his undoing. He charged in, aiming a closed-fist punch at Takao's massive neck.

Takao dropped his hands and accepted the blow to his throat without evasive action. The karateka's punch would have felled any normal man and finished the match right there; certainly *I* could not have withstood it. But the judoka only laughed. "Don't play games, child; it makes us look bad for the TV audience when you pull your punches."

Jesus showed his teeth in a snarl, but there were chuckles from the men watching. Pulled his punch? Hardly! Whale was there; he had no love for Takao, who had kneed him in the crotch. But he also had been knocked out by the same punch Jesus had just used, and obviously felt better watching than receiving. And he appreciated repartee on his level. Perhaps he hoped the two rough men would kill each other.

"Try it again," Takao said. "A little more force this time, if you please. And extend one knuckle. I have an itch right here." He indicated a spot on his neck. I didn't like it, because such an invitation was foolhardy even against a poor karateka, and Jesus was, for all his temper, one of the finest in the world. Very, very few men would have had the nerve to taunt him like this, and fewer would get away with it. Takao was showing off, carried away by his successful comeback, too certain of his power. I knew why he was doing it: to humiliate Karate the way Karate had humiliated Judo in the first round. But how long would he laugh if Jesus delivered the tile-breaker blow to his heart?

But Jesus, foolishly, struck again at that invulnerable neck— and was met with a louder round of chuckles as Takao swatted the place of contact as though stung by a mosquito.

Something snapped. The karateka was not able to believe that human flesh could withstand the fist that shattered bricks. In his preoccupation with his own successes he had never properly studied those of the other martial arts. To him, Takao was a ghost:

impossible yet evident. He had to assume that it wasn't Takao's strength, but his own weakness that balked him. The young man was completely unnerved.

Then Takao moved. He gripped Jesus in a *hane goshi,* the spring hip throw, his bent leg lifting the other man's leg. When the hapless karateka was high in the air, Takao executed a *sutemi hane maki komi,* turning during the throw and falling with all his weight on the other.

Both men lay still. I bit my tongue, fearing that Takao had overreached himself and stopped his heart. But in a moment he lifted.

Jesus Granda was unconscious. Whether he would recover in time to make his next scheduled match was problematical; quite possibly he had suffered internal injuries, and certainly his self-confidence had been gravely wounded.

Judo now had undisputed command of the tournament, with a 6-1 record. But I felt little pleasure in the accomplishment. Men were being destroyed, emotionally as well as physically—and what did it really prove?

Kung-fu took on Wrestling next, and I stayed to watch. It was Wang Hsu against Whale. The wrestler tried to grab the other, having learned respect for throws and blows and wanting none of Wang's tiger's claws. But Wang met him with just one blow: the crane's beak with thumb and two fingers extended and clenched together, the three nail-spikes leading, driving into the solar plexus. Whale managed to squirm aside slightly, but even so he collapsed unconscious as the beak made contact.

Then we all noticed: the wrestler no longer breathed.

Takao jumped up, brushed Wang aside as though he were a bystander in the way, and put his hands on Whale. The Wrestling judge started to protest, but the other judges cautioned him back. Takao hauled on the prostrate man, trying to get him into a sitting position. When I saw what he was doing, I went to help. We got Whale up, and Takao kneeled behind him and reached around to massage his huge belly, but there was no response. We were supporting a dead man.

Then Takao kneed him in the small of the back and gave a tremendous *kiai*! that blasted my ear and made me jump involuntarily. But Whale jumped too—and took a breath.

It was kwatsu: the secret judo art of resuscitation. I had tried it on Jim Blake, after I strangled him, but with only partial success. How would we fare this time?

We helped the huge man to his feet, making him walk, forcing him to get his circulation back. I saw the puncture marks the crane's beak had made, just to the side of the nerve complex. Had Wang's strike been true, no art we knew could have restored this man to life.

I looked up to see the TV camera covering our faces. I knew Takao had performed a feat that more than made up for the brutality with which he had brought Whale down in his own match. The American audience, probably antipathetic to Takao and perhaps judo itself, might now have a change of heart. I felt it in myself. Takao had shown me another side of his personality, and it made up for all the rest.

Wang merely watched, smiling as always. But I wondered what was in his mind. Had he intended to kill Whale? With Karate's loss and Kung-fu's win, Kung-fu was now in a three-way tie for second place with Karate and Aikido. And Kung-fu's next two matches were with those same two arts. Was a new leader in the making—via a trail of dead men? The top prize money—$240,000—was a big temptation. But more than that was the glory of vindicating one's own martial art, proving conclusively that when the fighting was serious, that art was strongest. Even second or third place would be impressive, if a number of Kung-fu's opponents were dead.

I hoped I was being unduly suspicious. But I liked this tournament less and less.

*

My own next match was with the second boxer, Pibe Rosario. I had admired his horsemanship during the jaguar hunt, but now he had metamorphosed back into the brutish slugger. He had a broken nose, scarred eyebrows, cauliflower ears and monstrous fists. He was the current Latin American champion, ranked about third in the world, and had never been knocked out in regular boxing. He was a bleeder, and also seemed a bit punch-drunk, but I knew Pibe could take a great deal of punishment. In fact he had done so, here in the tournament. But he had still managed to play a good game of chess, which suggested more brain to him than normally showed.

I had no desire to exchange dull blows with this brawler. My finger continued to bother me, for it had had no chance to heal and set between marches, and my wrist was not much better off. So I needed a fast, simple win. The kind this man seldom yielded.

Before Pibe could approach me, I made a high leap and went into the *kani-basani*, the flying scissors or flying crab-pincers. I turned my body sidewise in the air, one leg going to his front, the other to the back of Pibe's legs. He was thrown back, and I dropped with him, holding that clamp. I squirmed around and straddled him, taking his head in my two hands. My weak right hooked onto his forelock, my strong left caught the shorter hair on the back of his skull, and I twisted, gently.

The judges were on their feet, but Pibe was already screaming capitulation. This was smart of him, for I could easily have broken his neck had he resisted. He was great for absorbing punches, and no doubt he had given Karate a hard fight, but the tactics I had used were foreign to him, and deprived him of his will to fight.

*

"Will you order a girl tonight?" Takao inquired gruffly. I saw he had a bruise where the karateka had hit him; his neck was tough, but he *had* been hurt.

I shrugged, surprised. Normally Takao did not make suggestions of this nature. "No. I thought I'd go out for another training run."

"In the nude, past pretty pools?" He shook his head. "Our esteemed host would undoubtedly feel better if you took a girl. *You* are not married."

Oh. Because Pedro thought I was out to seduce his niece. "Maybe you're right," I agreed, knowing very well he *was* right. Pedro surely knew which contestants were indulging in what entertainments, and my abstinence had to seem suspicious. Probably he was saving Amalita for his own pleasure, being restrained only by her youth and kinship. Or, more likely, he was *unable* to have her, except in the most mechanical way, so had to take the long difficult route of gradual seduction. Meanwhile, he wanted nobody *else* to have her. Which was really his own business, and hers. Perhaps he had a right to her if he proved able to win her active cooperation through gifts and persuasion. I didn't like it, but I had no authority to interfere. "This will be the first time I ever stayed out of trouble by making out with a hired woman!"

So I put in an order for a girl, any description. I didn't ask for Lufita, my date at the dance, because now I thought of her as a person, and this was an impersonal business.

Takao departed discreetly to play some music in the lounge with his friends—it was amazing how quickly friendships were developing after his act of mercy-saving Whale—and I turned out the lights, stripped, and lay down. I didn't really want a girl, and didn't plan to make actual use of what showed up. Sex is not an end in itself to me, but a part of a larger relationship, a situation that did not exist here. I suppose if Thera were present . . . but fortunately she wasn't. Everyone would assume I *had* used the assigned girl, and Pedro would be off my back. I had a tournament to complete, and rough matches were coming up; I needed no trouble on the side.

There was a light knock. I grunted from the bed, and she

entered: a female shape, her face covered by a veil. I could not see her well through the mosquito netting, but she wore a suggestive perfume and was young and full. She seemed familiar, and I was suddenly nervous. I knew myself for a hypocrite, selecting an anonymous female so that I could use the excuse of noninvolvement to pass her up.

Obviously Lufita had arranged to come. Still, I was having an attack of unmanly modesty, and doubted I could use her sexually.

She came to my bed in the dark, removed her robe, and sat on the edge just inside the netting. I felt her bare warm thigh against my flank as I lay on my stomach. I thought momentarily of pool nymphs—watch that!—and of matwork with the lively daughter of an industrialist, and I felt plaintive urges. The girl did not speak, but slid her hands up across my back and began to massage me. It felt astonishingly good.

After a few minutes she lay down beside me. Her arms snaked around my shoulders and her lips came close to find mine while her firm breasts pressed against my side.

Ah, well, I thought. She wanted to complete her business and retire for the night. I would do her no favor by making her wait indefinitely for nothing. What harm was there in it?

She was small, smaller than I remembered Lufita, and now she shivered a little, so I knew she was not a veteran call-girl. Probably she was paid a flat fee by the house for every man she serviced, and needed that money desperately for her proud but poor family, but was not experienced. Maybe five thousand dollars for a success, one thousand for a failure? No that was unkindly facetious.

I put her on top of me as I rolled over, so as not to have to be concerned about crushing her, and gently proceeded. She was ardent, driven by a rather pleasing passion, but she was indeed inexperienced. In fact, she was virginal. I did not realize I was hurting her until I felt her tears fall on me—and by then it was late.

"I'm sorry," I mumbled inanely. "I didn't mean to—"

"No, no, Señor Kane, I wanted it to be you!" she whispered fiercely. "I love you! I saw you fight—"

That voice! "Amalita!" I exclaimed, horrified. "How did you—
"

"I am not so naive as my uncle thinks," she said breathlessly. "Not anymore!"

Now I remembered the broken *katana* and realized what it meant. I should have broken my sword in some other living body! "I have drawn the blood I promised to spare!"

"Now you must take me away with you," she said.

I had a vision of tapirs, jaguars, riflemen, dogs, poisonous snakes and liver parasites. Broiling days and cold nights. Starvation in the barren pine badlands. "I can't take you anywhere! I as much as promised your uncle I would leave you alone. Now I shall have to tell him what—"

"He would kill you—and me!" she cried, her terror genuine.

Vicente Pedro probably would, I realized. There were a thousand ways he could do it, here on his premises where he was the law, or somewhere in the wild countryside where it would seem an accident. A knockout drop in a drink, men hired to haul the body out, use those metal tiger claws on it to make it resemble a jaguar kill, and leave it there in the sun. Who would ever know—or who, suspecting, could ever prove anything? Such a pity: his own niece, showing the guest from America the countryside, and both struck down by a jaguar! Three days of mourning, followed by a massive jaguar hunt and another feast.

Talk to Pedro? I doubted he would be reasonable. If I convinced him of the truth, he would have proof of Amalita's complicity, and only execution of both parties would salve his wounded pride. After his scrupulous warning to us both . . .

There seemed to be no alternative but to cover up. Amalita had done what she had done of her own free choice, and did not deserve to die for it, however covetous of her body her uncle might be. It galled me to be a party to such deception, but since I was already party to the damage, I had to carry it through with expedience.

If only I had been more alert before taking the supposed stranger to my bed! Such carelessness in a match would have cost me dearly, and the stakes were no less, here.

"Look, Amalita," I said, realizing with a lesser shock that we were still connected in the love-embrace. "I can not take you with me. Your uncle would never let you go, and if somehow we managed to escape his guards and get through the wilderness alive and make it out of Nicaragua, I still could not bring you into my country. You are not an American citizen, you probably have no passport—and even if we got around all that, how long do you suppose either of us could escape your uncle's assassins, anywhere in the world? There is no escape."

"There never *was* any escape," she said. "My uncle picked you for the tournament so that Judo would lose. You knew that, surely! But after the first match you changed your mind and fought so hard you made a fool of him! Now you can fight to get me out."

"Hey, hey, hey!" I yelped. "Pedro picked me? I thought—"

"You didn't know? About Uncle and his American business partner, Johnson Drummond? How most of the Pedro money is invested in the U.S.A. for safekeeping, a lot in Drummond Industries?"

"I didn't know any of that!"

"They're good friends," she continued relentlessly. "The American was here last month bragging about what a good instructor he had found for his daughter. An American judo champion. But Uncle knew how the U.S.A. is really a poor judo nation, and how big a difference just a few years retirement makes, so he was sure you would be no match. Drummond thought he was doing you a favor, pulling strings to get you in."

"God!" I exclaimed, appalled by what this innocent little girl knew. So Drummond had been my anonymous supporter, no doubt greasing his recommendation with money. On top of everything else, this indicated corruption in Judo's higher councils. No, better to believe that I really was the best of the poor lot that was American judo. My country had nothing to compare to the ranking judokas of the world, unfortunately.

That reminded me. "My original judo partner—was it the same deal with him?"

"The East German? Yes. Uncle knew they would not let him go, not when he told them about the Kipchak defector already signed up. And he thought the Japanese would try to fill in, but he was too old and fat to get far. So Judo had the weakest team." She hugged me, laughing. "Now my uncle can't admit he made a mistake! You both are so much stronger than he thought possible, he's absolutely furious! He—"

"We're lucky," I said. "I've gambled and won, but that can't last. And the moment someone realizes that Takao has a weak heart—"

"I knew you'd help me, once you knew," she said. "I showed you my body, and came to you, so that you would."

So even her first nude swim had not been innocent. Everyone had plans for me! But I was tired of serving other people's purposes. "Amalita, I'm *not* helping you! I'm staying here to maintain the honor of judo in the Martial Open. I would never be able to face myself if I let your uncle use me to defame my profession."

"The American said you had a moralistic streak," she said, tearful again. But I refused to rise to that taunt, which was an accurate one. The truth was that I found Amalita quite attractive, physically. Less so, mentally. I had no illusions about any lasting relationship with her.

"Now you go back to your room," I said firmly, "and fix yourself up so there's as little evidence as possible of what has passed between us. Fix this in your mind: it never happened. This is the only way either of us will last out this tournament alive."

She nodded, finally understanding that I meant it. At last we severed our embrace. She mopped herself in the darkness, put on her robe and veil, and moved silently out the door. "Make sure the girl whose place you took doesn't talk!" I warned her. She nodded as she disappeared.

Then I turned on the light and checked my bed. There was an incriminating spot of blood on the sheet, and more on me. I washed myself quickly, then scrubbed at the sheet with a damp cloth. I managed to get most of it out, leaving a dark stain. Then I spilled coffee over the place, hoping that stain would conceal the remaining evidence, and took a long shower. I felt like a criminal.

Suddenly I remembered the intercom. Had Pedro been listening the whole time? Disaster! But when I checked it, the wire was loose; Takao had taken care of that detail before he left, thoughtfully, not suspecting how important it would be. Whew!

*

The first match of the ninth round was Karate *vs.* Boxing. Makato the Korean; Mustapha the American stylist. I did not expect to meet either Karate or Boxing again, as both Judo's matches against these arts had been completed; but a problem I could not discuss with anyone weighed on my mind. I needed distraction.

Makato, surprisingly, elected to *box* with Mustapha. I was surprised, and Mustapha himself was amazed. His nose had never recovered from my partner's smash, and he had taken humiliating beatings in every match. His early arrogance was gone; he no longer expected to win. I had to give him credit for courage in adversity for staying in the tournament. But I found it hard to fathom Makato's purpose. The karateka had never shown inclination to waste motions; he had been a single-minded engine of destruction throughout. He was one of the two undefeated men remaining in the tournament (the other being Takao) and he evinced no heart condition. Why was he fooling around now?

Mustapha, after his initial surprise, was more than ready to accept the Korean's gambit. He was taller and had a much superior reach. He began displaying pretty combinations, dancing around and scoring to Makato's head and shoulders. Those had to hurt; they were not light taps. But Makato ignored the punishment, advancing relentlessly.

Mustapha was the first to realize that this could not last long. He became wary, watching for the Korean's real move. And he tried his best to finish the fight, his way, while he had the chance. What an upset, if the winless boxer brought down the invincible karateka! He wound up for his best punch—and Makato delivered the bull-stunner blow. Mustapha reacted instantly, bringing up his fists to block while jumping back. It was a good try, but neither move could foil that knockout express. It crashed through his guard as if through light kindling wood and struck the top of his head. Mustapha was out cold before he started to fall.

Takao was watching, and I saw him scowl. Could he be jealous of the karateka's success? A little of that had showed during the halftime festivities. Makato had just demonstrated that he could absorb a boxer's best punches without seeming effect; that nullified Takao's performance with Jesus. Would Takao try something new with his next match?

I hoped not, for that was with the kick-boxer from Thailand, Suphon Kitisathorn. I sat watching the two men. The Thai was the larger of the two kickers, being about five-feet six-inches tall and weighing 160 pounds. Still small by the standards of this tournament—but Suphon was the champion of Thailand, and therefore the world. Kick-boxing had not been doing well here, winning only two matches, and those against Boxing and Wrestling; but this was not because the art was inferior. Wrestling, Boxing and Thai Kick-Boxing all suffered because they were essentially sport arts, normally governed by stringent protective rules. Had Aikido or Kung-fu been similarly restricted, with penalties given for injury to the opponent, this tournament might have had a very different complexion. Karate and Judo were dual-aspect disciplines, sport *and* business, so had the best of both. But complacency would be foolhardy. Takao had done extremely well so far, though his very brutality could indicate his own lack of confidence in his skill and stamina. If he tried to play around, showing up Makato, and got smashed by a hard kick—

Suphon kicked. Takao dodged aside, caught that foot one-handed, and struck with his other fist, one knuckle protruding. Struck at *the sole of the foot!* It was a powerful blow, but represented exactly the kind of foolishness I had feared. Suphon would twist away in a moment and counter devastatingly.

But Suphon was not twisting, he was falling. The judges and spectators stared as he lay unmoving. Then there was a smattering of applause that swelled as others realized what had happened.

Takao had successfully executed one of the most difficult of all *atemi* blows: a strike to a nerve center in the bottom of the foot. The shock and pain had knocked out the Thai.

The applause continued, but I did not join it. I knew Takao could only have mastered this rare technique by practicing against Chinese prisoners already sentenced to death.

*

"That girl!" Takao demanded abruptly that night. "Pedro's niece—you have not seen her again?"

"I have no need to answer that," I said.

"The rumor is about," he said, concerned. "False, surely, yet if Pedro hears it—he is a jealous and vindictive man. All his pride is tied up in that girl."

Somehow the news had leaked. The girl whose place Amalita had taken—she must have talked. No one could know what had actually passed between Amalita and me, but the mere suspicion was enough to undo us.

Takao, watching me, swore in Japanese. "I thought you had better sense! You accepted the *katana!*"

"I thought I had sheathed it," I said simply.

"You had—so long as you confined it to the whore on order. Do you know she is dead?"

"Dead! When? How?"

"This morning. It must have been very soon after she left you, or after *someone* did! Small *kris* to the heart."

The *kris* was another exotic blade, originating in Java. There were many variants, straight and wavy, the larger ones up to two-feet long in the blade, the smaller only five or six inches. These were typically used on women, and often the blades were poisoned. Like the *katana,* the *kris* had a venerable history, and was surrounded by important conventions. Such a weapon would not be employed for a routine murder today.

I had told Amalita to make sure the other girl did not talk. Now I knew she had done so. She was a true niece to her uncle, lacking only his more experienced subtlety.

Takao shook his head and said no more.

Oleg Usk, the Kipchak sambo wrestler, was not as large as his partner Whale, but at six-feet two-inches and 250 pounds of muscle he was no midget. He sported a shaved bullet head and a ferocious mustache.

Sambo is distinct from American wrestling, and superior, being more scientific. It is closely related to judo, having borrowed many techniques from it, and on occasion judokas crossed over to compete successfully in sambo tournaments. The wrestling team had won three matches and lost six, so was not in contention for honors, but if Oleg got a proper hold on me, I'd be finished.

I had been fortunate so far in completing my matches quickly. This time my luck ran out. Oleg had learned things during this tournament, and must have had prior experience against judo, and was careful to avoid giving me any easy openings. I had to grapple him his way, and he was a bear. He was stronger than I, crushing me again and again in his ursine hugs. I broke his grips only with difficulty, by striking him repeatedly until he had to relinquish a given lock. He was also wary of the nose-finger Hiroshi had used against Whale, and I was unable to use my weak right hand to good effect. Oleg had the advantage, and wore me down implacably.

The only thing that saved me was an inhibition of his own: in sambo, strangleholds are considered unsportsmanlike, so Oleg was not well versed in them. He knew they were legitimate for this tournament, but his reflexes and inclinations were not attuned, and under battle stress a man does what is most natural to him.

There was a thirty-minute time limit for any given match,

with provision for overtime periods if required. Few bouts had come near this limit, but this one did. I was unable to put the big man down, and only continuous evasive maneuvering on my part prevented him from finishing me. He took *me* down, though. He grabbed my leg and pushed me back in a sambo takedown, then tried for a leghold that almost wiped me out. He had used the same techniques defeating the young aikidoist, gripping one of his legs and lifting it while sweeping the other foot from under. Then a leg-twist combined with pressure on the knee, forcing surrender. I foiled that, but remained at a disadvantage. The judges finally called time, and we broke, tired and sweating.

There was a five minute rest before the first ten-minute continuation. No draws were permitted; each match had to continue until a victor was determined. I was not optimistic; I was so tired I was bound to make a mistake. Oleg, used to this sort of combat, seemed stronger than ever. It was no longer difficult to appreciate how this man had defeated Sato, the second aikidoist: Oleg was about to do the same to me.

Normally Takao was on hand when I fought, but for some reason he was absent this time. This irritated me; didn't he care whether Judo won or lost? Or was this his way of expressing his disapproval of my situation with Amalita?

Amalita. If word of that affair were circulating, how long could Pedro himself remain ignorant? What would he do, once he learned? Even without proof, he would act.

The break was over, way too soon for me. I went to meet the sambo wrestler, and was taken down by surprise. He bent to grab one of my knees, lifting and pushing and forcing me to the floor. I grabbed for his hair, dim-wittedly, for he was billiard-bald. He fell on top of me, giving me another good thump in the process, and tried for a leg lock. I managed to foil that, but I was pinned, and remained so, struggling futilely, until time expired again. In any sport match I would have been counted out.

The wrestler was trying to wear me down to the point where I could no longer interfere with his win, and he was succeeding. I was escaping more narrowly, and every minute on the mat was draining my scant reserves of strength.

In the next overtime period I summoned what remained of my energy and went for broke. I hit Oleg several times about the face and body, boxing him with my leaden-heavy left arm. Then we grappled again, and I got on his back and suddenly put a *hadaka-jime* on him, a naked strangle, assisting it with a scissors hold on his body. I could not have set it up had he been more conversant with the form. I passed one arm in front of his neck, and with the edge of my right hand I pressed against his windpipe. This was painful for me, because of that infernal wrist, but this time I refused to let that deter me. I seized that hand with the other to increase the pressure. This was a combination choke, interfering with the flow of blood through his carotid arteries and also stopping his breathing. It would not have worked against a neck like Takao's, and it almost failed here, because of Oleg's strength and my weakness. But he just didn't know how to handle a strangle, and finally he made the signal of submission. Rather to my surprise, I had won.

I checked my room, but Takao was not there. I was worn out, but could not relax, so went to watch the Aikido-Boxing match following mine.

Aikido was still in contention, with a 6-3 record, but it was in trouble. Sata had been eliminated through injury to his knee in his losing match with Oleg two days before and was no longer able to compete. *O-Sensei* Hiroshi was carrying it alone. The man was capable, as my painful finger attested, but he was sixty-two years old, and so tiny! How long could he maintain the grueling match-a-day pace? Yesterday he had defeated Kung-fu; today he met Mustapha the boxer; tomorrow he would meet Karate, and the final day, me. Takao had planned to take the second Aikido match, but with Hiroshi now certain to appear, that was out. I had strong sympathy for the gentle, honest, discreet, indomitable old man, and I liked him personally, but I would have had to go for the win regardless.

At least I had no decisions to make at the moment. I could watch this match dispassionately, knowing that the best man would win. If Hiroshi had a tough schedule, Mustapha had his own problems. There was a band about his head, probably because of the bull-stunning blow Makato had given him. There could easily have been a slight concussion, perhaps not so slight. Actually, Mustapha himself should have rested today, but his own partner appeared to be ill. Pibe's last match had been with me, and I had not hurt him, I thought. I hoped.

What decimation was occurring. Yet this was to be expected, three quarters of the way through a no-rules tournament. That was part of the point of it. A martial art that looked good in the opening encounter but could not keep the pace after absorbing some bruises did not deserve acclaim as a world leader. This was the savage but fair law of the Martial Open.

Mustapha was dancing again, his guard up. I had thought he would be slow and dispirited at this point, but he was actually quite swift. He had real grit, for I knew his head was hurting, and Hiroshi had dumped him before, with the corner drop. Mustapha circled the old *sensei,* and when Hiroshi tried to catch an arm, Mustapha snatched it away. He had really studied his man this time, and was not walking into the same mistake as before. All the time he was moving and jabbing, peppering Hiroshi with light blows.

The old Japanese was nothing if not patient, awaiting his opportunity. Too patient, it seemed to me. He was small and light, and Mustapha was strong, and that constant barrage was telling. Was it possible that the boxer could do it this time? I doubted it; Hiroshi was as deadly as the karatekas, in his way. Once he found his opening . . .

But the opening never came. Mustapha avoided all but the fleetest contact of his flashing hands on Hiroshi's head and body, never trying for a knockout punch. The punishment was becoming severe; the *sensei's* eyes were puffing and his nose was bleeding.

Suddenly Mustapha unleashed a brilliant combination to head, face and body, finishing with an uppercut to the chin, and Hiroshi fell to his knees. Mustapha stood back as if waiting for the referee to count to ten, and of course there was no count, here. It was a mistaken gesture, and foolish too. "Finish him!" the Boxing judge shouted.

But Mustapha shook his head. "Not that way," he said.

Hiroshi was already finished. His eyes were swollen almost shut, and he was having difficulty orienting. He had won his victories without injuring anyone, applying his techniques slowly and carefully; now, ironically, he was injured himself. He made the signal of submission.

Mustapha jumped to help him up. "I'm sorry I had to do that," he said. "You beat me before, so I couldn't ease up. But I just *had* to have this win, for the brothers and sisters back home."

Hiroshi smiled. There was blood on his lip and teeth. "It was well-earned," he said politely.

Indeed it was, for Hiroshi was no easy mark, however impotent he had seemed in this one match. Any single mistake by Mustapha would have reversed the outcome. But all I could think of, as they walked away, was that tomorrow, with impaired vision and insufficient rest, that nice old man would have to face Makato the killer karateka.

*

The third match for the day was Karate against Thai Kick-Boxing. But I had had enough. The whole show had become gloomy for me, and every match seemed part of a building tragedy.

I returned to my room, ate alone, and watched television. Latin soap operas and *I Love Lucy* reruns. I wondered what had become of my formidable roommate, whom I had not seen since morning. My depression intensified. I wanted to go home, or at least out for a run and swim, but was certain that would not be smart. It wasn't just Pedro's ire I feared now, but Amalita's. He with his *katanas*, she with her *kris*.

Sleep would not come. Finally, late in the evening, I walked about the interior premises, searching for someone—-anyone-— to talk to, to play chess with, or to share a film with. But no one was around. The private rooms were empty, the entertainment halls deserted. The entire building was unnaturally quiet.

Now I knew something was wrong. No special event had been scheduled, and no one had told me of any change. Where had everyone gone?

I listened, then walked, and listened again. After several tries I heard faint voices. There was some sort of meeting going on in one of the projection rooms.

I was about to try the door, but hesitated. Feeling like the sneak I was, I listened—and was stunned.

Takao was talking: " . . . not need to repeat what I did during the war. You all know that . . ."

What was this—a confession session?

" . . . so I have no claims to honor, no claim at all." Takao paused, and someone else said something I couldn't make out. It sounded like Japanese. Then:

"But I have told you the situation here, and told you again. You know it was an accident. You know he is a decent man—more decent than some of us here. You know he is worth our support." Who was he talking about?

Then Takao's voice became loud and strong. "Every man of you who lets this pass is worse than I was! How can any of you lay claim to martial honor? Have you forgotten the social and ethical precepts of your rank? Do you call yourselves *sensei* and *sifu* and judge, yet stoop to this? It is a mockery no one could believe! You are gluttons and cowards!"

There was a chorus of protest. Then I recognized Mustapha's voice. "I'm American, same as him, so I figure I understand, some. It could've happened to me just as easily, or Whale, here. I saw that li'l girl swimming bareassed."

Then I understood. They were discussing Amalita and me! I was the one on trial. That was why I hadn't been told.

" . . . but we can't prove a thing, or stop it anyway. He was warned, fair and square. I told him myself to watch that sword of his. But he played dumb. Now he'll just have to watch out for himself. I'm betting he will. I wash my hands of it. It's the same as a match."

More hubbub. Then Takao again. "I see I cannot move you by reason. I plead no more. Then understand this: the man who stands aside I hold in contempt, but I let him be. But any man who participates will owe the blood debt to me. Anywhere, anytime. So deal with me first, because I shall not stand aside, and it shall be an eye for an eye, a skull for a skull, and a life for a life. Who stands with me in this oath?"

Now there was silence. Takao had gone way out on a limb, threatening this assemblage of the strongest warriors of all the world, calling them cowards and meaning it. He had invited them to kill him, if they would not yield to him. And they would not yield. But what was he trying to accomplish?

Then someone walked across the room toward Takao, and stopped beside him. The first challenger? The tread was so light as to be almost inaudible, but because of that, and the rustle of a skirt, I recognized it. Hiroshi!

The one man Takao could not oppose.

But there was no encounter, just silence. I realized that the O-Sensei had not come to oppose, but to join. No other footsteps came, and slowly more hubbub developed. I suspected that the meeting was about to break up, so I departed quickly.

I had a lot to think about!

CHAPTER 8

VENGEANCE

The eleventh round, first match: Aikido against Karate. Hiroshi's face was remarkably improved, with the swelling diminished, but I knew he should not be fighting again so soon. Particularly not against the sledgehammer fists of Makato. But it was out of my province.

They circled cautiously, the aikidoist balanced to avoid the killing smash, the karateka careful not to extend himself vulnerably. A powerful fist counted for little against so experienced a warrior as Hiroshi, who knew every trick of evasion and counter. Makato was not fool enough to assume he could take the old man for granted; if he missed his shot, he would find his arm locked, and he would not recover it short of submission. So he was careful, and by no means assured of victory. One of Karate's two losses had been to Aikido, Sato beating Jesus. Now the stronger representatives of each discipline were up against each other.

Makato feinted. Hiroshi caught the arm anyway, winding into a devious hold that could readily be the finish, and Makato countered with a terrible smash with his other hand, whose edge was so calloused and hard it could shatter a tall pile of bricks. The blow landed midway between Hiroshi's wrist and elbow, which were held firm by his own grip on the karateka—and the bone snapped like matchstick.

Hiroshi's eyes glazed with pain, and he sagged, making no outcry. The Aikido judge signaled capitulation. Takao rushed in, and for a moment I thought he was going to strike the Korean and initiate the death match that would settle their rivalry right then. But he controlled himself and turned away, and put his arms about Hiroshi, and picked him up as tenderly as he might a child. I saw tears streaming from Takao's eyes as he walked with his burden toward the infirmary.

Makato stood impassively, watching them go. I remembered how Hiroshi had stood beside Takao the night before, sharing his oath and the invitation that went with it. Takao had at last obtained his pardon—but what was to be the price of it? Did Makato's brutality stem from that situation?

Then the Korean looked at me, and I felt the chill of death. What was on his mind? Our matches were over.

Takao returned shortly for his own match with Kung-fu. Something had gone out of him. He was grim, and I was nervous about what he might do, but I knew better than to interfere.

Both kung-fu specialists remained in fighting order, but it was the younger Chinese who appeared for this match, Pung Lii. He was an ex-Red Guard, said to be the equivalent of the kung-fu champion—though even any unofficial title was arguable—who had entered the United States illegally after deserting the Communists. He had remained in San Francisco's Chinatown, serving as bodyguard to the Tong racketeers. He had been promised Nicaraguan citizenship, making his stay in this hemisphere legal.

Whatever his politics, there was no doubt of his fighting competence. I deemed him less dangerous than his partner Wang Hsu because he lacked the refinements of deception of the smiling *sifu*. Nevertheless, Pung Lii was 170 pounds of very wiry, strong, fast fighting ability, conversant with the tiger's claw and other terrifying kung-fu weapons.

Pung made a tremendous leap, did a reverse somersault, and

landed with both feet on Takao's chest. I winced. Takao was strong, but this bowled him over. Ordinarily such gymnastics are less effective than they look, because the intended target has merely to step aside. But on occasion they work well enough.

Before Takao could right himself, Pung kicked him in the nerve center under the armpit. I winced again; my partner had an invulnerable neck, but was not adapted to withstand such punishment elsewhere.

My misgivings seemed well founded. Takao recovered his feet, but his arm was half paralyzed. Pung, with true killer instinct, took immediate advantage of that liability, battering the wounded judoka with heavy blows.

Takao maintained a tight defensive shell, so that his massive neck and shoulders took the brunt. But I knew the punishment was getting to him, and I feared for more than the mere loss of the match. I had seen him waver during his battle with Whale, and I knew that only the brevity of his other matches had kept him out of serious trouble. He was tough and skilled, but he was also too old and stout for prolonged exertion of this nature. Soon he would tire; he lacked the stamina, the staying power necessary for a long contest. The abilities remained, but the wind is the first to go.

Pung Lii was well aware of this. He was in fine physical condition, with excellent endurance. He wanted the match to be long, for every minute increased his advantage. He did not bother with the tiger's claw or crane's beak, knowing the attempt would be futile against a judoka of Takao's experience. A failed strike was always an invitation to a devastating counter, and Takao, like Makato, could shatter bricks with his fist. So Pung kept moving, moving, avoiding Takao's attempts to grapple, dodging Takao's punches, presenting no good target, not even the sole of his foot. Twice more he slammed the judoka with flying kicks, kicks that should never have landed had Takao been properly alert. He shoved him mercilessly about the room, weakening him further. Then Pung deemed the moment propitious and tried a frontal charge.

Mistake! Takao dropped, and came up with a *kata guruma*

shoulder wheel throw. Suddenly the complexion of the match changed. Kung-fu had fallen into Judo's power. Experience and patience, once again, had told. Takao lifted him high into the air, heaved, and threw him crushingly to the floor.

Pung struck and bounced. He lay there stunned, wide open for the finishing kick. The Kung-fu judge was already standing, beginning the signal of capitulation. The victory was Takao's.

But Takao staggered, clutching at his chest. I saw the bruise marks forming, from the repeated strikes of the flying feet and leopard's paw. Pung had really worked on that chest.

Then Takao toppled.

Pung struggled upright and came dazedly to attack again. But he halted. Then he turned away.

He had seen what we now saw. Takao's heart had failed, and he was dead. No *kwatsu* would bring him back.

*

I spent a bad night alone. It was not that I liked Takao; my feelings about him had been strongly mixed, though I had learned considerable respect for his prowess and candor. It was not that Judo, by that defeat snatched from victory, had now dropped into a tie with Karate. It was not even my own bleak situation, linked mysteriously with Takao's oath. It was a general, deep-delving disgust with the entire tournament, that had seemed such an excellent idea but turned out to be so ugly in practice. What was being settled, really, by all this injury and death? Was this any more than a bloody Roman circus, a spectacle put on by paid cutthroats for the sadistic amusement of jaded masses? Could any amount of notoriety be worth the brutal snapping of a nice old man's arm, or the death of one of the leading judokas of our time? Where were our values?

In the morning I went to visit Hiroshi at the infirmary. I had been scheduled to meet him in combat again, but that match was now mine by forfeit. I was surprised to find no other visitors. Then, remembering that secret meeting of two nights ago, I was angry. Was the *O-Sensei* being ostracized even now for his stand beside Takao?

Hiroshi smiled when he saw me. His arm was in a complex hanging sling, and his position looked uncomfortable, but I was sure he had been peacefully meditating. He was not one to complain about discomfort.

"Will you see that Takao's share of the prize money is delivered to his widow in Japan?" I asked him. "In fact I don't want any of it, so the entire Judo allotment should go there. But don't tell his wife that, or she might not accept it. There should be close to two hundred thousand dollars."

"No," he said. "She would not accept any payment associated with his death. You must find another way."

Another way? I set that aside for future consideration. I intended to see that Takao's family got its share.

"It appears likely that there will be a tie in the final rankings," Hiroshi said. "Perhaps it would be expedient to let it stand."

I shook my head. "Vicente Pedro will insist on a playoff. He demands a single winner to this tournament."

"So," Hiroshi murmured reflectively. "Yet there may be a positive approach."

What was he hinting at now? I knew better than to ignore his warning, however discreetly couched. This had to connect with that secret meeting, where the two men had stood in defense of me—and suffered grievously in their following matches. I had thought it the misfortune of battle—but Takao had obviously had another opinion, when he almost attacked Makato out of turn. Then Takao's own demise—had it really been an accident? Pung had attacked him brutally, not even trying for the quick win, but blasting him about the chest at every opportunity.

If these two had been struck down because of me, what could I expect when I entered a match myself? There was now no one to settle any blood debt. Hiroshi seemed to be suggesting that I stay clear, even if it meant forfeiting the top prize.

Had I been marked for death?

It was paranoid to think so. There was no conclusive evidence. But it made sense out of many of the ugly mysteries of the past few days. Pedro could not avenge himself directly. and neither could he have a guest killed out of hand. Not with the proceedings being televised worldwide, and that guest a contender for the top spot in the tournament. He would have to depend on a legitimate match to accomplish his purpose. If, say, a man knew he would receive a large bonus if his opponent died, rather than submitting or being knocked out.

There would be a playoff match, and surely I would meet Makato again. There was death in that karate fist. My only safe course was to stay out of that encounter.

Yet there were other sides to it. I was no helpless innocent. I was a fifth degree black belt in judo, a former world contender, and I had won five of my six matches here. I was in fact guilty of the crime accused, shedding the blood of Pedro's niece. In judo a mistake is just as bad as inferior skill; the best fighters are the ones who make fewest mistakes. I had been given warning, yet I had acted carelessly, and now there was a reckoning to meet. But Pedro himself had conspired against Judo, wronging me before I ever heard of him, so he had invited trouble. Both of us had justice and error.

"Should a man flee the consequence of his action?" I asked.

Hiroshi shook his head, not answering. I knew he was not surprised.

We remained a time in silence. I would have left him to his rest, but there was something uplifting about his company that dispelled my own depression, and I could not yet make myself go. He was the ill one, yet also the healer.

"You said something about a positive approach," I reminded him. "I would like to understand."

"Our host is a complex man," Hiroshi said. "It may seem that he is antagonistic to judo, but this is not so. If he could be freed of his liability, he would forget the scapegoat. Then he would find other interests, and perhaps forgive the past. It would be kinder to assist him, rather than to inflame his misery by opposing him."

"My absence would not cure him," I said. "Not even my death."

He only shrugged, and I knew I had missed the point. But if he would not speak directly, I would just have to work it out for myself. And if I could not, I would have to settle with Makato, the hard way.

I got up to go. "I thank you for your efforts on my behalf," I said, meaning it. "And for the support you gave to Takao." I put my hand momentarily on his.

"It is easy to support a good man," he said politely.

Something was nagging me. I concentrated, and realized what it was. *Hiroshi's hand was burning hot!*

"You're sick!" I exclaimed. *"Really* sick! You're running a terrible fever!"

"It is not important," he demurred.

I brushed that aside. "This can't be from your arm! It must be a hundred and six degrees! What is it? Is Pedro's doctor trying to—"

He laughed weakly. "Jason, such suspicion does not become you. The doctor is excellent, and he is doing his best, and he has remained silent at my behest. The siege must run its course. Do not be concerned."

"I *am* concerned. Here I am, taxing your strength. What do you have?"

"Malaria. I have lived with that parasite many years; we are old acquaintances. Patience is all that is required."

"Malaria!" I reviewed what little I knew of this scourge, perhaps the most widespread and devastating disease in the history of man. It was practically incurable, and the terrible fevers and chills were almost impossible to ameliorate. Hiroshi was a very sick man. "How long has this siege been?"

"Only a few days. Perhaps I overtaxed myself."

A few days . . ."You fought Makato—and Mustapha—during an active siege of malaria?"

He closed his eyes. "If one may make a request—do not let this fact be known. It would not bring honor to these men, and would neither help me nor give me pleasure."

I stared, at him. He meant it. He was not a nice old *sensei*, he was a holy man. "I shall keep silent," I said heavily, feeling my burden increase almost intolerably. I had been laboring over grassy knolls while this man surmounted glaciers. "But why did you fight, in such condition? In fact, how *could* you fight? Malaria—"

"There was no one else," he said, answering my first question in the simplest way. When there was a job to be done, he did it without excuse or complaint, regardless of how he happened to feel "Many things are possible, with the *ki*."

The *ki*! That mysterious inner power that some men claimed to be gifted with, that made them stronger and somehow better than others. I had heard of it often, but never experienced it myself, and never verified it in another man. *Ki* required complete discipline, intense practice, absolute faith, and a proper mental attitude, and even then it manifested only erratically. I had often doubted its existence. Yet surely, if any martial art possessed *ki*, it was aikido. And if any man had it, that would be Hiroshi. Yet . . .

"I do not mean to scoff," I said. "But *ki* is not a thing I understand. Surely you did not use it when—"

He shook his head. "I would not use it in a match."

"But if you *have* it—"

"No. Not to harm another man. Only to preserve my own well-being, or to aid someone in need, or to accomplish a necessary labor."

"By entering a match despite malaria?" I asked incredulously.

"This is not readily explained," he reminded me gently. He meant that if I could not clarify it on my own, no one could clarify it for me.

I stood there numbly, certain I was on the verge of the most important understanding of my life, if only I could fathom his meaning and share his faith. But it would not come. His philosophy was alien to me.

Then he took my hand, and now somehow he had become cool. Physically cool. His raging fever was down. No doctor's medicine could have done it so soon. And I felt the incredible force of *ki* passing into my fingers, warming them with a heat that was not of the flesh. He *did* have it.

And I did not. My hand, my spirit grew cold as that contact parted.

With a regret verging on the deathwish, I left his presence and his power. In grief I returned to my lonely room.

*

The last matches were finished. Judo and Karate were tied at 10-2, with match awards of $52,000. Part of that had been paid during the halftime show, of course. Kung-fu was third, 8-4, $44,000; and Aikido fourth, 6-6, $36,000, because of Hiroshi's three terminal losses. Then Wrestling, 4-8, $28,000, and Boxing tied with Thai Kick-Boxing for sixth, 2-10, $20,000. But all that was the small change.

The team prize for first place was $240,000. Second was $120,000. Kung-fu got $60,000, and Aikido $30,000, in addition to their match awards. The prizes continued to halve each time, so that the bottom teams received only $7,500. But even that last-place minimum, when added to the match awards, totaled $27,500, or almost fourteen thousand dollars per man. Losers seldom got that kind of money for two weeks work.

There would be a playoff match, where I would meet the bull-stunner, contending for that top money and the dubious honor of winning the Martial Open. I had a weak wrist and a broken finger. But I doubted I could take Makato even in my best condition; he was devastating, and had beaten me before.

Yet it seemed to me that judo was inherently superior to karate, for judo is a broader martial art, with better worldwide organization and continuing research for improvement. There is no fixed set of rules for judo; it is a state of mind, drawing the best from all other fighting disciplines and developing steadily, not stratified in set patterns. Every strike in the karate arsenal belongs to judo too, as Takao had demonstrated; every kick of the Thai kick-boxers is valid for judo, and every leg take-down of sambo wrestling. I could use the kung-fu tiger's claw, had I the fingers for it, and the aikido arm-locks, and wrestling's strangles and boxing's punches. Nothing limited me except my personal knowledge and ability.

But I also knew that everything else would fall aside the first time Makato's iron hand scored. I might never wake from that smash. I represented the superior martial art, but I was not necessarily the superior man. And in the end, it is always man to man, not art to art. Japan had judokas who could lay Makato low, and so did Europe, such as the East German who should have been here. But I was American.

I reviewed the films, searching for potential weakness in my opponent. I had seen the Karate defeats by Judo and Aikido, but they were not enough. Now I looked at Karate's victories, to see how they might have been converted to losses.

Jesus Granda the Puerto Rican karateka had had a difficult time with Pung Lii, the kung-fu Red Guard who had slain my partner. They had traded terrible blows, and Pung had scored with the leopard's paw knuckle blow to the middle of the chest, cracking the sternum. It was the very sort of blow he had used to weaken Takao, and had brought blood to Jesus' face. But Jesus had finally won with a powerful but quite risky high kick to the chin, for a knockout. He had gambled and won. But I doubted that Makato would gamble with me unless I was beating him.

Makato himself had met Wang Hsu in the other Karate-Kung-fu match, and that had been the karateka's closest call. Wang scored early with the tiger's claws that ripped open Makato's forehead and barely missed his eyes, the streaming blood interfering with vision. That strike had been enough for Wang to win over Aikido, I remembered, but not in this case. Makato had managed to duck, so that his eyelids were not touched. Now he pressed forward with terrible fury, delivering a remarkable series of punches, chops and kicks. But Wang avoided most and foiled the rest with an equally remarkable defensive series. Later Wang scored again with the tiger, this time nearly ripping off Makato's left ear. Then the karateka scored to the shoulder, knocking the *sifu* back a good eight feet. He then made the mistake of following with a high kick. That tactic had been risky against the junior kung-fu specialist, and was foolhardly against the senior one.

Wang dropped into the "horse stance," knocked the foot up for a near miss, pivoted 180 degrees, and whipped out his right arm in a backfist attack to Makato's groin. It was the complex movement known as the "black dragon's thrashing tail," and it very nearly finished the karateka. But then Wang himself made the mistake of failing to make certain of his victory by an immediate follow-up, and Makato shot a desperation kick from the floor that smashed into the *sifu's* own privates. This time the fight really was over.

I shook my head. That was perhaps the best match of the tournament, and the deadly Chinese had gone all out, yet Makato had prevailed. My nails were nothing compared to Wang's, so I could hardly hurt Makato with the tiger's claw, and in any event that had not stopped the powerful karateka. I could execute the thrashing dragon's tail, but not nearly as well as Wang had. Imperfect technique would be disastrous. And again: the *sifu* had actually struck the karateka's groin, probably doing serious damage, yet Makato had hung on long enough to win. So that too was a losing strategy. I could also dodge straight punches and kicks, as Wang had. But despite all the fancy opposition techniques, the Korean had prevailed before, and surely would again.

Punches and kicks . . . I put on the films of the two Boxing-Thai Kick-Boxing matches. Mustapha took on Suphon of Thailand, and managed to block or avoid most of the kicks rather neatly, so that it looked like a win for him, but then the Thai went into a clinch, seized Mustapha with both arms around the waist, and rammed a terrible series of head butts to the face. Blood spurted and Mustapha's face became a mask of sausage before the judges jumped in and made the Thai desist. Mustapha was already unconscious, held upright only by Suphon's hugging grip.

Poor Mustapha! If the Thai had tried that on me, I would have boxed both his ears with my cupped hands, bursting his eardrums, or knocked him out with a knuckle blow to the temple, and he would not have butted more than once. But Makato certainly would not try butting me, and I would not try it on him, for that reason.

In the other film, Filo the Philippino kick-boxer actually did try the same butting technique against the Argentine Pibe Rosario. But Pibe, more canny in the clutch, let go with a savage rabbit punch to the back of the neck even as the first butt opened his cheek. Filo dropped unconscious, and Pibe mopped his bloody face, unconcerned.

All of which did not help me much. The other fights seemed to have no unique keys to victory. How could I handle Makato? The answer was that I couldn't—unless I could foil his terrible fist.

And there, perhaps, *was* my key. The karateka had many punches and kicks in his arsenal, but the thing that distinguished him was the iron fist. If he wanted to kill me, seemingly by accident, before the television cameras, that fist was a certainty. A kick that incapacitated me and ended the match would not suffice; he had to use the bomb.

That was his weakness: the win had to be fatal. Only his fist could do it properly.

Foil the punch, and I foiled Makato.

*

There were feasts and games and parties, for the tournament was over, for most of the combatants. I hardly paid attention. I ate moderately and tried to rest, with little success.

I did not see how it started, but suddenly there was a commotion several places down the table from me. The Whale stood ponderously, swayed, and picked up a bowl of noodles. He was obviously drunk.

Then he flung the bowl across the table—into the face of Pung Lii, the Red Guard.

The others just sat, amazed, while the kung-fu fighter wiped the juice out of his eyes. There were noodles tangled in his hair, giving him a comical appearance, but nobody laughed. A lot of odd things had happened, but this seemed more like a challenge. What had brought it on?

Pung Lii's face was burning, and not merely from rage. Those noodles were hot. Yet he retained control, as a trained warrior should. Slowly he stood, and his pretty Caucasian companion for the evening stood with him, taking his arm. With perfect aplomb she picked splattered noodles out of her bosom.

"The gringo is intoxicated," Pedro said loudly from the head of the table. "Pay him no heed."

This was all we needed, I thought sourly. Another clumsy scene by a white-skinned North American.

Whale lunged across the table and caught the woman's arm away from the Chinese. "No white woman touches the likes of *him!*" he bawled.

Pung Lii whirled about, assuming the horse stance—and Whale lifted his knee and boosted the entire table into him. The dishes and drinks crashed to the floor, inundating the seated warriors all along the line, including me.

But from the gross confusion, Pedro's voice emerged supreme. "Bring the cameras to bear! Ten thousand dollars to the winner, no holds barred!" He sounded gleeful.

"Stop it!" I cried. "Whale's drunk! He's in no condition to—" But I was drowned out by general applause. The majority wanted to let them fight.

And fight they did, while the rest of us cleared back, food and liquor dripping from our formal clothes.

Whale picked up a gooey yam from the rubble and hurled it at Pung Lii. "Choke on it, killer of heart patients!" Whale cried.

Suddenly I comprehended. My partner Takao had saved Whale's life, and Pung had killed Takao. Whale had a blood debt to settle, not to mention the humiliation he had suffered in his tournament battle with Wang Hsu. That Crane's-beak blow to the solar plexus.

Actually Whale should never have challenged kung-fu again. Pung Lii was the lesser member of that team, but he was still a deadly man, as he had shown Takao. Whale was a blubbery mountain, 325 pounds, the weaker member of a weak team, and he was drunk. I feared he had just brought death on himself, and there was nothing I could do to stop it.

Pung Lii's formal dress was stuck with noodles and spattered with yam. He had been publicly insulted and assaulted. But he was not drunk, and he had an iron control He wanted only one thing: to kill Whale.

One moment he was standing, soberly brushing himself off, while the Whale poked amid the garbage of the banquet. The next, Pung Lii was in mid air, his feet thrusting forward to strike Whale in the chest.

Whale stepped aside, and the kung-fu warrior landed square on the table, crashing amongst the dishes. He skidded on through the wreckage, his course greased by butter, wine and gravy. The sight was ludicrous, but still no one laughed.

I realized then that Whale was not drunk at all. He had been clowning, as was his habit, and had suckered Pung Lii into this messy combat. It was, like all the others, a fair fight.

Except for one thing: Pung Lii was a much more brutal customer than Whale. He weighed little more than half as much, but all of it was deadly.

Whale found a roast on the floor. He heaved it at Pung Lii, and followed it up with a foot stomp. That was a mistake; Pung grabbed the foot and twisted. Whale fell on his side. As he went down I heard the table boards snap under his weight. Immediately Pung was on top of him, trying for a nerve pinch on the trapezius muscle of the shoulder. But that was his mistake. Whale was too big, and had too much fat overlaying his muscle; the pinch was obviously painful, but not incapacitating.

Whale got up very quickly, and shook himself. He bucked like a bronco, surprising Pung, and threw him against the wall. Sweat poured like water from Whale's body, mixing with the grease that coated him.

Whale flung himself after Pung, and the kung-fu warrior's snake-fang fingers plunged at Whale's face. The blow was swift and horribly effective: one of Whale's eyeballs bulged half out of its socket, and the other was covered with blood. He had been blinded.

But Whale had contact. He pulled Pung's head down and opened his mouth. Pung screamed as their two faces came to-gether. Then they broke, and I saw why. Whale had bitten off Pung's nose.

Pung's face was now a mass of blood, but he had not quit. Goaded to maniacal fury, he leaped on Whale, raining punches on his head and face. The kung-fu sophistication was forgotten now; this was elementary savagery.

He would have done better to retain his training. Whale, sight-less, could only grapple—and grapple he did. He caught an arm, then Pung's whole torso. Suddenly, with insane strength, he lifted the Red Guard up, up, high in the air, one hand on the man's shoulder, the other on his thigh—then brought him down across his bent knee.

Pung's spine broke with an audible crack, and he lay still in the garbage. If he were not dead, he would wish to be when he woke. Whale was little better off. He stood there swaying, blood streaming from his face, from his two eyes.

The whole thing was brutal and unnecessary, a butchery that never should have been allowed. Yet behind my horror, enhancing it, was a certain guilty satisfaction. For I too raged at Takao's death, and now he had been avenged.

And where did that leave me? With another circus massacre, to no more purpose than the others? No, there was purpose: I had to win the big money, so that Jim's medical bills could be covered. I had to sacrifice one man to save another.

The servants moved in to clean up. Whale stood there, eyeball hanging, blind. I returned to my room, numbed.

A long telegram was waiting there, delivered in my absence. It was from Jim. He had suffered a spontaneous recovery, and was now, he claimed, as good as ever. Or would be, soon, with a little practice. There would be no colossal medical bills.

"You're doing great!" he finished encouragingly. "Wrap it up for Judo!"

"Yeah, sure," I muttered, feeling twisted inside.

CHAPTER 9

CHAMPIONSHIP

The playoff match was set up in the ballroom, so that everyone on the premises could attend. The *tatami* had been placed beside the wall, where the orchestra had been. I saw to my dismay that the girls had been invited, each dating a fighter or judge. Furthermore, they were all formally dressed, as they had been at the halftime banquet. The TV cameras were in place as always. Though I knew that millions were paying to watch this on closed circuit, the magnitude of the publicity hadn't been brought home to me until I saw the incongruously elegant attire of the audience.

Vicente Pedro himself arrived in his wheelchair, flanked by his niece. Amalita looked wan, but she kept her gaze level. I would have had more sympathy for her if it had not been for the *kris*-murdered innocent girl. As it was, my primary interest was in protecting myself; Amalita knew how to take care of herself.

Pedro settled in his chair at ringside, and his fair niece sat at his right. Another wheelchair was brought to rest on his left.

It was Hiroshi! I had not seen him enter. What determination had brought him from his bed? Surely he had no particular fascination with this death-match!

Pedro was here to watch me die. Hiroshi must be trying his

positive approach, however that might work. And Amalita was neutral.

Very likely Pedro would be satisfied, much as I intended to resist the denouement of this long bloody contest. My finger still hurt, my stomach rumbled, my gut was flatulent, and I had not slept well. Makato, in contrast, seemed to be in top shape. Only faint scars marked his forehead where the kung-fu *sifu* had raked him, and there was no sign of the crotch strike or his other injuries. He did not exude confidence or swagger, as that was not his way; he was merely a quiet, stolid Oriental with a square face and an irresistible fist.

This time there was a live announcer to puff up the match. He reviewed the fights we had had, speaking English, and I knew that translators were working from his broadcast. He dwelt unnecessarily, I thought, on my prior loss to Makato and on the bout I had won by forfeit because Makato had incapacitated my Aikido adversary. How I wished I could tell the world about Hiroshi's malaria, but naturally I could not. The announcer's verbal picture made Judo mediocre beside Karate. Was this intended to make me mad? If so, it failed, for I had more pressing problems. Mainly, staying alive. If I could accomplish that, the image of Judo as a martial art would take care of itself.

The contestants were interviewed, briefly. Makato did not speak English, so a translation of his prepared statement was read for him. It was all about the glory of karate and the uses to which he would put the grand prize he had virtually won. Obviously he had not written it, for no ranking karateka talked like that.

"And now the American judogi, Jason Striker," the stout announcer said.

"Judoka," I said, annoyed. "Not *judogi*—that's the uniform." Had he confused it on purpose?

"And what are you going to do with the prize money?" he said with something like a sneer. I saw that it was not just me they were gunning for, but judo itself, and America. Everything I stood for was to be brought low tonight.

I looked about, and saw Hiroshi again. He had tried to tell me something, and he had shown me his ki. Now he was here, and not to watch me die. He had shared Takao's oath. What had he meant, about being positive?

"Striker!" the announcer said, snapping his sweaty fingers under my nose. "Little punch-drunk, maybe? I asked what you thought you'd do with that quarter-million dollar prize."

"Two hundred and forty thousand dollars. It shall be divided evenly among the families of all those eliminated prematurely from this vicious tournament," I said before I thought. "The crippled and the dead." I had had Hiroshi and Takao in mind, but I realized now that this also struck at Pedro himself, a judo cripple. I saw his face freeze.

The announcer was taken aback. No one had told him I had a mind of my own, and he seemed to find it awkward and unfair. "But Mr. Striker—nothing for yourself?"

"The honor of representing Judo, and all serious martial arts," I said. Was that more positive?

The men were beginning to nod agreement. Pedro made a signal, and the announcer cut off the interview immediately. Naturally they couldn't have the loser looking more decent than the winner, or foster undue underdog sympathy. But I saw the ghost of a smile on Hiroshi's face.

The next item on the agenda was the selection of the three judges. Karate's was there, of course, and the neutral one was the Kung-fu, who had shown partiality for Karate in matches not against Kung-fu itself. No hope there. I would have to select the Judo substitute judge from the remainder, as if it made any difference in this stacked deck.

Think positive! I reminded myself—and suffered an inspiration. "I can think of no more qualified judge for this important match," I said clearly, "than our esteemed host, Vicente Pedro, himself a third-degree black belt in judo."

Pedro's mouth dropped open, but there was spontaneous applause from the audience, especially the girls, who thought this was a signal compliment to their employer. Many of the men knew better, but joined in after a moment, appreciating the irony. I knew then that the other contestants were not against me, but merely impotent to express their views. Whatever would be, would be; they were standing aside, and would abide the settlement with clean hands.

Pedro, committed by the applause, said nothing. I knew that a certain perverse pride was warring against his fury, for he had to like the notion of participating in this ultimate match, even indirectly. He would not dare to show bias against Judo now. Also his own pride and martial training would force him to be fair; the code had to be ingrained, or he would never have achieved his third dan black belt, and would not so carefully have warned me about staying clear of Amalita. So I was not exactly throwing away my choice of judges. Perhaps I had neutralized my major opposition.

"Vicente Pedro, the judge for Judo," the announcer said, and again Hiroshi smiled.

It was time. Makato removed his robe, and I did likewise. Now the scars on his face stood out in the strong light necessary for the television cameras, and his torn ear had not yet healed. He looked like a brute, though the judogi concealed the extreme musculature of his upper torso. I doubted I looked much better. My face was unmarked except for bruises, but my lack of sleep probably made me hollow-eyed. Yes, we were gladiators, both.

The starting gong sounded. The crowd hushed.

I closed slowly. Of course I did not look at his eyes; that was a foolhardy amateur tactic. I looked at what could hurt me: his body, his arms, his hands.

Makato was in a slight crouch, one leg a bit ahead of the other, one hand lifted shoulder high, the other waist high. His weight was balanced and he was ready to move rapidly, hitting, kicking or taking evasive action.

His hands were extended in the "knife" position, fingers together and straight, thumbs on top and laid alongside the palms for protection. He was relaxed; this was not overconfidence or carelessness, but a state of superior readiness. The options were always narrowed by tenseness.

I had drilled for much of the night on my counter to Makato's kill-strike, until it was very nearly an automatic reflex. If he confined himself to that one type of blow.

Makato did not attack immediately. Was he waiting for me to attempt another *Harai goshi* throw? Fat chance!

We circled each other. Where was the punch? I was primed for it, yet it did not come.

Well, if he wasn't going to mix it up, I would show him some judo. I'd force him to use his weapon.

I faked the *Harai goshi*, gambling that the karateka had done some priming of his own. And he had. His left fist shot out like a pile driver, straight for my head. But my right arm came up, striking his hand with the bony edge of my forearm and deflecting the thrust as I pulled back and turned to the side to present a smaller target.

There was such power in his blow that my arm was swept back to smack into my head. I had to jump away to escape its fury, and even then my whole body was propelled across the ring. My right forearm, where his fist had actually struck, was numb from wrist to elbow. But I had foiled his kill-shot by adapting the knife defense to my purpose.

Makato came after me as I tottered off-balance. But I surprised him by trying a dangerous maneuver that succeeded: a flying kick to his chest with both my feet. Had he been on guard for it, he would merely have stepped aside and let me fall, perhaps hurting myself. But he had been intent on the attack, off-balanced himself, and so momentarily vulnerable. I saw Amalita watching, her eyes bright, her lips parted.

She liked this. Pedro's face was serious, as if he were analyzing the particular motions. Hiroshi seemed neutral.

We closed again. I noted the concentration of the other spectators. They were trying to fathom how I had foiled the fist, and wondering whether it was a fluke. Makato himself was not confused; he stalked me just as he had before, seeking his opening.

I didn't allow him undue time to set up. I watched for my own opportunity, when his weight was balanced just so, and tried a foot sweep, *De ashi barai*, combined with a kick to the ankle. I caught his right leg and brought him down in such a way that he had no leverage for his fist. My blow had strength enough to break a normal man's ankle, but Makato's was not normal. It was a massive column of muscle and bone. I had hurt him, but hardly decisively.

I seized him as he fell, and whipped into a stranglehold, the *okuri eri jime*, the sliding lapel strangle. My right hand gripped his lapel—but my broken finger hurt, weakening the choke, and it was extremely difficult to cut off either his air or his blood.

Makato grabbed my hair and pulled savagely, unseating me and throwing me to the right. The pain was sharp, and I saw the hair between his fingers; he had pulled some of it out by the roots. I had to let go.

He threw a flurry of punches as we disengaged, stinging me, for even minor strikes by those hardened hands hurt. But he was unable to deliver the killing punch, for a blow is only as strong as the thrust of the body behind it. Makato had broken tiles and boards not with his fist alone, but by using his fist as the leading edge of his dynamic body. He had to be set for it.

I backed away, parrying, seeking room to maneuver. He followed, stalking me as he would a peccary, getting his balance. Now he was primed. His fist shot out—and again I struck with my arm and thrust against it, jumping away. Again that freight-train collision. Arms flopping, I was flung back. Hard. I crashed into the wall, and the white plaster gave way, collapsing around me and powdering me with fine dust. My head overlapped the painted frieze, and I felt the imprint of the carved relief against my neck.

Half-conscious, I hung there, supported largely by my own imprint in the wall. Makato came at me, his great fist firing to-

ward my face like a cannon ball. I wrenched my head aside—and
that juggernaut smashed into the frieze and through it, to the
elbow.

Momentarily, he was caught. His hand was trapped in the
crotch of a supine nymph who surely had not anticipated any
such rape when she was painted there. But I came to the defense of
the lady, lifting my knee high to strike him in the groin. I braced
myself against the wall so that there was no recoil; all my power
went into that flesh-crushing, bone-splintering blow. But he
twisted aside, and dropped, so that it caught him in the stomach.

His right fist ripped out from the wall in a shower of plaster,
carrying a section of wood with it and destroying the nymph. A
loose flap of skin dangled from his knuckles, scraped off by the
jagged break in the wall. My strike should have knocked him out;
just a little higher and it could have caved in his rib-cage and
squeezed his heart, giving him a taste of Takao's final agony. But he
would not go down.

I saw Pedro staring, amazed at the punishment the karateka
had survived. I was amazed myself.

Or was it that Pedro was surprised and chagrined to see me
putting up a decent fight? Well, he had some more surprises coming.

I charged Makato, trying to finish it while I had the chance. I
rammed his belly with my head, hunching my shoulders and covering my own ears in defense against counterattacks. I butted him
back across the room, working on that weakened section where my
knee had hit, keeping him groggy. But his stomach muscles were
like rock and still he would not go down.

Makato brought up his hands, too slowly. I ducked down and
hit him at knee-level with my shoulders in a *kuchiki-taoshi* dead
tree drop, my hand catching behind his ankle as I lifted him. He
had no chance to chop at my kidney this time.

I got him in a *ude-garami* figure four armlock and leaned into
it, forcing him to capitulate or have his elbow dislocated, but he
would not give in. My weak hand betrayed me again. Makato,

with a surge of strength, slowly bent his arm, escaping the lock. He sat up and drove his fist at my face, again forcing me to break the hold or suffer a concussion. As it was, my nose was smashed. Blood streamed from my nostrils so that I had to breathe from my mouth, although in the heat of combat I felt no pain. *He* might be indestructible; *I* was not!

I disengaged and did a back roll, but not quickly enough. The fist of death came through to catch me on the thigh, numbing my leg. Now my nose was hurting, and I licked the salty blood, trying to mop up enough so that it would not splash into my eyes on the next maneuver. I hopped and staggered, trying to recover proper use of my leg—and Makato flipped to his feet and followed, scoring on my shoulder as I hunched to protect my head. My arm became numb too, moving with difficulty, and I dropped and rolled again, still trying to escape him. It was a replay of our first encounter.

There was no escape. He kicked me, and I thought I felt a rib break. It was painful enough for a fracture; the agony was like a knife stab in my side. But I had no time to worry about details. I somersaulted, spun about, and got caught by another kick that barely missed my groin and drilled into my upper thigh. I must have slowed him up, or he would not have missed.

I managed to catch his foot and pull upwards, upsetting his balance and throwing him on his back. He aimed another kick at my face. But I was rolling, carrying his ankle with me, throwing him off, and his horny sole only grazed my ear. I caught his lapels for another *Okuri eri jime* strangle, but it was even less effective than before. He reached for my hair again, and I spun my face about and caught his fingers in my teeth.

Then, for the first time, he made a sound of pain, for it was no love-bite I clamped on him. My teeth cut through his flesh to the bone, and I felt the gristle grate, and my mouth filled with blood. His other hand came up to smash my face yet again, but I toppled him sidewise and put a third strangle on him, as my teeth ripped free. The blood flowing was no longer mine alone. This time my strangle was a *kazure okuri eri jime*, a variation of the sliding lapel strangle, and my weak hand did not subvert it. But still he would not yield. He elbowed me in the ribs, tore away my hands, and as I jumped to my feet, that fist scored yet again, this time to my solar plexus.

My breath left me, my heart missed a beat, and I blacked out momentarily. I had a vision of Takao falling to the mat as his heart failed, and I thought I would join him. I fell on my back, and far, far away I saw Makato falling toward me, his fist leading, middle knuckle protruding. That descending punch would crush my temple like an eggshell.

I lifted my feet for the stomach-throw, but they were too slow, they would not respond. I was exhausted; my limbs felt as if each weighed a ton, and my heart was beating so hard it seemed it would burst. So I jabbed just two fingers at his neck, left-handed: the kung-fu snake's fang, stiff and swift.

One fang hit his wind-pipe and collapsed it.

Makato's fist missed. His body fell across mine, but he was breathing yet. His neck was strong, so the trachea had sprung back, but he had suffered a hell of a shock. I hit the side of his neck with the edge of my hand, trying to score on the nerve center that controlled the flow of blood to the brain, thereby knocking him unconscious. But his neck was too tough, and my arm too weak. He rolled off and started to climb to his feet.

I had to get him now, while I had the chance. He was partially dazed too; his whole effort was to disengage and stand. He was open for a terminal strike—if only I could make it.

I tried. I reached up to grasp the right side of his head with my good left hand, and with my cupped right I smote his left ear. The sudden explosive pressure was calculated to rupture his eardrum.

It did. Makato leaped up, and I knew that soon blood would dribble from that ear; he had no calluses inside his head. But still he did not yield. He would go on fighting as long as he was conscious, no matter what injury I did him.

I sat up, my head spinning, and looked about the room. I was braced to catapult into action the instant the karateka attacked, and I wanted him to come to me. But for the moment he stood back, shaking his hurting head and kneading his bitten hand. Now he knew that judo was no easy match; his own life was at stake too. And he knew that Jason Striker could fight.

Everyone in the audience was sitting silently. There was no encouragement for either judoka or karateka, and no condemnation for the tactics employed. Only a tense waiting for the outcome. Amalita sat beside her uncle as if hypnotized; perhaps her fate also hung on this match. There was no expression on Pedro's face, and Hiroshi's eyes were almost closed.

But I could not afford to dwell on the spectators. Makato was stalking me again, more carefully now, for I had hurt him and might do so again. Another man would have yielded, with the injuries he had suffered so far, but not the Korean. I found myself on my feet, stepping back. Did he know how much he had hurt me with that iron hand? I could not last much longer. My hand, my leg, my chest, my face . . .

As I circled, my eyes crossed the room again, involuntarily seeking some escape though I knew there was none. I had to kill—or die. My eyes took in fast details as they swept the faces there. I saw the two wrestlers, Kipchak and Whale, uncomfortable in their formal costumes; Whale's eyes were heavily bandaged, so that he could not see at all. Next to him was Mustapha the boxer, one brown fist clenching spasmodically. Then Wang the kung-fu *sifu*, for once not smiling. All the men were deadly sober. The girls were uniformly pale, whatever their physical colors, some frozen-faced, some not looking. What had they expected, a Ping-Pong game? Then my roving eye caught Hiroshi's eye—and I felt something remarkable.

It was as though a star shone in his face, though there was no special light. It was the power of his ki, imbuing him despite his illness, making him more than a man. The power I had not believed, until I discovered it in him.

Be positive! I thought, reminded of Hiroshi's advice. But what was positive about death? Only the removal of Pedro's grudge against me could stop this killfest, and how was that possible, when I had given him cause? No power on Earth could expurgate my act with his niece. Makato was getting set again, and all the good will in the universe would not stop the fist of karate at this moment.

I saw the fist, as if it were in slow motion, rising from his springing body. Makato was hurt, yes, but the whole of his intolerable might was in that final blow. It was driving toward my face like a wrecking ball toward a condemned building.

Yet I did not move. My feet seemed rooted, my arms hung down. Some strange rigidity was spreading through me, pulsing outward from my eye, as though I had seen the gorgon Medusa and was being transformed to stone. My face hardened, my neck became stiff, my torso crystallized. All feeling left my body, and only my brain functioned, deep within thick layers of leather, gristle and bone.

The blow struck my jaw just below the left ear. The impact was tremendous. I felt bone giving way, nerves being crushed, flesh being pulped, blood vessels bursting hydraulically.

I watched Makato's hand fall away. I heard a groan of utter agony, not mere pain, but the loss of the certainty of a lifetime.

Then I understood. It was the *ki*.

My flesh and bone and brain had not been crushed; *Makato's* had. His hand hung loosely, like his spirit, shattered.

I moved. Every muscle in my body glowed with smooth power, and there was no pain anywhere. I was invulnerable.

I stepped toward Makato, raising my right hand, now stronger than his. He merely stood, watching me dully, knowing what was coming but taking no evasive action. He had lost, and knew it; he had not thrown it away by error, but had been conquered at his height. The penalty for his failure might be a crushed skull or a burst heart, or merely an arm snapped like kindling wood, but he refused to flee from it.

"Kill him! Kill him!" It was Pedro's voice. He did not realize that Makato's strength was gone.

I turned on our host a glance of contempt, and saw him straining at the arms of his chair. How badly he must want me dead. Amalita put out a hand to restrain him, and Hiroshi also put his hand on Pedro's. It was pathetic: the cripple so eager for the kill that he had to be stopped from falling out of his wheelchair.

I returned to Makato. He remained as he had been, pleading no mercy. Killer he might be, but no coward.

I turned away. The *ki* was the most remarkable thing I had ever experienced. I could not use it as a murder weapon. Better to forfeit the match. That much, now, I understood of Hiroshi's philosophy.

But Makato did not follow. He also was through. We bowed formally to each other, terminating the match.

The experience of the *ki*—Hiroshi's gift to me—was more important than all the glory and all the prize money. But now the *ki* drained away, and I felt my wounds and fatigue. I would be out of action for weeks, healing. It was all I could do to continue standing. But I had to remain for the decision.

The three judges did not confer. "Karate!" the karate man cried. "On points."

The kung-fu, or theoretically neutral judge, considered longer. He had been alert to the kung-fu tactics I had used, and he had recognized the *ki*. "Draw," he said.

Pedro, the third judge, struggled again in his chair, throwing off Amalita's hand but not Hiroshi's. "There is no draw!" he said. "It's a plain win!"

Still Hiroshi's hand was on him, and I wondered whether any of the *ki* was touching the incorrigible despot.

"A win for whom?" the announcer asked, perplexed.

"For *Judo!*" Pedro cried, standing up. "That is the best match I've ever seen! Three times the fist was launched—and three times countered! By knife, by snake, and by—" He stopped, realizing that everyone in the hall was staring at him.

Only the announcer failed to comprehend. "One vote for Karate, one for Judo, one Draw," he said. "The result is a draw. Folks, you have just seen—"

But the rest of us were watching Pedro, and Pedro was facing Hiroshi, feeling the *ki*, realizing what had happened. Amalita was studying Pedro with new appraisal. It had not been him she disliked, but his crippled state, and that had changed.

"Come on," I said to Makato. "Let's go clean up."

Then the applause began, swelling tremendously. Was it for the combatants, or for Pedro, or for the true victor in the true contest, Hiroshi? Did it matter?

CHAPTER 10

DEATHBLOW

Jim was up and about when I returned, and he was full of praise for my televised performance. "But you should have put a better strangle on that karateka," he said. "I know you can strangle when you really try."

"Get out of here!" I yelled, making a motion as of a kung-fu strike at his groin.

He got serious. "Speaking of kung-fu—did you realize that our local practitioner died?"

"Died!" I exclaimed, shocked. "Kolychkine the *sifu*? What happened?" I remembered how Kolychkine had beaten off Dato's raid last month. Had there been foul play?

"Heart attack. In front of his own students. Just like Charles Smith."

So abruptly, the muffled dread of the local situation returned. I had supposed everything would be peaceful once I got free of the Martial Open and back to familiar haunts.

Smith had had contact with Dato, and so had Kolychkine. Now both were dead, similarly. Could there be a connection? I had the growing and awful certainty that there could be, and was. "What has Dato been doing?" I asked warily.

"Nothing special. He entered a tournament while you were gone—jealous of you, I'm sure—just a small local affair, and he was matched up against Cohen Worthen. But Dato stopped after a few motions, claiming he was ill. So he lost by forfeit. Nobody can figure why he entered in the first place; at his age he's in no shape to compete."

I shook my head, remembering how people had thought the same about little Hiroshi. "Dato is eccentric."

"He's a clown!"

And I had called Takao a clown. How terribly we wrong good men by our superficiality! But long after Jim had gone, I lay on my bed, thinking of Dato and of the rumors I had heard about him. I didn't like the situation at all, but still I hesitated to believe the ugly notion that pushed at my mind. Next day I still couldn't let it rest. I was recuperating from the beating Makato had given me, but I just couldn't lie about my house while this thing obsessed me. It seemed ridiculous to vocalize, so I didn't try to phone. But I had to get over to see Cohen Worthen, the other local judo *sensei*.

I stepped out of my door, and into the arms of a chic young lady. "Thera!" I exclaimed, gladder to see her than I should be. "What—?"

"Just checking on you between trimesters," she said brightly. "Never did get raped, so I thought you and I could—" she paused. "Jason—you look awful! What have you been doing, headstands on a bed of nails?"

"I—"

"That's bad for the complexion. I know."

"Don't you watch TV?" I asked, bemused. "Or check the sports pages?"

"Never. I have no time for current events. I'm studying hard at college, remember? So I can get smart and impress a certain dumb— Jason, did *you* get raped?"

So she didn't even know about Nicaragua. That was deflating. "Yes, I got raped," I said, only half joking. "Come on over to the *dojo*."

"Are you sure it's a safe place for a nice girl?"

"The *dojo*? Of course! Thera, I've got something on my mind—
"   •

"Well, then, I have no business at your *dojo*!" she said, taking hold of my arm and nudging her firm young bosom against it. "Let's just get that something *off* your mind, at my place, after a drink, and—"

"Thera, we've been through all that," I said, though privately flattered and tempted. I had experienced a lot in the past few weeks, and she was a lovely girl.

"And I've kept up my judo practice, too," she said. "Want to see de assi bare?" She wiggled her rear.

"*De ashi barai*," I said, correcting her atrocious pun. "There really is something I have to attend to. Possibly a matter of life and death."

"I love life and death! I'll drive you there!"

"Uh-uh! The way you drive, you'd *better* love one or the other! Last time you took me to a bar, remember?"

"I was young then." But she joined me in my car.

It was nice being with her again. I wished I could take time to socialize, but this thing about Dato simply would not let go. The Martial Open had taught me that exceedingly strange things are possible.

Jim met us at the entrance to the *dojo*. "What's this, Chief?" he joked. "Picking up broads in broad daylight?"

Thera bristled. "Who let that loudmouth in?"

"Wait a minute, kids!" I said quickly. How like that age, to enjoy making but not receiving sexual puns. "Thera, this is Jim Blake, my assistant. Jim, this is Thera Drummond, visiting from college."

"College?" he asked. "What does a piece like that want with college? She'll never use what little mind she has!"

Thera stopped short on the edge of the *tatami*. "What would an oaf like you know about a mind?"

"Come off it, tart! I'm in college myself. You girls think you can wiggle your bottoms and get high grades."

"Better both than neither!"

"Look, folks—" I began, surprised by the vehemence of their antagonism. They were scoring on each other better than either knew, for Thera did tend to solve problems by displaying her anatomy, and Jim's grade point average had suffered somewhat because of the time he put into judo.

But there was no stopping it. "Listen, sister," Jim said angrily, putting a hand on her arm.

Thera executed a neat *de ashi barai*, sweeping Jim's foot with the side of her own while pulling on his sleeve. Caught by surprise, he fell.

She turned to me. "See? De assi bare. He's certainly an ass!"

Jim sat up, amazed. "She knows judo!"

"Brown belt, oaf," she said. "Have you heard of it?"

"I thought you knew," I said belatedly to Jim. "She was my tutoring student. Six weeks, and then she kept it up in college."

"I'll be damned!" Jim said, getting up.

"Will you clean up your language?" Thera snapped. "What's so strange about a girl learning self-defense?"

"Doll like you *needs* it, for sure," Jim said.

"Only against free-handed oafs!"

I had to cut in. "Jim, I have some private business this morning. Can you handle the *dojo*?"

"You mean you leave *him* in charge?" Thera demanded incredulously.

Jim's face darkened. "Sister, you are pushing your luck. You think you're the only female who ever made brown belt?"

"I didn't notice *you* making anything of it!" she said, pointedly eyeing the spot where he had landed on the *tatami*.

"Why don't you put on a *judogi* and try it again?"

"You think I won't?"

I started to protest, for Thera could be no match for Jim's second degree black belt and great strength. But I stopped myself. Thera had more than judo going for her, and Jim knew enough to avoid serious trouble. Two young, bright, short-tempered college kids, both my students—let them work it out by themselves. There would be fireworks before they came to terms, but that was all part of growing up.

I ducked out. They didn't even notice.

I drove across town to Cohen Worthen's *dojo*. I was in luck; I caught him in his office. He was a short, rotund and very hairy man whose huge mane of hair was shot with gray. He was about forty five, fat but strong, an outgoing type. I rather liked him, though he had a number of annoying mannerisms and a thick hide.

"Jason the Strike!" he bawled as he always did, never tiring of the supposed humor.

"Cohen, this is important," I said. "You had a run-in with Dato, didn't you?"

"Nothing like yours with that karateka! I don't mind telling you, Striker, I didn't think you had the stuff to pull it off. But you did judo proud, winning that tournament."

"I didn't win," I said. "But about Dato—"

"I couldn't have done better myself!" he continued with blithe conceit. "You must be hurting, though! Broke a rib, didn't you?"

"Yes, and then some. But I got even. I bit his finger." He laughed at that. Then I continued: "Look, Cohen—this is serious. Are you feeling well?"

"Am I feeling well!" He shook his head, his hair flying. "All right, Striker. I'll give you a rundown. I took a couple fouls off Dato, but when I really came to grips with him he was weak, and quit right off. So I won, by forfeit, technically. But I'd've taken him easily anyway. Dato's old, and kinda kooked, and his technique is like nothing known!"

"That's what I'm worried about!" I said. "When he hit you—"

"Oh, sure, it was sore for a few days where he hit me on the upper thigh, and it had a funny kind of bruise, but nothing crippling. You expect to get bruised, in this business. Hardly a day when I'm not hurting somewhere, but I never miss a day, and right now I'm better'n ever. So if that's all's bothering you—"

"Cohen, Dato hit a student of mine, and maybe six weeks later that boy died, with no illness in between. He hit Kolychkine the *sifu*, and several weeks later he died, right in front of his own students. Now he has hit you."

"Striker, I get your drift," Worthen said. "I know all about those cases; hell, Koly was a friend of mine, after hours. But it has to be coincidence. Dato just isn't that good! When he tried to match me—"

"He doesn't have to be good!" I said. "At least, he doesn't have to seem good. Maybe he's faking incompetence, so that nobody will believe he has actually mastered—"

"The delayed-action deathblow?" Worthen shook his head, slowly, so that the hair stayed in place. "The blow itself is folklore, Striker! Just like the ninja mythology. Might as well start believing in old Fu Antos while you're at it, and the Tooth Fairy! How could Dato master a technique that doesn't exist? He might fool himself into believing it, but who else?"

"I'm not so sure," I said. "I thought at first I was making a wild conjecture. But the pattern fits. There are strange things in the old Oriental texts."

"Work it out for yourself, Striker. How would such a blow work? I mean physically? What would go on in the body of the victim, over the course of hours, days, weeks? Does such a thing make any conceivable sense, in terms of the physics and biology we know today? Maybe it was possible in the old days, just as witchcraft was possible, and voodoo. I'm not fooling; I really believe those hexes worked—when people believed in them! We'd call it hypnotism today, or faith-healing, or neurasthenia, or maybe even *ki*. All how you view what you can't understand."

"*Ki* works," I said. "It's not superstition. I know."

"So does faith-healing! But my point is you've got to believe in it before it can work for you, right? And I don't believe in any delayed-action deathblow, okay? So it can't hurt me, right?"

"I hope it can't!" I said. "But look, Cohen, humor me. Go to your doctor for a thorough physical tomorrow. Just to make sure. Have him check your heart especially. And if you begin to feel at all funny, especially three, four or five weeks after Dato struck you—"

"Forget it, Striker!" he said, laughing. "My doc's booked up on routine physicals for two weeks ahead; I'm not going to waste his time on any phony emergency. You can see I'm healthy! Don't try to voodoo me with that crap!"

I had to let it drop, because I was trying to scare him, whatever my motive. What irony, if my very warning should start him brooding himself into a heart attack.

In any event, he had reassured me, and made the specter of lurking death seem ludicrous. I went home.

Jim was still at the *dojo*, but Thera was gone. "Fool girl said she was sick," he said disgustedly. "I had to drive her home. Ritzy estate she lives at!"

"Her father's Drummond of Drummond Industries," I said.

"So I learned. Spoiled rich kid. But she knows her judo! Not surprising, considering you taught her, but what a pain, with her stuck-up ways. How did you stand it?"

"I had my moments," I admitted.

"How'd you make out with Worthen? I never did catch what your business with him was."

"Morbid notion of mine," I said. "I was worried about his health."

"Him? Constitution like a polar bear, and every bit as smart! Never gets sick."

"As I said: it was a morbid notion. Thanks for holding the fort."

He looked uncomfortable, for no reason I could ascertain. "Do me a favor, huh? Don't bring in any more coeds!"

I laughed. Thera was a bit hard to take, initially, especially for someone as short of patience as Jim.

*

Thera had the flu. She was sick all week, and I didn't see her at all. Even phoning her never worked out conveniently, which was perhaps just as well; I had no business associating with her anyway. Teen-age rich girl; Jim had her pegged pretty well, actually.

I felt better. Jim was running things well enough, so I could recuperate at leisure. Several reporters interviewed me, picking up new slants on the Martial Open, but I discouraged that for the most part. I had done what I had to do, and now it was over, with no money and some bad memories. Maybe I shouldn't have been so generous about donating my share of the winnings, but I didn't regret that part. It was the Roman circus aspect, the brutality and death, and I had been as brutal as anyone. I still felt unclean. The best thing I could do now was keep my nose to the *dojo*-business grindstone.

Then the phone, as usual, pulled the rug out. It rang; I answered. Then:

"Johnson Drummond here," the familiar voice rapped. Thera's father, whose Midas touch could mean trouble proportionate to its wealth. Well, now I would ask him whether he really had pulled wires to ease me into the Martial Open.

"Drummond, were you the one who—"

"Right!" he said. "Striker, have you been laying my daughter?"

Sock! to the solar plexus, or maybe the groin. I suppose I could have gotten clever and inquired which daughter, but my brain was less nimble than my judo reflexes. "No."

"Thought not," he said, and disconnected.

I had hardly assimilated the dubious meaning of that when the phone rang again. This time it was the police: "Cohen Worthen is dead. You're another judo instructor; do you know anything about it, Striker?"

I mumbled something ambiguous. I would be laughed right out of town if I made known my real suspicions. Dato—his delayed deathblow had struck again. Now two of his three major competitors were dead, and I was the third. There was only way to resolve this mess. I phoned Dato. "Jason Striker!" he cried before I could say why I was calling. "I have wanted to call you! I was a zebra last time I spoke to you. A pony."

"An ass," I provided helpfully.

"Ass, ass, yes! I was an awful hole, and I apologize! I want to make it right! And I have something urgent to talk about. Come see me tonight at *dojo* and I'll open good *saki* and we'll talk, very well?"

"Good enough," I agreed, since this was exactly what I wanted to do. I wasn't fooled for a moment by his friendliness; that was how he had been with Charles Smith. But this thing had to be settled: had he really rediscovered the delayed-action deathblow, and if so, how was it executed? I couldn't let him go on killing with impunity, eliminating all rivals or fancied rivals. Such murder could not be tolerated, and judo should not be abused this way. Also, who had taught him? Suppose a plague of such killings developed, with half a dozen renegades perpetrating them? "Nine o'clock?"

"Come alone. What I have to tell you, no one else must hear!"

That I could believe. I agreed to come alone. When the day came that I was afraid to see a man alone, I'd know it was time to retire. I'd doubted that he'd try anything so soon after the other killings. Certainly Dato wouldn't admit to murder in the presence of others. Probably he'd swear me to complete secrecy first. But that was a separate problem.

I called Jim to let him know where I'd be. "Don't wait up for me," I said. "If I'm not home by morning, check Dato's, that's all."

"Sure thing," he said uncertainly. Did he suspect what I was up to?

Dato's *dojo* was closed when I got there a little before nine. But there was a light on in back, so I went around there and knocked. There was no response.

I waited a few minutes, but he didn't come. It was a cold night, and with my usual foresight I hadn't dressed for it. So I tried the door, and it was open. He must have meant me to enter and wait until he came. He was a funny guy, even allowing for the attraction the martial arts had for far-out characters. So I entered.

Outside, the *dojo* was run-down. Inside it was elegant. This was an attractive display room: many *senseis* are connoisseurs and collectors of rare weapons. There were Chinese lacquered shields and battle axes, assorted daggers, a number of *katana* swords, and even a few pistols. Police clubs were laid out on a table, not ordinary ones, but—

I heard a step behind me. Before I could turn I was struck hard in the back. The blow was not crippling, but it felt strange.

I reacted instantly. I turned, seized him about the waist, and threw him violently? over my head in an *ura-nage*, the inside-out throw. Dato was old and small, weighing only about 110 pounds, and I was jumpy; I put more power into it than I would have otherwise. An attack from behind, when I had come to talk! He flew over my head as I fell back against the table, and he crashed against the wall just under a huge samurai sword.

Dato dropped to the floor, heavily. The wall trembled, making the sword quiver on its mountings. He was still conscious. He started to get up, his arm swinging around to bang into the wall, while I stood there dumbly, braced against the leaning table.

That small extra vibration did it. The samurai sword slipped off its nails and fell. I tried to shout a warning, but the force of gravity was faster than my reaction time. My cry still forming, I saw that immense blade crash down edge first.

It sliced across his neck and clattered to the floor. Then I was over there, scattering police clubs, lifting Dato up, trying to stanch the flow. But there was blood spurting all over and his clothing was in the way, half cut, half intact, so that it was impossible to get it off neatly, and the light was poor and I was half in shock. As I looked, the spurts diminished and the pool of blood grew. An artery had been cut.

It was not that injury or blood unnerved me unduly; I've seen plenty of both. But the sheer malignancy of the inanimate preyed on my mind as I struggled ineffectively to help him. Witchcraft, voodoo—it was as if Dato had been ensorceled and struck down by his own weapon. I was powerless to interfere. Where could I apply a tourniquet, when the gash had opened both jugular and carotids?

Yet, amazingly, he spoke. "Jason! Jason Striker! I am dead, but the laugh is mine! I struck you with the fist of doom, stronger than that karateka's, and you will die."

That first blow. That had been it! The delayed action death-blow!

"When?" I demanded. "When does it take effect?"

"You will never know, until the end!" he whispered. And be-gan a liquid laugh. In the midst of his laughter the blood bubbled out from his mouth, and he died.

I ran. All I could think of, in that awful moment, was that I was a man-killer. For the second time. That Vietnam memory—how long was it going to haunt me? Who would believe that this had been an accident, self-defense? I had entered Dato's *dojo* at his secret invitation, and he had attacked me, and one of his own weapons had killed him. But any jury would say that my hand had wielded that blade, even though there were no fingerprints. The blood could have obscured prints, so I could not prove I had not touched the sword.

But no one knew where I had been. I might never come under suspicion. So I was far better off to leave, once more fleeing the consequences of my action.

The deathblow! No matter who suspected or what the law decided, I was doomed. The evidence had pointed to it, and Dato had confirmed it as he died. When would it strike? In a day? A month? A year? I would have to have a thorough medical examina-tion, the same one I had urged on Worthen.

Then I remembered. I was *not* free of suspicion. I had told Jim where I was going. He would make the connection as soon as the news of Dato's death got out.

I knew it would be better to report to the police immediately and tell them everything. I was a law-abiding man. But Diago had also obeyed the law, and look where that had led him. The flight-reflex was too strong, and other objections crowded in. How would it look, to have the near-winner of the fabulous Martial Open booked for murder so soon after his success? What a reputation that would give judo! Nothing Dato had done could approach the harm I might do to my profession. And suppose the deathblow took effect while I was in prison awaiting trial? I couldn't tell the police about that; they would be sure it was the ranting of a man too eager to get out, or to fashion a defense of insanity. And Thera—what would I say to her? After all my talk about the ethics of judo.

Thera. I needed her now! Why had I held out on her? Age was no sufficient barrier to love.

I had to talk with Jim. He at least had to know the truth, so he would keep silent. I had to catch him tonight, before the story broke.

First I stopped at my own place and took care of all the blood. I washed it off and changed my clothes; they would have to be burned. But first—Jim.

I drove to his apartment, but he was not there. Was he working out late at the *dojo*? Sometimes he did that, practicing special techniques in privacy. Yes, that was it.

I went there, keyed up by nervous energy, wishing the whole episode with Dato had never happened, wishing I'd spent the time with Thera. I'd passed up romance—and killed a man with a sword. Make love not war!

I had been a fool. There were worse things than having an affair with a girl like that.

Jim's car was outside, and there was a light on in the *dojo*. I was reminded for an ugly moment of Dato's light, but I quelled that. Nothing sinister could happen to me in my own place. I used my key and entered quietly at the front. Once I talked to Jim, everything would be okay.

He was on the *tatami*. I was about to call to him, for he did not know I was there. Then I realized he was not alone, and not practicing. There was a girl with him.

I was furious. This was a profanation of the *dojo* and an abuse of the trust I had placed in him. A *dojo* is more than a martial arts training hall; it is a temple to the *budo* spirit, the gentle way of judo. Jim could have whatever affairs he wanted, but not in my *dojo*!

But I needed his cooperation, so it was a poor time to condemn his lapse. Obviously he still hadn't mastered the proper attitude, but I couldn't hold myself up as any example, after killing a man and fleeing. I did not want the girl to overhear our conversation, either. So I would have to pretend I knew nothing of his little exploit, and catch him after he had gotten rid of his night's entertainment.

I shook my head, watching them a moment more. They were really going at it. She thrust up her torso in time with his lunges, so it was a fifty-fifty proposition with both contributing effectively. The sight helped take my mind off the outer gloom that pervaded me. I could not see the girl's face from this position, but she certainly had nice legs. Firm, healthy thighs, no flab, but good form.

I ducked out before working myself into a state. If Drummond's daughter were here at this instant, I'd soon be in the position where I'd have to give a different answer to his query. Just who had he thought was making it with her?

Jim would be furious if he realized someone had seen him in action. So he wouldn't know. And I hoped he would keep my secret as well as I kept his.

I sat in the car, lights out. Twenty minutes passed. At the rate Jim had been exercising, he should have wrapped it up long ago. Were they trying for a second go?

Then I heard the back door open. At last! They were walking around to Jim's car. Mine was on the street, not obvious; I had to catch him alone, not now.

They passed through the glow of the streetlight and I saw the girl's face. And I froze in shock.

Thera.

There was no mistaking either her identity or the nature of her relation to Jim. She stopped to kiss him as they reached his car—a lingering, intense caress. Not the sort given a partner on a one-night stand. A fiancé-kiss.

I had introduced them to each other . . .

The car drove off, and still I sat. I had thought the worst had happened when I killed Dato, and perhaps it had; but this second blow, in the moment of my vulnerability, hit me harder. I was not now in the throes of action; I was sitting still, completely open to the thrust. Thera obviously had not been as sick as she had claimed—if, indeed, she had been sick at all. How long had this been going on? Now, in retrospect, Jim's attitude of the past week seemed suspicious.

How could I talk to him now? The answer was that I couldn't. If I met him now I might have a second murder on my battered conscience, and I was no Pedro, who could calmly contemplate that prospect. Yet I had to see Jim, because of tomorrow's news. What else could I do?

For the moment I was numb to pain of any type. Tomorrow I would suffer; tonight I could concentrate on only one thing: home. Nothing further could happen to me there.

I made it home and let myself in. I fell on the bed without undressing, seeking refuge in instant sleep.

And dreamed of murder. I was fighting someone in the dark, interminably, knowing he was killing me. Strange weapons hung all about, S-shaped blades, boomerangs that fired bullets, crazy things that seemed quite possible and menacing in that trance state. Finally I lifted my mortal enemy with the *ura nage* inside-out throw and hurled him against the wall. Then a sword was in my hand, stiff and cylindrical like a—like a—and he was split in half, the bamboo split, famous Japanese sword technique. But when I looked closer, only his neck was cut. I saw his face. It was Jim.

I struggled awake, but sleep held me like a demon in its straitjacket, an endless suffocating canyon from which I could never quite rise. Despairingly I sank back into the depths of the nightmare. I was in a church, kneeling in prayer, begging forgiveness for my sins—and the priest was Dato, laughing in falsetto glee as he poured unholy water on me that burned like lava, melting me into another blackness. Once more I tried to rise, but I was floating in an ocean of warm blood, drowning in it yet not dying fast enough.

Then I saw Thera, more beautiful than she could ever be in life, naked. I had a powerful reaction, and I reached for her, accepting all offers, and I knew that her affair with Jim had been nothing more than an irrelevant suspicion on my part, jealousy on a par with Dato's resentment of competitors, unworthy of me. But as I touched her vibrant flesh there was a terrible pain in my back, spreading through my chest to the heart, and in front of my amazed judo class I fell dead.

It began again. The night was years long, eternally morbid. I lay supine, looking up at Diago, he of the *kiai* yell. "What are you doing in this particular nightmare?" I inquired.

"I saw the headline," he replied, holding it up. JUDO TEACHER SLAIN. "I knew you needed me, Striker."

"We murderers must stick together," I muttered, knowing it was too soon for the morning paper to have the news. "What's in it for you?"

"I want to go home," he said.

"Japan?"

He nodded. "Now you understand my position."

I began to fear that this was not dream-nightmare but reality-nightmare. I peered at the paper—and discovered that it was the afternoon edition. I had slept late. "Diago, I can't help you! We did shiai—"

"Your friend in Nicaragua. Call him."

"Pedro? I cuckolded him!"

"The way your student cuckolded you?"

"What do you know about that?" I demanded angrily.

"That girl is my distant cousin. I know what goes on in the

white-sheep branch of the family."

"Why didn't you teach her judo yourself, then?"

"Drummond didn't want her sleeping with my color."

"That isn't funny!" I snapped. "Thera doesn't—"

"That same day they met, he came to her house."

"She was sick! He took her home!"

"Sick with lust. They did it in the garden. I watched from behind the fountain. An appropriate metaphor! After their urges were spent, they were sorry."

"You mean she was avoiding me because—?" But of course it was true.

"Jason, there is nothing for you here," Diago said. "I came to give Drummond good advice, and I gave it; now I do the same for you. Call Pedro, have him fly you to Japan. My old *sensei* Hiroshi understands about *ki*, and—"

"Hiroshi!" I exclaimed.

"Do not sneer. He may be aikido, not judo, but he taught me to extend my own *ki* through my voice."

My mystery was solved; now I knew where Diago had studied. Of course. Hiroshi would have been the one to put *ki* into his *kiai*! But I could not dwell on that now. "Diago, that was a snort of recognition, not of disparagement! I know Hiroshi! But *ki* can't get me off a murder rap! And it can't bring me back my girl, or undo Jim's betrayal."

"It can make you able to live with these things, though, as I have lived with racism and American justice. Go see the great teacher! And take me with you; I cannot get out alone, and I need healing too."

Suddenly I found it easier to understand his position. I had reacted against attack, and killed in the process, and fled the law. So had he. I was no better than he.

"Dato claimed he struck me with his delayed-action death-blow," I said. "Do you know anything about that?"

"The blow itself I never learned. But Hiroshi—"

"Yes." The notion was growing on me. It was the sort of thing

Hiroshi should know about. Takao might have been familiar with the delayed deathblow. Too bad I had never thought to ask him. But Takao was dead, so it was time to seek the man with the *ki*. There was joy in that thought.

I placed a call to Nicaragua. There was no direct line, and it had to go by radio telephone, but there was not actually much problem. I reached Vicente Pedro's mayordomo. That had to do; I left a message that I was on the same judo team with Diago and needed some fast training in Japan before the event. I knew Pedro would get the real message, for anyone linked with Diago was in bad trouble with the law.

Then I gritted my teeth and phoned Jim. No answer. I felt black rage, knowing whom he was with. To do something, I went to the door to check for my mail.

Jim stood there. He must have been trying to get up nerve to knock. I stared at him, but couldn't bring myself to speak my mind.

Diago came to my rescue. "You will have to run Mr. Striker's *dojo* for a time," he told Jim.

Jim looked blank. I had some notion what had brought him here. It was either his conscience, or the afternoon headline. But what could I say?

"Mr. Striker will be away," Diago explained.

"I know," Jim said. "I—"

The phone rang. I went to answer it, fearing the worst. I still wasn't sure I had come out of my nightmares, and nothing seemed completely real.

"Striker, he'll be at my airstrip at six," Johnson Drummond said abruptly. "My office is making out papers for Japan for you and Blake and Diago. Be ready to board."

"Wait!" I cried. "Only two are going!" But he had hung up. Appalling efficiency.

"You know what to do," Diago told Jim.

"No," Jim said, agitated.

I had not yet spoken to Jim, and he had not spoken directly to me. Diago was filling the vacuum, both ways. Ridiculous situation, but the vision of the bare figures on the *tatami* last night tied my tongue.

"You cannot run the *dojo*?" Diago demanded, businesslike now that he had an immediate function.

"I—I want to come along. With you."

Still I couldn't speak. How had Drummond anticipated this? Obviously he had known about Jim and Thera.

"To Japan?" Diago asked. "Don't you have business enough here?"

"If I stay here, there will be questions," Jim said. "I'm not good at lying."

"When you are good enough at other things," Diago said meaningfully, "you had *better* be good at lying!"

I realized that Jim was in the same situation as I had been with Pedro. He was sorry, but he couldn't say so. Probably he hadn't even known Thera was involved with me, until too late. Now he just stood there, mute, miserable.

Diago threw up his hands. "You wish to travel with murderers—why not!"

"You're not murderers!" Jim said. "And I—I'm not . . ." Which seemed to equate it nicely. Was it nightmare, or comedy?

*

Pedro's private plane landed at the Drummond Industries private strip on schedule. Neither Drummond nor his daughter showed, fortunately; a lawyer-type drove up with our papers just as the plane arrived. The three of us bundled on, and the vehicle took off again immediately.

"My uncle is piloting himself," a voice said as we settled hastily into seats. "We are proceeding to Managua, then to Japan. Is there anything you need?"

"Amalita!" I exclaimed. She looked fuller, more mature, though less than a month had passed since the tournament. But it was not her young beauty—more buxom than Thera's—that I saw, so much as the image of a *kris*. This girl, directly or indirectly, was capable of murder without qualm.

Jim looked at Amalita with immediate interest. I wondered whether I should warn him. But the devil in me kept my tongue still. Let him find out for himself.

CHAPTER 11

HOKKAIDO

The city of Sapporo has a million people, but the interior of the great Japanese island of Hokkaido was rugged indeed. We drove through large uninhabited forests, but finally had to leave the car in the foothills of a mountain range.

Makato grunted something as he studied the trackless snowy waste, and I needed no translation to know what he was thinking. Who would have expected to find the two of us together in the wilderness, so soon after our death match? I had been amazed to discover him at Hiroshi's *dojo*, training like any novice. But it made sense, once I worked it out. Makato had recognized the *ki* that had defeated him. Hiroshi, despite his broken arm, had wrought his miracle regardless, protecting me in a fashion Takao never could have done. The cause of Pedro's vengeance had been lost from the moment Hiroshi stood beside Takao that night, sharing his vow. Makato could never have hurt Hiroshi had the *O-Sensei* chosen to extend his *ki* in combat. Makato, recognizing a superior force, had decided to make it his own.

Now we were on a private quest to solve the problem of Dato's deathblow. Hiroshi, at his *dojo*, had performed a remarkable demonstration. He had set up a concrete tile, placed a soft pillow on it, and a second tile on top of the pillow. Then he had patted the upper tile gently with his hands in a peculiar and building rhythm, and suddenly the bottom tile had cracked across. Not the top, not the one touched, but the one protected by the pillow.

We all gaped. "How—?"

"The vibrations," he explained. "I establish a pattern, a harmonic reinforcement, that increases until the object at the focus is sundered. A similar process can be started in any object, even a living one, and arranged so that there may be a considerable delay before the proper harmonics manifest."

"A delayed deathstrike!" I exclaimed. "But Dato didn't pat on me that way. He *hit* me, once. Could that have started the vibrations?"

"Not under such conditions. You are fortunate."

"Fortunate? Why? He *said* he had—"

"Because there is no cure for the pattern I have demonstrated. Once it is started, only its natural culmination can end it."

"Oh. Yes. But still—"

"He must have used a cruder technique. A gradual nerve-damage attack, or a strike on a vein such that an embolism is formed, a clot of blood, that travels through the system until it reaches a critical point."

"Such as the heart!" I exclaimed. "That would account for all the cases in my area. That should be curable."

"Unfortunately it is very difficult to locate a small embolism, or to anticipate its progress through the body," he said. "Exercise would facilitate its motion, but I doubt a doctor could abate it, short of open-heart surgery at the instant of crisis."

"Uh-uh!" I said. "I can't afford to hang around a hospital for months just waiting for—"

"Then I think you must see my *O-Sensei*, Fu Antos."

Makato passed the map along to me. We seemed to be on course. We had many miles to travel on foot, but at least we knew where we were going.

We climbed. It was slow, because we were not sure of the way despite the map, which was not detailed. There is a big difference between knowing a precise path in trackless wilderness and knowing to the nearest few miles.

This was central Hokkaido, near Daisetsuzan National Park, whose environs encompassed one peak of seven and a half thousand feet and others not far short of that. Not exactly Everest, but quite sufficient challenge for the duffers we were, particularly in winter. Climbing is a different kind of exercise from level running, and I knew there would be specialized stiffnesses in my muscles tomorrow.

Pedro was worse off. He had not been walking long, and despite his program of exercise the muscles had not had time to redevelop completely. How could he manage a heavy pack? But he was proud, and sensitive on this point, so that it was awkward to lighten his load.

Pedro stumbled, and had to sit down in the snow before he fell. Jim leaned over him. "You okay, sir?"

"Of course!" Pedro snapped.

Jim didn't seem to notice the tone. "Hey, look at that snowman!"

Down the slope was a snow-covered shrub that did resemble a child's creation. "Take care," I said. "The abominable snowman is following us."

"I'll knock his block off!" Jim said, making a snowball. "I'm the best pitcher this side of the Mississippi!"

"Insufferable Yankee arrogance," Pedro muttered.

"Oh yeah?" Jim said. "Bet I can score on that head before you can!"

Oh-oh! Jim's usual lack of discretion was operating again. He had already aggravated Pedro by paying undue attention to Amalita, though she had given him a chili shoulder. But still there was that in me that held me back.

"Shall we establish a small wager on that?" Pedro said, not smiling.

Jim glanced insolently at him. "Wouldn't be fair. I know I'll beat you, but it's not right to bet you money when I couldn't pay in case I did lose."

"I'll loan you enough!" Pedro said, fashioning a snowball himself.

Worse and worse. If only Jim would learn to stay out of sensitive situations!

"No, I—" Jim paused. "Hey, we don't need money! I'll bet you my pack to yours for the next mile that I can beat you!"

Pedro was perplexed. "What would I want with your pack? Your things don't fit me, and your abominable American food—"

"To carry," Jim explained. "I win, you have to carry yours and mine. And vice versa. Those are real stakes, that'll make you sweat no matter how much loot you have in the bank."

This was too much! "Jim, leave him alone!" I said. "Can't you see—"

"Keep out, Striker!" Pedro cried furiously. I had muffed it, only antagonizing him further.

"Chicken?" Jim inquired.

Pedro's face was red with rage. He stood up, hefting his snowball. "Throw, gringo!"

Jim smiled confidently. "Sucker," he said, and hurled.

His ball, thrown too hard, overshot the mark.

Now Pedro threw, using a sidearm motion. His aim was low, but he struck the base of the bush, knocking down some snow.

Diago chuckled. "Counts!" he said.

"Sure wasn't dead center," Jim grumbled. "Lucky shot, too. Wouldn't happen again."

Pedro smiled with all his teeth. "Then you shall have a chance to earn it back, youngster. Throw again."

"Okay!" Jim made another snowball, sighted carefully, and threw. This time his aim was true, and he struck the edge of the mound.

Pedro, almost nonchalantly, flipped his second. It struck just inside Jim's.

"Closer, again!" Diago said, grinning.

Jim glowered. "Okay, that's two. Double or nothing, this time!"

"Very well," Pedro agreed.

They fired off another round apiece. Jim clipped the other side; Pedro scored dead center.

"Hey!" Jim cried, suddenly realizing. "The shrunken! The throwing knife! You've had practice."

"*Shuriken*," Pedro corrected him. "You should have thought of that before you challenged me. Care for another try?"

Jim shook his head. "I'm four miles in the hole now, and I'll never beat you! I'd better quit before I'm stuck for the duration!"

"The professional always defeats the amateur," Pedro said smugly. "I would not have wagered had I not been certain of success."

Jim picked up the second pack and held it in his arms. "Man! I see how you made your money!"

Pedro nodded, and we resumed the climb. Diago winked at me, and then I realized what Jim had done. He had relieved Pedro of his load, with honor. But he was lucky Pedro hadn't caught on to the ruse.

Pedro fell back to walk beside me. "That young man has a future," he murmured. Then I knew he hadn't been fooled, either.

*

We came across a small stream, and there was a black Asian bear, there for water or fish. I was surprised, supposing the creature would be hibernating in this cold, but apparently hibernation is a variable among bears.

Pedro brought out his *shuriken* and let fly immediately. "Hey!" I protested. "That bear's harmless; he'll run at the sight of us."

Too late. The little dagger had already winged the animal, and a wounded bear is not at all the same customer as an untouched one.

The bear stood on its hind legs, pawing at its face. It roared, showing a mouthful of saliva-moist teeth. I saw that the *shuriken* had actually scored in its eye. I was revolted at this senseless brutality.

It ripped the blade out so violently that its eye socket became a mass of blood and torn flesh. It howled in pain. Then it charged.

The bear had appeared to be not large, but now it loomed much more massive than a man, with sleek muscles under the black fur, and gaping jaws.

Pedro threw again, and the blade sliced into the creature's snout. The bear's fury only intensified. It rose again on two feet.

I stood helplessly. Then something swished by my ear. Makato had thrown his cleaver and it scored in the middle of the bear's chest.

It took the animal time to die, but after that it never had a chance. Jim hit it right over the gaping eye-socket with a hard ice-ball. Diago threw two knives that caught it in the stomach, ripping it open so that the guts began to spill. The men started carving it into bear steaks before it even stopped shuddering.

I said nothing. Why was it necessary that an innocent creature be bloodily slaughtered—in the middle of the quest for my life? How could I condemn these men who were helping me—yet how could I thank them?

At dusk we reached a primitive native village. The houses were frameworks of wood roofed with grass or bark; it was hard to tell under the snow. Each had an entry shed with a low doorway.

"Ainu," Makato said, and that needed no translation either. I had heard of the Ainu: aboriginal white men amid the Oriental hinterland, separate in culture from the Japanese. They were supposed to have lived in northern Japan for something like seven thousand years, and once were spread much more extensively. Had the Caucasians once dominated all Asia, before losing out to the Mongoloids there? No one could say for certain, but here were the Ainu, with their distinct physique, language and culture.

A man emerged from one hut and approached us. He was about sixty, with a large white mustache and beard. As he came near I saw that his skin was almost as pale as mine, his eyes were round with prominent brows, dark brown, and the lobes of his ears were long. No Japanese, certainly. Trim the whiskers and put him in a Western suit, and he could have walked the streets of my hometown without being distinguished from any other citizen.

He spoke Japanese, greeting us. Diago translated. "He greets us, inquiring our business."

Makato was already answering, and I knew he was explaining that we were warriors from many lands, looking for the castle of Fu Antos. It occurred to me that Pedro and I would be in trouble without Diago's linguistic services, for we did not speak Japanese and Makato did not speak English. So it wasn't just Pedro's money and my mission that made this group functional.

The Ainu representative frowned. "Evil men," Diago translated. "We know of no Fu Antos, but there are fierce warriors, brutal killers, in the mountain yonder. Do you come as friends of these?"

Makato looked at us. "Those must be the ninjas!" Pedro said. "Fascinating!"

The ninjas: those fabulous warriors of old whose exploits enhanced Japanese folklore for centuries. "And deadly," I reminded him. "It's one thing to admire their exploits from the viewpoint and safety of distance and time. But in the flesh it may be quite another."

"Yes, indeed," he agreed, looking eager. Jim wasn't the only impetuous fool on this mission.

"Tell him we may have to fight the ninjas," I said to Diago.

Actually, I doubted the presence of legitimate ninjas here. Their fortunes, like those of the Ainu, had faded as Japan modernized, perhaps in part because they eschewed the use of modern weapons like guns. Theirs had been a rigorous existence, and few of today's luxury-softened citizens had the gumption for the lifetime devotion to privation and combat that was required for the true ninja. So while I had no doubt there was danger out here, I was more alert to conventional forms. Storm, avalanche, wild animals, or modern bandits whose presence might terrorize the backward Ainu.

But Hiroshi had told us that this was where the man he called *O-Sensei* dwelt: Fu Antos, ancient mystic. The man who could help me—if he would. And if we could reach him despite possible ninja resistance.

The Ainu, understanding that we were not of the ninju number, smiled and invited us to stay the night. Gratefully, we accepted.

Our party of five was too large for a single family to entertain, so we agreed to split up. Makato, who seemed to know something about the Ainu, assured us that they could be trusted, and I was glad to accept his judgment. Thus I soon found myself in the *chisei*, the traditional Ainu house, with a family of four with whom I could not speak. These people had learned Japanese—quite different from their own language—but knew nothing of English. The single family room had a packed-dirt floor and open fire pit, but was surprisingly comfortable.

The Ainu wife was a shock at first. She was a portly, kindly woman, but her lips were grotesquely tattooed. Purple stain extended all about her mouth like a reverse whiteface clown's makeup. This was the Ainu female's sign of marriage-ability, probably quite painful to apply, outlawed by the more civilized Japanese but obviously still practiced in remote colonies such as this.

Supper consisted of conventional rice in bowls, eaten with pointed Japanese chopsticks—a real hazard for me—hot soup, tea, and pickled white radish. I was so relieved that it wasn't chocolate covered ants that I ate with all the gusto my inept sticks permitted. My bearded host apologized for being out of bearmeat, the Ainu staple—a huge bear hide stretched on the wall—but I assured him by gesture and example that what he had was fine with me.

After the meal, the husband settled crosslegged on the floor to rock the baby to sleep, while the wife played her *mukkuri*—a musical instrument like a jew's-harp, with a thread to make it vibrate properly. The infant was tied by cords onto a wooden hammock suspended from the ceiling, so that the whole thing swung gently. The older child was like any American little girl, alert and eager to play. She possessed a pair of homemade wooden stilts that she used in summertime.

It was a pleasant night. I wished I had the education to appreciate the significance of the intricate decorations on their clothing, and the curved sticks that were thrust into the ground near the fire pit, and all the other oddities of their unique way of life. I knew these were all symbols of a vanishing culture, for only a few thousand Ainu remained on Hokkaido, and most of these were not pure blooded. Soon this primitive village would be absorbed by the reaching Japanese culture, and the Ainu, the "hairy ones" of Asia, would be gone. They had no written language, and had to transmit their history and teachings through story and song. But they were cheery people, and hospitable. This, despite the fact that for centuries they had been harried out of their homeland by the Japanese, just as the American Indians had been ousted by the European immigrants.

In the morning Makato amazed our host-villagers with his demonstrations of board-breaking and ice-breaking. He placed several blocks of ice one over the other, first shattering them with his hand, then his elbow, and finally with his forehead. The Ainu reciprocated by doing an intriguing bear-hunt dance. That may seem minor, but after sharing the hospitality of these friendly people, I found their parting gesture meaningful.

When we separated, the men raised and lowered their hands and bowed. The women uttered mournful whining sounds of sorrow at the parting. It was all exaggerated, yet expressive and touching. It was strange to think that all my life until yesterday I had known virtually nothing of these people—and had been content in my ignorance.

*

We plodded all the remainder of the morning through the deepening snow, seeming to make little progress. It would have been better to have a native guide, but no professional had been willing to enter this region, and the Ainu stayed well clear. The ninja, or whatever menace inhabited the mountain, had inspired fear throughout the area.

Diago stopped abruptly, cocking his head. His hearing was acute, for he could extend his *ki* into that sense. "Animals!" he said.

"Here in the snow?" I asked. But predators were hardly confined to the jungle. Bear abounded in this region, the totem beast of the Ainu.

Before he could answer the pack was upon us. Five huge dogs, larger than German Shepherds and with more fur, silent and swift. No barking, no snarling, no baying; just wolflike muscle and teeth and single-minded mayhem. We were on the steep slope of the mountain, unable to maneuver freely or form a defensive circle; we had to fight where we stood.

I stepped to the side, where there was a brief level spot—and my footing gave way. It was a concealed pit, bridged over by sticks and straw and hidden by subsequent snow. A ninja trap! My arms windmilled, but I was falling.

Jim grabbed my arm and hauled me back. But in the process he yanked himself into the deadfall, his boots skidding on a sheet of ice, hidden beneath the snow. I was falling away from him toward safety now, but could not get hold of him. And the great dogs were charging.

The first canine leaped at Pedro, striking his chest and bowling him over, for the man's legs remained uncertain. The two rumbled down the slope, the animal going for his throat, but Pedro got one hand up and rammed it far into the beast's mouth. He got bitten on the arm, but his thick jacket protected him and the penetration of the teeth was slight. He crossed his legs over the dog's lower abdomen where the ribs did not extend, and squeezed. Pedro felt weak, and his legs were tired, but with a desperate effort he crushed the dog until it expired.

The next two attackers were already in the air as the first struck Pedro. These hurtled at Makato and me. Both of us used our fists. I barely regained my feet and shot a fast blow to my dog's nose, an especially sensitive target. The shock was hard, for about eighty pounds of dog was behind that nose, but my knuckles were tougher than that tender flesh, and the beast fell, dead. Makato flashed the karate stiffhand chop and crushed the dog's skull in like the shell of an egg. A fighting dog is an object of terror to most people, but a trained man can readily kill a dog if he knows how.

But the fourth dog also launched at Makato. The man turned rapidly—I remembered from painful experience just how fast he could move—and delivered a tremendous kick with the front of his boot. It connected to the chest of the dog, caving in its ribs.

At the same time the last animal attacked Diago, who stepped nimbly aside to avoid its rush. He hit it a downward blow on the shoulder, breaking it. Then he pulled a hidden knife from his sleeve and finished the canine off with a thrust to the heart.

The complete action had run its course in under five seconds, except for Pedro's action. Five dead dogs lay in the snow. Pedro was the only one injured: some scratches around the arm, not deep. But already they were an angry red.

Jim had by this time climbed out of the pit. He had managed to avoid the sharpened stakes beneath, by sliding down the side. He had saved me, and himself.

I regretted the ugliness that stood between us but still I could not make it right. Doing good isn't enough; a man has to avoid doing harm, also, and Jim's impetuosity still had to be controlled.

"Look at those teeth," Diago said. "Filed sharp!"

"No wild pack, then," I said. "Someone trained those dogs to kill men!"

Makato muttered something, shaking his head, but Diago did

not translate. "Let's get you cleaned up," Diago said to Pedro. "Blood could attract more animals."

"Doesn't matter," Pedro responded. "It'll dry soon." But Diago spent a lot of time washing off the arms with snow until they were absolutely clean, despite his own coldness.

We went on. We knew we were getting close to our destination, because the dogs must have been set on us by the ninjas, or whatever. Hiroshi had not said the castle was defended by ninjas, or explained why anyone should try to prevent us from visiting old Fu Antos there. But Hiroshi was a master of understatement. It was obvious now that there was malignant opposition to our mission, and we would have to be on guard at all times. Those dogs would have wiped out any ordinary party, with no chance for discussion or retreat.

But what was the threat of death to me, when I was doomed anyway by the delayed deathblow? Diago hardly cared about life, after the betrayal of his half-adopted country, America. But Fu Antos might be able to help him, too. Pedro claimed he just wanted the adventure, having read about the ninjas a great deal. But more than that was driving him, I was sure. Makato, dissatisfied with his progress in mastering *ki*, thought Fu Antos might in one simple gesture present him with what he needed. I was cynical about that, too, but glad to have his powerful fist along. And Jim, well, perhaps the truth was that we all needed to get away from the world and interact with each other, coming at last to whatever accommodations we might; Fu Antos was merely the pretext.

The mountain became steeper. We plodded on, following the tracks of the dogs. Certainly we were not going to give up after such an attack; it united us in a bond of anger. Why should such obstacles be put in our way? Was old Fu in fact being held prisoner by the ninjas?

The trail led up a ledge hugging the side of the mountain. We went single file though there was room to go abreast. We came around a turn.

The ninjas were there, rising up all about us in their snow-white tunics. I knew their traditional garb was black, but that would only make them obvious in the snow, so they had wisely adapted to their environment. Ninjas were never fools about combat, and there was now no doubt these were ninjas. Even their weapons were white, and they carried an appalling variety. Sword, axe, pike, bow, and more devious instruments whose nature I could not grasp at first glance. They had lain in ambush despite the cold, and no wonder we hadn't spied them sooner. They had been buried in snowdrift.

Diago was in the lead. He looked up to see the bowman taking aim, while a little behind was another man with a contraption like a flamethrower made of bamboo. Diago recognized it as a watergun probably filled with poison or acid. Ninjas did not like to use firearms, but were ingenious in inventing devilish devices of their own.

There were nine of the ghostly white figures, so they outnumbered our party almost two to one. They had assorted weapons, whereas we had, except for Diago's knife, only our hands. They could mow us down from a distance with bow and spear and jets of poison and thrown knives. Diago knew he had to act.

He gave his devastating *kiai* yell. The rest of us, warned by his stance, covered our ears, muffling that awful shriek to some extent. It was not completely effective in this open air, with the enemy protected by wool and armor, but it was still an extraordinary shock to the unsuspecting ninjas. Diago concentrated on the worst immediate danger: the man with the watergun. That man twisted and fell to the ground in an involuntary reaction to the *kiai*. His watergun discharged a stream of liquid full on the face of the archer, who was just drawing on his bowstring. The archer screamed and clawed at his eyes, his arrow driving into the snow as the bow dropped.

But there was one ninja who was not set back by the *kiai*. An older man, sharp of visage and with his head enclosed in some kind of protective turban. His weapon was a *kusari-gama*, the chained sickle. On one end of the long fine chain was the L-shaped sickle, ready for its anchored throw. It was almost impossible to stop safely. On the other was a silver counterweight suitable for entangling the opponent's weapon. Diago's knife was in his hand, but before he could even lift this feeble defense the silver weight shot out and wrapped about it, pinning both knife and hand and holding Diago captive for the flying stroke of the sickle. Not even his voice could save him now.

Pedro was familiar with the *kusari-gama*, however; he had several in his Nicaraguan collection of weapons. He whipped out one of his star-shaped *shuriken* throwing knives—actually a ninja weapon. He skated it at the sickleman's face just as the ninja was ready to skewer Diago. But Pedro's shot went wide, merely grazing the white turban. The man whirled around, taking aim instead at Pedro.

Pedro swore in Spanish, ready with another metal star. He squatted to emulate the position he had practiced in the wheelchair, and fired again as the ninja's arm flashed back for the throw. This one caught the man in the upper biceps, tearing into the muscle and making the sickle fly wild.

"That's the way!" Jim cried. "Good thing I practiced you up for this!" Pedro's lip curled, half in anger, half in mirth.

But now the ninjas had recovered from the momentary shock of the *kiai*, and were charging upon us in a mass. The fallen watergunner had rolled down the slope until almost upon Diago, and now was drawing a knife. Diago blocked the thrust and kicked him on the jaw, breaking it and knocking him out more lastingly. But the first of the charge was upon him: a ninja armed with tiger's claws. Even as Diago dispatched the knife-wielder, the metal talons raked him from forehead to jaw: four parallel gouges down the side of his face. Diago did not even exclaim with pain; he gripped that arm and threw the ninja with a *ko-uchi-gari*, minor inner reaping throw. He shoved the man backward while pulling down on his sleeve and reaping his heel. Even so, the ninja managed to rake him again, this time on the abdomen. Diago put a *juji-gatame* cross armlock on him and broke the arm at the elbow.

Still the ninja fought, raking him with the other claw on arm and chest. Diago had to kick him repeatedly in the head until at last he was unconscious. There was no quarter given or asked here.

Makato, meanwhile, was right at home. A ninja came at him with a battle-axe, lifting it high for a devastating downward chop. Makato stepped in and blocked the descending arm with one hand. With the other he smashed a powerful punch to the sternum bone of the chest. The man wore a mail shirt under his white tunic, but this was almost useless against the karateka's iron fist. The ninja fell unconscious, lucky to be alive.

The swordsman was there almost at the same time, trying to score with a rapier-thrust though it was a *katana* he wielded. This was because he didn't want to decapitate his own man with a wild swing. Makato saw him and dodged swiftly to the side, letting the sword pass so close that it severed the threads of his heavy cotton jacket, then grabbing for the hand. But the ninja, no clumsy amateur, was already whipping the weapon away, and Makato caught the blade instead. It cut into his hand, but his calluses resisted enough for him to grip it anyway and use it to pull the ninja forward. With his other hand he delivered a terrible open-handed slap to the swordarm elbow.

The ninja's arms were protected, but it made no effective difference for this blow. The arm broke. Makato had shown good judgment in not going for the neck, for that was protected by a barbed chainmail throat-guard. But the joints remained vulnerable, for too-heavy armor would have hampered the ninja's movement.

Without letting go the sword, Makato kicked the side of the ninja's knee with the side of his foot. This too was vulnerable; the ligaments and inner cartilage tore, and the man fell screaming. There is nothing more painful than a broken kneecap.

Already the warrior with the pike was going for the karateka's unprotected back. This ninja was in full plate armor in the ancient Japanese style, with lots of gold and silver filagree, all lacquered. He was completely covered, and moved comparatively slowly. But he would be a demon to stop; blows would not hurt him and the only part of him that showed was the eye behind the tiny eyeslit.

Pedro had saved Diago from the *kusari-gama*; now he did the same for Makato with the pikeman. He produced a special *shuriken*, like a very small, very thin knife. He squatted to gain his once normal posture, then hurled the miniature blade at the armored face. This time the range was short and his aim unerring; the metal penetrated the eyeslit and lodged deep in the eye, felling the ninja.

Another warrior came at Makato with a knife. The thrust was low, to gut him from beneath, and the stroke was fast and sure. Not one of these devotees of the ancient discipline was weak or slow. But Makato was ready for this, having faced experienced knife fighters many times before. He stepped in and deflected the knife-arm outwards, at the same time lifting his knee to give the man a solid blow on the testes. The ninja collapsed in agony; the only thing that saved him from death was his mail crotch protection, a kind of armored underwear. In a moment he was mercifully unconscious.

At the same time, I faced the ninja armed with spiked brass knuckles. His punch came at my face. I threw up my shoulder, but he twisted his fist as it landed, to mangle my upper arm. My heavy jacket protected me somewhat, but the sharp spikes were excruciating. Maddened, I turned and executed a throw forbidden in judo competition: *yama-arashi*, the mountain tempest. My leg swept both his legs from underneath him, while I lifted him high with a *harai goshi* hip throw, then jumped into the air myself, turning and falling on top of him with my entire weight. He managed to strike me while he was in the air, however, wounding my trapesius muscle; I could hardly believe the tenacity of these fighting men. Then the fall, and he was knocked unconscious, perhaps severely injured. That was why this throw was normally forbidden: the terrible fall, like the thrust of an avalanche down the slope of a mountain. Even as this man slid down and out of sight, making his own small avalanche.

The *kusari-gama* man, wounded in the biceps by Pedro, was

not out of the fray. The ninjas were hardened to suffering and trained to fight to the finish. They were professional killers, while we were amateurs. This one now went for Jim.

Jim still did not realize what he was up against. He was much larger than the ninja, weighing two hundred pounds to the other's hundred and twenty-five; and Jim was in the pink of condition, facing a wounded older man. So he didn't really try, at first. Had I not been occupied myself, I would have screamed a warning at him.

The two grappled. Jim threw the ninja with a *harai goshi,* the same throw I was using simultaneously. But he did not, convert it into the savage mountain tempest. He used it straight, just as I had done so foolishly against Makato in our first tournament match. Of course the ninja clung to him and brought them both to the ground. But the ninja maneuvered so that Jim was on his stomach, with the other on his back. Then the warrior seized Jim's head with one hand on each side and, ignoring the bleeding pain of his own arm, twisted rapidly and with extreme force.

This, and all the other action about me, I comprehended in full only later, when I had opportunity to organize and assess the diverse and simultaneous impressions of the melee. I actually turned from my execution of the *yama-arashi* mountain tempest throw just in time to see that ferocious wrenching of Jim's head. His bull neck, his longstanding pride, was no protection against the savagery of this attack. I charged the ninja, kicking at his back.

But as I reached him there was an awful snap! and Jim's neck was broken. His head lolled awfully to one side. At the same time all his natural functions let go, and he soiled himself.

My heavy boot struck the ninja's lower back, in the middle of the spine between the kidneys. This blow broke his back, and he fell away, living but done for. But I kicked him again, and yet again, and I stomped on his face as he rolled over, grinding my icy heel into his eye socket and again and again into his mouth, breaking all his teeth, until his entire face was unrecognizable. Just a

hamburger mess with a hole where the mouth had been. I didn't
stop until Makato's strong hands hauled me off.

If I had doubted before that I was a killer, no better than my
companions, I could doubt no longer. But though we had won the
battle, it was too late for Jim, as I had known when I heard that
snap. He was dead, and as my rage abated I became numb again.

Then my fading fury changed to horror. Pedro was leaning
over one of the dead ninjas, carving open his body as he had that of
the bear. He cut out the liver and held it up. He brought the hot
morsel to his mouth and bit a bloody hunk out of it.

He had reverted to cannibalistic ritualism. Makato and Diago
looked on impassively, as though this were nothing out of the
ordinary. They had probably seen it before.

Could my own life possibly be worth it, to lose a friend like
Jim? I would not be able to judge this until months or years or
perhaps even decades had passed, assuming I lived that long. For
the moment only peripheral thoughts registered around the raw
central wound: if only I had talked to Jim, let him have Thera,
who was really his type. What was the worth of any girl, compared
to true friendship? Surely I had killed him.

Now there was nothing to do but go on. Though the mission
no longer seemed to matter.

CHAPTER 12

FU ANTOS

We attended to our wounds, buried Jim, and moved on, pausing only to pick up the more useful weapons of the ninjas. Makato took the battleaxe, I took a fine long dirk, Pedro picked up the *katana* and Diago hefted the long pike. We noticed the cave from which both dogs and ninjas must have issued, but shunned it; it was probably thoroughly booby-trapped.

We climbed farther, weakened by our injuries but unable to give up now. The footing was treacherous, the elevation cruel; one slip here could send a man sliding far down the mountain, perhaps to death or at least a roughing that would force him to turn back. Diago used his pike to brace himself and assist his climb: smart tactic.

The notion of the cave became more tempting; could the traps be more hazardous than this challenge of nature? But I knew the answer: deadfalls and sharpened stakes were the least of the obstacles the cave passage would present. There might even be other ninjas waiting in ambush there. Out here, at least, the cold numbed my wounds somewhat.

At last we crested the windy pass and had our first view of the castle. It nestled among snow-covered pines high on the far slope of the mountain. We were above it now, but there would be a difficult traverse to achieve it this day. We had little choice, however; a night out here, in our condition, could be disastrous.

This was not the round-turreted stonework of the medieval European castles, but the stately square multistoried pagoda type of the Orient. From this height it appeared to be in ruins, with three tumbled-down towers and only one major edifice still standing. Most of the walls were fallen, but the main keep rose from the rubble and might still be habitable.

"The Black Castle of legend," Pedro breathed. "I have read of it, but thought it was destroyed centuries ago."

"*Wasn't* it?" I asked, staring down at the ruin. "Who would live there now?"

"Fu Antos," Diago put in.

"The Black Castle was the home of Sumita Takawa," Pedro said, oblivious to our remarks. I had not realized he was this much of a ninja fan. "He was an evil lord of the sixteenth century who ruled with an iron hand. But he incurred the displeasure of the emperor, who laid siege to the castle. For six months he held out valiantly, until he was defeated by treachery."

"You tend to identify with the villains," Diago remarked, smiling as he leaned on his pike.

Pedro only nodded affirmatively, and continued: "Then Sumita Takawa was taken and skinned alive and doused with vinegar, living. His castle was sacked and left with its corpses unburied. No one would approach it thereafter, as it was believed damned, and in time even the authenticity of the tale came to be doubted. Yet here it is: the Black Castle!"

But *I* doubted it. There had been sieges and betrayals and slaughters in Japan's history, and certainly this castle had suffered pillage and ruin—but there was no proof that this was the Black Castle of the legend. Yet it hardly mattered, so I kept silent.

We descended toward it. The structure was in a place of early shadows and darkness, despite the brightness of the surrounding snow. The forest encroached closely: pine trees and—gingko? I remembered that the gingko, or maidenhair tree, was one of nature's oddities: a survival from the time of the dinosaurs. But I recognized it only by its fan-shaped leaves, and these were gone in winter. So perhaps these were not gingkos, and I was merely reacting to the growing aura of the castle. Old, reminiscent of things extinct.

We crossed a frozen stream, breaking through the ice to fetch up chill drinking water. "Sometimes the ninjas poison streams," Pedro warned.

"This feeds into their own water supply," Diago pointed out. "And the snow here hasn't been disturbed in the past few days." So we drank, reassured.

The distance to the castle was greater than it had appeared, and I was becoming more tired despite the downward trek. It is actually harder to march downhill than on the level; I had heard that somewhere, but now I believed it. It has to do with the body fighting gravity. The closer we got, the more formidable the castle's ramparts loomed. The stones were black with dead moss, paint, age and perhaps even smoke smudges from the final burning. Hell, incarnate.

Many things were illusory about this castle. For one thing, more of it was in repair than had appeared from a distance; obviously men *could* live here, if they chose to. The moat was in order too, representing a formidable barrier even in winter. The structure was not actually on the slant of the mountain, but in a pocket, a high valley. Our little stream fed the moat, and the moat drained into a marsh, and there was insufficient ice near the castle to sustain a man. We could not afford to fall in and get soaked; the chill would greatly hamper our fighting ability, already impaired, and a wet night could kill us. Where could we safely change?

There was just one dry path through that marsh. Diago located it by poking through snow and ice until he found land, then prodded ahead with the pike step by step. He was getting better use from that erstwhile weapon than I had anticipated. It was dusk now, but we could not rush it.

Progress was faster, now that we were on the right path. Actually it was better to depend on our sense of touch, rather than sight; there could be more deadfalls. A patch of water opened out on one side, with dead reeds sticking up like broken spears. Evidently it was warmer in the immediate vicinity of the castle; maybe the heat of the daytime sun was reflected off the fragmentary walls, warming the moat and keeping the ice clear. Smart arrangement. Now that it was evening, a thin sheen of ice was reforming, but it would never support our weight.

Suddenly there was motion. A figure rose from the water, to my amazement, and flung a series of knives—*shuriken*—so rapidly I could hardly see his arms operating. Pedro was a rank amateur compared to this tenth ninja.

We were vulnerable. We had been caught off guard, and could only cower away from those shooting blades. I threw up my forearm automatically to protect my face and neck, and a sharp pain in that arm told me I had acted barely in time. Diago could not move his heavy pike fast enough, and Pedro was entirely outclassed; I saw him falling already.

We could not charge the attacker because he was ten feet away, in water. It seemed ludicrous, but we four specialists in martial art were helpless before this lone ninja warrior. He had made his ambush well, and now was submerged to his chest in the freezing water.

Then there was a kind of thud, as of metal striking bone. I saw the ninja sinking. Makato's axe was buried in his forehead.

The light was fading, but we were able to reconstruct what had happened. The ninja had broken the ice beside the path and swept the edges to make it seem natural and cover his tracks. Then he had submerged himself, using a bamboo tube for breathing—a favorite ninja trick, Pedro assured us—and waited. It was an incredible feat, for he must have been there, unmoving, for several hours while the marsh slowly froze over. I could not have survived such a vigil, yet the ninja had emerged to fire six *shuriken* at us before the axe struck. Two had hit Pedro, opening his cheek and sticking to his chest, not serious in themselves, but weakening him further. One had hit me in the forearm, the padding of my jacket protecting me from the worst. One had hit Diago in the back of the shoulder, giving him one more reason to be slow with the pike. Two had missed Makato, who was already in motion with the axe. One of these lay in the path we had made, one of its points blunted; it must have struck the blade of the axe itself. Astonishing accuracy, considering the diversity of targets, his speed of delivery, the poor light, his disadvantageous position for throwing, and the chill of his limbs. What might that warrior have done had he been on land, and warm?

I feared we had killed a better man than any one of us. Only superior *ki* could explain the ninja's performance, both during the long cold wait and in the sudden action. Just a little lower on that one *shuriken*, and he would have hit Makato's eye instead of his axe, and won the battle.

Again I wondered whether it would not have been better for all concerned if I had simply stayed at home and suffered whatever fate was destined. Better, even if Jim had not died. Still, we had not come to kill ninjas. We merely wanted to see old Fu Antos; the killing had been in self defense. Why weren't these hardy warriors content to let us pass, or at least to meet with us, ascertaining our mission? Why did they set killer dogs upon us, then attack with the same canine fury? None of them need have died.

All of which suggested that our mission was not as innocent as we supposed. I could not believe Hiroshi would have sent us into such a merciless situation. Not knowingly. He had said he visited Fu Antos here upon occasion, perhaps once a year. Could it be that the ninjas turned a different face to Hiroshi, so that he considered them innocuous?

Yet he had warned us, with his characteristic understatement, hinting at danger. He must have felt the mission was worth the risk.

What could possibly be worth the lives of perhaps ten men, so

far? We were exterminating the last of a vanished type, the true
ninja. And dying ourselves.

The moat, after all, was largely filled with debris. We picked
our way across it, stepping from stone to stone, avoiding those
that were precariously balanced—another ninja trap?—and stood
at last under the ragged but forbidding wall of the castle. This
difficult crossing set us up for attack, and we made it singly and
nervously, but none came. Now it was dark, but we did not dare
use a light. Some faint glow developed from the rising moon, reflected by the snow, however, and our eyes became adjusted to
that level.

There was no sound as we passed the rock-strewn outer wall
and made our way through desolate open courts. We saw great
piles of rubble, and holes leading downward, suggesting an exis-
tent system of cellars and other passages. I thought I spied a skel-
eton at one point, but avoided that as scrupulously as the rest.
Anything could be booby-trapped.

We passed an empty kennel: this must have been where the
dogs had been housed, for there was the smell of recent occupancy
about it. And at last we came through the ominous stillness to the
massive central keep, where Fu Antos should be.

Had the ninjas turned against their *O-Sensei*, imprisoning him
and finally murdering him? He had come originally to the castle,
Hiroshi said, to reform this wild remnant of an extinct martial
tradition. He had ninja training himself, and in his youth had
been a mighty warrior, but had grown beyond that. Yet, he could
not have had much success here, as these ninjas were manifestly
unreformed. If they were determined to cover up their crime—

Makato pried open the keep gate. Pedro drew his new *katana*.
Diago prodded inside with the pike. And I cautiously poked my
head inside.

Nothing happened. If other ninjas defended this place, where
were they? Diago was listening, but there was a night wind whistling past the broken stones, making it hard to hear anything meaningful.

There was faint light inside, and the chill was less severe. I smelled burning incense and some Oriental spice. But the inner walls were bare; it was a stark severe residence here. The glow was from a flaming torch set in a hole in the wall, deep in the keep.

I proceeded into the keep, amazed at the sheer mass of its walls. There were very small windows, and the actual door aperture was tiny, so that we had to stoop to pass through, alert for further traps. Makato followed me, and Diago, tapping the floor stones.

"Check above," Pedro warned. "Sometimes—"

Something hairy dropped on me. I flailed wildly. A reddish demon was clutching me, chattering, biting. Others were landing on Makato and Diago and Pedro, clinging too tightly for the metal weapons to be effective.

My demon was small—perhaps twenty five pounds—but powerful. Its teeth fastened on my forearm painfully. I shook it loose with a great effort and tried to wrestle it around, in hitting range, but its muscles were like furry steel springs. Finally I got the thing around its hairy throat and strangled it.

It was a monkey. The gloom and surprise had provided it with a special terror. I threw the body aside and grabbed for the one on Pedro. I did not draw my long knife, as I was not accustomed to its use and didn't want to risk stabbing a friend. Bare hands sufficed.

The monkeys were vicious and tenacious. They had been trained to attack relentlessly, like the dogs and the ninjas themselves. We were more massive than they, and trained in hand-to-hand combat, but they were superior natural fighters. I had seen cheap adventure movies in which men defeated apes in unarmed combat; the truth was that a man could not even out-fight a chimpanzee. But these were smaller, and the sixfold to eightfold weight advantage of the men sufficed. Makato soon killed three, breaking their skulls with hammerfist blows, and I took care of two more, and the rest suddenly fled. We had more wounds, but still nothing serious.

"What are monkeys doing here?" I demanded breathlessly.

"They're tropical creatures!"

"Macaques," Diago said. "Cold-adapted. They live here and in Tibet, too, I think, as well as in the tropics. Good guardians."

I shut up, embarrassed at having shown my ignorance. The monkeys had done us one favor, at least: they surely would have sprung any further traps within their reach. If we looked about, we might discover monkeys crushed under stones, pierced by sprung barbs.

We continued on down the gaunt stone hall, moving from torch to torch. I took down the first and used it for more specific illumination. In an emergency, it would also do for a weapon.

Silently, Diago pointed. There was a closed chamber ahead; he meant that his sharp ear told him it was occupied. More monkeys over the sill—or armed ninjas?

Diago piked it open, while Pedro stood by with *shuriken* in each hand. Makato and I stayed back, ready to cover our ears, for if an attack were sprung here Diago would surely blast out with his devastating *kiai*. Even so, I had the premonition that men would die in this chamber.

But there was no action. By the light of my torch we saw a very old man sitting on a dirty mat. Beside him stood a young boy, bareheaded and barefooted. Fu Antos and his body servant?

We filed in and stood before them. And found ourselves somewhat at a loss. The primary mission was mine, of course, as my fear of Diago's delayed deathblow had brought me to Japan and served as the focus. I should be the spokesman, but could not speak Japanese. Did the old man know English?

One way to find out. The ancient sat absolutely still, not even seeming to breathe. He looked to be about ninety-five years old and in poor health. His flesh was dessicated, his skin stretched parchment-taut over prominent bones. His body exuded a sickly sweet odor, as of corruption. Could this really be the fabulous trainer of ninjas, *0-Sensei* to Hiroshi? No sign of physical prowess remained.

"I'm afraid he doesn't understand me," I said to Diago, after a couple of halting attempts.

Diago spoke in Japanese. The sunken eyes did not even glance up, and I realized with a small shock of horror that the old man was blind, and probably deaf. He wasn't even aware of our presence.

But the boy should not be similarly mute. He seemed to be about seven years old, yet he stood with glazed eyes, making no more response than his master.

Hiroshi had said he would send word of our mission ahead, perhaps by pigeon. Obviously he had, for the ninjas had been well prepared for our coming. So Fu Antos had to know of us. Was this a fake, a decoy set up to confuse us?

I turned to Diago, about to voice my suspicion. But at that moment the old man's hands came up. They gestured in a strange, wobbly pattern. It seemed to be some kind of sign language. I hoped one of us could read it.

Makato spoke and Diago translated. "Fu Antos says we must kill him."

"*What?*" I demanded, suspecting that old Fu was senile after all. "After all the trouble we have taken to save him from the ninjas? Tell him he has nothing to fear from us."

But before Diago could retranslate, the ancient mystic addressed himself directly to me. One withered finger made a half circle about his ear, while the thumb of the other hand jerked down. "Crazy? Not me!" those hands said in plain colloquial American. He understood me well enough; not my words, but my thoughts.

Then one finger pointed to Diago, and returned to slice across the *O-Sensei's* scrawny neck. Diago had been selected for the murder.

"This is ridiculous!" I said, speaking for us all. "We came only to talk to you, Fu Antos! To—well, you see, I was struck by this delayed—"

Fu Antos' feeble hand gestured me to silence. His fingers, though hardly more than papered bones gnarled by arthritis, were so expressive that I understood him perfectly. "Wait," they told me. "I will attend to you in due course."

After Diago killed him? Something prickly crept up my back and tugged at the short hairs of my neck.

"The ninjas would not kill him," Pedro said, evidently reading his own message in the moving fingers. "They knew that either he would die, leaving them without their honored teacher, or he would reincarnate in too strong a form, depriving them of their way of life."

I nodded. I knew the Buddhists did believe in reincarnation, with the soul occupying a new body after the old one had passed, until through right living it became purified and joined Buddha in nirvana, that ultimate state of unity.

"And it is against his religion to commit suicide," I said, reading those amazing fingers for myself. "Leaves a burden on the soul. So he will help us only if we render this necessary service." I stopped short, hearing my own words. "But how can a dead man help anybody?"

There was a noise behind us. I whirled, and saw more ninjas in the passage.

"Do not fear," Diago said. "Those are the remaining guardians, who were with their families in the neighboring villages. They could not travel swiftly enough to join the battle on the mountain, so followed us here. They dare not intrude upon this holy chamber."

"Not while Fu Antos lives," I muttered darkly. "But if we are fools enough to—"

"I must do it," Diago said, still reading the fingers. "He promises me release, the right to stay here with him."

"Stop!" I cried, whirling on him. But he had already set down the pike and approached the *O-Sensei*, and I was powerless to prevent him. It wasn't the ninjas outside, or even my own wounds; rather, something within me bade me abide what came.

Diago gave his *kiai*, half-stunning us all. I found myself propped against the wall, while Makato stood shaking his head somewhat stupidly and Pedro sat ignominiously on the floor. The ninjas beyond the door were in a tumble of bodies and weapons. But Fu Antos merely smiled, showing blackened gums bereft of teeth, and made a gesture signifying a creditable performance by a promising pupil. He had not been affected by the yell, perhaps because of his deafness.

Diago, dismayed but not finished, got down on his knees behind the seated man and applied a respiratory strangle, the *hadaka-jime*. He placed his left forearm around the front of Fu Autos' thin neck and caught his hand on his own right upper arm. His right arm went back so that his right hand was braced behind the old man's head.

Fu Antos was old and weak, surely near death already. This strangle would be effective against even a robust athlete. I knew it would be over soon. Then what?

Diago tightened his hold, pushing the bald head forward as his left forearm pressed firmly against the throat. Fu Antos did not even attempt to resist. I was sickened at this calculated murder of a helpless oldster, yet still could not bring myself to interfere. Those fingers were still moving, as though nothing of consequence were happening.

Strange. Fu Antos breathed easily, while Diago became red in the face and began gasping. His eyes bulged, the veins in his forehead throbbed, and the four stripes down his face made by the tiger claws were burning bright. Diago had taken a beating on the way here, but I had not realized that he was this far gone. He seemed about to pass out himself.

Suddenly Diago let go. He panted as if the strangle had been on him, not the other man, and fell to the floor. Yet Fu Antos sat unmoved. Diago's attack of faintness had prevented him from ever putting on real pressure.

Diago recovered in a moment, however, and shook his head. There was a red mark on the front of his neck, perhaps a welt just rising from the monkey attack.

Now Diago knelt in front of Fu Antos and tried a sanguineous strangle. He put both hands on the man's neck, fingers to the back and thumbs to the front, a bit to the side. The neck seemed almost too small for a decent grip. He probed until he found the carotid arteries throbbing under his thumbs, then gently applied pressure against them. Still Fu Antos did not resist. This strangle would knock out an ordinary man within five seconds, for it cut off the supply of blood to the brain.

One, two, three, four, and inexplicably Diago desisted, letting his hands fall limply as he sagged. He had not applied enough pressure to make the old man waver, yet the *O-Sensei's* thin hands were talking again in that marvelous way of theirs, congratulating Diago on an excellent try.

Diago, with what must have been a supreme effort, recovered again and set up for a third strangle. He seized the lapels of the old man's kimono at both sides, his thumbs inside and his fingers outside, then twisted both hands so that the knuckles were pressing into the neck. This was the nerve strangle, *eri jime,* forbidden in normal competition because it was extremely dangerous. He found the spot on each side of the neck, a little below and to the front of the ears, and bore down savagely.

There was a cry of anguish and Diago fell again. He was not breathing.

"The ninja poison!" I exclaimed, suddenly realizing. "They are experts at poisoning! On the tiger's claws!"

Pedro stared at me. "Poison! Of course! And he knew it! That was why he insisted on cleaning my wounds so carefully. The dog's teeth could have been coated too. I wondered why I felt so weak and ill."

"Why didn't he say something!" I cried. "He must have felt it working on him, yet he—" But by his own admission Pedro had felt the effects too. Why should a man burden others with his weakness? Both had kept silent.

Fu Antos gestured benignly to Makato. I gazed upon the scene with helpless horror: the decrepit old man, the unmoving boychild, the fallen Diago. Those parchment fingers speaking in intricate patterns, saying that our friend was now at peace and inviting the karateka to kill the *O-Sensei* next.

I had my second awful realization. Those fingers—they were not just talking in unique polylingual sign language. This was *kuji-kiri*—the ancient ninja hypnotic exercise. Fu Antos was not sitting passively, he was actively hypnotizing us all. That was why we were unable to move, and had to attempt to kill him at his directive, when in the normal course our reactions would have been quite different.

My respect for the *O-Sensei's* powers increased considerably, but my comprehension of his motives diminished. Surely he had no need of our services, when he possessed the ability to control men this way. And why should he want to die?

No, I could answer the last question myself. Confined to a decaying body, unable to leave this bare chamber or to read or listen or walk. To be isolated from all meaningful experience was to be condemned to hell.

"Not so," those fingers said to me. "There is no greater experience than *Zen!*"

I shut my thoughts up, abashed. I had to believe either that he was telepathic, or that I was losing my sanity.

Now Makato approached. He made a formal bow to Fu Antos, who merely inclined his head in response, those fingers still weaving their intricate tapestry in air. Diago might have been poisoned, but Makato remained strong. He stood over the seated man, setting his stance as he might for a difficult karate exhibition. Then Makato cried "*Saa!*" and brought his terrible fist down in the punch that smashed ten concrete tiles simultaneously—and struck the *O-Sensei's* head.

I blinked. Makato was falling, his head bloody. Fu Antos sat unharmed.

"It's supernatural!" Pedro exclaimed, unconsciously crossing himself.

Now the thin finger gestured to me, and I felt something. "No!" I cried to Pedro. "It is the *ki!*"

For the old man had *ki* like Hiroshi's, but much more power-ful. Now I knew: poison had not killed Diago; God had not frac-tured Makato's skull. Fu Antos' appalling power of *ki* had done it all. Now that compulsion was directed at me, and I had to set my torch in a niche and respond.

I walked up to the mystic and bowed. This man had been the greatest warrior of his age, when he was young, and he remained so today. No man proficient only in the physical martial arts could ever overcome him. The little touch of *ki* Hiroshi had loaned me once had made my flesh invulnerable; Fu Antos had a hundred times that power.

Why hadn't he used that phenomenal *ki* to control his own illness? The answer had to be that he had. He could be much older than we had guessed, salvaged from the grave decades ago by that force of personality. Now his body was rotting about him, but that same *ki* would not permit his vitality to abate. So he had to be helped to die—though all of us might perish attempting to imple-ment that need.   .

Those hands spoke again. "As you do to me, so I to you," they said. "Grant me freedom from my bondage."

"But I came here to save a life, not take it!"

The hands shrugged. The inscrutable ninja.

"He uses *ki* to change!" Pedro cried, openly terrified. "Diago strangled himself! Makato stove in his own skull! We can't touch him any more than the ninjas could."

"*Ki* and hypnotism," I agreed, contemplating the *0-Sensei*. To attack him was to die, yet he insisted on being killed. He had set us an impossible task!

I turned to peer through the doorway at the waiting ninjas. Some held drawn swords; others had more exotic devices of mur-der. One had several caltrops: spiked objects to pierce the feet of the unwary. No hope there.

How would Fu Antos' death help us? I did not know, but perhaps he was wiser than we. Was it possible to kill him?

With a new shock of horror, I realized that there was one incredible technique, that no one had ever tried before. Did I have the courage?

What choice did I have? Anything I visited on the *0-Sensei* would react against me. To leave this room with the job undone would be suicidal, because of the ninjas. Even if Pedro and I fought our way to freedom, the delayed action deathblow would still bring me down at its own convenience. So three of my four choices meant death.

The fourth . . . was also fatal

"Pedro," I said. "I will need your help."

He was standing nervously near the door. The lordly confidence he had affected as master of his estate in Nicaragua was gone now, and he was a pitiful figure of a man, more crippled than he had been in the wheelchair. "It won't work," he whined. "If we attack him together, we'll *both* die!"

I concealed my disgust at his cowardice. He had done well until Fu Antos had unnerved him. To cover my own fear I demanded brusquely "Are you familiar with the ritual of *seppuku?*"

"*Hara-kiri.* Japanese suicide. Yes, I know it. But—"

"Good. You have the *katana.* When the time comes, strike off my head."

He stared. "*Dios mio*, Striker, at least die fighting the ninja! Are you such a coward?"

He accused me of what he felt himself. "*Seppuku* is hardly cowardice," I said, though there was a tight cold knot in the pit of my stomach. "It is an honorable procedure, if the ritual is properly executed. But you must witness, and perform, the *todome*, the coup de grace."

"Striker, you are crazy!"

I found a small, ragged *tatami*, a Japanese straw mat, in the corner and hauled it to the center of the room. "What direction would you say the Imperial Palace is from here?"

"South." He saw I was serious. "Striker, don't do it! You're not even Japanese! Don't leave me like this! I am weak from the poison, I must get to a hospital, I could never do it by myself."

I set up the mat before Fu Antos, who was facing north. I knelt, my eyes meeting the blind orbs of the *O-Sensei*. From his open mouth came a stench like that of a sewer. I brought out my dirk. It was a *wakizashi*, or Japanese short sword, with razor-sharp edge and point and a blade nine and a half inches long. The ninjas carried good weapons.

"Striker," Pedro started again. "Amalita must have someone to take care of her. *Florecita*, tender flower that she is. If I don't get back—"

"Please don't interrupt my concentration," I said, annoyed. "Just be ready with that sword, because I sure don't want this botched at the end! You don't get a second chance on this sort of thing."

Pedro stuttered into silence. I saw the suggestion of a smile on Fu Antos' brittle lips. Did he comprehend my strategy?

The Japanese ritual of *seppuku*, disembowelment, was a special form of suicide, difficult to perform correctly. The lowbrow term for it was *hara-kiri*, "belly-slitting"—an unkind but accurate description. The person who successfully performed seppuku established his innocence of the charges against him, or his rightness of cause. If I succeeded, would I win my suit?

I had forgotten one important detail. I stood up, set down the knife, and stripped away my jacket, sweater and undershirt until I was barechested. I loosened my belt and slid my trousers down somewhat, exposing my abdomen. The air was cold, perhaps forty degrees, but I was sweating.

I took up my white shirt and wrapped it about my middle. It was not a proper band for this purpose, but like the dagger and mat it would have to do. The spirit of *Seppuku* was far more important than the trappings. Then I kneeled again and took up the *wakizashi*, holding the point toward me with both hands.

Now it was time. If my blood stained the *tatami*, I was vindicated. Perhaps. I bowed my head, staring at the small sword poised before my tensed belly. My arms quivered.

I thrust the blade deep into the left side of my abdomen,

sidewise. Pain exploded in my body, yet somehow stopped short of my brain. I was aware of it intellectually, but my thoughts and perceptions were clear. An excellent beginning.

I drew it slowly across my stomach to the right. Then, before I could faint, I turned the blade in the wound and jerked the point up. This was the motion of *kappuko,* and very few could complete it, even among the pure Japanese. I was rather proud of my performance.

I drew out the knife and my blood poured out, soaking over my trousers and overflowing across my thighs, red and pure. With dazed gratification I saw it drip onto the *tatami.* Now the pain was up to my brain, but I reached in with one hand and drew my entrails out from the gaping wound, and I was falling over.

But it was not finished. I fought to recover my posture, to sit erect. Where was Pedro? *You wanted to kill me,* I thought fiercely at him. *Now strike, strike!* But all that came from my mouth was the agonized rasp of air. I stretched out my neck.

Then I saw it coming: that bright, beautiful sword. It flashed toward my neck, true and sharp, with Pedro's terrified face behind it. Contact!

Pain abated abruptly. I was lying on the stone floor, my eye near a thin spattering of blood. I stood up slowly and saw the severed head lying where it had rolled to the corner. Clumsy; the decapitation should have been incomplete, so that the head remained fastened to the body by a strip of flesh and did not roll away. Pedro was sobbing like a woman, the gore-encrusted *katana* behind him on the floor.

The corpse of Fu Antos sprawled across the mat, headless. His belly had been slit open gruesomely by some hand stronger than his own, and he had been truly disemboweled. I was physically untouched.

"You have succeeded, and you shall have your reward," a voice said. It was high-pitched but resonant: the voice of one born to command.

I turned to face the source. The small boy stood there, no

longer immobile or blank of gaze. His fingers worked in the *kuji-kiri* technique, and there was now a dominating quality about him, a nobility.

"*O-Sensei* Fu Antos," I said, inclining my head.

He nodded with the bare acquiescence of high rank. "Released from the bondage of age," the child said with that astonishing timbre of maturity. "Restored to youth and sight and hearing and mobility, given lease on another century of improvement and meditation. A few more months, and this body would have grown too old and set for the transfer, and the ninjas would have prevented me from acquiring another. But you came. Give me your hand."

Amazed, I held out my hand. His small fingers took it, and I felt that same vibrant force of *ki* that Hiroshi had shown me. "There is nothing I can do for you," he said.

"I—but my—"

"You have cured yourself," the child *sensei* continued. "Your act of *seppuku* expunged the curse visited upon your heart, and you shall live. In two weeks you will feel a momentary pain and your heart will skip, making you faint for a few seconds only. By that token will you know that the threat is over; the embolism broken up." He paused, and when he resumed his voice was more compassionate. "The American jury will rule you killed in self-defense. Yet might you better have died."

He turned to Pedro. "You have not lived an exemplary life, and you may not return to it. But that which you craved has been granted."

Pedro lifted a streaked face to him. "Does that mean I'll die? I have to take care of—"

"She will bear your child," the boy said.

And I saw that Vicente Pedro had, indeed, been granted his ultimate desire. Not life, but an heir.

"Diago, Makato—" I mumbled. "They did not deserve—"

The boy stooped to touch Diago. "This man remains with me." He moved on to Makato, stepping with uncommon grace, and laid his hands on the fractured skull. "You abused your power when you conspired to kill for money," the *sensei* said to the karateka. He withdrew his hands and resumed the finger-motions of *kuji-kiri*. "*Ki* is denied you. Return to your world, your accounts balanced."

Makato rose, his head miraculously clean again. No language could portray the mixed relief and hopelessness of his countenance. I knew he had heard Fu Autos' message in Japanese. He had sought absolution from his crime, so that he might master *ki*. Now he had that absolution, at the price of losing any hope of achieving *ki*.

"Leave me to my meditations," the boy said. He sat on the mat I had used, crossing his legs in the posture of Zen meditation, oblivious to the gore of his former housing.

Makato and Pedro and I departed. There was nothing else to do. I could not even tell whether Diago was sleeping or dead; either way, he would remain here, and perhaps this was the place he had subconsciously searched for all his life.

We walked the cold hall as I re-donned my shirt and jacket, and the ninjas let us pass unmolested. They had lost their valiant bid to prevent Fu Autos' transfer to a fresh body, and now were subject to his restored power for the next century or so. He would reform them at his convenience.

As the swirling snow outside struck my face, I saw that it was dawn. How much of what I had witnessed and done inside the Black Castle had been real? Had I really killed the *O-Sensei* by taking advantage of his *ki* to transfer my own suicide to his body? Had he really killed two men through similar transfers, then resuscitated one or both? Or had he merely hypnotized us all to believe such magic, and trained the dead-eyed boy to assume his authority after we killed him? There should be a natural explanation for all of this, if I could only work it out. Even that sensation of *ki* when the boy's hand touched mine could have been subjective.

I suspected my doubt would never be completely resolved. Meanwhile, I had the burden of informing Thera that her lover was dead, when theoretically I did not know about the relation between them. I did not look forward to it. Perhaps it would have been better if Jim had survived in my stead.

Yet might you better have died . . .

We started the difficult climb to civilization, Makato leading the way. Pedro took a few steps after him, then keeled over. "The poison!" he muttered as I rushed up. But he was smiling. "I will everything to my child . . . bear witness, Striker, as I did for your *hara-kiri*. Take care of them, and name the child Vicente. You owe me that much."

"Yes," I agreed.

MISTRESS OF
DEATH

Piers Anthony and Roberto Fuentes

28-ANTH

CHAPTER 1

RAID

The door crashed open and they poured in: hell's own collection of deadly freaks. I knew in a moment they were doped, high on "Kill-13"; their eyes blazed orange.

"Class dismissed!" I bawled. "You kids get out of here—fast!"

But this was my karate class. It was a wilder bunch than my judo group, and less disciplined. A number of them had the notion that one *kiai* yell and a swift punch would overcome all threats. They had never had first-hand experience with hard-core martial-drug addicts. Startled but unalarmed, my boys halted their practice and stared at the intruders.

There were eight, demons with wild long hair and bright orange cloaks. The color of their clothing chillingly augmented the pigmentation of their eyeballs. They spread out from the door, forming a glowering line.

"Don't try to fight!" I yelled to my students. "Move out the side doors. Avoid contact!"

The leader of the demons took one step forward. "Do as the coward teacher says," he cried. "There isn't one of you sniveling bastards who could stand up to a real man!"

That stung. I saw half a dozen of my students stiffen. I felt like going up and pasting the insolent demon myself. But that would have been playing into their hands. They had come to disrupt my class and turn it into a brawl, at the very least. What might happen in such a free-for-all I dreaded to contemplate.

"You there, with the chicken-yellow hair!" the demon said, gesturing to my black-belt assistant Tom Sellers. "You must be color blind! Where's your white belt?"

Tom bristled. Conventions vary, but a white belt normally indicates the lowest level of competence, while the black belt is the highest. Ordinarily Tom had good control over his temper, but he was being challenged in front of the class. That made him sensitive. "Why don't you druggies go home and sleep off your fit?" he asked pointedly.

I started forward, ready to haul my students individually out of the hall. Avoidance of a fight in these circumstances was not cowardice, it was excellent sense. A man doped on Kill-13 is dangerous to himself and others. Safer to go after a rabid dog.

Then I saw, the other demons: two more for each door. There was no way out without a fight. And my students hardly knew what they were in for.

"The Kung Fu Temple would reject this child," the demon said. And spat at Tom.

Tom glanced at me. Now we knew where this bunch had come from. The Kung Fu Temple was a new establishment that had wasted no time in establishing a singularly bad reputation in the neighborhood. Little but the name connected it to any genuine kung fu school. I had suspected it of traffic in the violent new drugs, but had not had proof—until now.

I began to hope that the intruders would move on, once they saw how little effect their insults had on us. Any student of the martial arts knows that the best self-defense is to avoid a fight. Especially in a situation like this. The demon leader had tried to bait Tom and failed.

"All right: reject me," Tom said abruptly.

I barely refrained from gnashing my teeth. If only Tom had

controlled himself just a little longer.

The demon grinned and rolled his eyes, making the orange flash. Kill-13, so named because it supposedly has thirteen fatal ingredients, somehow impregnates the eyeballs so that the person under its influence cannot be mistaken. It is a horrendous effect, but is deemed a badge of distinction among the addicts. It normally fades as the high wears off.

The demon squared off in the horse stance. He made a frightful scream, his face twisting into a grotesque contortion. The purpose was theoretically to scare his opponent, but I knew it was really to rev up his own energies. People, like car batteries, often need to be charged for the major effort.

The cloaked figure aimed a punch at Tom. The voluminous clothing served to obscure the thrust of the blow, but Tom blocked it easily. Tom countered almost simultaneously with a knuckle punch to the solar plexus. This looked like an effective blow, but Tom, used to harmless ritual sparring, pulled his punch up short as it landed, so that there was no force at all.

The demon made a flurry of knife-hand shots, and again Tom parried easily. Tom countered to the shoulder and the side of the head, and it was apparent that he could score at will, but each time he pulled his punches harmlessly.

Even the demon audience was beginning to realize that their man was no match for ours in sport combat. They began to move restlessly. The drug gave them a feeling of power and invincibility, but they were not stupid. This stimulated the demon to extra effort.

Tom scored again with a punch that could have crushed a cheekbone, had the effort been real. The demon countered with a terrible dragon stomp. He kicked out with the flat of his foot—and it was booted!—to Tom's stomach. This blow was not pulled; it landed heavily, making Tom grunt and stagger back. But he managed to catch the foot and twist it, making the demon fall ignominiously to the mat.

I knew that the demon had been out to hurt Tom, while Tom

was obeying sport rules. But this could go on only so long.

Tom bent down to give the other a friendly hand up. It was a mistake. The demon pulled a dagger and, sliced across Tom's stomach. It was a savage swing, partly concealed by the man's cloak and Tom's position.

For a moment Tom stood there, not seeming to be aware of the injury. Then, too late, his hands grabbed for his abdomen. He pitched forward, and as he rolled his intestines spilled out onto the *tatami*.

Still, he was conscious. "Why? Why?" he cried.

For an answer the demon lifted his foot and stomped on Tom's face, again and again, making a gory ruin of it.

Kill-13: that was the other source of the name. For a man under its influence had very little conscience and a lot of savagery. The murder had happened so quickly that there had been no chance for me to interfere, and now it was too late.

Such a sight might have terrorized an ordinary group. But my students tended to be over-bold, and they had witnessed an act of treachery and needless brutality. As a man they spread out to meet the demons, the black belts and brown belts in front. It was as though a voice had cried in each of their minds: Avenge the murder! There would be no more pulling of punches.

The demons, as though responding to a signal of their own, moved almost in unison. From under every cloak came a weapon. Knives, chains, clubs, ice picks, an awful array of back-alley instruments.

Now it was twelve against twenty-three. Twelve deadly weapons against twenty-three unarmed students. A possible contest, if the demons were as inexpert with their devices as they were with their unarmed combat. But no matter what their skill, more people were bound to be killed.

I ran for the back wall and dived for the phone. "Operator, emergency!" I cried. "Get the police! Send a riot squad to—"

The phone box clanged as something struck it, and the line went dead. A cleaver quivered in the wall before my nose.

Evidently someone knew how to throw well enough, unless that cleaver had been intended for my head. I turned.

There was a moment of stillness, broken by the massed scream of the demons. It was an awful sound, calculated to bring the fear of death to the hearer.

Then the demons charged.

"Get back!" I cried to my students. "Form a wedge! Bull out through the front door!" But my voice was drowned out by the multiple screams of attack and agony: theirs and ours, respectively.

The massacre was on.

My students were fighting bravely, but there was little they could do against these weapons. In movies one barehanded hero may overcome half a dozen swordsmen, but in life one swordsman is more likely to decimate half a dozen unarmed men. My boys didn't have a chance.

I ran to the display case near the phone. There were ceremonial Japanese swords and several ancient daggers, and a *nunchaku*. I ripped down the last.

The *nunchaku* is like two police billy-clubs linked together by about nine inches of cord or chain. It doesn't look like much, but it has its points. I had learned to use one through an anomaly of circumstance, and never thought I would have occasion to draw upon that skill in this country. Now I was glad to have it.

I gripped one stick, letting the other hang loose. I flexed my wrist a couple of times, getting the feel of it.

My students were trying hard. I had of course drilled them in defense against assorted weapons, but had always stressed that they should flee a weapon whenever possible. Now it was not possible, and I saw that I had taught well. Several of the attackers had already been disarmed.

But that was the small positive side of a black situation. Even as I fetched the *nunchaku* and got set for action, I was aware of several devastating encounters. One student faced a demon with a chain; he tried to grab the chain, but it whipped around his throat, choking him and dragging him down. The demon then stomped on his back, breaking it. Another student launched at him with a two-handed blow to the solar plexus. But the chain was already free. It wrapped around his two wrists, dragging him down to the floor on his back. The demon stomped with his heels on the fallen man's ribs, caving them in.

One demon with a sickle faced two students. One tried to hit him with a *shuto* blow to the head. The blade flashed, cutting into his wrist and finally severing the hand. A fountain of blood spurted through the air. Still the student tried to close in. He struck with the other hand, with deadly force. But he trapped himself; the sickle jammed point-first into his chest. His body flopped against it, impaled. The demon hauled the thrashing student in, and this gave the second student his chance to apply a naked strangle, the *hadaka-jime*, on him.

Then that second student was rolling on the mat, screaming. All I could see was what looked like a handsome black woman standing over him, obviously a confusion of my sight. There were no women here.

Several other, students were lying on the mat, and a great deal of blood was visible. The battle had raged only thirty seconds, and it was obvious that another thirty would cost the health or lives of several more. I had to break this up rapidly.

So I charged. "Disengage!" I shouted, hoping my students would recognize my voice and catch on. I wanted to be free to strike without hindrance. This is one of the few advantages a single man has in a fight against a crowd.

I swung the loose segment of my weapon around my head like a bolo and angled it to strike the head of the nearest demon. There was a satisfying *thunk* and he groaned and went down. Probably I had fractured his skull.

The next demon was wrapping his chain around the neck of one of mine. I looped my cord about his own neck and jerked hard with both handles. As he staggered back I bashed him on the forehead, and he was out.

Then there were three men at once—and they realized that

they no longer faced an unarmed man. One lunged at me with his knife, while another struck at my legs with his club. This was no time for niceties; I swung one stick on the end of the cord in a short arc that smacked across both their faces, breaking at least one nose. But the third got me with his chain.

Fortunately it was not a critical blow. The thing wrapped around my waist, smarting but not striking anything vital. He jerked me toward him, but I had already recovered my swinging stick. I snapped it at his ear, end-wise. He didn't cry out; a man high on Kill-13 normally feels no pain. But his brain must have rattled within his skull, and he went down.

Some fighting sense warned me, and I ducked. A cleaver whistled over my head. I whirled and raised one stick to block the return sweep, while the other stick swung wide and carried the cord around his hand, disarming him.

Then the demons drew back, preparing to rush me. They were natural cowards, hesitant to engage in single combat the moment real resistance developed. Obviously these were not well trained; the drug gave them extraordinary strength and speed, but could create only the illusion of genuine skill. Only years of disciplined practice could make a man a professional.

They paused, afraid to attack me even in a mass. Then a high-pitched voice urged them on, and they charged.

I squatted down, whirling my *nunchaku* fast and low, striking them in the shins, knees and feet. The wood hit solidly, and I heard bones crack. They might be numb to pain, but they could not get at me if they couldn't walk.

For a moment there was confusion. Some action continued elsewhere in the hall, as my remaining students tackled the remaining demons, but in my vicinity there was chaos. Then a new figure strode through the melee: a black face above the orange cloak, with long black hair.

I whirled the *nunchaku*, knowing that this would be a dangerous opponent, summoned from the reserves. His eyes were barely discolored, meaning either that his fit was wearing off, or that he had developed a tolerance for the drug. That could mean that he would attack with less ferocity, but greater finesse. Probably much greater, because he was a veteran; his nose was disfigured by a healed-over break. I waited to see what weapon would come from beneath that cloak.

His hands went to the neck, and suddenly the orange garment fell free. I accelerated the *nunchaku*, preparing for a rapid and devastating strike—and saw that my opponent was a woman. The same one I had seen before, and not believed had been there.

She was in a kind of spangled two-piece outfit, her black midriff bare, and she had the shape of a sculptor's model. But it was her face, seen in this changed context, that stunned me. It was firm-chinned yet delicate, framed by hair too long to hold an afro. A beauty; a classic in any race, except for that broken nose. It reminded me of someone.

She was unarmed. The *nunchaku* drooped from my hand; how could I mutilate this impressive woman with such a weapon?

I hardly saw her motion. Then her foot connected to my groin in a swift, accurate, devastating kick. There was an instant of unbearable pain before my consciousness mercifully departed.

CHAPTER 2

CAMBODIA

I flew backwards in time. I was in the Green Berets, back when American military commitment was quasi-official in Southeast Asia. I had private doubts about our involvement in that war, but the brass never inquired my opinion, and I knew better than to volunteer it. I had a job to do, so I did it, as well as I was able. It was not a nice job, and I never look back on that experience with any pride.

It was blind luck that got me in trouble, but that was the way it was, in that region. The Cong and their allies were everywhere, and no one was to be trusted. I had known that sooner or later I'd catch it. My mission was to infiltrate the Cambodian jungle, avoiding the paths and roads, so as to observe the enemy movements along the southern end of the Ho Chi Minh trail complex. After I'd made a count of people and vehicles, so that I knew when a given trail was in current use, I'd plant a little sensory device that would generate a continuing signal for the bombers to home in on. If I were mistaken, and had spotted only a stray column instead of a main trail, the sensor would have a low count in the following days or weeks. But if it counted many troops, pretty soon the bombers came and—no trail.

Of course there were hitches. Sometimes a congregation of

animals triggered off a bombing mission, since the sensors did not distinguish between forms of life. Sometimes a sensor was discovered and moved, causing much mischief, especially when it was moved to the vicinity of our own forces. And of course the Cong were expert at rerouting and repairing, so that one mission never did the complete job. But they had to work mainly at night, and the more accurate the bombing the greater the inconvenience and delay for them. In a good sequence, we'd plant a new bomb-lure almost as soon as they got a new trail ready, and they'd have to start all over, while their supplies sat and waited.

I worked with Cambodian mercenaries. These were Cambodians who had lived in Vietnam, who were trained for such missions. They could not afford to fight; the Cong would get their families if any of them were identified in association with me. But I didn't want to fight either; I had to remain hidden as long as possible. Until my tour of duty was up, I hoped. The Cong did not even know who I was, but they knew what I was doing, and they wanted me. Badly.

It was grinding, boring work. Whenever we plowed through the jungle the leeches fastened to our legs, or wherever they could find skin. We couldn't pull them off; that just left the heads connected while the rest of their bodies ripped apart. We had to make them let go by burning them, as is done with the ticks on dogs. I kept a pack of cigarettes and a lighter on me, though I don't smoke, just to handle those leeches. A couple of my cigarettes I never used; they were booby-trapped with mercury fulminate. I had cut apart detonator caps and inserted the business ends into the cigarettes. The moment flame touched those . . .

We were careful, but not careful enough. The enemy must have placed ambushes all over the jungle, hoping we'd blunder into one, and one day we did. Those Cong must have stayed motionless for two days, letting the wildlife become acclimatized to the intrusion; we had no hint of their presence until their guns fired.

Actually, we outnumbered them, but it was no match. As the

Cambodians went down I charged the baffle and landed with both boots on someone's face. No room here for a rifle; I laid about me with my knife, slashing at anything that moved.

Then something struck my head, and I was out.

I woke in a cage of bamboo. My head ached, and I had a welt where I had been bit, but that wasn't the worst of it. The cage was small, so that I couldn't stand or move effectively. I had to squat, my knees and buttocks jammed up against the bars, while the biting flies multiplied freely. By the time I swatted one, several others were sucking my blood elsewhere, and I had to go after them too. It did not help that my captors would not release me for calls of nature; I had to relieve myself in the cage, and bask in the growing odors of my own refuse while the flies bred in it.

They did take me out for questioning. The guards had socks filled with sand. One spoke English. "Why are you here?" he demanded. "Where are your associates? Sign a confession!"

Of course I did not answer. They had not expected me to. This was just a formality before the beating. They pounded me methodically with the socks. I took it; there was nothing else to do. Their object was to soften me, not to kill me. They wanted to make me feel miserable, more amenable to their will. And of course they hated everything I stood for. This was routine. In their position, I probably would have had the same motives and hates.

Comprehension did not make it much easier to bear. Eventual death, probably by torture, was my likely lot, if I did not manage to escape. I was dumped back into my cage to meditate upon my pains.

A guard approached, carrying my lighter and cigarette package. He was smoking with evident relish. "I learned to smoke when I fought the French," he told me. "Too bad these aren't marijuana. You want one?"

"I don't smoke," I said, realizing that the truth would be the last thing he believed. "I only use them for burning off leeches."

He took a languorous puff, evidently trying to tease me. I licked my lips as though secretly eager for a cigarette. Let him think he was torturing me this way; it might postpone the real torture.

"I am the only one here who speaks your language," he confided. "So I get the easy duty: to question you. I get to smoke your cigarettes. Tell me the truth, and I will give half the pack back to you."

"I won't talk even for the whole pack!" I said.

"Too bad for you, good for me," he said, lighting another. "The longer this takes, the more smokes I get for myself. I am in no hurry! But we must make this look good, for the others are jealously watching. They want so much to cut you up!"

Surely the truth. But dead men seldom give valuable military information. So their natural appetites had to be restrained, for the time being.

He poked the new cigarette toward me, intending to burn me with it, another standard torture. Suddenly I saw that it was one of the special ones; I had tried to make them indistinguishable from the rest, but this was impossible, and of course I did need to know the difference myself.

I jerked away, genuinely horrified.

"Ah, you are brave with the socks, not so brave with the butts," he said with satisfaction, taking another puff so that the end glowed brightly. "Your weak point, your Achilles' heel, eh?"

He prodded my leg with the glow. I tried to get away, knowing my leg would be blown off if the thing exploded at that instant, but the cage was too confining. He scored on my thigh; and the pain was sharp. I yelled, but that, too, was for a purpose. He thought it was the pain alone that set me off.

He puffed again, enjoying this. "Yes, you Americans are all such cowards. A little burn—I would not fear it! But you, with your decadent soft life—shall I burn your white nose first, or your white pizzle?" He pushed it toward me again.

"Wait!" I cried. "I'll talk!" Actually I was doing some feverish calculating. I had set those traps to explode in about a minute from ignition, but it is hard to be accurate in a home-made job, and there were many variables. That cigarette could help me or kill me. It all depended where it was when the trap sprung.

If he were just poking it through the bars of the cage at the time, not too close to my flesh—escape! I would suffer burns and other damage, but he would lose his hand—and the cage would be blasted open. With luck, I could make it to the jungle before the others collected their wits. It could hardly be worse than another beating. And if the explosion were too close, and I was killed—at least it would be quick and clean.

"So talk," he said, holding the ember half-way between us.

"Well," I began, acting as if I were going to balk after all. He moved the cigarette toward me and I speeded up. "I'm on a mission for the Green Berets. Planting sensors to mark your trails, for the bombers to home in on." I was telling the truth, gambling that it would make no difference after the blast. They would assume I had been lying merely to buy the precious time, if they even guessed about the cigarettes. Meanwhile, my talking encouraged him to hold the cigarette right where I wanted it: close enough to serve as a threat without actually burning me. Near to the bars of the cage.

But it didn't last. He listened attentively, bringing it up to his lips for another draw. Half a minute had passed, and the cigarette was too far away.

"Aw, give me one puff," I said, interrupting myself. "You promised me half the pack."

He started to bring it toward me as I wanted. I didn't expect him to give it to me, but to tease me with it—but that would place it exactly where I wanted it.

"*After* I am satisfied," he said. He held it toward me a moment, then slowly returned it to his mouth for another lingering puff.

The blast tore his head apart and momentarily blinded and deafened me. When my senses cleared, the whole camp was standing around us, amazed. But I remained confined, and he was beyond help.

They were confused and angry, and so was I, for rather different reasons. To have escape so near . . .

But there was one small benefit. Evidently he had spoken the truth about being the only English-speaking one, and they did not realize that I knew some of their language. They could not figure out how I could have smuggled a bomb into my cage, since I was obviously helpless. So they let me be; there was no one left to interrogate me.

I was taken to several villages. That was the only exercise I got: walking with my hands bound behind me, yoked to the cage, hauling it along behind me. I knew better than to stall or try to run; there was no escaping such numbers when they were on guard. If I tried, they would put me back in the cage and haul it themselves, and the battering would leave me in much worse condition than I was.

They fed me the same rations they gave themselves: a bowl of rice with a stinking fish sauce. I could hardly choke down the putrid mess, but there was nothing else. As it was, there was not enough. They were giving me the same amount each of them took. But they were small men, weighing about a hundred pounds; I weighed 180. It took more to sustain me. So I went hungry, in time might have starved, on the same rations that kept them healthy.

They were brutal even when they didn't intend to be, in another of those ironies of war. There were, however, plenty of times when they did intend to be brutal. At each new village my cage would be set up in a public place, and the natives would pelt me with anything handy. Overripe fruit, clods of earth, roots, dung. Nothing really dangerous, because they were saving me for interrogation by the experts. I knew I would have to escape, or die trying, before that happened. There would be torture, and probably a combination of drugs and brainwashing that might or might not leave me sane, but *would* get the information they required. The pelting was child's play, when viewed in proper perspective.

Literally, for it was the children who participated with greatest glee. I suppose flinging dung comes naturally to youngsters the world over. Good, clean fun.

For two weeks I traveled, most of the time cooped in that cage, my legs numb from the position, my scratches smarting from grime and dirt and sweat. No one had pity on me. I knew that anyone who showed me the slightest open favor would be killed or tortured. *They* did not have to be preserved for interrogation.

Yet there were those who seemed to show that they lacked the force of hate that was expected of them. They threw dung with the others, but arranged to miss me; they shouted insults that lacked conviction. None of them would help me, of course, but if I should escape, their pursuit would not be as vigorous as it could be. These people were good at that sort of thing; they really did not like trouble.

One of these was a girl. She was young, perhaps sixteen, and petite, with long black hair. She stood about four feet ten inches, and might have weighed eighty pounds. Her figure was childlike, or more correctly doll-like, for it was all there and extremely feminine, accentuated by her long black pajama-like uniform. On her feet were crude sandals fashioned of tire rubber.

She would have been a beauty, were it not for her crooked nose. It must have been broken in childhood and never set correctly. Too bad.

She traveled with the Cong, and there was no mistaking her profession, but none of this showed in her aspect. She was just a girl trying to get along. Maybe her home had been bombed, her family killed, so that she had no support and no one to turn to. So she was using the one real asset remaining to her: her enticement of form. When that faded, she would be finished. But for that nose, she could have had a far better life.

She came to me at night, hesitantly, afraid of this huge white stranger. She carried a bucket of water. I thought she was going to offer me a drink, but then one of the guards saw her and approached. She swung the bucket with all her force, and the water drenched me.

The guard laughed, and the girl laughed too, but in her eyes there was sorrow. The guard took her away, into a nearby hut, and she seemed to go with him willingly enough, but she sent one glance back at me that reversed the meaning entirely.

Or did it? I could not ignore the possibility that they were trying a subtle or not so subtle gambit to get early information from me. Let the little whore play up to the prisoner a bit, discovering how much he really knew of their language. If she got me talking, I might give her news to aid my supposed escape—news that would close that escape forever.

No, I could not afford to trust her, unfortunately.

She came again the following night, bearing her bucket. This time no guard interrupted her. She must have given him a warning, last night. I took the drink she offered, gratefully, and used the remainder of the water to wash myself off somewhat. She smiled at me, and the shadows concealed her nose and accentuated her white teeth, so that it was an extremely nice smile. I was tempted to throw away caution; I wanted to believe in her. I knew that two weeks in the cage, suffering and slowly wasting away from the inadequate diet, had distorted my judgment. Still, she *was* a pretty girl . . .

She put her face to mine, just beyond the bars. Her hands came up to caress my cheeks. "Do you understand me?" she asked. "I am here to help you escape."

She had rushed it, making the ploy too obvious. Now I knew she was no friend of mine. I shook my head as if in incomprehension.

She continued to caress me. Her touch warmed me despite my distrust; it was so gentle, so feminine. Her face came closer, until I could kiss her, and I did. Meanwhile I put my hands through the bars, placing them about her slender throat, lightly, then tightly.

I strangled her. I intended only to knock her out so that I could get her knife; I was sure she had one somewhere. They all do. Then I could cut my way out of the cage. But she struggled like a fighting cat, pulling away strongly, trying to get her teeth into my hands. I tightened up instantly, struggling to hold her still, determined to prevent any outcry while I searched her body for the knife. I did not realize how strong I was in my desperation, or how frail she was.

I heard a crack, and she hung in my two hands, limp. Her black pajamas became soiled; her bladder control had vanished. I had broken her neck.

She was not quite dead. She jerked about as I held her, her body twitching in involuntary spasms the way a beheaded snake does. I had no choice; I held her up one handed while with the other hand I searched for the knife.

My fingers wormed into her loose top, exploring her warm breasts. They were not large but well formed, and no knife was there. I continued down, feeling her smooth belly and firm thighs, intensely regretting my destruction of this beauty. Finally I found the knife strapped to her waist, concealed by the slack in the uniform. I ripped it off, then let her drop. She was all the way dead now.

I cut the cords and the bamboo rods separated. I was free. But at what price, what price! True, she might have intended to betray me, but I could have stopped that without killing her.

Now what? I hesitated to leave her there. Better to have my escape a mystery, so that their pursuit would be uncertain. If they thought an agent had come to free me, or better yet, a traitor— what havoc with their intelligence system. And I just didn't like to implicate her, rightly or wrongly. If any of her family lived, they would pay the price of her supposed treachery.

Perhaps it was that I was thoroughly ashamed of what I had done. Murdering an innocent girl. *How* innocent, I didn't know.

I picked her up, feeling the wetness in her clothing, and hauled her into the jungle. I knew I didn't have time to bury her, but if I could hide her—and then I heard the cry of alarm. My escape had already been discovered.

Actually they would have been smarter to organize their pursuit silently, so that I might have been lulled into carelessness. This way I knew exactly where they were. I threw the body into a tangle of brush and took off. My chances were fairly good; it was almost impossible to track a man in the jungle, if he had any ability in covering his traces. And I did.

But I took the further precaution of ambushing the two guards who were hottest on my trail. One had a Russian automatic rifle with bayonet attached, an AK-2; this was much lighter than the American equivalent, and superior for use in the jungle. It did not jam as readily as the American M-41. I wanted that weapon.

The other man had a machete. I jumped out behind them as they passed and plunged my knife unceremoniously into the side of the nearest, the machete man. The other whirled, swinging his rifle about to cover me. My mistake; I should have gone for the rifleman first.

I jumped at him, deflecting the barrel as the weapon fired: The bullet hit my side, but what annoyed me at the moment was the noise it made. Now everyone would have a clear notion where the action was.

I grabbed the bayonet with my bare hand and pulled it toward me. I hit the man with a karate chop to the head. He grunted and fell, and I finished him off with a couple of hard kicks to his throat and face.

I kept the rifle, of course, and also the machete. Now I was doubly armed, and my pursuers knew that, for the hue and cry had died out. While they hesitated I made good my escape. Ten minutes was as good as a week, for they would never find me now.

Certain of my reprieve, I suddenly felt my personal state. I was weak from hunger and the cage, and my side was bloody, and my right hand was a mess where I had gripped the bayonet. I did not look at it; I kept my fist tightly clenched. But blood was leaking out and it burned terribly.

The same wilderness that hampered the pursuit would make my private survival difficult, especially in my condition. I was not familiar with this region and had no supplies. I staggered on, uncertain of my course, thinking dizzily of the girl I had killed. That sweet little form . . .

My footing gave way. I windmilled for balance, realizing that I had blundered into a river. Then my face struck the water. I gasped for breath instinctively, and took in a lungful of liquid. Choking weakly, I faded out.

CHAPTER 3

KILL-13

I must have faded in and out several times. I knew that hours, perhaps days, had passed, and I had jumbled memories of stretchers, motion, sirens, doctors, jungle—no, some of *that* was years ago.

It is not my way to collapse after one blow. I might have been out at first, but hardly for this length of time. I knew the doctors had drugged me, putting me back under again and again. That bothered me; I don't like drugs, particularly when they are used on me. I seemed to be whole; my arms and legs were present and responsive, and my senses were all right. Why this hospital treatment?

As if on cue, a doctor entered my room. "Good afternoon, Mr. Striker!" he said jovially. Well, on his pay I'd be jovial too.

"Afternoon? First I knew of it."

"Two o'clock." He seemed to have a slight British accent.

"I remember there was a fight," I said.

"Some fight! You physical training roughnecks certainly make a job of it, you know."

Roughnecks. He classed us all the same, demons and martial artists. Typical ignorance; no point arguing. "I got kicked, that was all," I said. "No cause to run me broke in a place like this. What about the others?"

"Kicked!" He shook his head, making a soundless whistle. "Evidently you don't realize—"

"I realize." The drug they had dosed me with hadn't worn off entirely. I felt numb in the crotch area, and was in better spirits than I suspected I ought to be. "That black woman was an expert at her trade. She would have gotten me, if I hadn't—"

"*Would* have? I did the surgery on your testicles, Striker! You'll be lucky if you're not sterile. I may have saved one."

This medic lacked something in bedside manner. No doubt he figured me for a charity patient he could talk down to. No sense in reacting too strongly to his attitude, however. I picked up my sentence where he had interrupted it. "If I hadn't learned the trick of drawing them up into the body cavity for emergencies. It's an almost involuntary reaction to danger, now. The last thing I did as I saw that kick coming—"

He looked at me with a certain grudging appreciation. "You did that deliberately? I assumed the kick had luckily driven them there."

I nodded. "I would have done better with more warning. It certainly hurt!"

"Because you were only half successful," he said. "Some parts of the body don't heal, Striker. I can't promise—"

Even through the euphoria of the medication, that hurt. How far had I been unmanned?

"Time will tell," he concluded with his damned mock cheer. "The saddle-block will be wearing off soon, and you'll feel pain. The more the better, frankly; it'll mean the nerves are sound. If there's *no* pain, you'll really be hurting! Ha ha."

"Ha ha," I echoed sourly.

"The nurse will give you a shot when you ask for it."

"I don't drink, Doc," I said. "Ha ha."

He frowned. He really wasn't much for his own medicine. He

got up and headed off to his next case, no doubt to gladden other hearts as delicately as he had mine.

The pain did get bad, fortunately, and in due course I gave up and drew on my *ki* to suppress it. *Ki* is a wonderful inner power, but not to be abused, and for me it was erratic. But this time it worked.

The nurse came with her needle, and was amazed when I waved it away. Nurses don't understand *ki,* unfortunately.

I must have slept another hour or two, for I felt better when I awoke. I swung my legs off the bed and stood unsteadily, glad the numbness was gone.

Ouch! I had had surgery, all right. That woman had really scored, and it had all been unnecessary. If I hadn't stood bemused by the sight of her—

I could walk. It required strenuous discipline to contain the agony of every step, but that was all. My muscles had not been damaged, after all. Obviously I had suffered crushed veins or nerve damage, and a substantial bruise, as well as the surgery. All that would take time to heal.

So I walked spreadeagled, trying unsuccessfully to summon the *ki* again. I hoped no one would see me and inquire whether I had been gang-raped. You get some sick humor in hospitals.

I was sure I was not supposed to be out of bed, but there were things I had to know. I got into my robe and marched out the door as though on routine business. Naturally the nurses ignored me. I walked down the length of the hall, stopping at the double doors to the lobby. I could read the sign backwards from my side: *No admission.* Cut out the *Adm* and it would read the same forward or back. *noission.* Not that it mattered.

I turned about, trying not to grimace from the sensation that shot through my groin with this twisting motion and ambled back. I had glanced surreptitiously into each room as I came down, and verified another suspicion: several of my students and at least one demon were also here. From the look of it, they were all considerably worse off than I, and only one seemed to be conscious. I couldn't tell who, because his face was bandaged, but I saw his brown belt and part of his judogi hanging over the foot of the bed. He must have insisted they be close, to give him moral support, so the hospital personnel had obliged him just that much. I liked that fighting spirit.

I walked boldly in. "Hello, karateka!" I said in a professional tone, a parody of the doctor's. "I did surgery on your brain. I saved one hemisphere. You're lucky you're not senile!"

He recognized me immediately despite the masking of his eyes by the bandages. "Mr. Striker! How'd you get past the guards?"

"Didn't have to," I admitted. "I'm in two, two rooms down. Walking wounded, though I'd rather *not* walk! Who are you?"

He smiled beneath the bandages, knowing I knew his voice. I know all my students; they are not mere meal-tickets to me. "Andy Jones. I feel like hell."

"You *look* like hell!" I told him, putting the right amount of cheer into it so that he would know I was joking. The irony was that he did look bad.

There was another patient in the room, an old man with a cast on one scrawny arm. I thought he was asleep, but now he laughed. "'Bout time somebody told the truth around here! He looks like to die, and I don't want his ghost haunting me."

I smiled, though I wasn't sure I appreciated his remark. "What happened to you, Andy?" He was a good student, a sincere worker, and I hated to see him in this condition.

"I think I'm blind." His chin was firm, but there was a quiver to his lip.

That was my fear for him also. "They wouldn't have you in here like this if they didn't figure they could cure you," I said.

"Now you're lying, just like the rest of 'em," the old man said.

I decided to let the old bastard have it. People with the foulest tongues are apt to be the most sensitive to incoming foulness. And I wanted to verify certain impressions of the past few hours. "How about your memories of the fracas?" I suggested to Andy. "Details, I mean."

For an instant he smiled. There was an understanding between us, though I felt a tinge of guilt too. The old man probably wasn't responsible for his lack of tact; he might be in pain, or even senile. People in their declining years often do not realize how loud they talk or how badly they come across. But Andy and I were in pain too, more than physical. We needed catharsis.

"It was pretty bad," he said. "You know how those demons came after us with weapons, and all of us barehanded. We tried to fight, but—"

"I know," I said grimly. I knew the oldster was listening closely. "How'd the others make out?"

"I didn't see all of it. Things were pretty wild and crowded. Just one I watched, with an ice pick; he lunged at Joe. Joe blocked it the way you taught us, the same as the knife defense. And then Joe tried the *uki goshi* floating hip throw, and threw him, but Joe didn't hang on to the armed hand."

"Oh-oh," I said.

"And on the way down the demon stabbed him in the kidney. God, those bastards are fast! I don't think Joe made it."

I hadn't seen Joe in the hospital. Either he was dead, or in intensive care. "I'm afraid not many did," I said.

"Hey, what kind of a party *was* this?" the old man asked querulously.

Andy ignored him. "Someone else caught at one of those chains, and punched the demon in the nose with an inverted fist blow, the *uraken*. Smashed it flat! But then a demon with a knife got him in the side. The blood spurted out all over the two of them and on the floor—"

The oldster had had enough. He clutched for the basin beside his bed. We had torpedoed him, but I found no pride in it. Sick men teasing other sick men, and the sickness was multi-leveled.

"You," I said. "You, Andy—how did you catch it?"

"Two of us came after the demon with the sickle," he said. "Matt and I. Matt went in first, trying for a *shuto* blow to the head."

"I saw that," I said. "That sickle took off his hand! Then the point went right through his body."

"Yes. I jumped in—I was almost crazy with rage, and fear too, I guess. Never felt that way before. Always thought I'd run from trouble."

"Smartest possible move," I said.

"I put a naked strangle on him and twisted his head. I had the pleasure—this sounds horrible, but I swear it *was* a pleasure—I pulled back and heard his neck crack, and then—" He paused.

I remembered my first glimpse of the black woman. The karate mistress. I had then thought it a trick of my imagination. "What then?"

"Someone caught me from behind. A woman, by the feel."

"A *woman?*" I challenged him because I wanted to get it exactly straight.

"I didn't see her, but her long nails raked across my face. I—my eyes—"

"How did you know it was a woman, if you didn't see her?" I demanded, morbidly fascinated. No doubt about it now: this was the female who had scored on me. It hadn't been imagination.

"My head collided with her body as I fell back." The blank bandaged face turned toward me, and I could almost feel the buried eyes searching my face. "I—I felt her breasts on the back of my neck. If I wasn't dreaming it—"

"You weren't dreaming. I saw her. I fought her."

He licked his lips, relieved. "That's about all I remember. I woke up here."

"That's about all there was *to* remember," I said. "I mixed in with my nunchakus—but that same black bitch kicked me in the crotch."

"Ouch!" he said. "But you always told us how to guard—"

"I guess I didn't follow my own advice!" I said. "I was amazed by the sight of her, there among those demons. Never saw a female demon before. And she had a swift motion. Fastest kick I ever experienced."

"That's some demon," he murmured.

"Some demon," I agreed ruefully. "I didn't see long nails on her, though. She must have been using metal claws, artificial nails, and took them off later. Maybe you're lucky; she scraped your eyes, instead of gouging them. The eyeballs should be in place and intact. The doctors can fix that sort of damage."

"You think so?" he asked hopefully.

"I think so," I said, believing it.

By this time the nurses had discovered my absence. They were standing in the door, frowning in a manner calculated to intimidate the most resistant patient. "Okay, wardens, I'll go quietly," I said. "Don't take it out on my friend. He didn't know I was an escapee."

Andy grabbed my arm. "Thanks, Mr. Striker," he said. Thanks for coming! You've given me hope."

"You've helped me too," I said. "We'll talk again soon. Get some sleep." I almost said "shut-eye," but that remark would have been a disaster for a man concerned about possible blindness.

Back in my own bed, my thoughts were not quiet. I lay awake, pondering the problem of drugs in general and Kill-13 in particular. For there was no avoiding the fact that this drug had cost me the lives or health of a number of my students, and perhaps cost me my manhood too. I had figured it enough to stay off drugs myself and to keep my students off them, but the drug problem had suddenly come out to find us anyway.

Drugs have been around a long time, perhaps as long as man himself. We in the martial arts can usually handle them. In fact, judo has been used in a limited way as a cure for certain addictions. If a person has nothing special to live for, and he falls into the crutch of the alternate reality of drugs, participation in a good martial art can provide the meaning he needs. Yoga can do that too, and religion, and perhaps any other disciplined interest.

But it couldn't, it seemed, deal with Kill-13. This drug was to other drugs as a grand prix racer to a go-cart. It seemed to be addicting within the first week of use, and it had a special appeal for athletes and martial artists.

There has always been a drug problem among athletes, with both individual performers like weight lifters and team performers like football players. Not because they crave hallucination or escape. The opposite: they are aggressively competitive. They want to succeed outstandingly, to win. Every contestant wants the trophy, and his ultimate goal is the world's record for his class. Some of the worst offenders are the muscle builders, the Mr. America competitors and similar types. These pretty boys really go out for the muscle-tissue drugs, because in this way they can make tremendous physical gains in a much shorter time than would otherwise be possible. In fact, they can put on more muscle than any non-user can, though there is some question whether they can put it to good use. Appearance is everything, not performance. It is said that a good percentage of them are homosexual. This sort of drug use flowers because there are no regulations governing it in professional sports.

It is a different matter in the Olympics. After the contests, the players have to give urine samples to be instantly analyzed, and there are always a few caught even though they know of the procedure. There are periodic rumors of un-analyzable drugs, developed by the Communists, that enable them to do so well in competition.

The thing is, the athlete who comes in second after rigorous training and maximum effort could come in *first* with judicious use of certain drugs. Quite possibly he comes in second only because the competition is drugged. So the users become winners, and the practice inevitably spreads. The athletes themselves may not like it, but they have little choice in a world that loves only winners. A competitor has three choices: he can use drugs; he can be an also-ran; or he can drop out of competition. It is that simple and compelling.

The main drugs used in athletics are steroids, amphetamines, and barbiturates, often in combination. The steroids are related to the male hormones. They facilitate the growth of muscle, much more and much faster than normal. But this must be accompanied by much exercise, so a stimulant is used to prevent fatigue and sleepiness. This is an amphetamine, "speed," "bennies," etc. But then it can be hard to relax, so a depressant drug is taken: barbiturates, "downers," "red devils," etc. Thus the training routine amounts to amphetamines in the morning, steroids in the day, and barbiturates at night.

Of course there are certain side effects. Amphetamines depress hunger but increase thirst. The user drinks much more than normal, and urinates more. He develops a tolerance, so that heavier doses accomplish less. Hallucinations are possible, waking nightmares. Eventually irreversible brain damage is done, as cells die and brain tissue shrinks. Sexual abnormalities may develop in the male, such as priapism: sustained and painful erection without real desire. Weight is lost, and the user gets extremely nervous.

The steroids deliver the muscle, but also cause the man's breasts to enlarge, and his testes may shrink. He loses his sexual appetite. His whole life tempo seems to accelerate, so that he matures more rapidly—but by the same token, he seems to age faster. Body hair is lost. He can suffer liver and kidney damage and is prone to cancer, often of the prostate. And so, gradually, he is emasculated.

That's why I believe such drug dependence is bad, quite apart from ethical considerations. It is measurably, physically harmful to the body in the long run, and perhaps the short run too.

But the effects of Kill-13 are worse, in proportion to its potency. It builds muscle so rapidly that the whole body is put under severe strain. Vital nutrients are drawn from the system, impoverishing everything else in favor of the large muscles being developed. Massive infusions of vitamins, minerals, protein and other foods can alleviate this somewhat, but an addict is not the sort to bother with a healthy diet. Not a Kill-13 addict! So this drug can be fatal, leaving behind a muscle-bound body.

"Live fast, die young, and have a handsome corpse," I muttered to myself, remembering the saying that once had been humorous.

"Eh?"

I looked up, startled. I had been alone in my room, but now I saw that I had acquired a roommate. I recognized him, too: the obnoxious old man who had been with Andy. "What are you doing in here?" I demanded.

"Got moved in while you was snoozin'," he said.

I hadn't been snoozing; I had been thinking. But the effect was the same: I had failed to protest the addition of a roommate. My fault. "Why didn't you stay with Andy?"

"They took him to surgery. Guess they wanted to clean up the room."

So they moved a patient out? Could be; the rationale of hospital procedure was not my strong point. I hated to be ailing, ever, and to be confined however briefly to any such institution—well, I knew I was prejudiced. It was just possible that they considered this man to be a bad influence on Andy, so had moved him in with a less critical patient. If I could get up and walk around, I was a prime candidate.

"Well, let me snooze some more, okay?" I said.

"Just one thing, youngster. I didn't puke in there because of what you kids were talking about. I got a stomach condition. Nothing fazes me except hospital food."

"That figures." I closed my eyes, dismissing him.

He shut up, and I resumed my consideration of Kill-13. Its addictive properties only make its side effects worse. So long as an addict was on the drug, he hardly felt the damage. But when he stopped, those months of neglect hit abruptly, often fatally. This was not generally known yet, as there were no long-term addicts; the drug was too new. But I had researched it as well as I could, and this seemed to be the pattern. Even mild withdrawal symptoms could be loss of the sense of touch or even blindness, because of the destruction of blood vessels in the eyeballs. That orange effect.

The numbness to pain is actually a slow destruction of certain areas of the brain. Perhaps that accounted for the hallucinogenic effect, too. This was a seeming paradox, since the reflexes of demons were notoriously fast and accurate. I had talked with a doctor about it, and he conjectured that the strength of the nervous signals was multiplied by the drug, so that the reflexes were good despite the deterioration of the controlling brain tissue. Like using a sledgehammer on thumbtacks: not good for the tacks or the wall, but devastatingly effective anyway.

The demons gradually or not so gradually lost their gentler emotions, becoming like spoiled children: imperious, short-tempered, quick to physical violence, and without remorse for their mischief. They seemed to have no feeling but hatred and anger. Of course I had not known any demons personally; possibly they had better qualities when among their own kind. But I doubted it, and I never expected to see an old demon, unless he *started* old.

Kill-13 had appeared on the scene only six months ago, though probably it had been around longer in the underground arenas of the world. Its popular impact had been immediate and, to my mind, catastrophic.

Martial arts is my profession. I hate to see any aspect of it perverted. When the vast improvement in body, mind and spirit that proper training and discipline can bring is destroyed by a debilitating drug, I hurt.

The demons of the so-called Kung-Fu Temple were indeed hellish. Not because of their ferocity; because of the mockery they made of the philosophy and integrity of all martial art.

So I had tried to abolish Kill-13, at least in my own area. I allowed no demons in my judo or karate classes, and warned all students against the use of any of the other drugs, including alcohol and nicotine. I don't smoke or drink myself, and my reasons are not moral but physical: these vices weaken the body.

I am not much of a public speaker, but I spoke out against Kill-13 wherever I could. Church groups, civic clubs, high schools—they wanted to hear how it was possible to kill a man with one blow, but I gave them warning about the killer drug instead. I hadn't thought my effort was having much effect, but evidently it had, because it had aroused the demons against me.

Now those demons had struck back, viciously. Probably half my class was dead or permanently mutilated. Only luck had spared me. The police must have come before the demons could complete their massacre or I would have been dead too.

If the demons thought they had silenced me or scared me off, they had misjudged their man. After this, I was going to go after the drug full time. I would not rest until I had eliminated Kill-13, and not just from my neighborhood. From the face of the earth.

CHAPTER 4

AMALITA

I slept again; I needed it. I woke, ate, slumbered. I had, I
learned, received other wounds, and lost some blood. That accounted for my unseemly weakness. The cuts on my arms and legs
were healing nicely; I had not even noticed the bandages during
my first illicit walk. The bruises about my torso hurt more. But
the off-and-on numbness in my groin bothered me most. Would I
ever again be able to. . . ?

Then a female vision trotted in. The old man in the next bed
whistled wistfully. Long black hair, angelic face, figure like Miss
Latin America. Young, but full. She wore a pair of white calfskin
boots up to the middle of her thigh, and they fitted as tightly as
gloves. Her pants were as close and short as a tank-suit, made of
some kind of rubber or plastic. Above that was a skimpy halter,
almost transparent, leaving her midriff bare. I'm a belly-button
man; I notice the midsection. A faint line of black hairs went up to
her navel, suggesting the contours in the other direction. Most
women shave their bellies, so that most men do not realize that
pubic hair extends, faintly, up to that area, but as I said, *I* know.
Her eyes were blacked with thick mascara; her lips were ruby red—
with modern lipsticks, that's no hyperbole!—and her long finger-

nails were painted to match. Her lustrous black hair was braided down beyond her buttocks, which showed a certain cleavage as she turned. And a red beret perched on one side of her head, with a white pom-pom ball on top.

I looked her up and down, and vice versa, checking and re-checking, and then I realized who she was. I hardly concealed my groan. "What in God's name are you doing here, Amalita?"

"How could you be ill, and near to dying, in need of comfort, and I not close by your side?" she said, pouting. She was enveloped in a cloud of musky perfume; I could almost see it wafting over me. "After what you did for me, lover . . ."

"You're a married woman!" I reminded her urgently, acutely aware of the listening ears in the next bed. "And the mother of Pedro's child. You should be home in Nicaragua."

"Pedro's child in name only," she said. "As well you know, handsome man."

"Pedro's child in name and in fact," I said firmly. "Amalita, what's past is past, and I'm not up to—"

"I left it with the nurse at home," she said. *"Pegado a la teta.* So I could come here."

Some mother love! "Where's Pedro?"

"Uncle is having a long—"

"He's your husband now!"

She shrugged. "In name."

"In *fact!*" I shouted.

My elderly roommate sniggered from the other bed. "You sure know how to string along the girls," he said. "Married ones, yet!"

Brother! I had to lay it on the line. "Amalita, you and I had an acquaintance in Nicaragua—"

"I thought you Americans called that an affair," she said.

"We Americans," the oldster said gleefully, "call it good old-fashioned f—"

"Shut up!" I yelped. Then, to her: "But after that your uncle recovered from his paralysis, and learned to walk again, and you married him and bore his child." This was rough, considering the audience, but I continued determinedly. "Vicente Pedro is an extremely jealous man. You should not be here."

What I didn't say was more complex and significant. I had met Amalita on Pedro's vast Nicaraguan estate over a year ago. She had joined me in a naked swim, and I had thought her to be an innocent Indian servant girl. The last thing I had imagined was that she could be my wealthy crippled host's intended bride. When I learned that, I tried to keep away from her. But she had come to me at night, impersonating another girl. My folly; that episode had aroused Pedro's deep, implacable wrath, however unwitting my part in it had been. Amalita had killed a servant in an effort to cover up, but my own life had nearly been forfeit before that entanglement eased.

I knew this young girl—she was still hardly sixteen—for a conniver and murderess, and the wife of a justly jealous man I now called friend. Beautiful she was, but she was bad trouble in several ways, and I wanted no part of her. It was my misfortune that she appeared to retain a certain idle hankering for me.

Once I had thought her shy and naive. *I* had been naive, in the manner of so many men. But not anymore.

"So thanks for the visit, and please go home," I finished aloud.

My roommate cackled. "But the lass is trying to tell you something, hero!"

I glanced at him in annoyance, then back at Amalita.

She had removed her jacket—I had not even noticed it before, which showed where my attention had been—and was starting on her halter. Or perhaps it was better termed her blouse. I could hardly think straight, with my eyes playing tag with those contours beneath it.

"What are you doing?" I demanded foolishly, knowing very well what she was up to. I had seen her strip for action before.

She paused, leaning forward impressively. "I am bringing you news of *muerte* thirteen."

"Amalita, you can't—" Then her mixture of language penetrated. "Do you mean Kill-Thirteen?"

"She'd kill more than that, with that outfit!" the oldster said. "They don't make 'em like they used to, they make 'em better! Look at them boobs!"

"Mind of an adolescent," I muttered.

"Mind of a connoisseur," she said, her breasts bursting into full view as the meager covering came off.

"What a body!" the oldster remarked. "If I was you, I'd get her under the covers before she gets tired waiting. Don't get a shot at stuff like that often."

I realized it was useless to argue about her dishabille. Soon enough a nurse would check in and put a stop to the show. And she had known how to hook me verbally. "What do you know about the drug?"

She continued undressing, with somewhat more motion than was strictly necessary, particularly in the torso. "It is a mixture of poppy and coca and mushroom and chemical," she said. "Ancient Mayan formula, very potent. The priests used it—"

"Wait, now, wait!" I exclaimed, concentrating on her words so I wouldn't have to concentrate on her body. She had filled out some since I had known her, especially in the bosom. Her pregnancy must have done that. Did she nurse her baby now? Her breasts were high but solid, like two pointed pears. "Poppy—that's opium. Coca is cocaine. Cactus is peyote. But chemical—are you talking about acid? LSD?"

"*LSD!*" the oldster repeated, savoring it. "Wow!"

Amalita sat on the edge of the bed and peeled off her boots. Her legs, too, were—Never mind! I told myself. But my eyes wouldn't cooperate. Now her panties came down. No stretch marks, I noted; her abdomen was as smooth as I remembered. "That and more," she agreed. "I do not know all the ingredients, but together they are very strong. Pedro said—"

"Don't you see," I said, "that it *couldn't* be any ancient Mayan formula! They didn't have LSD."

She glanced at me sidelong over one breast; my angle of vision from the bed made this a remarkable effect. Black of iris behind purple of nipple. "Didn't they, Jason?"

"No! LSD is manufactured in the modem laboratory."

"The priests had many things. Their secrets are not all known, even yet."

She believed, or wanted to believe, in her Indian heritage. There was no hard evidence the Maya had had anything like Kill-13, and the notion was dubious at best. But that hardly mattered. The present-day Indians in Central America certainly could have something to do with poppies, coca and peyote. And maybe LSD, or worse. I knew that at least one mushroom-related drug was so strong that it emerged virtually undiluted in the urine. So the tribesmen would drink the urine and get high all over again. And in Central America such drugs were not only smoked, but chewed and even drunk as tea. Something natural very well might have a similar effect to LSD.

The Mayan region of Central America was Pedro's domain. He could indeed know something about it; he had a finger in many lucrative and quasi-legal pies. If he were sick, he could have sent Amalita with the news, not trusting the mails or telephone. I doubted it, but it *was* possible.

"All right," I said. "What's your news?"

She was now completely nude. Where *were* the hospital nurses? Even a floor sweeper would be welcome now!

She lifted the sheet of my bed and eased herself under the cover beside me, her long leg sliding along my thigh. I could smell the woman-odor of her, distinct from the perfume. "It has been a long time, judo-man," she said.

"Not *that* news!" I wailed as her lithe torso snuggled up against me. I reached for the emergency buzzer.

"No one will answer," Amalita murmured as she wriggled even closer. "I made a small gift to the boss nurse."

I froze, aghast. "You bribed the head nurse?" But of course she had; such things were nothing to her.

The oldster cackled. "Wait'll I tell my grandchildren! They

sure don't make men like they used to! In my day I'd a had her laid and paid before the—"

"Paid!" Amalita flashed, facing me. "You expect to be paid?"

That shut up even my obnoxious roommate.

I grasped at the straw. "Not a bad idea," I said. "You're a multimillion-dollar heiress these days. How much is it worth to you, Senora Pedro?"

But she was not to be baited out of her hot-blooded mission. Her hands ran knowingly over my body. "It is worth some information about the drug of thirteen deaths," she said. "About its source, perhaps."

I had to bite. "You know its source?"

"Not exactly," she demurred, moving against me like a great friendly python. She knew exactly how to do it. She must have had good practice recently, for she had not shown such talents in Nicaragua. Had Pedro hired experts to tutor her? His illness might have made him slow to respond.

"What do you know?" I demanded.

"A name, perhaps." Impatient, she squirmed about and climbed half over me. "Remember how it was, how we did it before?" she whispered as her breasts slid across my chest. "I was so young then, and you were the first."

I remembered. I hadn't even known it was her that time, it had been dark and she had covered her face. In fact I had thought I was dissipating Pedro's jealousy by taking an anonymous woman. But clever Amalita, substituting in the dark . . .

She was a desirable woman, no doubt about it. But far more trouble than any woman was worth, as I kept reminding myself. Her husband Pedro seemed farther and farther away. "What name?" I asked desperately.

"One kiss," she said, bringing her angelic face up to mine. She did not wait for my acquiescence.

"Look, Amalita," I said, my lips moving against hers. "Apart from everything else, I got kicked. In the crotch. Hard. They did surgery. The bandages just came off today."

"Oh, let me see!" she exclaimed. "I will kiss it well again."

"For God's sake, no!" I squawked.

"Now Jason," she said reasonably. "That is why I came to help you. I knew you needed me."

"You came here *because* I was kicked?"

"I will give you the name. Of a man to see about the drug. But I could have telephoned to tell you that. What I bring to you in person no telephone can do."

"That's for sure!" the oldster agreed. "Not even one of them banana phones, though I bet you could try."

"Try it on yourself!" I yelled at him.

"What is this banana phone?" Amailta asked.

"Never mind! I'm probably impotent! The last thing I need is—"

"The *first* thing you need is!" she said with certainty. "You must do it now, or the nerves will atrophy and then it will be nevermore, and such a waste! So love me, Jason; I do for you what you did for me. I awaken you to new potential. I make you a man, as you made me a woman."

That made me pause. I didn't want to be impotent, and there could be something in what she said. Muscles atrophy with disuse, especially after injury.

I had suffered a serious blow, in more than one sense. How could I know whether any part of my manhood remained? The doctor thought it would work out, but surgery is never certain in a matter like that. If my crotch was numb now, would it ever change completely?

Still, this was not the occasion to find out, and Amalita was not the girl to experiment with. I had betrayed Pedro once, unwittingly; I would be doubly criminal if I betrayed him again, knowingly.

"Give me the name and get out," I said gruffly. She had a temper, and now it flash-ignited. "Jason Striker, I am not your wife! You cannot order me about!" And her fingers curled, their long nails like claws. I thought of Andy's eyes, and wondered momentarily how he was doing. And that cooled me somewhat.

"Not my mistress either," I said.

Those nails went for my face. I was ready for that. I grabbed her wrist, and we struggled under the covers in silence. It was not that I was weak or she strong; apart from my injury my health seemed good, though I still tired easily. But my will power was weakening, for I was profoundly uncertain of my continuing masculine ability. Why not test it out, since she had made it so convenient?

Because of Pedro. Her husband and my friend. Yet—

"Wait a moment," she said abruptly. "I cannot make love with a full bladder."

I was as glad as she for a pretext to end this struggle. "There's a bathroom down the hail," I said. All I wanted was to get her out of my bed and out of my room; I'd have a nurse in there before she returned.

Amalita got out, but did not leave. She reached into the bedside stand and drew out my bedpan.

"Hey!" I cried. "That thing hasn't been emptied yet!"

She peered into the pan. "You think I am blind?" She sniffed. "Or numb in the noise? But never mind; our urine shall merge first, then our bodies." She took it to the corner and squatted over it.

"You can't use it here, in plain sight!" I protested.

"Why not?" the old man asked, his eyes shining as he watched her. "Nothing gets it up like watching a shapely nude pissing!"

I shut up, realizing that this was another aspect of Amalita's seduction strategy. Some men *are* stimulated by the sight of a woman urinating. She was stopping at nothing.

I forced my eyes off her—and saw a shape in the doorway. Two shapes. Male. In robes. Doctors?

They came quietly to my bed, perhaps assuming I was asleep. The robes opened, and I saw the weapons.

They were demons.

One was wounded, the same one I had seen in bed down the hall. His arm was in a cast, but his other hand carried a long, sharp pair of hospital scissors. He must have raided the nursing supplies. The other seemed to be a fresh demon; he uncoiled from his waist a length of telephone cable, copper wire with black rubber insulation, flexible but heavy and tough as hell.

I had no time to think, but somehow realized instantly that the healthy demon had sneaked into the hospital with a dose of Kill-13 for his injured companion, and the two of them had then come to finish the job on me. I was in trouble.

I was not about to yell for a nurse now. Hospital personnel would never comprehend the situation: two fanatic addicts out to kill me while a naked woman squatted in the corner. If a nurse tried to mix in, she would get herself killed. I had to deal with this myself, and silently.

Furthermore, the demons would want it silent too. So would Amalita. We were all united in this, for widely divergent reasons. I wanted to protect lives and avoid embarrassment; the demons wanted to kill me and get away; Amalita wanted to make love, and no doubt the old man wanted to watch it all, like a living X-rated movie put on just for him.

But I had no time to meditate on this understanding, for the battle was on.

The demon with the cable advanced on my bed, his hand lifting for a devastating strike. I grabbed at my top sheet, seeking to throw it over him, if I had time. Naturally it caught on the bed, making my attempt useless.

The other demon held back momentarily, ready to stab with the scissors the moment his partner had set me up for it. His broken arm would not pain him now that he was in his Kill-13 fit, but it remained a disadvantage, hence his caution. Demons were not, after all, berserkers; they could bide their time when they needed to.

I was hung up on the sheet, trying to yank it loose while the demon prepared for a killing blow. Amalita was the first to act. In one quick motion she stood, scooped up the bedpan, and hurled it at the leading demon. The heavy metal hit him on the back of the head, making him fall to his knees in a shower of warm urine. The other demon got splashed too, and so did I.

"What a shot!" the oldster in the other bed chortled. "Crap all over you!"

The demon swept the bedpan away, then flipped something at the old man, supposing him to be another enemy. An object the size and shape of a large brown carrot flew through the air and struck him in the face, splattering like dough. Fecal matter from the pan.

At the same time, the second demon lunged for me with the scissors. But the diversion had given me time. I used my pillow as a shield. The scissors ripped through it, but did not reach me. I kicked with both feet at his middle, shoving him back.

I jumped from the bed, but got entangled again in my own sheets and fell to the floor. Some fighter I was turning out to be! The demon stabbed again with the scissors, but was hampered by the cast on his arm. I rolled on the wet floor, trying desperately to free myself from the sheet before I got stabbed. He kicked at me with his bare foot. Fortunately he was not trained for this, and did not know how to really hurt me. But he did score to my chest, midsection and thigh. My groin felt the shock, putting me in severe pain.

Then one of my hands felt a different kind of cloth. It was Amalita's blouse or halter—I still wasn't clear what that transparent bit of material should be called—and I grabbed it. There was elastic in it somewhere, so I stretched it almost as tight as her bosom had, and snapped it at him. It wasn't much of a weapon, but I wasn't in much of a shape to quibble. The end flicked against his skin with stinging force. Even a handkerchief, properly snapped, can be effective, and this had bits of metal in it. Fasteners or a zipper. I let him have it in the face, repeatedly, not letting up. He was unable to fend it off, because one arm was immobile and the other held the scissors. Finally I scored directly on his left eye.

Demons don't feel much pain, but this was more than pain. His eyeball burst, and the fluid ran down his cheek. He dropped the scissors and put his hand to his face.

I rushed him, thinking I could put him away now. I was wrong. He was half-squatting, bending over with his face in his hand as I came at him, and he hit me savagely with his cast.

The blow caught me on the hip. Something cracked. I hoped it was the cast. It was a terrific wallop, catching me entirely by surprise. I kept underestimating these demons!

He raised his cast to finish me off. I did a backward somersault and landed crouched on my feet—a spectacular but common judo maneuver—and it felt as though I had ripped out my own crotch. Oh, that surgery!

My action surprised the demon, so that he did not follow up immediately. His mistake! I launched myself in a half-tackle that caught him on the hip, under the cast. It lifted him up and threw him back against the open window—and suddenly he was gone. Five stories down.

Meanwhile Amalita was occupying the demon with the cable, bless her! She was no frail flower to sit out the action numbed with terror. She followed the thrown bedpan and leaped naked onto the demon's back just as he made his throw at the oldster. Her weight made him fall on his face. She grabbed his cable-arm and did a reverse *juji-gatame,* the "crossmark hold." She lay on her belly with his arm trapped between her thighs, both her hands holding on to his wrist. She pulled on the arm, trying to dislocate the elbow.

He was immune to the pain, and stronger than she. He fought out of it, rising to his knees and lifting his arm. She rode it up, and just as he seemed about to break free, his elbow dislocated and the cable fell from his fingers.

The fight was not over. Amalita tried to hit him with her fist as they both stood up, but he blocked it with his bad arm and back-handed her across the face with his good one. She almost fell, realizing that she could not match a man, particularly a demon, at his own type of fighting. He cared nothing about her splendid nudity, and neither pain nor injury would distract him from his intent.

So she switched to her own type of combat. Her braid was a good yard long, weighted at the end with a heavy metal ornament, a replica of the Aztec god of war. She flicked that braid across his body like a weighted chain, whipping him with surprising force. Her breasts danced with the impact of her body motions as the ornament cut into his chest, arms and face.

But demons are not much for masochism, however attractively packaged. He grabbed hold of her braid and hauled her forward and down, and he fell on top of her. She bit the hand holding her hair, forcing him to let go before the very tendons were chewed through. Then she squirmed around to get above him, her braid trailing under his shoulders; it caught there, holding her back and preventing completion of the maneuver.

She tried to achieve a leg lock, pulling his foot up with her ankle braced behind his knee, but couldn't get the leverage required. In a moment he would wrestle her around, and then he would have her.

With a fit of inspiration she caught the other end of her own hair and jerked it up around his neck. She looped it tightly and hauled back on it. The demon was held in place by the partial leg lock, and was unable to throw her off his back. As that braid constricted about his throat he turned purple—even his eyes!—wheezing for air. His tongue protruded; his good hand clawed at his throat. But he could not get a purchase on that slick braid.

And so he died, suddenly, in the way that demons do. They have little reserve for recovery; all their energies are expended in the activities of the moment.

All this had occurred in almost complete silence, and it ended as suddenly as it had started. I watched as Amalita's demon made his last gasp. The oldster was wiping stinking matter off his face.

I went to the basin and washed off my face and hands. "We must hide him," Amalita said, indicating the demon on the floor.

I slapped water across my eyes, but it didn't help. I had over-extended myself; I need a lot of rest in a hurry. "Hide him *where?* The hospital will never understand."

"Put him back in his bed. Who will know?"

"It's the wrong demon!" I said, exasperated.

"Let *them* explain it," she said.

The notion was ridiculous, but I could not think of anything better. The police would make their own kind of investigation in due course, and the hospital would keep mum, so as not to disturb the other patients. So maybe Amalita's simple logic sufficed for the occasion.

I carried the demon to the other demon's room and made him comfortable in the bed. What a surprise awaited the next nurse.

I staggered back, so tired I could hardly find my way, but relieved to have made it without attracting more notice. The demon threat was over for now, at least here in the hospital; I was just lucky they hadn't come upon me sleeping. And they would have, if it hadn't been for Amalita. She had saved my life a couple of times today. Next time I saw her, I would have to thank her.

I climbed into my bed, puffing up the wadded sheets. There was urine and dirt on them, but I lacked the energy to object. Ah, rest!

Arms grasped me. I jumped with alarm.

"You conquering hero!" Amalita murmured. "I am yours!"

Oh, good God! I had thought she had gone home. She was still naked, still hot, with none of her ardor diminished. What a creature of passion.

I was tired, but not in that fashion. "To hell with it!" I growled. I owed her something, and I knew what she wanted—and the truth was that I wanted it too.

I crushed her in my embrace, hurting her. She writhed and groaned, loving it. I suppose that to her, sex wasn't natural unless it had some pain in it. That was why she had married a man like Pedro. The preceding fracas had only made her more eager.

We struggled in a physical connection rather like that of combat. Her breath was hot upon my shoulder, and her hips moved to bring me in and force my response. Slowly, slowly my passion reached down from my brain and funneled into my groin; the nerves might be damaged, but they *were* functioning.

It was too slow for her. She had to help me some; but of course she liked that too. Her fingers grasped, massaged, kneaded, shaped, hardened and placed. I felt like a sculpture, fashioned by her hands—but when she was finished I was as hard as stone.

She sat upon me. Her braid fell across my chest. It conjured an awful vision. "Please . . ." I said. So she loosened her hair, and it fell in a fragrant curtain over my body and face. Much better.

Still the sensation was dim, as though there were still a bandage on my genitals, preventing completion. Amalita worked indefatigably to force performance. There was a tantalizingly slow culmination, with very little pleasure, and some pain for me. It was almost as if I were ejaculating blood. I was afraid I was hurting myself. I hardly enjoyed the sensation.

But the issue had been decided. I remained a man.

CHAPTER 5

KOBI CHIJA

As soon as I was safely out of the hospital, I got on the trail. The doctor had told me to rest a few more days. "Some very strange complications have happened to some of the other patients," he said, and I knew he meant the dead demon. But rest simply wasn't possible. Not with the searing memory of six dead students, one blind, and several others mutilated for life. My karate class was finished, and I didn't feel up to facing my judo classes yet. I had to do what I could to wipe out Kill-13 *now*.

I still did not know who the black karate mistress was, she who had maimed me. Only Amalita's heroic efforts had saved me, in more ways than one, and now I felt a somber guilt over that situation. I had a private (no pun!) score to settle with the black woman.

No use going to the pseudo-kung-fu temple; that had closed down while I was in the hospital. It would re-manifest under another name, with different front personnel, when the heat was off. The real urge behind the demons lay in the source of the Kill-13 drug, not in the doped acolytes.

That source would not yield to direct assault; neither police nor government agencies had made a dent in it. Arrested demons knew little, and refused to talk, and their withdrawal pangs often killed them in prison. This had led to cries of police brutality, and the police had become reluctant to make further arrests. So the matter rested; no one was going to do anything about it, while the muggings and killings went on and the Kill-13 cult grew.

No one would act but me. And I wanted to get to my new contact before it, too, dissipated. The name Amalita had whispered, in the throes of our slow, tortuous, sensuous embrace. Kobi Chija, a true kung-fu master from the orient, just setting up a school in a neighboring city. I did not know him, and had not heard of him professionally, but of course I was not conversant with kung-fu as I was with judo. There are so many variations and schools, and so many masters that never came to America. America is not the land of martial art; its citizens lack the patience to become really proficient.

Well, I would judge the man when I met him; the true professional cannot be mistaken, whatever his discipline. I certainly hoped he could help me run down Kill-13.

The address was in Chinatown. I took a bus to get there, fearing that the demons would be watching my car. I bought a newspaper, but was unable to read in the swaying vehicle. I don't usually suffer from motion sickness, but I was still a bit weak from my hospitalization, and the combination of bus fumes, jolting, and eyestrain was too much. So I concentrated on exercising my hands, using a pair of polished steel balls. These are employed by many martial artists; held in one hand and squeezed against each other, they strengthen the muscles of fingers, hand and arm.

The dojo was several blocks from the bus station. I ambled along, still feeling twinges from my surgery, still idly working the balls, newspaper tucked under my arm. There were throngs of people, by no means all Chinese. Tourists and others flocked to Chinatown to shop.

Indeed, it was an interesting place. Posters bore Chinese symbols advertising Chinese food and Chinese cinemas. People were standing in line to eat at what I presumed to be the better or cheaper establishments. The movies had English subtitles, I knew, for many Chinese had become largely Americanized no matter how they tried to cling to the old ways. Bilingual posters urged people not to be taken in by Communist China. There were many souvenir stores, and from the look of it some had excellent Chinese goods. And food markets with whole smoked ducks, chickens and geese hanging in the windows. Crows watched the fish being cut and gutted; for a moment I wished I were a crow.

I was glad I hadn't tried to drive in. There was absolutely no parking place, every possible space was full. People were walking, shopping, or just standing around talking at a great rate, and I couldn't understand a word. I passed a Buddhist temple, with its statue of Buddha in the middle of the street. And a Chinese museum, evidently a tourist trap, with a fake dragon inside. Even the telephone booths looked Chinese, with Chinese roofs.

My resistance to the blandishments of the merchants expired as I passed a pastry shop. I stopped and tried ineffectively to bargain down what I knew to be a steep tourist price, but the aroma was horribly good, and I was hungry, and the wily proprietor knew he had me hooked. Never tackle a professional at his own game! I bought a fancy pastry whose name I did not know, and ate it while I glanced over a newsstand full of Chinese magazines and books, and listened to Chinese music. There was even a Chinese liquor store with several kinds of *mai-tai*, whatever that was. Fierce, I was sure.

I heard something. It sounded uncomfortably familiar. I stopped to listen.

The sound came again. Yes, it was the eerie attack cry of the demons!

I gulped down the rest of my pastry, dismayed. Demons, here? Had they followed me after all?

No, they would hardly have warned me by making that sound from such a distance. They were up to some other mischief, and suddenly I had a notion what that might be.

I broke into a run, heading for the sound. Soon I saw the

source: a group of demons were closing in on two people. The region was quickly becoming cleared; though there were hundreds in the area, no one wanted to get involved. Old Chinese men, muttering in their native language; young Chinese girls with long black hair, speaking English; a few walking skeletons from an opium den; all pretending not to notice, while beating an expeditious retreat down the narrow, crooked streets.

This was partly mass cowardice, but mostly good sense. Demons could maim and kill, and seemed to have some immunity from the law. Why risk everything for a stranger?

My lip curled with contempt. I understood the attitude, but I also knew that those who tolerated such things would find no help when they themselves were abused. Each man had better be his brother's keeper, if he fears anarchy.

Meanwhile, seven, no, eight armed demons were attacking what I now saw to be an old man and a young woman. The man had a hand fan, the kind that used to be popular on hot days before air conditioning became rampant. The girl had only a handbag. I was still two blocks away; I knew I would not arrive in time to fend off those demons, and was not certain I could do anything against such a number, anyway. Even in top condition, which I was not, and with a weapon, which I had not. I was already panting, and my *nunchaku* was at home.

A weapon: perhaps I was not that badly off. I began folding my newspaper as I ran.

As the distance narrowed between us, I could only watch, knowing I was too late. Demons needed no more than seconds to kill. That could be another origin of the name of the drug: kill in thirteen seconds?

I saw the attackers make a circle about the two, cutting off escape, and the victims didn't even seem to be trying to run, knowing it was hopeless. The first demon came at the old man with a small knife. It looked like an *aikuchi tanto,* a Japanese blade that was ordinarily concealed within a wooden tube. It was dangerous, however. An ancient switchblade.

The old man made what seemed to be a futile gesture: he slapped the demon's face with the fan. But the demon fell back, his hands going to his head, and I saw even from my running distance the blood welling from an ugly cut across his cheeks and nose. Cut? No, his nose and cheekbones were smashed, his lips pulped against the stumps of his teeth. How had that happened?

A second demon lunged. The old man folded his fan with a flick of the wrist and drove it into the chest of this attacker. And, amazingly, the demon crumpled to the pavement.

Meanwhile the girl was busy too. A demon came at her with a knife. She made a half-turn and raised her handbag, intercepting the blade with it. The demon tried to punch her in the face, but she kicked him twice in succession in the stomach, and continued with an upward knee blow to the same area. She grabbed his shoulders and pulled downward to add force to the blow. That demon was finished.

Those were quite some kicks, not only in their effect on the demon, but in their effect on me. They were straight and swift and hard, beautifully executed. More than that, she had a beautifully structured leg. She was wearing a long Chinese dress, slitted to mid-thigh so that her legs could move freely despite the tightness of its fit. The knee-blow was especially provocative. That sudden, spectacular exposure was out of place in a street brawl, but my mind should have been on more important matters. I was still obsessed by my marginal masculine ability, so that many innocent things took on a sexual context. Any accidental display of female anatomy . . .

But I think that leg would have impressed me anytime.

Three demons had been downed, and now the girl had the knife she had captured with her handbag. She used it to slash the next demon across the cheek, a deep gash, not enough to put him out of commission although his teeth were visible in the hole made by the dangling flap of cheek. The pain would have been enough to disable a normal man, but these were not normal.

Then another attacker struck her forearm with a blackjack and disarmed her. At the same time a demon stabbed at the old man from behind with a huge butcher knife. The man jumped aside alertly, but he was hemmed in by demons he had just overcome, and the knife cut deeply into his forearm. His fan fell; the man was now helpless, perhaps bleeding to death. Not that the demons would give him time for that.

But this action had given me the chance to catch up. In the last block I folded and refolded my newspaper, forming it into a lengthwise rod, then bending that over. The result was a short, solid club about a foot long. Few people realize how deadly a folded newspaper can be. I held it by the loose ends and swung the folded end at the arm that held the butcher knife. I connected to the side of the forearm, breaking it.

I was in the thick of it now. A face was above me, and I whipped the newspaper up to strike him under the chin. He went down. Anybody would have, clubbed like that; even a brain that feels no pain can't maintain consciousness in the face of concussion.

I whirled and bashed another demon on the shoulder, I must have broken his shoulder bone, but I had to hit him twice more before he fell. The demon tried to seize my leg, and I kicked viciously backward, stomping him with my heel till he let go.

But this gave the demon armed with the butcher cleaver a chance to approach me. He swung. I dodged and managed to hit him on the side of the head by releasing one end of the folded newspaper like a whip. It was not enough. I lunged with the end, using the paper like a rapier, but it was battered now, and bent, and lacked rigidity. He sliced down, cutting the newspaper in half. Well, it had been a good weapon while it lasted.

Then I felt strong arms grab me from behind. I was momentarily helpless, and the demon with the cleaver was swinging again. I tried to move, but the arms about me were like iron. I never ceased to be amazed at demon strength.

Luckily the girl came to my rescue, using her umbrella to hook one foot of the demon from behind and pull him down. I hadn't seen that umbrella before; she must have had it behind her when she handled the other demon. The demon's swing fell short of me, as he tumbled down. He turned on the ground and aimed at her legs. She jumped back, releasing the umbrella. That gave me time to reach up and grab his hanging flap of cheek—this one holding me was the demon she had cut before—and I pulled it down to the jawbone. That completed the ruin of his face, which had not been pretty to start with. If the pain didn't faze him, the destruction of his body did. He released me and felt for his face with both hands.

I whirled and punched him hard twice on the jaw, but did not have the balance to put him away. I grabbed the two steel balls from my pocket and put one in each palm. They weighted my fists, an unfair advantage I would not have taken in friendly sparring. Then I hit him in the nose, my hand wrapped about the ball, and it was as if a stone had struck him. The pounding of my buttressed fists completed the demolition of his head, and finally he went down forever.

Even in the throes of struggle, this amazing determination bothered me. These demons had to be literally destroyed before they gave up. They could suffer horrendous wounds, yet keep fighting. There simply was no reasonable limit; the only not-dangerous demon was a dead one.

Now I turned to the cleaver-wielding man, the one the girl had distracted in time to save my life. He had her cornered against the wall, and evidently was immune to her kicks. She had hold of his wrist, but one of her arms had been injured by the blackjack blow, and she could not match his strength. The cleaver was bearing down.

They were too far away; I could not get there in time.

I threw one of my balls, hard. It grazed his head. The aim of the second was better; the cleaver dropped at the feet of the girl, and he followed it down, as well he might.

I started to go after him, to recover my ball, but saw that it was embedded in his skull. I would have to pry it out of his head, with bits of brain clinging to it, and I really didn't want my ball that much. I was not hardened to killing, or even to violence; how much better it would have been to have avoided this entire battle.

But then two people would have been killed by the demons.

I turned to the old man, who was holding his torn arm together as though it were a mere scratch. "Kobi Chija, I presume," I said.

He made a little bow. "It is an honor to meet you, Jason Striker," he murmured. He could not shake hands; already the blood was welling through the fingers holding his wound together. To release that hold was to bleed, copiously.

So he recognized me! But of course my face had been widely televised at the time of the Martial Open last year.

"This is my daughter, Chiyako," he said. She bowed solemnly, a demure and quite pretty Chinese girl.

Kobi Chija was tall and slender, almost bony, with a wispy gray beard, mustaches and fairly long gray hair. He had a mole under one nostril, and was missing a front tooth. It was typical of such men that they lacked the vanity to have false teeth made. He seemed to be over sixty years old, with skin stretched taut like yellowed parchment across his cheekbones, though he had a certain ageless quality.

His daughter was something else again. She too was tall and slender, almost as tall as her father. But she was in the peak of youth, with luxurious black hair piled up high, ivory skin, rosy cheeks, black eyes and a perfectly proportioned figure. The fight had messed up her appearance so that her elaborate coiffure was coming apart, her *cheong*, or ankle-length Chinese dress, was torn, and one arm was bruised. But her beauty transcended details.

I had already admired her leg; the rest of her measured up.

"Please enter my humble abode," Kobi said, making a small half-bow. Then he stepped over a body toward his house. I walked beside him, while his daughter followed about five paces back, in the Chinese way.

We entered his dojo. As with many such establishments, home and school were one. He had rented a large old house and converted the big front room into his kung-fu hall, with a *tatami* or exercise mat covering the floor. There were folding chairs along the walls, silk banners above them, and a display of assorted weapons. At one end was a high wooden chair, almost like a throne, from which he would normally conduct his classes.

We continued on through the hanging curtains that set off the living quarters, passed a couple of smaller rooms he evidently used as offices, and entered a large kitchen-cum-dining room with adjacent bathroom.

We exchanged pleasantries as though this were a social visit and there had been no savage battle in the street. The girl took care of her father's wound, cleaning it out and binding it competently, and he never flinched or interrupted his speech despite the pain. I knew that "face" was vitally important to Chinese; proper appearances, had to be kept up no matter what. So I ignored the proceedings as well as I could, knowing that any reference to their evident poverty—Kobi had no maid or other help, and probably had refrained from calling a doctor because of the cost—would be gauche.

I acquainted him with my campaign against Kill-13, omitting only certain details about the hospital fracas. Kobi nodded wisely. "These demons are powerful adversaries. So determined, so swift I am ashamed for my art, that I went out with my daughter so carelessly and was so readily wounded."

"They're swift, all right," I agreed. "They are immune to pain, and they don't much care whether they live or die. One demon is more than a match for one normal man; you faced eight, and they were armed." I did not add the obvious: he was old, they young.

"But I too was armed," he said. He brought out his fan, holding it in his good hand. Meanwhile Chiyako was pouring some strong-smelling antiseptic in the wound; I saw the skin redden as the stuff burned through.

"The fan?" I asked, not wishing to appear incredulous.

"The *tessen.*" He passed it over to me for examination. The thing had iron ribs covered by special decorated paper. The edges were razor sharp, and when folded together the thing was like a knife. No wonder those two demons had collapsed so suddenly!

"Your weapons, too, are admirable," Kobi said.

I shrugged, remembering the newspaper and steel balls. "One must use what is available, especially against the demons." Now the girl took out a needle and thread and began stitching the wound closed. I did not want to be too obvious in averting my eyes, so I had to look, casually. I'm hardly squeamish, but I had just had a rough fight, and I began to feel faint at this surgery. Kobi had taken no anesthetic, and Chiyako had no special equipment. How could they stand it, both of them?

"Yet these people have many admirable qualities," Kobi said after a moment.

"The *demons?*" I demanded.

"Certainly. A martial artist must train rigorously for many years to achieve the speed, power and control that these demons exhibit from the outset. Their selfless devotion to their cause, their fearlessness in the face of battle."

"Maybe so," I said, amazed at his generosity. I had not seen it that way, but now recognized it as an attitude in him that impressed me. Small men—and I don't mean physically—are not generous. "Yet you seem to be in trouble with them."

He nodded agreement. "I intended only to set up an honest kung-fu dojo, but they oppose this." Chiyako was binding his arm in gauze. Some man—and some girl!

"No mystery about that," I said. "The demons call themselves members of the Kung-Fu Temple, mockery as that is. A legitimate kung-fu establishment, with a genuine *sifu*, that would show them up for the fakes they are."

"Perhaps," he agreed. "I did not at first concern myself with them. But first they threatened, then intruded, as you have observed. They would not let me go in peace, and so, necessarily, I opposed them. It was not my choice."

And that opposition had brought the two of us together. It was evident that Kobi did not know any more about the demons or their source of supply than I did; Pedro's informant must have assumed that anyone the demons wanted to get rid of was a real threat to their operations. Thus Amalita's information was worth less than we had thought. But somehow I didn't mind at all; I was exceedingly glad to have made the acquaintance of this fine man and his daughter.

Chiyako departed silently, but soon returned with a plate of Chinese delicacies. I wondered how they were able to afford good food, but remembered that many established Chinese would feel it a privilege to make gifts of food to a genuine *sifu*. I was sure Kobi would not accept anything else. So he would be forced to eat unaffordably elegant meals, when simplicity was his style.

We moved into a moderate Chinese meal during our conversation, and I was mystified how she accomplished it, for she had had almost no time to prepare. First there was dried seaweed, green like spinach but salty tasting. Then jellied jellyfish. And small pieces of raw fish with vinegar, salt and oil. Some fruits in heavy syrup. Then some nice shark-fin soup with pieces of the dark fin, showing. And finally some fierce *mai-tai* liquor, the same kind I had seen in the store. I only tasted that, out of politeness. I was glad I knew how to handle chopsticks.

At some point Chiyako had slipped out again and washed her face and let down her hair. She had applied makeup: white powder on her cheeks. Now her hair flowed blue-black down her back, perfumed and straight. She wore a silk kimono tied at the waist with a red sash, and tight white pants underneath. She looked younger.

I was struck again by her beauty, and was constrained to analyze it. She was handsome of face and form, true, but it was more than that. She moved with an unobtrusive grace, with a perfect precision and balance, but it was more than that, too. She knew how to fight, and fight well, and had the courage to perform a kind of surgery without fuss on her own father. But even that was not it. There was something she shared with Kobi, a composure in adversity, a dignity, but not ordinary dignity. A special nobility, with indefinable yet unique attributes.

"If I may ask," I said carefully, concentrating on my chopsticks as though they symbolized something of life and death importance, "what is your school of kung fu?"

"Shaolin," Kobi said.

But there were many forms of Shaolin. "Northern or Southern?" My hands were so tight I was afraid the chopsticks would break.

"Northern."

Then it fell into place. I had had experience with Northern Shaolin kung-fu, and had developed a fundamental respect for it. I had met men like Kobi, men that shared that aura, that philosophy. I had deep memories of respect, power, horror and grief.

I covered my face, but there was no concealing my abrupt emotion. It is no shame in the orient for a man to cry; Samurai warriors in Japan do it, and Chinese too. But it was acutely embarrassing for me.

"Please tell us your story," Kobi said, taking no more notice of my condition than I had of his.

I told:

CHAPTER 6

SHAOLIN

Somebody was hauling me through the water. For a confused moment I thought it was a crocodile. But it was a man, whether friend or foe I could not tell. He brought me to the overgrown shore and pumped the water out of me. Then he doctored the gashes in my hand and side. I lay there and let him work, though I was now conscious; he seemed to know what he was doing. He was a powerful, silent man.

But he was on to me. "Up, friend," he said in Khmer, the Cambodian language. I decided not to pretend ignorance; I was weak, in no condition for resistance, and I owed him my life.

He was a monk. He had a shaven head, was on the thin side, and seemed to be about fifty years old. His face was lined, his hands were gnarled with two fingers missing, from the left, and he walked with a limp. Yet he was strong and competent. He wore long saffron robes and wooden sandals, and carried a wooden staff and a begging bowl. His name, I learned later, was Tao.

He led me miles through the jungle to his monastery. It squatted on the slope of a mountain, and even though I was largely ignorant of the nuances of Eastern architecture I could tell that the style was primarily Chinese. It seemed old, very old; perhaps it had been built centuries before by Chinese missionaries. It had a wide front entrance, an outer court, an inner court, a chapel, and a number of small chambers for the residence and activities of the monks. It all seemed rather ordinary as monasteries went, but I was soon to be disabused of that impression.

For this was a Shaolin temple, and the monks practiced that aspect of the faith known as "Northern" though this was in fact well south of China. A Northern Shaolin monk is not an ordinary man.

They fed me a bowl of brown rice with fish heads and tails in it, and of course the wretched *nouc nam* sauce. Also an appetizer of a bowl of clear soup with small round quails' eggs in it, and a few Chinese beans and bean sprouts. The monks, it developed, were vegetarians; they consumed fish, eggs and milk, but no meat, and rice was their mainstay. But I was hungry, tired and wounded, and this was a feast. I struggled with the unfamiliar chopsticks, for there was no spoon.

Then I was conducted through narrow corridors, past a statue of Buddha, down to a stone cell with one high window opening onto ground level outside. A monk took care of my wounds, applying native dressings with seeming competence; at any rate, I felt better. My bed was a straw pallet on the floor, comfortable enough. We can do quite nicely without the amenities of civilized, technological life when we have to, perhaps better than *with* them. I slept well.

Next morning I was awoken at five A.M., the monks' normal time of arising, and I joined them in their communal dining hall for a frugal breakfast. There were about thirty monks in all. After prayers and food they dispersed to their several occupations. Some went to the fields beyond the monastery to work until afternoon; others took their begging bowls on a trek to the nearest village. A simple, stifled life, as I judged it. Mistakenly.

I had an audience with the head monk, Yee Chuen. I wasn't sure of his exact title, as it was rendered in Chinese, but he was obviously the man in charge. He was a tall, spare old man, his skin leathered by the sun. His entire head was clean shaven: beard, brows, hair. His skin was taut parchment stretched across the cheekbones. His teeth were not good. But he was spry and moved rapidly and with certainty. I could not know it then, but his face and form were to have a profound effect on my imagination, so that whenever afterwards I saw a man like him, certain emotions were evoked.

"It is good to have you with us, Mr. Striker," he greeted me in Khmer. "We very nearly lost you."

I stiffened. I had told no monk my name.

"No, no, be at ease," he said immediately. "We know you because we came to free you from your captivity. Unfortunately, there was some confusion. We had not expected you to escape by yourself. You are a resourceful man! Your trail was devious."

"You were going to rescue me?" I demanded. "I thought the monks took no part in the fighting." But I realized that if these were Chinese monks, they might well be refugees from the Chinese Communists. They could have renovated this old building, that no one else wanted. They would have no brief for the Vietminh.

"That is true. But we had a vision, and knew that you could not be permitted to die at this time."

I pondered. "What do you want from me?"

"Nothing, friend," Yee said.

"I can't give you any information about my mission."

"We do not want it. We are simple folk, largely unaware of external matters."

Now I was good and suspicious. Simple folk seldom think of themselves that way. How clever were the Cong getting? This seemed to be a legitimate monastery, but it was possible that money or terror had subverted it. Had they agreed to take me in and use gentle persuasion to get military information I would not otherwise yield?

"This rescue mission," I said. "How did you propose to get me away from the Cong?" I was sure they would have a cover story, but perhaps there would be holes in it, clues that would betray their collusion with the Cong, Vietminh or whatever.

For though I was wary, I was not entirely satisfied that I was in enemy hands. These monks were difficult to corrupt. Sometimes such establishments did help downed American pilots. It depended on the individual situation.

And of course I wanted to believe in my freedom. I knew that the instinct for survival could be my own undoing, but still I wanted to live.

"We sent an agent to release you," he said.

"No agent came," I said flatly.

"It was difficult, because the enemy is vigilant. They must have discovered her despite our precautions."

Every nerve charged. *"Her?"*

"A young woman. You did not see her?"

A young woman. I felt suddenly sick. "Did she have a nice figure and a deformed nose?"

He nodded. "We are celibate, but your description is accurate. She was comely, and her nose was crooked. Her family had been killed by the enemy, and we fed her, and she asked to help us. She could not help us in her normal fashion, but was ideal for this particular task." Delicately put, the girl was obviously a part-time prostitute, hardly a service honest monks could afford. But she had been an excellent infiltrator among soldiers. "She was to wait a few days, diverting suspicion, then release you at night and lead you to us. But she did not return. We found her body where they had left it, carelessly thrown away, after they had beaten her to death."

Beaten to death . . .

Even if this were all part of a plot to make me talk, it had been wrong for me to kill her. I could have gone along with the plan, just as I was doing now. The issue was still to be decided, but at least she would be alive.

And if these monks really were trying to help me—how much

worse that killing was! In that case, I could not ethically accept my freedom from them. I would have to stand trial for murder.

To hell with it! I was not about to start lying to protect my hide. "Father, the Cong did not kill her. I did."

He did not show emotion. "Why?"

"I thought she was an enemy agent."

He did not respond, so I blurted out the whole story. "Take your vengeance now," I concluded, sure that if these people were legitimate, they would.

"Vengeance?" he looked puzzled.

"I killed your agent, when she meant me no harm. My life is forfeit." I was aware that this sounded like a masochistic streak in me, a wanting to be punished. But it was the way I felt. I have never killed with equanimity; there is always a deep remorse, an impossible desire to wipe the slate clean.

Yee shook his head. "Jason Striker, you have much to learn."

"No use to spare me. I will not tell you my mission. So you will gain nothing by keeping me alive."

"Indeed, we *shall* keep you alive," he said firmly. "And we shall teach you what we must. Only now do I comprehend the second level of the vision."

This hardly reassured me. "You can torture me, but I doubt if it will help you. You don't have the facilities to get my information, and I don't think the Cong do, either, or they would not have tried anything like this."

Still he looked at me sadly, as though I were an erring child. "It is not enough for us to free you; we must prepare you for your true mission."

"I won't tell you my mission!"

"How could you? You do not know it, as we do not." A strange ploy, but it wouldn't work. "Many years will pass before that mission comes clear. We shall not live to see it, but you will do it in your own time, if only our instruction is good. Therein lies our justification for existence."

I stared at him. "I don't understand!"

"Jason Striker, it is seldom given to a man to understand, yet he performs as he must. Had you comprehended our philosophy before this, that girl would not have had to die." That was as close as he ever came to reproving me on that score. Not that he needed to; my guilt was already deeply embedded in my conscience.

"I'll try to escape, if I get the chance!" I warned him.

"There is no escape from destiny," he said. "Not for any of us, however we might wish it." And he seemed mortally sad. I did not comprehend his reason until much later, way too late.

Yee clapped his hands and the monk Tao appeared. "Show Mr. Striker our demesne. Do not hinder him; he will remain with us of his own accord."

"I will do no such thing!" I protested. "Are you naive?" He gave no answer to that. I followed the monk out of the chamber and down the narrow halls. The monastery was a large stone building, more intricate than I had thought the day before. It was like a small town, self contained, with big courtyards devoted to little vegetable and flower gardens. Statues of Buddha were everywhere. There were cisterns to collect rain water, and it was always pure, but when I got a bucketful myself I discovered giant water cockroaches in it.

We entered the central court, with flowers growing around the fringe. There was a modest fountain in the center, and assorted fish in the water: huge black and gold goldfish and others I couldn't make out. Monkeys perched atop the walls, watching us and crying out reproachfully.

"It is time for my practice," Tao said. "Will you indulge me, Ling?"

Another monk stepped from the silent shadows, nodding.

Tao turned to me. "Would you care to watch?"

I shrugged. Whatever he was leading up to, I would have to go along. "If it is all right with you," I said to the other monk.

He did not answer, and I thought my Khmer was inadequate; I was hardly expert in that language. "Ling does not speak," Tao explained. "The Vietminh cut out his tongue."

Oh.

Tao and Ling removed their robes to reveal surprisingly well-developed bodies. I had been unobservant before; these monks were muscular, not flabby. I realized that if I had tried to bolt for my freedom, I could have been brought up rather short. No flaccid ascetics here.

Of course I had judo and karate training, third degree black belt in judo, second in karate. I could handle myself. But I was weak from my Cong experience and my injuries. Unless I put such men away quickly, I would be in trouble. Not that I intended to start anything at the moment.

At any rate, Tao had already succeeded in showing me one hazard in my potential escape. I would not underestimate my bodyguards.

Ling got a spear. Tao picked up a pole about four feet long with a giant curved blade attached to the end, rather like a scimitar. I had never seen a weapon like it, and was amazed to see such devices in the hands of these monks.

"Quando," Tao said, noting my puzzlement. "Feel it." And he held it out to me.

I hefted it. The thing was heavy, like an axe, but well balanced. A weapon, surely, but unusable for close quarter combat, as it would be far too slow. No doubt it was used for cutting high vines out of the way during maneuvers; the blade was razor sharp.

Tao took it back and faced Ling. The two bowed formally to each other. The ritual was slow and precise, almost like a dance.

Then Ling lunged forward, the sharp point of his spear driving for Tao's stomach. I leaped up involuntarily, my mind's eye seeing Tao treacherously skewered.

But Tao was already moving. Smoothly he parried the strike with the shaft of his quando. I was amazed at the facility with which he handled the heavy implement; I could hardly have done it, even in top condition.

Tao raised the rear portion of his weapon so that it was level, just above his opponent's spear. He changed his footing; amateurs don't realize how important the stance is in combat, and swung the great blade about. Right for Ling's neck.

As the flat of the blade threatened Ling's head, Tao made a high kick to Ling's ribs, then jumped back into what I recognized as the kung-fu cat stance.

Kung-fu. Something clicked. I knew little about it, except that it was a Chinese form of karate, many of whose schools affected religious overtones. Shaolin, that could be a form of the martial art.

The mock battle was over; I recognized it now as mere practice, every aggressive move and defense scripted in advance. No wonder lunge and parry had been coordinated so beautifully; these two monks must have done those same motions a hundred times before, just as we practiced the judo *katas*.

Still, I was impressed. Precision drill is as close to genuine combat as you can get without doing the real thing, and any mistake can be fatal. "You must be terrors in battle," I remarked.

"Battle?" Tao looked blank.

"Well, when a bandit attacks you, and you have to fight for your life. Those weapons—"

"Bandits do not attack us," he said. "We do not fight with weapons."

I stepped back mentally and took stock. Something was funny here. More language trouble? "You are expert with weapons! I just watched."

He smiled comprehendingly. "You see no use for a weapon except combat?"

"That's right," I said, feeling inexplicably defensive.

"Take up the quando," he said.

"Now wait a bit!" I exclaimed. "I'm no match for you with the—"

"Peace, friend! Trust me, as I trust you."

These words were like a stab in the gut. I *didn't* trust him, or any of these monks. Yet suddenly I knew I *ought* to, and I wanted to. They had no reason to kill me treacherously; they could do the job openly, anytime, and call it an execution. After what I had done to the girl . . .

I, on the other hand, had plenty of reason to kill any monk I could. I had nothing to lose, and my freedom to gain. One savage swipe at Tao, and a swift kick to Ling's groin, and I had a fighting chance. I had not agreed to stay here; I had promised to escape, any time I could.

I took the quando. It seemed lighter now, and its balance somehow extended out from its wood and metal and transfused into my arm, lending me strength.

"Move it," Tao said softly.

I moved it. The head swung about smoothly, reminding me of a comment about, of all things, a car. The Mercedes. One did not steer it, one aimed it. That was the way of this fine weapon. Like the precision machinery, a touch would guide it true.

"You feel it," Tao said.

"I feel it." I shook my head. "But *what* do I feel?"

"The spirit of the weapon."

At another time I would have disparaged this as fantasy. Now I could not.

"Is it a malignant spirit?" he asked me gently. "Do you have the urge to kill, to destroy?"

"No," I said, at a loss to analyze it. "I only—I only want to— to experience it. As well as I can."

He moved to stand squarely before me. "Kill me."

I hefted the quando again. I was amazed at the sensations within me. He was offering me escape, but the weapon resisted as though enchanted. "No, I can't do that. This is, this is not for killing."

"You have taken a step," he said, smiling. "A weapon is for training, not killing. You know that now. For building up the body, not destroying it. Each weapon emphasizes a slightly different aspect of the user's body." He took the quando again. "This builds strength, a living, moving power, all in perfect proportion. It develops the elbows along with the biceps, so that neither will be injured when ultimate force is assayed."

"Yes, I understand, now," I said, realizing the truth of his words as he spoke them. The weapon was a bit like a ouija board, in which the subject's smallest inner motives were translated into physical motion that in turn offered clues about the person. And perfect control of the weapon led to control of the man, for he could not make the weapon perform properly unless the inner being of the man was proper. The men who spoke of beating a sword into a plowshare failed to comprehend the true nature of the weapons.

"You are very quick to comprehend," Tao said. "Some never do."

"I pity them," I said. And I meant it.

"Would you like to watch the other weapons?"

I could only nod affirmatively. Tao had opened a horizon to me that was miraculous in its implications. In all my life I had never understood the fundamental nature of weapons, until now. And there was so much more to learn.

*

The bigger they come, it is said, the harder they fall. My ignorance had been enormous, and the implications of its dissipation were staggering. I had thought I had known something about martial art, and I had known considerably less than I suspected. The man who recognizes his ignorance may be better off than the one who doesn't realize his limits.

That day I went to the head monk, Yee Chuen, and begged to become a student of the Shaolin art. I was ready to sweep the floor and wash the pots and grub in the earth like any novice, and practice the horse-stance until I could maintain it indefinitely, no matter how great the pain in my cramped legs became. Better that than keeping a cramped awareness. There were mysteries here that it was worth a lifetime to learn; I knew that now. The revelation of the quando . . .

But even in these expectations, I was naive. "We do not spend years on difficult positions," Yee said. "Southern Shaolin monks do, but there we differ with our brothers. If a man can move, he can stand still. It is motion we teach, and it is pointless to delay it. We do not understand the style of the South; here we concentrate on what is important, without hindrance or pain. Those who master the weapons, the motions, also achieve a powerful stance."

So I proceeded directly to practice with the weapons, to my joy. First I worked by myself, because I was a complete novice. There was no discrimination against me; in fact the Shaolin monks went out of their way to assist me. But it would have been a waste of time for me to attempt the paired exercises too soon.

I worked on the staff first. This was nothing more than a pole. In fact, I made my own implement by going out into the forest and cutting a sapling. I could have run for my freedom right then, but the head monk had known what he was talking about. I remained of my own accord. No physical bonds could have been as effective as the emotional ones that held me. I had to master this unique nonviolent science of weapons.

My homemade staff was not straight, strong or well-balanced, but in fashioning it myself I came to understand it better. Slowly the ungainly thing became a part of me, and I a part of it, for the sweat of my effort was in it. I practiced the forms, and the staff was a good teacher, because it magnified my errors. If one of my hands was a fraction out of place, the tip of the staff could be a foot off course. My whole body had to be just right, or the forms were impossible to complete. Even the slight misalignment of one leg, which I did not notice, became critical with the staff.

This was discipline: not harsh but exacting. I worked a week on the staff, many hours a day, before I had confidence to try another weapon. It was some of the most intensive training I had ever had. I learned to breathe the way of the true martial artist: into my lower abdomen, displacing my diaphragm. I emulated the life of the monks, going out to labor in the fields, for I felt that only thus could I assimilate the full spirit of the weapon. Weapon, Shaolin, and hard work, all were facets of this way of life.

Meanwhile, my body healed. These martial monks practiced yoga to limber the body, and I went through these gentle exercises too. The ravages of my imprisonment by the Cong faded; not only was I whole again, I was a better man than I had been. Not merely physically.

I worked on the quando, the trident fork, the chain, the double hook axes, the *tonfas* and the other weapons of the monastery. I also sparred with the sturdy monks barehanded, using my judo and karate techniques. Here I was competent; I could take down most of the monks, and knew some techniques they didn't. They had things to teach me too, however. One was the ability to draw the gonads up into the body cavity, so that they could not be injured by a blow or kick. This sort of thing does not occur to most Western fighters, as the groin is a forbidden target. But elsewhere in the world this is not so, and any street fighter will go for the groin too. So I practiced? gonad control, especially during the yoga sessions, and trained myself to do this whenever I took on a living opponent. It became an almost automatic reaction; I did it without conscious control. One could never tell when such an ability would come in handy.

But my surpassing interest was the weapons. I had never had use for a double-edged sword before; now I handled it with an almost spiritual reverence. It no longer seemed strange that monks should be martial artists; weapons and religion were highly compatible.

I had, however, some unfinished business with the Cong. I told the head monk, that I needed to take a couple days off, and he merely waved his hand amenably. "You are our guest," he said. "You may go as you wish, without consulting any of us." No one questioned me, and no one followed me; I retained enough caution to check on that. I really was free to go.

I made my way to the place where my party had been ambushed. Sure enough, the Cong had ransacked our supplies, removed all our food and money, and thrown away what they couldn't use or didn't understand, including two of the tiny sensors. Not surprising, since these were disguised as spent explosive shells. I carried both kinds, regular and camouflaged, so the Cong would not realize how many I had. In case of capture.

I didn't know whether these two were still operative after weeks of exposure to the rigors of the jungle, but I couldn't leave them there. If any knowledgeable Cong happened across them, one of our prime military secrets would be exposed.

I did what I had to, but my heart was no longer in it, if it had ever been. This war had never appealed to me, and now it sickened me. All I wanted to do was get back to the Shaolin monastery. Oh, I was not about to betray any secrets; I just wanted to get quit of destruction and return to positive things, like yoga and weapons-discipline.

I couldn't just hide the two sensors; the Cong might have metal-detecting equipment. I couldn't bury them or throw them in the river; they might corrode into "ON" position and summon a useless bombing raid. I couldn't even destroy them; they were designed to be tough. I simply had to keep them with me until I could either use them, which I had no intention of doing, or return them.

So I fastened them in my trousers and forgot about them. The monks would not pry; they had strict covenants regarding personal privacy.

I returned and resumed training. And one day Yee summoned me and gave me a remarkable gift: a weapon of my own.

This was no casual gesture; I was free to use and keep any weapon in the monastery's considerable arsenal. But such acquisition would not have been proper. I needed that particular weapon that was right for me, for my physique, mentality, and future. For my fighting soul, though the weapon was really a symbol of my peace of soul. That no longer seemed paradoxical. The head monk had spent months studying me, as he studied all his flock, and now he had decided on the appropriate weapon.

"You have done well, Jason Striker," he began. "Never before has a man progressed so rapidly from novice to trainee. You have considerable natural talent and an unusual devotion, and your mind is responsive."

I bowed my head. "There is so much more to be done, Venerable."

"You will do it with your ideal weapon."

I nodded my head affirmatively, eager to know which instrument he had chosen. The fierce double-bladed sword? The mighty trident? The staid *tonfa*? How had he judged my character?

"The nunchaku," he said.

This fell somewhat flat. I had never heard of it.

He brought out two thin clubs tied together by a short cord. The arrangement looked inefficient as hell. I tried to conceal my disappointment. Maybe he was testing me, before unveiling a real weapon.

He smiled benignly. "Come to the practice court."

At the court, he stripped to a white loincloth and took the awkward sticks. "Take any weapon," he told me.

I had not before practiced with the head monk. He was doing me a signal honor, yet I did not know how to react. He was an old man, however well preserved, and much smaller than I. Yet I could not tell him no. He was the Master.

So I chose the sword, intending to make a show of technique without really pressing the attack. Even the ritual motions can be dangerous, and this was *not* a ritual. I did not want to hurt him accidentally.

We bowed and commenced.

I jumped at Yee with my sword held high as I gave a *kiai* yell. Unfazed, he swung his linked sticks overhead and down in a figure eight, checking my thrust. I drew back, momentarily baffled by the intricate maneuver. He followed, maintaining the pattern, the heavy wood blurring with the speed of its motion. Daunted, I gave ground cautiously.

Suddenly I lunged under his swing with the tip of my sword, like a fencer. But Yee swung aside nimbly and the tip of his weapon tapped me lightly on the head. Even that token contact had me reeling. The wood was solid, capable of smashing a skull, *my* skull; I had suddenly been made aware of that.

Yee laughed ringingly. He was toying with me. I had never heard him laugh before, and it was annoying as hell. My head still stung from the blow; my brain had been jarred, and I did what I had thought was unthinkable: I got mad at the head monk.

I screamed "Kiiii!" and started a furious series of overhead and downward cuts. I wanted to kill him!

Yee gave ground, blocking each cut expertly. Suddenly he executed a *taisa baki* sidewise movement. The chain of the nunchaku wrapped around my sword. He heaved; the sword went flying through the air. I was disarmed.

He put his feet on the blade, bent down, grabbed it, and threw it back to me. "Is that the best you can do, novice?" he demanded.

I saw red. I stooped, gathered a handful of dirt from the garden, and threw it in Yee's face. He was momentarily blinded. I took the sword and charged him. But he continued to swing those linked clubs in a dazzling pattern, and I could not get close enough to strike effectively. I was astonished; he could not see me, yet he was impervious!

Then one stick shot out, under my guard, and struck me in the stomach. The breath went out of me and I pitched forward. He clubbed me again on the head, not so gently this time. It hurt awfully, but did not knock me out, and I knew that was the way he had intended it. He had humiliated me.

"My son, you need more patience," he said. "And more practice. Never let any man taunt you into carelessness; never allow anger to blind you." He put the devastating weapon, the nunchaku, into my hands and left me.

It had been a most effective lesson.

*

So I practiced with the nunchaku. It still seemed clumsy in comparison to the other weapons, but now I knew that this was not the fault of the sticks but of the man. After all, only a few weeks ago I had been clumsy with chopsticks, but now I was adept. What I could do with the little sticks, I should be able to accomplish with the big ones. It might take years to become proficient, but they would be worthwhile years.

When I did master it, I would have one hell of a powerful weapon, suitable to counter sword or knife or even a crowd of armed men. Not that I would ever face such a thing, in my life here at the monastery.

I did not have those years. Once more I was summoned to the presence of the head monk. "There is now opportunity to return you to your people," he said.

I was stunned. "I want to stay here!" I blurted. "To master the weapon, master myself—"

He shook his head. "That is not your destiny, Jason Striker. This is our life, not yours. You belong in the great outside world, in America. It was for this that we saved you."

It was foolish to argue, and extremely bad form, but I could not help myself. "What is there in America that's better than this?"

"Nothing," he said. "But your mission is there."

"*What* mission?" Even as, I spoke, I knew it was futile. The issue had been decided long before this interview, perhaps even before they rescued me.

"We do not know. We have prepared you, as our vision directed. You will know when the occasion arises." There was nothing I could do but go. However politely couched, however sadly made, his decision was final. They would not force me out, any more than they had forced me to stay, but it was inconceivable that I should oppose my will to Yee's. I was not to be a celibate monk, whatever I might wish.

We went down the river at night by boat, transferring from

one boat to another as we left the monastery further behind. I wore the robes of a monk, so that my identity would not be evident. My head was shaved, I wore sandals, my skin was stained yellowish by dye and I carried a begging bowl. It was not a difficult impersonation, for if I had had my way it would have been no impersonation, but a way of life. Alas, I knew I would never again see these good men.

A hundred miles down the Mekong I remembered the two sensors, sewn in my trousers back at the monastery. I should have brought them with me.

Well, nothing could be done about it now. With luck they would never be discovered, and of course the monks did not understand the sensors' purpose. It galled me to have forgotten them like that, but it probably made no difference.

How wrong I was!

We passed the capital, Phnom Penh, then proceeded on through the monsoon-flooded plains down the swollen river, that overflowed its banks and covered the countryside in a sheet of brown water. It was dusk as we reached the frontier of South Vietnam, but we pushed on. Another hundred miles would bring us to the general vicinity of Saigon. We joined a convoy of five river barges and continued our leisurely pace. One was a bigger power boat towing a barge full of merchandise.

In my guise as a monk, I had to play along with the deference shown me by the natives, who did not know my real identity. I suspected that Cong were among us now; they would have had my head, literally, if they had known. Instead I blessed them and comforted them in priestly fashion, and somewhat to my dismay found that they, too, were human beings, with human feelings and cares. They believed they were throwing out the invader, fighting the oppressor, righting great wrongs, and they gave me food in my begging bowl, though they hardly had enough for themselves. I supposed they were off-duty.

Suddenly, at dusk, we were attacked by American or South Vietnamese gunboats. They were small fast launches carrying 20mm rapid-firing guns and .50 caliber machine guns. I had been doz-ing; I had not seen their approach. Evidently the engagement was a surprise to our people, that is, the native sailors, too. An am-bush; no doubt the South Viets needed a body-count, and we were it. Several people were killed before they could scramble for cover.

I took cover too, such as was available. What did those trigger-happy bastards think they were doing, gunning down innocent natives? Tracer bullets passed right through the thin shell of my raft-cabin. Every fifth bullet was a tracer, lighting the evening sky. In that moment I thoroughly sympathized with the Cong; this invader *needed* to be driven out!

Then one of the barges exploded. I recognized the stigmata of an oil fire: the typical roiling smoke, the spreading slick on the surface of the water. Innocent natives? They had no business carry-ing hidden oil in such quantity. That was contraband!

Ironic, that this ill-motivated government massacre should actually strike a legitimate enemy shipment. Doubly ironic, that I should be in that convoy. But right now I had to worry less about irony and more about my own hide.

Now there was answering fire from the boat towing the barge. Someone there carried a P-40 rocket launcher, no innocent native artifact. A rocket streamed toward the leading gunboat, hitting it in the bridge. There was a big explosion, and the twin 20mm gun was knocked out.

The other gunboat concentrated its fire on this resistance. There was an exchange of automatic rifle fire, but it was obvious to me that the Cong were overmatched. They had hoped to sneak through; now they were fighting because they had no choice.

A shell struck the barge, and there was a tremendous explo-sion as all of its smuggled load of fuel went up. A brilliant fireball appeared, glowing red and white; it lit the entire river. The thing was both awful and beautiful, an animate mushroom cloud rising into the sky. The towing boat was engulfed in the burning oil, the sailors shriveling like moths against a bright flame. Some tried to jump, but it was too late; they were burning torches.

The gunboats fired at the flaming men; whether this was brutal sport or an act of mercy I could not tell. Both, perhaps.

Then they began firing at the other boats of our little convoy, mine among them. A dum-dum bullet entered our guide's head from behind, and spread out to destroy the man's entire face as it emerged. Dum-dums were illegal, but both sides used them.

The craft caught fire. A shell hit our rudder; our boat started to turn and head for the burning oil. Our sailors were falling as the bullets found them.

I dived into the water, taking a deep breath on the way. My voluminous cloak hampered me as I tried to swim. I twisted desperately to get out of it, wasting precious seconds while the flames spread above me along the surface. In a moment, stripped, I stroked for the shore. The only thing I retained was my weapon, the nunchaku.

When I came up, gasping for air, I found myself in the company of a crocodile. I tensed, choking on smoke, the acrid black stuff searing my lungs; vomit filled my throat.

But the big reptile was not after me. It was fleeing the burning oil slick, just as I was. Behind us, my boat was in the midst of that flame.

We struck land almost together. I followed the crock up the bank. A government patrol was there, armed with M-3 submachine guns. "Don't shoot, I'm with this crocodile!" I yelled.

They were American, fortunately. They laughed, recognizing my accent. "Which one's the crock?" one asked.

I was home free.

*

It wasn't until several days later that I learned the rest of the story. One of my sensors had begun broadcasting a day after I left the monastery, signaling a large group of bodies. The planes had gone out and bombed the hell out of what they presumed to be an enemy fortress.

The Shaolin monastery was rubble. There were no survivors. The planes had dropped napalm, just to be sure.

Napalm. Jellied gasoline. I knew what it was like. I had seen its terrible effect many times. That was part of what I didn't like about this war. Carbonized bodies with all trace of sex burned away, impossible to tell whether the victim was man, woman or child. Pull at the body and it might become carbon dust. Somehow the flesh melted away till the bone showed. Once a little girl had come running at me, one of the innocent victims of a blind bombing; I had tried to halt her by seizing her arm, and the whole skin of that limb came off like a glove. In my mind's eye I saw the noble head monk, burning, burning; smelled the stink of incinerated body fat, the peculiar sweetish odor that scorched human meat gives off, the eyes melting in their sockets leaving only a skull, still burning.

I hoped the first strikes had been by B-52s instead of fighter-bombers, and that their big bombs had been accurate. At least the monks would have died rapidly without suffering. But I feared it had not been so, and that they had been caught in the firestorm, in the collapsing ruins, suffocating slowly, the air getting hotter until their lungs burned away.

Someone must have taken my trousers for washing, and either the heat or the vibration had jogged the sensor setting to "ON." The monks had never known what was coming, or why.

My carelessness had wiped out Shangri-La.

I was awarded a Silver Star for bravery in action, and the Purple Heart. I put them away, accursed things. I never told the truth to the authorities; what point would there have been in that? I hung the nunchaku in my trophy case, and let the entire memory of the experience for which that weapon stood become encysted in my brain. It was as though the monastery had never been.

Except for unhappy moments when some stray reference summoned a portion of the experience to consciousness. I always reburied it as fast as possible, a shameful thing.

CHAPTER 7

CHIYAKO

"Until this moment," I concluded.

Kobi Chija shook his head. "Not so, Mr. Striker," he said. "Kung-fu had been with you all the time. Setting the nunchaku aside could not remove that experience from your being."

"I have not been aware of it," I said.

"You held a third degree black belt in judo and second in karate," he said. "What do you hold now?"

"Fifth in judo; third in karate."

"You tried to steer away from karate, but even in your judo you felt the kung-fu influence. Could you have achieved your fifth dan so rapidly otherwise?"

I had never thought of it that way, but now I realized he was right. The experience at the monastery had improved me in many ways, and that had translated into success on the *tatami*. The signals were all there, in retrospect; I had been willfully blind to them.

"I caused the destruction of the Shaolin monastery," I said. "How can I accept any benefit from that?"

"You are mistaken. They knew when they took you in that it meant death for all of them; their vision had foretold it. The head monk made a deliberate and conscious decision. You cannot overturn that. You cannot call him wrong. You become culpable only if you waste the effort they made. Do not spurn their tremendous sacrifice! You must seek your mission."

"You sound so much like Yee!" I said ruefully. "Did you, did you by chance know him?"

"I knew *of* him," he said. "I am not a monk, but I know how he thought. I know he never feared destruction. I see his handiwork embodied in you; *you* were his mission."

"I know my mission, now," I said. "It is to abolish the demon drug Kill-Thirteen from the face of the earth."

"Perhaps so. It has visited much the same devastation on you as the airplanes visited on the monastery. That is omen enough."

"No. Until I saw you, it was only revenge. I never thought of the Shaolin mission."

"Yet it is the drug that brought us together," he pointed out.

I spread my hands. "I can hide nothing from you!"

He smiled. "Why should you wish to?"

"I am afraid you will be hurt, because of me." I was surprised to hear myself say this, but it was true.

"How much better such a hurt," he said, "than the failure to know friendship." He looked at his arm. "Already I am wounded, because of you." He paused. "Instead of dead."

Was that a hint? I stood up. "I forgot how weary you must be. I shall leave, so you can rest. Thank you for your excellent hospitality."

He too stood, and I knew I had done the right thing. He would never have allowed his wound to interfere with politeness. "My daughter will see you out," he said.

"In a moment," Chiyako said, taking Kobi's arm as he wobbled on his feet. Yes, he was weak, and close to passing out. "Please wait."

"Of course," I said. Naturally I had to take no notice of my host's discomfort. Chiyako would make her father comfortable, and then she would usher me to the door as though nothing were amiss. No face would be lost.

They were gone for several minutes. I stood with my eyes half-closed, trying to analyze the strange exhilaration I felt. I had finally unburdened myself of my darkest secret, and met with people I could really believe in. Was it a major turning point in my life?

"He sleeps," Chiyako said, emerging from her father's room. "There is no infection, I think."

"I'm glad," I said. Then, feeling the awkwardness of being alone with a beautiful girl, an awkwardness I would not have felt, had she not appealed to me so strongly, I turned to go. "I shall phone you tomorrow, to hear how he is doing."

She put her small hand on my arm, and it was as though that contact was charged, positive on negative. I had never felt that before. "Please, Mr. Striker. I know you are tired, and that we hardly know each other, but would you stay a little longer?"

There was nothing I wanted more. "If I can help you in any way, "

"I do not like to impose."

"No, *I* have imposed on *you*, with my private history. I'm sorry I talked so much, when your father was too polite to interrupt." That embarrassed me increasingly, that I should have made a severely wounded man listen to something like that.

"He has been long away from China," she said. "When the war with Japan ended, it seemed that Communist victory in China was imminent, so many monks departed, refugees. I was born in exile, not so very far from the monastery you described. My father was a *sifu* in that region, working with them." Her eyes drifted upward, as though she saw a distant object. "Your words took us back. I was only a child, but I remember these things; I too long for the peace of the monastery, but know there is no peace. My mother died of malaria, while we traveled; my father—"

Why hadn't I seen that? If I missed the monastery, after only a few months residence there, how much worse was the agony of separation that those trained to it felt! I should have thought of Kobi's feelings.

"I spoke unwittingly," I said. "I'm sorry."

"No, it was wonderful!" she exclaimed. "You are the Chosen, chosen by the vision; that power is in you, and it is an honor to be with you."

"You're way too generous," I said, embarrassed again. "After all the trouble my presence caused—"

"Please," she said. She left the room for a moment, then returned with two weapons. One was a kung-fu practice sword, the other a set of *tonfas*: oblong boards with handles. "Will you practice with me, as you did at the monastery?"

I was caught completely by surprise. Here she was in her Chinese clothing, as pretty a girl as I had seen in months, who had just tended her father's gruesome wound and served an excellent meal, and now she wanted to practice with weapons.

I humored her, glad for the pretext to remain with her a few moments longer. I would indulge in a token exhibition, then go home. I took the sword.

The sword was wood, cleverly painted to resemble steel. The monks had used similar devices in place of the real weapons, particularly for the novices. After all, the purpose was practice, not mayhem. Still, a wooden sword could pack a nasty clout.

Chiyako assumed a defensive posture with the *tonfas*, and I made an overhead cut with half my strength, not wanting to risk hurting her. I should not have been so cautious; she caught my blade on the crossed boards, then with a flick of her wrists sent my sword flying. And whacked me across the chest with one *tonfa*.

Something happens to me when I get hit. I come out fighting, and I do things I may later regret, such as knocking a pretty girl on her butt. I picked up my sword and approached her, but she confused me, whirling the *tonfas* overhead by their handles and doing figure eights with them. Then she clashed them together with a considerable clatter, and jabbed me with the end of one in the solar plexus, so hard I gasped.

I had practiced against the *tonfas* before. The reason I was falling for her ploys was because of *her,* not *them.* I simply had not anticipated such technique from a girl.

Now I took more competent steps. Despite the pain in my torso, I struck her on the chin with the flat of my sword, shocking her so that she dropped one *tonfa.* When she bent to recover it, I whacked her hard across the derriere.

She made a little exclamation. I thought it was of pain, but it turned out to be laughter. "So you told the truth!" she cried. "You *do* know weapons!"

I knew weapons. More than that, I was feeling once more their magic, the exhilaration of weapons in motion. It was a good feeling, and I liked it, and I liked Chiyako too. This little mock battle had been more exciting than a kiss, and not alone because of the sword.

"Take the *tonfas,*" she said, holding them out to me. "You have won them."

"I would rather have won the girl," I said.

She did not quite blush. "Perhaps another time," she said. "Please, I want you to have these; I have a premonition that you will need them."

I did not like such premonitions. They smacked too much of the old head monk's vision, the one that had led him to destruction. But I could not say no to her, so I accepted her gift.

*

Next day I called on them again, but Kobi was absent. "He has gone to have an acupuncture treatment," Chiyako explained. "I am alone."

This was awkward. I did not want to enter the house in her father's absence, but I did want to see more of Chiyako. "Would you like to take a walk?" I inquired, not certain how Americanized she had become in her decade or so in this country.

It was that easy. We walked in the nearby park, then went to a movie. It was a Bruce Lee picture, and we both laughed at some of the junk that passed for kung-fu. It is a fighting art, not a ballet or trampoline act. Bruce Lee certainly knew that, but had evidently been corrupted by the big money proffered for such distortions. The irony was that kung-fu needed no exaggeration; it is deadly enough without the phony stuff.

Afterwards, we stopped at a Chinese tea house and had tea. And pastry full of cheese. An old Chinese with an ancient camera took our picture. Back on the street we passed a tourist trap, and I bought her a jade Buddha to hang from her neck. We watched them gutting fish expertly at the market and ate mango ice cream, and I found myself holding hands with her as we walked. We smelled burning incense and entered a temple, but it was a fake, a tourist souvenir shop with a Buddha in front as a facade. So we went on to a Chinese museum, and it was another disappointment, with an imitation dragon belching flame.

I had seen these things before, but now they bothered me more. Everything was artificial, except Chiyako.

Next day I talked again with Kobi, telling him the details of my encounters with the demons. Kobi was looking better; evidently the acupuncture treatments were helping him recover. "A black woman," he murmured. "Tomorrow I will investigate."

Sure enough, he was gone again the following day. This time Chiyako invited me inside, and I accepted. Her father knew I was seeing her; he would have said something to one of us if he objected.

"I do not know your specialty," she told me as we entered the dojo. "This judo, is it like kung-fu?"

Could she really, be ignorant of judo? Well, I was happy to enlighten her.

"Judo is literally the 'gentle way'," I said. "Designed to subdue your opponent without hurting him, or yourself. That doesn't mean it is nonviolent, or that strength is immaterial. Sometimes judo is decidedly ungentle. And the stronger man has the advantage when the skills are equal. Judo consists mainly of throws, locks and holds, but it really is less of a physical arsenal than it is a mental attitude."

"That is true for kung-fu," she said.

"Yes. Kung-fu is a form of karate, an empty-handed striking. But all the major martial arts overlap to some extent. Judo experts know many of the karate blows, and a good karateka will know most of the judo throws. And of course a kung-fu *sifu* knows them too. I'm sure your father does. So the forms of the martial arts really aren't so different."

"That throw you did in the street, that was judo?"

"Throw?" I had trouble orienting on her question.

"When you stood on one leg and made a sweep with the other." She made a little demonstration, very attractively executed, so that I still couldn't really concentrate on her words.

"That looks like the *harai goshi*," I said. "Yes, that's judo."

"Will you show it to me? It certainly was effective on that demon."

"Well, if you really want it," I said. We changed into judogis for practice, then returned to the hall. My uniform was conventional for judo, but hers was a bright scarlet kung-fu outfit, very pretty on her.

I approached her on the *tatami*, and went into the *harai goshi*.

Rather, I started it. She resisted with the *hara*, or "strong stomach thrust out," then grabbed me around the waist and swept my supporting leg so that we both fell to the mat, she on top.

"You gamine, you know judo!" I exclaimed ruefully.

She laughed so hard she fell over.

That nettled me. "I never did the *harai goshi* on a demon," I continued. "Why did you ask about it?"

She shrugged, avoiding direct response. "Maybe you did it wrong."

I stood up, grim. "Yes. Let's try it again."

She was still shaking with mirth, but my pride had been hurt. She tried the same defense as before, which was foolish. I let her counter by sweeping my leg and throwing me, as before, but this time I did not let go of her. She was carried down with me, and as we fell I passed one of my legs between hers, levered her to the side, climbed on top and held her down. She was pinned, but also, I realized abruptly, very close.

I let her go again, hastily. My leg rammed between hers, that could be misunderstood.

"But I can get up and attack you again," she said. "With kung-fu I would have knocked you out."

"Not if I put a *kesa gatame* on you," I said, smiling. I sat along-side her, my legs braced apart for balance; my upper torso held hers down. Her head was caught in the crook of my right arm, while my left caught her right arm.

"But I could break that hold!" she said.

She tried, but of course it was impossible. I could have held a three-hundred-pound wrestler firmly with this hold, and she fell far short of that weight.

Her breasts writhed against me as she struggled. I didn't want to hurt her, so I gave her some play, but that only made her motions more voluptuous. Her lovely face was close to mine, and I inhaled the fragrance of her hair.

I kissed her. I hadn't meant to do it, but it seemed natural in the circumstance. She met me with a passion that amazed me, a deep, deep kiss.

It was as though all my repression and guilt about the monastery fueled this quite different emotion I experienced with Chiyako. She was of the kung-fu line, heir to its traditions, yet she was a woman. She embodied both of the worlds I craved: the monastic and the romantic. For years I had been searching, unbeknownst to myself, for just these things, thinking them mutually exclusive. Now here they were—together.

And I realized that this was the reason for her mock queries about judo. It was like an American girl saying "I'm cold" on a warm evening. A Chinese girl, even one half-Americanized, does not simply ask a man to take her in his arms. She had maneuvered me to where she wanted me, in a rather more subtle manner than Amalita had. I had been slow to catch on.

Things proceeded naturally from that point. The loose exercise outfits were no problem, and the mat was comfortable. The culmination was exquisite, without pain, like nothing I had experienced before.

No, perhaps there was pain, for her. When we rose, there was a small bloodstain on the *tatami*, an embarrassing tattle-tale. She washed it out, but some stain remained. Then she went to clean herself up and change. I was amazed again at her composure, for now I knew that this had been a completely new and significant experience for her.

I changed too, returning to the front room before she reappeared. I had much to think about.

I heard a commotion outside. I looked and saw a car parked just across the street. Three people were inside, two men with a girl between them in the front seat. She was the one making the noise. They were squeezing her in, trying to hold her arms while getting her clothing off. In the cramped car it wasn't easy, and she was making such an outcry that the whole neighborhood could hear. And of course the neighborhood was paying no attention, though this time the men were not demons. All windows and doors were closing.

It was obviously an attempted rape. I don't like rapes, and I don't like public apathy. I was about to go to her rescue, but abruptly realized two things.

First, her screams were not so much of terror as of rage. She was cursing those men in several languages, calling them grandsons of dogs and pig fornicators and pederasts, however inappropriate to the occasion that seemed, only in more colorful vocabulary. *"Maricones! Hijos de putas! Castrados!"*

The second thing was that I recognized her. Amalita, whom I had last seen at the hospital.

So I paused. I knew from experience that pretty little Amalita

Pedro could take care of herself. And I wanted to figure out just what she was doing here.

Suddenly she stopped screaming, for it was doing no good. Her blouse had been ripped open to expose her bra-less bosom, and one of the men was working his hand up her thigh. He could not go far, as there was no room in the car, but he was getting one hell of a feel. I suspected that she didn't mind the feel half so much as the notion of having a man get the better of her in a public place.

Amalita's two elbows shot out sidewise, catching the two men just below the ribcages. I thought I heard their breaths whistling out explosively. Certainly the blows stung, as they were unprepared. One had been intent on her breasts (I couldn't blame him; her architecture was about as elegant as any) and the other had been watching the progress of his own hand along the smooth flesh of her inner leg (another compelling view). They had both been wide open for such punishment, but it did not knock either of them out.

The breast-man cursed and aimed a blow at her. Amalita blocked it with a sweeping motion of one arm, while with the other arm she delivered a second elbow strike. Elbows were really more effective in cramped quarters. This time she hit the face, catching him just over the eye. It broke the eyelid, drawing blood, making the flesh around it swell rapidly. The man opened the door and scrambled out.

Then she went for the other man's face with her claws. In a moment he, too, fled the car, leaving her alone.

Chiyako came up behind me, noting my preoccupation with the window. "Is something wrong?" she inquired.

I put my arm about her waist. "Well, there's an attempted rape in progress," I said. "But don't worry about it."

She was not one to overreact, but this brought her right to the window. "It *is* a rape!" she exclaimed. For the two men had not given up; they now stood in the street, one by the hood of the car ready to chase Amalita down if she exited from the far side, and the other putting his hand on the near handle. The car window was open, so she couldn't lock him out. The men had evidently decided that they could rape her better in the open street, and the indifference of the other people in the area facilitated this.

"*Attempted* rape," I corrected Chiyako. "Watch."

"Watch!" she said, shocked. "I thought you were a different kind of man, Jason Striker!"

"I *am*," I murmured.

The man at the car door now had a club, a piece of broken board from the street, with a couple of nails protruding from it. He held it in his left hand, while his right worked the handle. He intended to quiet Amalita forcefully, so that the rape would be easier. I held Chiyako near to me, making her watch though she was trembling with anger.

The man opened the door. It burst open, and Amalita's right foot shot out, catching him in the groin. I winced involuntarily, knowing how that hurt. We were treated to quite a flash of her bottom, for her other leg was braced against the car's floorboard, with her torso face down on the seat. At least she was wearing panties.

The man dropped his club. He was hurt. Amalita's foot came down. She landed on it and pivoted to face the other man, now on the other side of the open door. He tried to grab her, but she stooped, caught him about the waist, lifted him up and boosted him over her hip in an *uki goshi* hip throw. He landed across the hood, denting it. He was out of the fight. Then she kicked the man holding his crotch, this time in the face.

"That girl knows how to defend herself!" Chiyako murmured.

"Yes indeed!" I agreed. "Pity the poor rapists!"

She glanced at me sidelong. "You know her?"

"I'm afraid I do. Can't think why she's here, though."

"To watch you," Chiyako said. "I did not know you had an-other woman."

Oh-oh. "I *don't*," I said. "I have a long and nefarious past, but that's over." I realized as I spoke how true that was; this girl beside me was all the present, and possibly the future too, that I needed. "Anyway, Amalita is a married woman."

"It has not been your way to conceal the truth," Chiyako reproached me. "She came for you. She regards you as hers."

This was treacherous ground, so I tried to extricate myself delicately. "In a car with two men?"

"She was hitch-hiking. Perhaps the men were impressed by her outfit and manner and got the wrong idea."

I sighed. That was exactly the sort of fool thing Amalita would do. She was wearing another see-through blouse and no bra, and a skirt that barely covered her panties when she was standing. Such a hitch-hiker would attract only one kind of man.

But what claim did she think she had on me? I thought I had made plain to her that the hospital affair was strictly a one-shot deal.

"You are lovers," Chiyako said.

Brother! Her guesswork and intuition were as accurate as her *shuto* blows. "That's over!"

"Not over," she said firmly.

I turned to her, embarrassed and exasperated. "She forced herself on me. I didn't want it, and I don't want it now."

"I believe you," she said, surprising me. "I know how men are. But it is not over so long as she still wants you."

"Well, she won't want me after I talk to her!" I said. "I don't like being spied on!"

I stomped out of the house, but Chiyako followed me. Well, let her listen!

"It is natural for her to be concerned," she murmured. I wondered just what was going on in her mind.

The two rapists were still out of it, one collapsed on top of the car, the other alongside it. Amalita had really polished them off.

"Why Jason," Amalita said as if surprised to meet me. She patted her hair in place, though it was hardly mussed. She had had time to tuck her blouse back into the band of her skirt, not that it made a whole lot of difference to the view.

"You are a married woman," I said bluntly. "And your husband is a jealous man. Go home to him before he kills someone." I had had taste enough of Vicente Pedro's wrath before; I much preferred him as a friend.

But suddenly Amalita was paying no attention to me. Her gaze was on Chiyako. "So you throw me over for a Chinese!" she said grimly.

Another accurate assessment, by her lights.

"Come inside, señora," Chiyako said politely. "We shall talk."

I understand just enough Spanish to know that "señorita" means a maiden and that "señora" is an older, married woman. By calling her señora, Chiyako was putting her in the old-married category. Since Chiyako was not of Spanish descent, this usage was affected and insulting.

Amalita was abruptly polite, realizing that there was nothing to gain by making a scene. The contrast with the Chinese girl would only work to her disadvantage. "Thank you so much, Auntie," she said, making a deep mock bow.

We trooped inside. Each girl insisted on giving way to the other, as though to an older woman, with the result that I had to break the impasse by preceding them both into the house. I grabbed the wrist of each, dragging them both inside.

I had severe misgivings, but the matter was now largely out of my hands. At least whatever followed would be out of the view of the street crowds. We passed through the dojo, and the faint wet stains on the tatami were visible, where we had tried to wash out the blood. Amalita gave no sign, but I was sure she had seen them.

Chiyako served orange blossom tea and almond pastries with honey. "Jason says you were lovers," she said conversationally.

"Before she married Pedro!" I said quickly.

"And after," Amalita said. "Only last week, "

"Before I met you!" I said to Chiyako. But it sounded like a politician trying to explain missing records.

"But you are married?" Chiyako asked her.

"My husband is a cripple!" Amalita said.

"He is a fifth degree black belt," I said. "Karate."

"Not that sort of cripple," Amalita said. "Karate is no good in bed."

"Perhaps you should try judo," Chiyako suggested mischievously. I hoped I wasn't flushing. That stain . . .

"Well, I'm the same sort, after that kick," I said a bit lamely.

"No you aren't," Amalita said. And Chiyako nodded agreement. I wished I had kept my mouth shut; I was not in the same league with these cats.

"Such debate is pointless," Chiyako said. "I am glad to have met you, Señora Pedro."

I was aware that the subtle verbal battle was over, and that Chiyako had won. Amalita realized it too. Suddenly a knife was in her hand, a stiletto. I had not seen where it came from. She must have had it in her purse, and not even needed it to handle the rapists. She bounced to her feet and lunged at Chiyako.

Chiyako was a gentle, peaceful girl, but nobody attacks a kung-fu adept with a knife. Amalita held the blade low, going for the belly; she obviously knew how to use it. Chiyako pivoted to her right, grabbed the wrist of the knife-hand, and struck Amalita's forearm with the edge of her stiffened hand. That stunned the nerves, and the knife dropped to the floor.

Amalita, disarmed, was hardly out of the fight. She whirled around and caught Chiyako's hair, yanking her head back viciously. Those who disparage hair-pulling as a tactic have never seen it in practice; it is as effective as any other maneuver. Chiyako fell, but from the floor she hooked one foot behind Amalita's legs, and with the other she kicked. Amalita fell backward. She rolled in a somersault, while Chiyako twirled crosswise on her stomach so as to get out of reach. Both women stood at the same time.

I knew better than to interfere. They would have to settle this themselves. Each of these girls had saved my life.

Amalita tried to punch at Chiyako's head. No, I was thinking like a man; she wasn't punching, she was clawing for the eyes. Another tactical mistake, for the Tiger's Claw is a kung-fu tactic.

Chiyako knew exactly how to foil it. She blocked with her forearm, and countered with an inverted fist strike to the spleen, *uraken hizo uchi.* She followed that with another shot to Amalita's midsection. Chiyako was squatting slightly in a straddle stance, and she snapped the wrist slightly on contact. All good kung-fu style.

Amalita grunted; those professional blows were telling. But she knew karate herself, and was an indefatigable scrapper, as her hospital performance had shown. She delivered a front kick, *maegeri,* the ball of her foot making contact with Chiyako's abdomen. But the Chinese girl caught the foot and lifted it high, making Amalita fall on her derriere. Her skirt tore as she went down, exposing her thighs right past the panties, and Chiyako gave her one good kick on that bifurcation.

I winced. Such a blow has less effect on a woman than on a man, obviously, but Amalita would have bruises to interfere with tomorrow's love life. She was out of the fight, overmatched by a professional. She picked herself up with what remaining dignity she could muster and limped out of the house. She would be quite a sight on the street, but I couldn't bring myself to feel sorry for her. She had come here uninvited, and she had started the fight, and it had been a fair one. She had brought her humiliation on herself.

Chiyako now whipped up an oddball Chinese snack of fried caterpillars, canned sea urchin and fish eyes, the real thing, not the large tapioca slang—and really they weren't bad. Westerners have affected notions of what is edible; after all, what is caviar but jellied fish roe? But anything she served would have tasted good.

It had been a big day, and everything about it had increased my admiration for Chiyako. She had made love for the first time, dealt verbally and physically with a formidable rival, and served a delicious meal, all with perfect aplomb.

She was quite a girl.

*

At dusk we stepped out the back door, so as to avoid any possible confrontation with Amalita. I had to get home, and I didn't want to keep Chiyako up. She had to rest sometime. I planned to bid her goodnight with a minimum of fuss. There would be other days, and this one had been tarnished by Amalita's intrusion.

We stood on a small platform, protected by a thin metal railing. Several concrete steps led down to a narrow alley that dead-ended to one side in a disorderly crowd of garbage cans. A little Chinese diner or restaurant was next door, probably the source of the exotic food I had been served, so there was plenty of refuse for the alley cats I saw prowling. Not at all romantic, except for Chiyako's transforming presence.

We kissed. Kisses are part of male-female relations, and I have experienced a number of good ones in my day. But when my lips touched hers, I felt all of Shaolin infusing my being, the noble monastery and the kung-fu fighting art and the philosophy of weapons as builders not destroyers. Never before had I associated these important things with sexual romance. I held her closely, transported, adrift in an unusual and wholly delightful world. The shame and horror of my buried past became a thing of joy, for it had prepared me to properly appreciate this moment.

There was an earsplitting screech. Something leaped upon us, pushing us both against the rail. For a moment I thought it was a wild animal, maybe a monkey.

But it was human, and it was Amalita. She had not gone away, but lurked waiting for us with animal cunning in the shadow of the piled garbage cans. Our embrace must have driven her wild with jealousy. What a fury, for such unjustified cause.

Against a man I can handle myself. But against a woman I freeze up. So I stood like a statue, while again Chiyako defended herself. She used the one-arm back-carry throw, the *ippon seoi nage,* bending over and hurling Amalita right over her head. Amalita flew over the rail and landed in the garbage cans.

The crash was horrendous. Cans fell over and rolled noisily about, spewing their contents over the ground. Bottles broke in the pavement. The scavenging cats leaped out, fleeing frantically down the alley. I was afraid Amalita was hurt, but she leaped to her feet again and charged back up the steps. This time I moved to intercept her, but Chiyako was in front of me, and there was little room to pass.

There was another noise as of glass breaking, and a shower of specks glittered in the lamplight as they flew through the air. Amalita had found a large whiskey bottle and smashed it against the rail. Hardly pausing, she dived for Chiyako, the jagged circle of glass leading.

Chiyako tried to jump back, but I was right behind her and she could not move. The bottle thrust at her chest, a fiendishly sparkling thing in the partial shadow. She made a little cry as it struck.

Then Amalita went for the face. I saw the weapon come up, a hundred bright irregular teeth in a circular mouth, dripping blood. My paralysis broke and I reacted automatically. With one hand I reached over Chiyako's shoulder and grabbed Amalita's flying hair, jerking her head brutally back. With the other I struck at the attacking wrist, a descending blow with the edge of my hand.

My position was awkward, but my blow was solid.

There was a crack. Now Amalita cried out. I knew I had broken her slender wrist with my strike. The bottle dropped to the steps and shattered explosively.

Chiyako fell halfway over the rail and clung there silently. I jumped past her and down the steps, dragging Amalita with me and hurling her out into the alley. "Go tell Pedro whatever you want!" I cried furiously. "I never want to see you again!"

"Jason, I saved your life!" she cried pitifully as she staggered to regain her balance.

Guilt only made me more savage. "I'm saving yours by letting you go! Come near me and I'll kill you myself!" I hated myself right now, but I hated her worse.

She stumbled off. At any other time I would have felt sorry for her, knowing how badly she was hurt, and that she had no way to get home. But I meant it; I wanted her completely out of my life, lest I smash her to death with my fist. Now the break was clean.

I turned to Chiyako, and was horrified. Her white blouse was torn open, and her bosom was a dark mass of blood. Amalita had gone for the breast, and struck the left breast with a twisting motion. Chiyako had had to stand still for it, because of the obstacle of my body behind her.

"Let me see that!" I rasped, knowing the wound was serious. She did not resist as I drew her down into the light and ripped away the remaining fabric. I exposed both breasts and peered closely. There was still too much shadow, but I saw what I needed to.

Chiyako's right breast was unmarked, firm and beautifully formed. Her left breast had been cut in a horrible semicircle, many wounds that could be inches deep. Shards of glass were embedded in her flesh. There was so much blood I knew she would bleed to death in short order if I did not stop the flow.

But I couldn't put a tourniquet on. Not on a breast!

I swung her about to stand before me, facing away. Then I took hold of her breast with my left hand and pressed it in toward her rib-cage, hard. My fingers sealed the jagged slashes, obstructing the hot blood. Some would escape, but the worst had been stopped.

Suppose I was also trapping glass in the wounds? Couldn't be helped.

I had to get her to a doctor.

Walking down the streets like this was out of the question. Any person who saw us . . .

"Inside!" I said. I could tell by the wilting of her supple body that she was losing consciousness. How much blood was gone? I had to act while I could get some help from her or it would be hopeless.

We staggered up the steps and almost fell through the door. I trundled her into the parlor and found the phone. Both my hands were occupied supporting her. "Pick it up," I directed.

She tried, but the receiver dangled from her hand. Damn! She was fading fast. I hugged her in the crook of my left elbow and grabbed the receiver with my right hand. It was awkward as hell, as I dared not remove my left hand from her breast, now slimed with coagulating blood. Way too late I realized that I should have made some kind of bandage, with my shirt if necessary, and wadded that over her wound; it would have contained the blood better.

Anyway, I had the phone. Now all I had to do was dial. I stood there, breast in one hand, mouthpiece in the other. Chiyako couldn't help me any more; she had finally passed out. Her sticky blood continued to squeeze through my fingers; every motion I made let some more out. The dial tone roared in my ear. What could I do?

I thought of putting her down for a moment. But I couldn't chance it; the very act of removing my hand would rip the cuts open again and make the bleeding worse.

I scuffed off one shoe and tried to reach the dial with one toe. I almost dumped us both on the floor. With her dead weight, I could not keep the balance one-footed. Maybe at some other time it would have been simple, but at the moment I was overwrought.

She was bleeding to death while I struggled to dial.

Then the obvious came to me. I set down the receiver, off the hook, and dialed with my finger. I sure as hell didn't have to listen while I dialed.

The ambulance made it in time. There weren't even any tasteless wisecracks. They stitched her up right there, gave her a transfusion, and took her in to the hospital for further treatment.

She survived. I knew her breast would not be as pretty as it had been, but that is not a place that ordinarily shows. In any event, it could not change my attitude toward her, which bordered already on love.

Love. Why not admit it?

But I remembered: once I had found Amalita attractive, and

the consequence of that mistake had been gruesome. Before that, I had even thought of marrying another girl, and she had become the mistress of my top judo student. My judgment of women had always been suspect.

How could I be sure about Chiyako?

CHAPTER 8

ILUNGA

Kobi Chija returned with valuable information. "I have ascertained the identity of your black karate mistress," he said.

I was selfishly glad that Chiyako was still in the hospital. She could hardly be expected to understand my involvement with yet another woman.

"Tell me where she is," I said grimly. "I will deal with her."

He shook his head. "You are thinking like a warrior, not a monk."

A none-too-subtle reminder of my Shaolin experience. Why did he choose to call that to mind in this connection? "That woman nearly unmanned me," I said. "And she is tied in with Kill-Thirteen."

"True. Yet there may be redeeming qualities."

"Forgive my skepticism, but that sounds like a contradiction in terms," I said sourly.

"Permit me to describe her in my own way," he murmured.

I knew he wanted to go to the hospital to be with his daughter, yet he was insisting on taking time in dealing with this black karate matter. He had something special on his mind, and I was bound to respect it. "Of course."

*

Ilunga, at age twelve, was just budding into what would soon be classic beauty. Black haired, black eyed, and black skinned, she walked the street with pride. Already her swaying walk gave her an unconscious sensuality. She was the brightest student in her class, and last semester her science project on melanin and skin disease had won a prize. In the past few months the boys had started showing interest in her too.

She cut through the park, as she often did despite her mother's stern admonitions. What harm was there in trees and bushes, even at night?

"Well now!" It was a man, blocking the path. Huge and pale under the lamp, a red face and nose, brown stubble on cheek and chin, bloodshot eyes, and dirty fingernails.

Ilunga knew he was no friend. She turned to run, but suddenly there was another white man behind her. "Going somewhere, little Sambo?" he demanded. His breath reeked of cheap wine, and his clothes were grimy.

"I-I—" Anxiously she looked about, seeking some escape. But now two more men appeared, as old and dirty as the first ones. They must have set an ambush for her, or for anyone else who happened to pass by. "I don't have only fifty cents—"

"You got more'n that!" the first man said, and laughed. "You got two dollars worth, I bet!"

"Where you been the last twenty years?" one of the others said to him. "You can't get it for less'n ten dollars now!"

"No, only fifty cents—" Ilunga said, confused.

The nearest one grabbed her arm. "Have a drink, girlie." He put a bottle to her mouth and tilted it so that the burning alcohol splashed down her chin.

She was catching on. Terrified, she bit his hand.

He cried out in pain and fury. "All right, nigger—you asked for it!" He struck her backhanded, so hard she heard a ringing in her ears.

She tried to run, but he caught her and threw her to the ground. He put his fingers inside her shirt, ripping it open. Her modestly filled bra was exposed. She tried to turn over and scramble away, but one of the other men grabbed her hands and held her arms outstretched above her head, while a third caught at her legs and forced them apart. Hands hauled at her panties, pulling them down and off. Other hands fumbled over her breasts and pinched her buttocks.

Ilunga screamed. "Shut up, nigger," the fourth man warned, digging his nails into her flesh.

But she continued screaming, thinking they were going to kill her. Swearing, the last man clenched his fist and struck her once in the center of the face.

The pain was so awful she could never afterward remember all of it. She knew her nose had been flattened, and she choked on the blood that coursed through her nasal passages. Now she was sure she was going to die!

One man was on top of her, crushing her so that she could breathe only in pained gasps. Her legs were uncomfortably wide apart, and something big and hard was jamming up between them. She hardly felt this new pain, because her nose was so much worse, but she still tried ineffectively to squirm away. It was no use; she felt something rip, and knew that she had suffered some awful new injury. It felt as though someone were thrusting a thick stick inside her, hammering it in like a tent peg. Once, twice, three times—and then, mercifully, it relaxed.

The man got off, letting her breathe. But immediately a second one lay on her, and again her gut was wrenched by a driving intrusion.

The third man turned her over and got down on her back. But at that point she passed out. The last thing she remembered was the salty taste of blood in her mouth, mixing with the dirt.

She woke in pain, naked and cold on the ground. Her face and hair were matted with blood, and there was sand embedded in it. There was some blood on her thighs, too, and she hurt all over.

She seemed to have a number of bruises on her torso that she didn't remember getting, and evidently she had also been bitten in odd places.

Her first reaction was one of surprise. They had not killed her.

She got up, found the rags that remained of her dress, and staggered home. She was walking like a drunk, and almost fell several times. Her mother was out for the night, and she didn't dare bother a neighbor for help. She cleaned herself up as well as she could and put on a clean dress, but her broken nose would not stop bleeding or hurting. Sick and alarmed, she went to the nearby police station for help.

It was a mistake. "Kid, you better get to a doctor," the desk sergeant said. "Been fighting again? You brats ought to stay off the streets."

Now she had had time to work out what had happened. She had tried to hide it from herself, but realized that was pointless. "No. I was raped." She knew that carried the death penalty, if they caught the man. She could identify these ones.

"Hey, Joe," he called to another policeman. "Hear that? She was raped!"

Good; they were going to act on it. She had heard that they didn't, sometimes. Not when the victim was black.

The other man came out. He was huge and white, a clean-shaven version of one of the rapists. She repressed her jolt of fear, knowing that it was unreasonable. A physical resemblance meant nothing.

"Got to make a report," he said. "Here, let's mop up that nose." He ripped a handful of paper towels, wet them, and dabbed at the blood. "What'd it feel like, girl?"

"I-I don't know," she stammered, confused.

"How many times?"

"There were four men."

"Feel sort of good, once he got it in there?"

"They *ask* for it, way they dress," the sergeant put in.

"No, I was just going through the park," she said.

"Maybe you better show us where they did it."

"I told you. In the park."

"On *you*. Makes a difference, you know. If it's regular or ped-erasty. Or something else. Let's have a look."

"Maybe you'd better re-enact the crime," the sergeant said. "Get it down straight. For the record."

Her eyes moved from one to the other. Abruptly she realized that these, too, were white men, and that they were baiting her. They got some warped vicarious thrill from making her repeat the details. And they wanted to *look*.

They would not help her. No man would. No white man.

She left the station. They did not stop her. She heard their laughter as the door closed. If she had stayed there much longer, they would have had her re-enacting the crime, all right. Young black girl—why not? They were all whores.

Her mother had hardly more sympathy than the police—but for different reasons. "I *tol'* you not to cut through that park at night! Bad men there! Bad men! Black as well as white—they're all the same."

"But it never happened before." If only her nose would stop hurting.

"Child, you weren't of age before. But some men go after little children, too, and not just girl-children. They're all pricks, when they get the chance."

"Daddy wasn't bad."

"Your pa's the worst of all. How do you think I got knocked up with you? Why you think we're living here alone?"

"My brothers—"

"Half-brothers. That man left his seed in half the whores of the neighborhood, till you have I-don't-know-how-many broth-ers. And the same time getting to my kid sister, so your cousin Danny is your brother too."

"Don't talk about Danny!" Ilunga screamed. The boy was her closest male kin, and she liked him.

But in this manner a harsh lesson was learned. In the following days and weeks, while the physical wounds healed, the emotional ones deepened. Danny got beaten up, defending her reputation against white boys, and even the blacks were cynical.

Her nose could never mend entirely. They had no money for plastic surgery. The beauty that was to have been would never be.

Men were evil. *All* men. Except her little brother down the street. The white ones were the worst. And most particularly the haunters of the night park. And policemen.

No one would do anything about it, because all the doers were men.

Gradually she worked it out, and came to a decision. *She* would do something about it.

But she knew she could not do anything by herself, without thorough preparation. She was too young, too small, too weak, compared to a man. A woman was vulnerable in every way, except one.

If she made a mistake, she would get raped and beaten again. Perhaps killed. So she moved very carefully. She enrolled in a karate class. Here, already, there were complications; she had no money for the lessons, and no hope of getting it. She had to pay in the only coin she had, and this was akin to the very thing she loathed.

Yet it was ironically fitting that she was using man's sexuality as the first step in abolishing it. The rape had taught her that she was physically desirable, even when not trying to be. With very little effort on her part, she was able to become much more desirable.

The instructor was unprincipled, and he tended to be brutal with her, but this only confirmed her prior knowledge. *All men were evil.* So she submitted to his sadism without protest, no matter what he demanded. It was an education in perversion. But she also learned karate.

He was not a top-flight instructor, but she supplemented the lessons by avid reading on the subject. She even profited from his ugly lovemaking, learning at first hand what blows and grips were most painful. She would have good use for those, and meanwhile she was inuring herself to such pain.

After three years she was through with him. She was fifteen now, and well filled out, and she knew more karate than he did. She came to him one night, as she had a hundred times before, and kissed him, then stepped back and put her entire effort into a kick that burst both his testicles apart.

He had been properly paid, at last. She was no longer anyone's concubine.

After that, her career began. She would walk through the park at night, tempting men, and when one came to rape her, she desexed him. Permanently.

She wanted to go after policemen, too, but held back because she realized that this would more likely stir up hornets prematurely. If she left the police alone, they would leave her alone, and that was what she wanted. It was tactical folly to tackle all enemies at once; some had to wait their turn.

It seemed to work. She considered any week wasted that she did not desex at least one enemy, and sometimes she got two. Her record was three. Not a word about it appeared in any newspaper that she was aware of. The police did not even seem to be looking for her. Which confirmed her judgment yet again: evil men did not even look out for their own.

Meanwhile, coeds started to walk safely in the park at night.

But as years went by, the flavor palled. She still went after any man she could catch alone, but this was no longer enough. There were fewer, now, and she had to go farther afield, to other cities. Even so, she could go a month at a time without catching any. Word was out among the sex perverts; it was taboo to touch lone women, especially black women.

She tried drugs, but none quite satisfied her need. She didn't want to be doped, she wanted revenge. Revenge on all men. Except, of course, her brother Danny.

Then she encountered Kill-13. She tried it as a matter of scientific curiosity, not expecting much. She joined one of the first kill-parties in the state. She was the only woman there, and she did not like that. The others were all bums of the type she liked to meet in the park. Four of them, a bad number for an introduction to a drug, which was normally a highly private matter. Maybe Kill-13 addicts were social creatures; she was not. But she had long since learned to control her reactions.

They joked with her about the party they would have, once the drug took effect. They thought she was one of them, a whore of the streets. They thought the drug would give them phenomenal erective powers. Well, she would cure that, if any of them got too smart.

Nevertheless, she expected to have to pay for her dose in advance, with the usual coin, and was ready. Sex was nothing to her, merely a useful tool. She knew how to make a man react, and would do so with whatever man she had to accommodate, but she would deal with him later in the usual way.

But there was none of that. The Kill-13 pusher was a renegade kung-fu "expert," a self-styled *sifu*. Obviously he knew little about his martial art, and had probably washed out of training. Ilunga knew she could take him, anytime. She had no rating in karate, because she had never sought any, but if she *had* wanted that sort of recognition, she could have had at least a black belt. Kung-fu had no ratings, but this man was still a novice and a faker.

First he took some of the drug himself. He put a tiny capsule, hardly larger than a grain of rice, into a metal cup, closed it with a tight lid, and heated it with a burning candle. "It takes a couple minutes to vaporize," he explained. "Meanwhile you can try the equipment."

They were in his so-called *kwoon*, a kung-fu dojo or practice hall. Actually it was hardly more than a shed. A long punching bag or practice dummy hung from a rafter, and there were a number of rusty weapons and a large bulls-eye target. Dutifully the four men handled the weapons and put shoulders to the heavy bag.

"Now," the pusher said with a certain tremor of anticipation.

"No dangerous, painful needle. No diluted oral dose. It is impossible to cut Kill-13; it's either all there or it isn't there at all. It's right here in the smoke." He uncapped a little spout on the cup and put his nose down.

A jet of vapor shot out. He inhaled it, capping the cup again almost immediately. "Never take more than one sniff," he warned. "This stuff is powerful; an OD will blind you for several hours."

Ilunga almost snorted her derision. What a cheap device to prevent sniffers from taking too big a free sample. But since she was testing, not using, she would keep her own sniff small. At least she understood, now, why the drug was taken in "parties": a certain minimum amount had to be vaporized, and it would be wasted on a single person.

The effect was amazingly rapid. The pusher's manner changed; he had been a bit shaky, but now he gained confidence. The timbre of his voice lowered. He moved more powerfully. He seemed to have better coordination than he had had a moment before. But most remarkable, his *eyeballs turned bright orange.*

"Now," he repeated. He took up a knife and flung it at the target across the room. The blade whistled under the noses of the startled watchers and struck the bulls-eye. He threw three more in rapid succession, and all scored in the center. He picked up a Samurai sword, tossed it in the air, caught it and hurled it also into the bulls-eye. He charged the bag and struck it with his fist and foot. It ripped off its cord and fell solidly to the floor.

"Kill-Thirteen!" he announced grandly. "*The* martial-art drug! I am invincible! Try me!"

There were skeptics in the audience, Ilunga prominent among them. A couple of the men were in martial arts training; she could tell one of those readily by his manner. One stepped forward challengingly.

The pusher dodged around him so rapidly that he hardly had time to move. Then the pusher caught him from behind, picked him up, lifted him high overhead, and threw him into the group.

They all sprawled, catching the man. Impressive, yes, for the victim outweighed the pusher by a good fifty pounds. But Ilunga knew that the man could have carefully rehearsed his weapons demonstration, developing a splinter-skill of marksmanship. Move the target, and he might not be able to hit it anymore. And the bag's cord could have been designed to snap on impact. And the martial-artist victim could be a shill, there to put up a bold front and take a quick fall.

Another burly man stepped up. "How are you for something slow, like arm-wrestling?" he demanded.

For answer, the pusher sat at a table and set up his arm. The other sat opposite him, grasped his hand, and applied pressure.

"If I were in my normal state, you could take me easily," the pusher said, his orange eyes flashing as his glance flicked across his audience. "And if you were a demon, I wouldn't try against you. But at the moment—"

He heaved—and the muscular challenger groaned. The veins stood out in his forehead as though about to burst. Then he gave way. That didn't look like a fake to Ilunga; the muscles were bulging.

"I can draw on resources you can't," the pusher explained. "Kill-Thirteen is the first true athletic drug. With it you can put on more muscle faster than any other way, and the muscle you have is twice as effective. I'm lazy; I don't exercise, so I don't have big muscles, but Kill-Thirteen makes me more of a man than any of you."

The men were convinced, but not Ilunga. Two shills were possible. That would still leave three customers, a paying ratio for an expensive addictive drug. She would have to test the pusher herself. Her way. If he were a faker, he deserved it.

She strode forward. "I'll try you now," she said.

He stood facing her squarely, legs braced apart, a perfect setup for a frontal kick. She lifted her hands as though to strike, then without warning let fly with her deadly kick to the crotch.

He was faster than she. He spun aside, caught her foot in his hands, and dumped her ingloriously on the floor. The other men laughed.

The humiliation was nothing; she had little pride, only determination. Now she was a believer. She had never seen a man move so quickly, so surely. The pusher could not have done it on his own; the Kill-13 had to have changed him. Just as he claimed.

"Even if you had scored, you could not have hurt me," the pusher said. He handed her a knife. "Cut me. Hurt me."

Ilunga accepted the knife and poked the point into his proffered forearm. He did not flinch, even when the blood flowed. "I feel no pain," he explained.

She was not fooled. She could tell by the subtle reactions of his body that he did feel pain. But evidently it was muted, so that he could control his reaction to it. She realized that such diminution of sensation would have its liabilities; how would a demon experience tactile pleasure? How would he perform in a sensitive task, such as picking a lock? Still, this certainly demonstrated the anesthetic properties of the drug.

"Now," said the pusher a third time. He went to the drug vaporizer and relit the candle.

No one needed a second invitation. They lined up, and each took a controlled sniff of the gas. Ilunga, still cautious, waited until last.

She took her sniff, a shallow one. The effect seemed instantaneous. Sensation shot up her nostrils and spread explosively to her brain. She had a tiny pocket mirror, one of the few feminine tools she carried for park-time preparations. She brought it out now and looked at her own eyes.

They were yellowing already, the color deepening into orange. The bright lights of the room made this quite plain. And she felt terrific.

She took a knife and nicked her own skin. There was pain, but it was slight. More drug, and she knew that the anesthesia would be good enough for any normal occasion.

The men were already playing with the weapons, throwing

knives into the target and tossing swords. Ilunga took her knife and casually flipped it at a knothole in the rafter. It struck and stayed, exactly where she had aimed.

Yes, Kill-13 was real. She had never had such a sensation of power.

But it would surely cost. No addictive drug was cheap. "How much?" she asked.

"Twenty dollars a sniff," the pusher said.

They were drugged, but not stupid. In fact, Kill-13 seemed to heighten intelligence as well. There was no sense of drowsiness, but rather a complete control, physical and mental. "How long does a sniff last?" one man asked.

"Variable. About four hours for the high if you relax; less if you're active. Residual effects up to three days, depending on individual chemistry. In time you develop a tolerance, but a deeper sniff takes care of that."

That was what she had suspected. This was a high-priced habit. To maintain it a person would have to have two or three sniffs each week, at twenty dollars a throw. Once a person was fully addicted, the price would rise. One always had to figure the eventual cost, and in this case it would be as much as a hundred dollars a dose, or worse. There was no way she could afford it except to go into hijacking or full-time prostitution, and not even Kill-13 was worth that.

"Of course," the pusher continued after a pause, "one of the residual effects is the muscle-building property. One sniff every two or three days will allow you to put on impressive amounts. And that muscle is real; it will serve you anytime, not just during a fit. If you've used steroids, you'll discover that this beats them hollow."

That was what would hook more athletes than anything else. The need to build muscle. "I'm on the muscle drugs," the man who had lost the arm-wrestling admitted. "I need ups and downs, too; can't sleep on my own. What about—"

"No ups, no downs with Kill-Thirteen!" the pusher said. "This drug gives you *control.* Will yourself to sleep, and you're out; wake up full of pep. No constipation, no lung cancer, no liver damage."

Impressive attributes, if true, yet what he didn't mention was significant. Such as eye damage and brain disfunction. "How long does it show up in the body?" she asked.

"It *doesn't,*" he said. "By the time its physical effects show, the trace amount of Kill-Thirteen absorbed has been used up. There may be some in the brain and muscles, but no known test will register so small an amount. There is no legal proof of its presence."

That was too good to be true. If it had a continuing effect, it had to be present in the tissues of the body. And some test would show it. But it might be an expensive test, not feasible for mass use in athletic contests.

Of course the orange eyes were a dead giveaway.

"Well, the sample was nice," Ilunga said. She walked out. She expected a last minute pitch, perhaps a reduction in price, but the pusher let her go as if he didn't care. Odd.

She felt good. She did shadow-karate as she walked, knowing that her movements were precise and powerful. The drug certainly gave a lift, and its effects were real and forceful. That pusher really had performed well, after his sniff; his strength and speed and accuracy had been no illusion. She meant to enjoy her fit while it lasted; she would never get another.

Despite the orange eyes, Kill-13 was bound to be used in athletics. Tennis players would wear dark glasses, and football players could hide most of it behind their face guards. For well-supervised contests, such as the Olympic games, it would be more difficult. But if the muscle could be developed during the fit and retained after it, demons could compete during their sober stages. They might not be as good as they were during the fit, but they would still be better than the non-users.

Too bad it cost so much. She simply couldn't afford to become addicted.

But as her fit wore off, she became depressed. She walked the park, and found a mark, and kicked him, but her timing was off, and she knew she had not finished him. He would hurt a long time, but he would probably recover his virility. Too bad.

Well, this was to be expected. The trouble with drugs, *any* drugs, was that they drew on the reserves of the body, and when the drug wore off, the body felt unusual fatigue, until it had a chance to recuperate. A drug as strong as Kill-13 naturally had a powerful hangover. The sensible thing to do was to sleep it off.

She lay down, but even sleep was difficult. "Damn liar!" she muttered, remembering the pusher's assurances on that score. She felt increasingly ill.

She got the shakes. She vomited. She had diarrhea. Her head ached. Her whole body felt painful, as if she had a bad fever, though she didn't. Her urine turned greenish.

She took a slug of tomato juice spiked with vodka. It didn't help. She tried a barbiturate, a Blue Devil. She felt woozy, but still couldn't sleep.

Suddenly she sat bolt upright. "Good God—I've assembled the suicide combo!" she muttered. "Alcohol and barbiturate!"

She went to the sink and poked one finger down her throat. She gagged unpleasantly, but there was not enough left in her stomach to make a good heave. So she gulped a glass of water and tried again. It came up blood red.

She stared at the puke, dizzy.

"Oh, the tomato juice . . ." she muttered, after the shock of alarm faded.

But the symptoms continued, complicated by the other drugs she had taken. She had not thrown it *all* up. Her hands shook; she sweated and felt weak. The room spun about her even when she sat still.

Finally she had to admit it: "I'm hooked."

She was addicted to Kill-13—after a single sniff. No wonder the damned pusher had let her go.

Who would have believed it: a drug so strong that one sniff addicted the user. And she had fallen for it; she had walked into the trap. She had thought a small sniff would protect her, but she had been a fool. Why hadn't she investigated more carefully, first? Twenty dollars a sniff.

She fought it for two days. Heavy cold sweat alternated with uncontrollable shivering. She had hot and cold flashes, as though entering menopause. Her sense of balance was shot. Her heart palpitated, and there were severe pains in various places of her gut. Her hearing became excruciatingly acute; any sound was painful, and the ticking of the clock got so unbearably loud she finally smashed the thing. Then her own heartbeat got just as bad. Everything smelled of vomit, even her perfume, even food and water. Even vomit itself.

Then the more serious symptoms began. She had convulsions of increasing severity, in the throes of which she bit her tongue and bruised herself. She was afraid to take a bath, lest she cramp up and drown. She became incontinent, unable to get to the bathroom in time for natural functions. Her posterior itched intolerably; only by scratching so violently that it bled could she stop the damned irritation. And she suffered nightmare visions, many of them disgustingly sexual in nature. She reenacted that awful rape of her childhood, and the irony was that now she enjoyed it. Until she realized. She could hardly tell dream from reality.

She fought it for two more days. The withdrawal symptoms abated, but the craving increased. Life without Kill-13 was impossibly bleak. The physical dependency could be conquered; perhaps her body had actually revolted against the alcohol-barbiturate dose. But the emotional dependency—how could she resist, when her will to resist had been sapped?

At last she returned to the kung-fu pusher. "What do I have to do?" she asked sullenly. "I have no money."

He had her, and they both knew it. There would be hard bargaining. It galled her awfully to find herself yet again at the mercy of a man, but she could not delude herself about the situation. "What can you do?" he asked.

"I can push," she said reluctantly. Her muscles were tightening, presaging another convulsion, but she was able to suppress it. To her, pushers were little better than pimps.

"I don't need competition," he said frankly. "You're younger and better trained than I; you'd have me out of business, and, without Kill-Thirteen, I'd have to shoot myself. No one else gets at my source."

Valid point. Like Ilunga, he had few delusions. He was in his fashion an honest man, and she respected that. Which didn't change the fact that she hated every other quality about him, and it didn't alleviate her need for Kill-13. "I can lure men."

"And flatten their balls? Fine lot of converts those would be! And it's all pointless; demons don't need sex anyway."

Demons. So that was what the addicts called themselves. Maybe because of their demonic eyes. She had heard the term before, but it hadn't registered.

And Kill-13 stifled their sex drive. Very nice. By using it, and tempting men to do the same, she could accomplish her purpose without having to go through the increasing bore of searching them out alone in the parks and streets. She might even be able to get some policemen, who might be trapped as she'd been: not realizing it was addictive with one sniff. In fact, it didn't have to be voluntary; maybe she could take a hot cupful right into a police station and let it into the air. Beautiful!

No, there were holes in that. Kill-13 hadn't stifled her own sex drive, it had aggravated it. Maybe the effect on women was different. And the police station caper probably wouldn't work, because the vapor would be too diffuse when it filled the room. No use burning a hundred valuable kernels of the drug for such a dubious experiment.

She didn't say all this to the pusher. He was right about her: she was younger and better trained, and a hell of a lot smarter. She would work on her own devices in her own time, not giving them away to the man who had trapped her. Now she had to make a separate deal with him.

"I can organize them," she said. "Teach them to fight. So that when the big crackdown comes, you have a decent defense."

"There's no crackdown. The cops are afraid to touch Kill-Thirteen!"

"Wait till the cops themselves start using it," she said. That much should not give away her notions. "Then there'll be trouble. They'll start raiding you to get a free supply."

"The supply will dry up the moment they do that, and they know it."

"Then you'll be out of business, won't you?"

"I'll move to some other area," he said uncomfortably.

"Where there'll be another pusher, who doesn't want competition." She paused. "The time will come when muscle is needed, to prevent any police raids, and keep your territory secure. Suppose the cops hold you in jail, incommunicado, until you talk? No drug, no fit, for two, three, five days."

"Suddenly you are making sense!" he admitted. "All right, organize. You'll get one sniff a day, on the house, so long as we're free to operate. The day we get closed down—the day I'm arrested—it stops. Even if the pigs made *me* talk, they wouldn't give any to *you.*"

"You won't get closed down!" she said, aware of victory. "But I'll need some for recruits."

"Free to your recruits, one sniff a day, as long as they stay in line. That's the best I can do."

In the circumstance, it was generous enough. "I say who's a recruit and who isn't," she said. "We'll have to have good, tight discipline."

"You say. But you have to have them on call. If I tell you to raid some place in six hours, you raid."

"A sniff before the raid," she said. "To get them up for it. There may be killing."

"Naturally. A bonus—for a raid."

They had worked it out. The pusher gave her a sniff, and the monkey was off her back at last.

She went out recruiting. It wasn't hard, because the properties of Kill-13 spoke for themselves. But she knew there was no way off. She would have to perform well for the demons; she had no choice. If the drug was busted, she was dead.

She hadn't expected to have to raid actual martial arts establishments, and didn't like it, because that played havoc with her richest recruitment lode. She needed trained men, not bums, and unfortunately had to settle for the latter. But when the word came, she did it. The first was the dojo of some high-ranked judo fink who had been making a noise against the demons, stirring up concern among the straight citizens. One Jason Striker.

This was to be an object lesson, and a major test of her new demon troops. She had to see that they did well, even if she had to step in and finish the job herself.

*

"I see," I said. Now it was clear why the demons had raided my dojo. They could not tolerate any focus of resistance, especially within the martial arts. Ilunga, conversant with the martial arts, had known of me, known that no mild measure would be effective. So she had done her job, and done it well.

I felt my groin. It still hurt, some.

"She is not evil," Kobi said. "She serves a purpose."

"Some purpose!"

"There are now few molestations in the park. And the demons do not bother women. They have little sexual drive; their parts degenerate. So she is accomplishing her mission, in her way."

I considered. "You are asking me to let her go?"

"Only to reflect. To understand. To be sure your action is proper from all viewpoints."

He sounded so much like the old head monk of the Shaolin monastery that I was moved to sorrow. If only I had thought things through, then, and taken care of those sensors . . .

"I will reflect," I agreed. "I will not attack her. I will try to talk to her, to understand."

He nodded, and gave me her address. "And accept a gift from me," he added, bringing out a bundle of cloth. "I suspect you will find it useful on occasion."

It was a battered old army armored vest, not even oriental. Mildew coated it. Nonplused, I accepted.

CHAPTER 9

ENCOUNTER

It was a ghetto neighborhood with very few white faces.

The streets were littered with garbage, showing the "benign" neglect of the Caucasian city fathers; collections were evidently irregular and rare. There were whole rows of abandoned buildings, and sometimes complete city blocks stood empty. Many of the boarded houses had been broken into, and stripped of everything sellable; they were glassless husks. Some had been gutted by fire. Slogans were painted on the walls: *Viva Che, Long Live the Panthers, Kill Whitey.* There were some abandoned cars on the streets, stripped of everything including tires.

There was life here, though. Garishly painted prostitutes paraded outside bright bars; they had tight dresses, high leather boots, miniskirts, and wigs of all colors. One gave me the eye as I drove by; I lacked the nerve to meet her bold gaze. A group of children watched one child twirling a *nunchaku.* That disgusted me; such weapons were hardly toys, as my own experience documented.

Several people carried carved African walking sticks, useful for self-defense. Others walked huge dogs. Evidences of a violent neighborhood, exactly the kind Kobi Chija had described. It gave me a feeling of *deja vu,* of having been here before.

Ilunga's address was an old brownstone building. The ground floor contained about eight stores, several with windows boarded or even bricked over. A telephone booth outside had all its glass broken. There was no elevator, and the interior hallways reeked of dirt, cooking grease and urine. The paint was peeling; I could hardly blame it.

I found her apartment, but she was not in, and no one would tell me where she was. I was white, and my eyes were white; no one trusted me.

I took a last look at the two padlocks on her door and departed. Even a black karate mistress had to lock all strangers out.

So I went to the park, and walked among the quiet trees. It was a chill November night, but pleasant in its contrast to the slum and in its solitude. A man needs to be alone, on occasion, and no doubt the same was true for a woman.

I thought about Chiyako, recovering now in the hospital, and about Amalita, so loyal a friend, so savage an enemy. Could things turn sour with the Oriental girl, just as they had with the Latin American one? No, the Shaolin philosophy provided a stability that others lacked.

Then I spied Ilunga. She was standing under a light, in a flowing African dashiki, and she was an ebony beauty. I had formed two mental pictures of her: first as the black karate mistress who had maimed me, a cruel attacker; second as a young girl, victim of multiple rapes and mutilation and injustice. Now the two images gave way to a third: neither maiden nor fighting woman, but a lovely, lonely figure, dark in the dark night.

"I am Jason Striker," I said. "I have come to talk to you."

Her head turned to face me, her black hair flinging out momentarily. All I could really see was her silhouette; her broken nose did not show. "I know you," she said.

"Yes, we've met," I agreed.

Her smile was white in the shadow. "Come closer, white man."

"I give you fair warning," I said grimly. "I promised a man I would try to talk to you, but if you make a move, I will break you in half." That surprised me; bluster is not my way. But there *was* a score to settle, and I knew how dangerous she was. Her first hostile motion would activate an automatic response in me, and not a gentle one.

"You are champion of the world."

Now I stepped closer. "No. You are thinking of the Martial Open. A formal tournament last year. I represented Judo, and the result was a tie with karate. Any of them could have taken it, with other breaks—kung-fu, aikido, even wrestling."

"Leave us alone," she said. It sounded more like a plea than a threat.

"I have a mission. I have to eradicate Kill-Thirteen."

"Because I kicked you?" she asked derisively.

"Because I owe it to the memory of a kung-fu monastery."

"Kung-fu. We *are* kung-fu!"

"You are *not* kung-fu. You are a sick imitation that disgraces the name."

She attacked without warning, a fast kick aimed at my groin. I had anticipated such a motion, but still that demon reflex was too swift for me. If it had been as accurate as the first one, I would have been gelded for sure. In the darkness I did not see it coming. But maybe it was that same darkness that helped me, throwing off her aim. The point of her shoe missed my crotch and connected to the inside of my thigh: painful but not disabling.

So it was to be this way. I was relieved; I had done my best to talk, and now she had started the fight I wanted so much to finish. This was one woman I would not hesitate to pulverize.

Yet that story of Kobi's nagged at me, and I knew I was doing wrong.

I tried to grapple with her, but she danced out of my reach, scoring to the side of my face with a half-clenched fist, *hiraken.* With a feminine twist: her long nails left a trail of blood down my cheek. That made me mad. I pursued her, throwing a series of fist-blows. Any reluctance I had had about striking a female had vanished. If that first disabling kick, the one that had put me in the hospital, hadn't changed my attitude, Amalita's attack on Chiyako had. Women were every bit as vicious as men. Now I was using a universal language Ilunga understood, the language of hard knocks.

She blocked my fists, but then I let fly with a kick of my own. I caught her on the left buttock with the side of my foot, and a handsome buttock it was, too. She was propelled forward, and almost fell before she recovered her balance. She would have a bruise there.

Then I had her. My arms went around her as I tried to wrestle her to the ground, where I could use my greater weight to advantage. But the bitch knew too much; a blinding pain hit me under the ears. She had dug her thumbs in and was pushing in the pain centers. I had to let her go, knowing I was lucky she had not chosen to strike instead, possibly breaking my ear drums.

I grabbed at her bright colored shirt with my right hand and went into a *morote seoi nage* shoulder throw. But my hand cushioned her fall, and she knew how to take a fall. Even so, she must have had quite a jolt. I fell on her, trying to get her in an arm lock, *ude garami*, to force submission. But she bit my armpit. It hurt, but I could have sworn I felt her tongue caress my skin for a moment.

She rolled free and stood up again. She tried a jumping front kick. I moved aside, caught her ankle, and brought her down. I forced her to fall on her stomach in the brush at the edge of the path, and I hooked my legs under hers as my body squashed her on top. I put a naked strangle on her, *hadaka jime,* to subdue her, but she struggled mightily, her buttocks flexing against me. My face was buried in her thick hair, fragrant and slightly oily.

Her struggles ceased. I realized I had strangled her too hard, and I remembered my promise to Kobi. In the dark I could not see how she was, so I gave her mouth-to-mouth resuscitation. I did not want her dead. Yet.

And she bit me, her teeth cutting through my lip. I tasted my own blood. "Now that Chinese bitch will know you were with me!" she whispered.

I pulled back, flipped her over, and put my weight on her torso again, pinning her to the ground. It was now mainly a matter of weight and muscle; my combat skill was becoming irrelevant to the situation. I had to have a moment to think.

Of course I am used to feminine anatomy in combat; I have trained many young women in self defense. Some very attractive ones, too. But this situation was special. First Ilunga was not my trainee; she was fighting in earnest (at least, I assumed she was). Second, she had wounded me in an exceedingly painful and embarrassing manner, and I was not thinking of the lip-bite. I had a special score to settle. Third, I knew her history, so compassionately narrated by Kobi Chija; that gave me a kind of perspective. Fourth, I hated what she stood for: a killer drug and the emasculation of men.

Hate is an emotion often akin to love, and the boundary can be vague.

I had an emotional involvement with Ilunga, however negatively, and now a physical one. She was one hell of a specimen, and we were in one hell of a position. My crotch was wedged hard against her generous buttocks. I couldn't let go of her; she might kill me. Literally. She could be trying to trick me by a few suggestive words, making me pause, setting me up again. Because she had found she couldn't overcome my black belt judo skill, undoubtedly the best she had yet encountered.

I couldn't reason with her; her mind was under the spell of the drug. I had the physical advantage at the moment, but Kill-13 gave her awesome reflexes and coordination. I had to see that she did not get into a position to use them again. Yet I did not want to hurt her unnecessarily.

I could knock her out and leave her; a simple renewal of my stranglehold would do it. But that would not get the information I needed. And it wouldn't stop her from coming after me later and trying to kill me by stealth. All my fighting skill would not avail me against a knife in the dark. And a Kill-13 addict would hardly stop at murder.

She struggled again, turning part way over. I let her have some play because that close contact with her posterior was extraordinarily stimulating. Forget about all the moralities of the true martial artist, and about Chiyako; there was a growing sexual compulsion.

"I hate you!" she gasped. She bared her teeth and bit my shoulder, hard. I shouldn't have let her have that much leeway. Now I had to jam down close again and force her back, and to hell with what it did to my groin.

She worked her jaws again, and I made ready to push her face down into the dirt, to break her bite. But I hesitated, moved by some intuitive impulse, and let her bite. And the sensation was more like a kiss, this time. Her teeth were resting on my skin, not painfully, and her tongue was moving.

Was she actually trying to seduce me? I hardly believed that; all she wanted was to subvert my guard, to give her the physical advantage. I sure as hell was not about to let go of her!

I bit her back, on the neck, not hard. I tasted the flavor of her skin, smelled the musky aroma. The effect was aphrodisiac. Then her face turned, and her chin lifted, and her lips met mine.

For a long, long moment we held it, that kiss of adverse passion. I felt her tongue, as lithe and strong as the rest of her, like a serpent probing my mouth. A suitable opponent.

"Honky, I know a thousand ways," she murmured as we broke. "Too bad you're castrated."

So that was what she thought. To weaken me by reminding me of what I had lost. "Yeah?" I shifted on top of bet, letting her feel my arousal. I had her right between the legs, right below the crease of her buttocks, and a little shifting about would shove aside the barriers of our clothing. "How sure are you that I'm castrated?"

Her eyes opened wide, so that even in this shadow I could see the orange. "You have to be!"

I drove, and not with my foot or fist. "Okay, I have to be, and that's my big toe I'm poking you with. Call my bluff. Get your pants down." I encouraged her by reaching down with one hand to do the job, exposing that magnificent posterior.

She called it. The fight was on another level now, but no less desperate. Her hips thrust violently. The impact was painful, because my injury still was not completely healed, but steadily I moved toward the completion of the connection. "What do you think I've been doing with my Chinese girl? Teaching her karate?" Judo, maybe . . ."Why did you want to mark me, if you think I have nothing?"

"I loathe you, I despise you!" she gasped, wrestling against that rigidity. "You white prick!"

I could have laughed, but it wasn't so funny. It was literal. She was cursing the whiteness of my erection, the thing she thought she had abolished. But it was the passion behind the words that counted most.

Her thighs opened and closed spasmodically, and I saw her tongue flick over her lips. Now she knew I could conquer her this way, too. It was a slight on her karate competence, that a white man should have survived her kick.

I put my arm alongside of her head and brought her face toward mine. I kissed her again, risking the bite, but it did not come. Her passion was stronger than ever.

And I realized that this was what she really wanted. She knew I wasn't castrated; she was merely goading me to prove it. She might hate all men, but she was still a sexual creature. This was one way in which the drug left her unfulfilled, for male demons lacked the interest and capacity.

In the guise of masochism, she could indulge herself. Then she could expunge her guilt by castrating her partner.

Thus I was playing into her hands, if that was the correct description. I had the advantage in this fight because she had carefully given it to me. I had the opportunity to rape her, here in the rapist's park, and prove I was no better than the usual bums.

My passion abated. I let her go and scrambled back. "I don't need to prove myself on you," I said. "When I want that kind of experience, I'll pay for it. Ten dollars. Or has your fee for perver-sion gone up?"

"You bastard!" Now she meant it.

"I'm a man. The terms are not synonymous."

"If they aren't, it's the first time!"

"If you ever went half-way to meet a real man, instead of bums in the park, you'd learn how twisted your values are."

She stood up, throwing off her remaining clothing. She was gloriously naked in the dim lamplight. "You sure you don't want it?"

I stayed well back. "Not your way!"

"I never wanted it before," she murmured wonderingly. "Not with a white man."

I knew better than to answer.

But she had not forgotten the situation, and she made no apologies. "Score a point for you," she said, her voice now bitter. "You made me plead for white prick." She set about repairing her scattered clothing. "There will be another time."

I didn't want any other time. "I took you fair and square," I said. "I stood still for your kick, and now you know I survived it. I beat you in even combat, on your terms, and I didn't cheat."

She made a harsh bark of laughter. "Yes you did. You didn't finish what you started."

"All I want is information. Then I will leave you alone. We could have saved a lot of trouble if you had only talked to me, instead of—"

"I will talk to you now," she said.

I was suspicious of this sudden appearance of reason. What was she up to? Surely nothing good for me. Yet, from all I knew of her, she was honest within her framework. I had beaten her openly, and she would have to respond openly. She was technically a woman scorned, but we had a détente. "I want the name of your supplier."

"He is dangerous."

"The fake kung-fu pusher? Just give me his name."

"No. Now I deal with his superior. He would kill you."

"Several demons have tried already," I said.

"This one is not a recruit from the streets. He is a weapons specialist. He will not meet you barehanded."

"I'll take my chances."

"Miko. He's lame, but he can fight."

"If I find this man and destroy him," I said, "you'll be out of Kill-Thirteen."

"Perhaps not."

"You're too smart to risk that. How do I know you're telling the truth?" I thought she was, but feared that her loyalty to Kill-13 might be stronger than her integrity.

She faced me squarely. "Because I want you dead."

That I could believe. She had accepted defeat at my hands, though the mechanism of battle had not been confined to those precise members, and now knew no other way to recoup. She had given me fair warning.

"Tell Miko I'm coming," I said.

"There is no need," she said as she walked away. I wasn't sure exactly how she meant that.

CHAPTER 10

MIKO

Miko's address turned out to be inside a rusty old ship, a World War II vintage oil tanker anchored alongside a crummy pier on the river port. The name on it was *LOLITA II*—surely a misnomer for a sexless demon craft. It had a long open deck, a superstructure at one end, a mast at the other. I could see a couple of lifeboats on board, and one modern speedboat. The ship was tied to the pier by ropes or big cables. It had a small bridge that could be lifted out of the way for privacy; it was out of the way now. That was all I could make out; there was no light showing anywhere on it.

I stood on the dock, considering alternatives. I could summon the police, but even if they came quickly and quietly enough to trap the demons, the Kill-13 supplies would very likely be destroyed or dumped overboard, leaving no evidence against them. Assuming there was any local ordinance against the drug. In fact, it wasn't even the drug I wanted, but information: where was the ultimate source? The police could arrest a thousand pushers and hardly make a dent on the drug trade—and the local police could very well be in the pay of the demons. This could be the branch of a great tree; unless I dug out the root, the deadly plant would always regenerate.

I checked myself over. I couldn't afford to be burdened with heavy tools or weapons, and wasn't sure they would be much use in this situation. All I wanted to do was reach Miko and make him talk, soon. I had come directly from my interview with Ilunga, knowing that even twelve hours could be disastrous. That meant scarcely an hour's rest while driving across town.

All I had was the armored vest made of fiberglass that Kobi had given me, and the pair of *tonfas* that Chiyako had let me have earlier. I had meant to add them to my display case, but had not yet gotten around to it. These were busy times.

The vest was bulky but light, designed to interfere minimally with the wearer's movement. I had used similar equipment in combat during the war. It would offer a lot of protection against shrapnel and certain hand weapons, but I hardly expected to sit still for such things anyway. What had Kobi had in mind? Well, I would gamble on his precognition, and wear it this time.

The *tonfas*—I didn't know. I had had practice with them, along with many other obscure weapons, at the Shaolin monastery, but they were hardly the weapon of choice for a swift, silent attack. Each *tonfa* was a heavy wooden board about eighteen inches long, with a sturdy peg-handle set at right angles in the flat side about three quarters of the distance in from the end. They had originally been used by the farmers of Okinawa for pounding rice and other grain crops. Later they had been adapted as a defensive weapon against the swords and spears of warriors, with such success that the tonfa had become a weapon in its own right. But would such a device serve me here in America, against the rabid demons?

I had to hope so. Ilunga would surely warn her supplier of my coming, but I hoped my immediate followup would foil that. I wanted to catch Miko by surprise. That was my only hope, for once he learned of my encounter with the black karate mistress, my life—and quite possibly hers as well—would be marked for rapid extinction. These were not sportsmen I was dealing with.

I tied the two *tonfas* to my waist and tucked them inside my pants in such a way that they would not bang together. Noise was unacceptable, with the acute hearing of the demons. I took firm hold of the guy-cable. It was much more than a wire, up close; it was a strongly twisted cord about two and a half inches in diameter. It offered good purchase for my hands and feet. But it was rusty, likely to cut my hands, and there was a sort of round plate on it, a little way along. A ratcatcher, I realized, to stop the rats from climbing the cable to the ship. "The rats are already aboard!" I thought. "Demon rats!" I had gloves to protect my hands, but it would be a struggle to get past that soup plate.

Well, I had to do it. I swung myself along, monkey-like, hand over hand. I almost fell, negotiating the ratcatcher; the vest didn't help, and I regretted having it on. Too late to take it off, though; the black water was waiting for me to try such a maneuver in mid-air.

When my arms got tired, I hooked my legs over and hung upside down, resting. Then I handed along for another stint. It was a grueling journey, but I reminded my self that I had just finished a hard fight with the black mistress, and that I had to conserve my strength as much as possible for the coming encounter. So I rested frequently.

By the time I got there, the palms of my gloves were in shreds, and my hands were hurting. That barbed cable!

I hoisted myself silently over the gunwale and dropped to the deck. My arms were cramped; I hoped I would have a decent chance to rest.

No one came. I proceeded along the long deck, looking for an entry to the interior. At this point, I was beginning to doubt that anyone was aboard. That was probably why I had boarded without being observed.

"Not quite," a voice said.

I jumped to face the sound, expecting the alarm to be cried at any moment. But this demon did not cry it. Instead I saw him assume a stance, in the faint light of the moon and the city. He wanted to fight.

He was a fool. His fit of Kill-13 had made him too confident, too eager to prove himself. He obviously knew or suspected who I was, and wanted the glory of dispatching me, alone. He should have held me at bay while he summoned others, or else ambushed me from behind. Or better yet, alerted the ship without even letting me know I had been discovered.

Not that I had any great confidence of my own. I was still tired from the long haul along the rope, and my vitality seemed low after my original injury. It was that it was tactical folly to give a trapped enemy a fighting chance. He just might expand on it.

This demon was fast and powerful, but I had anticipated that. He tried a reverse punch to my face, and I caught it on my forearm. I countered with a low strike to his spleen, which he parried as easily.

He was also a skilled karateka, obviously a black belt. A considerable cut above the other demons I had encountered, apart from Ilunga. This bothered me, not only because it indicated just how difficult my task was, but because it meant that the drug had already subverted some ranking martial artists. They must have been making a real attempt to bring in top men. Rabble and fakers were bad enough; real black belts were worse. Too much of this, and the entire martial arts movement of the world could be governed by the demon cult.

He fired a high kick at my head, and such was its ferocity and nicety of execution that it should have scored. But it missed. Not by much, but by enough to weaken its effect considerably. It grazed the side of my .face with enough force to make me dizzy. And I realized something significant.

The light was very poor, here, mostly deep shadow. My eyes had adapted to it, but it certainly was no help in combat. The orange of the demons' eyes had to reflect gross distension of the capillaries, harming the eyeballs, and adversely affecting sight. Night vision should be exceptionally poor. In bright light it made little difference, but in poor light, the demon had to be partially blind.

He couldn't see me as well as I saw him. I realized that all the demon encounters I'd had had been in daylight, except the one I had forced on Ilunga, and she had not fought as well as she might have, missing one of her kicks. Could this daylight activity be because the demons preferred not to operate at night? If so, good reason!

If this were true, it gave me an important advantage. I adjusted my strategy accordingly. I drew him out of position with a series of front kicks, which he parried with his forearms, trying to catch my leg. While he was bent over I jumped in fast and scored with a *hiraken, a* half-clenched fist, to the side of his head. My thumb was folded in, my fingers bent at the second knuckles. I struck his head hard with the palm area of that fist, right near the ear. My fingernails lacerated the side of his face so that it bled.

He might not have been able to feel much pain, but that blow shook him up. The brain itself feels no pain in the ordinary person, but when it gets banged it cannot function well, and a concussion can be fatal. He looked wildly around, having even more trouble locating me in the dark. Yes, his night-vision was a disaster.

I didn't want to close with him, because that would enable him to work by touch, nullifying my advantage. So I tried to psych him out, to force him into a tactical mistake that would enable me to finish him quickly and quietly.

"You're blind," I said. "The drug destroyed your eyes, and your sight is fading."

My mistake! I had just given him something else to orient on: my voice. His hands whipped to his sash with the speed of a striking snake, and suddenly I was struck in the chest: once, twice. Not by his hands or feet; he remained across the deck, glaring in my direction. By two small throwing knives.

I dropped to my knees, groaning. Both blades were embedded to the hilt.

The demon charged toward me. Then I struck back. I wrenched the knives out with my two hands and jabbed them at his belly.

I underestimated his speed. He didn't stop or dodge aside. The blades penetrated his abdomen. He fell at my feet.

I leaped clear. I was only scratched; the fiberglass vest had taken the brunt, absorbing the force and most of the length of each knife. My ploy had fooled the overconfident demon, who had not been able to see the vest on me. I was alive, thanks to Kobi's prophetic gift.

But now I felt that the vest slowed me down too much, and against these demons, maximum speed was critical.

So, regretfully, I took it off; it had served its purpose. I hoped.

I stepped on down the deck, but already another demon had spotted me. He carried a *manriki gusari*—a length of chain with weighted ends. The thing was hardly a foot long, and it was light, but the lead weights made it deadly in the hands of an expert. Other demons had used chains, notably in the attack on my dojo that had precipitated my active involvement, but they had been adapted bicycle chains, not tailored weapons like this one. There is a tremendous difference between a weapon of momentary convenience, and one that has been crafted and adapted with skill. For one thing, the tailored weapon often indicates the serious weaponist, one who has trained under professional supervision.

I wasn't going to gamble that this demon was a duffer. It was likely that this ship was the storage depot for all the Kill-13 drug supplied to this region, and it might be the entry facility for a much larger region. There was no way to tell how extensive the demon network was, or where their main supply route lay. Obviously the most skilled of their fighters guarded it.

I had guessed right. The chain whistled as he approached. No amateur bumbling here; the demon knew what he was doing. In a moment he would have the length of it around my neck, a garrote, or else my hands would be trussed securely, making me a prisoner. Neither alternative was inviting.

I dived to the deck. The chain struck me across the back, stingingly; the lead weight felt like a hammer-blow.

I twisted and twirled on the floor to escape further blows. My maneuver was partially effective; I got stung several times, but not critically. One strike across the face could blind me and break all the bones of my face.

The *manriki* was a Japanese Samurai weapon, popular with palace guards. It was sacrilegious to spill blood on the palace grounds, yet competent defense had to be made. So this bloodless weapon came into play, most effectively. It was also used to disarm unruly Samurai warriors; a trained *manriki* could handle all but the best.

I could not evade the chain much longer. I spun like a top, while that thing flashed above me, scoring my back like a whip. I dared not grab for it; my hands would be caught. All I wanted to do was get inside its radius.

Then the shadow came to my aid again. The demon misjudged my roll, and overshot me. I straightened out within the radius of the chain, jumping up, and delivered a roundhouse kick, a *mawashi geri*, to the side of his head.

The foot is reputed to be the strongest section of the body; the head the weakest. Much depends, however, on how they are used. An expert skull could break an inexpert foot. In this case the foot was expert. The ball of it broke the bones of his head, crushing his temple inward, and he was done.

The sound of this fight had alerted the ship. The demon sentry system had been incompetently organized; obviously they lacked proper discipline and direction. But that made little difference now. Four more demons charged me, their feet clattering on the rusty deck. All carried *bos*: long staffs, similar to those used the world over. Dangerous weapons, and a bleak prospect for me. One such weapon in expert hands would be enough to finish me. Four . . .

Still, the darkness helped me. I realized they could not turn on lights even if they had them, because that would attract attention from the shore. This was supposed to be an empty ship.

I snatched up the chain and struck the lead demon across the face with it—the very blow I had feared would be used against me. He staggered back, and I grabbed his *bo*. Now I had a weapon to match theirs, and thanks again to my brief Shaolin training, that had at least exposed me to such weapons though there had not been time to make me expert, I had some idea of how to use it. My odds had just improved significantly.

I was near the superstructure of the ship, a restricted part of the deck bounded on one side by a narrow iron stair descending into the bowels. A lifeboat was lashed in this vicinity, and there were bundles of heavy rope strewn about. A cluttered place, and that was just fine by me.

I stayed on the deck, where I had dived for the fallen staff. I might not have been a match for any one of them with this weapon, but they had made the mistake of rushing in together, crowding each other, hampering each other's motions, tripping over the ropes. A group is not better than an individual in all cases, especially when the locale is restricted.

They tried to draw back, to organize against me, but I gave them no chance. I poked the end of my *bo* like a rapier. I hit one demon in the chest, breaking ribs; I got another on the chin with the backswing, knocking him out. I twirled my staff around my head, seeking another opening.

Now there was one. He struck at my head. I ducked down, just as though this were a routine Shaolin exercise, so that the *bo* passed harmlessly over my head. Then I rifled a lengthwise shot to his crotch, using the *bo* like a spear. I hated to do it, after my own experience. But my chance to catch Miko was vanishing, and I had to move swiftly. This blow was incapacitating, regardless of how little pain he actually felt.

The last *bo* demon went down. Probably he would be up again soon, but not in condition to do me harm. I jumped out of the tangle of injured or unconscious demons, and braced for the on-slaught of the next, now striding down the deck.

And I fell on my face. My *bo* flew wide. One of those injured had grabbed my foot. Feeling like an idiot, I kicked backward and hit him with my heel, crushing his cheekbone, and he settled down again. I had underestimated the demon's resistance to the pain of injury, and it had almost cost me severely.

Time for a change of venue; if I stayed here my luck was sure to run out. I rolled for the rail and half-tumbled into the stairwell, trying to avoid the oncoming demon. I got my feet under me and charged downward, seeking a good place to hide. They certainly knew I was aboard, but if they had to spread out in a search pattern covering the whole ship, the advantage would be mine. I might yet be able to locate Miko and make him talk.

"Lights!" the demon behind me cried.

Blinding lights came on. I shielded my eyes with one hand— and made out a demon with a rifle, trained on me.

I froze, needing no command. Evidently the sudden transition to brilliance didn't bother demon eyes, perhaps because of that lack of night vision. "I thought you folks didn't use firearms," I said.

Now the pursuing demon descended the stairs. "Astute, judoka," he said. "We do believe in the power of our bodies, a power that cannot be properly exploited by the use of firearms. Any weakling can pull a trigger. We much prefer the manly ancient ways. In addition, firearms make a great deal of unpleasant noise, and our hearing is acute. There is a decided advantage in silent weapons. Finally, there are strong local gun-control laws. I fear our immunity to police interference would be severely strained if we violated those particular statutes. So we eschew such weapons, except in special cases."

I turned, slowly, to face him. He was about five feet eight but looked shorter because of his gorilla-like build. He weighed about 225 pounds, with long arms and short, bowed legs. When he walked, he limped. A scar ran along his chin, enhancing his ugliness. His clothing, in contrast, was bright and pretty: blue kung-fu trousers and kimono shirt.

"Hello, Miko," I said.

"You have gone to a great deal of trouble to find me, Striker," the demon said.

"Kill-Thirteen has been a great nuisance to me, Miko," I replied. I watched him carefully. He did not appear to be armed, but I knew better than to trust that. Anything could be hidden under his uniform.

"The terms of our encounter are simple," Miko said. "Defeat me in fair combat, and you shall go free. Lose, and you will become one of us."

"One of you!" I exclaimed, appalled.

"Come now, Striker," he said as though admonishing a balky child. "It is an excellent proposition for one of your stature. We make no secret of it; we desire to be represented by men of your reputation and competence. There is a substantial future for you, with us."

"Substantial future!" I echoed. "I am your enemy! You could never trust me!" But, my own words gave me a thrill of misgiving, for I remembered saying something similar long ago, to the head monk of the kung-fu monastery. How wrong I had been, then.

"All demons are trustworthy," he said. "They know there is no other source of Kill-Thirteen. Be at ease on that score. Also, we know you to be a man of integrity; if you agree to join us, you will do so."

"Then why don't you just shoot me down and dose me with it now?" I demanded, partly because I was afraid they would do just that.

"Two reasons, Striker. First, the drug is a strain on the system, initially. If you were dosed when wounded, it could be fatal, and that would be pointless. Second, we must have your acquiescence. You are strong-minded; dosed against your will, you would seek suicide at the earliest opportunity, and would be of no use to us. But if you agree, your strength and your honor would tremendously enhance our effort. It is worth some risk to us, to convert you."

"You talk of honor," I said. "What assurance do I have that your man won't simply shoot me dead, after I beat you?"

"Striker, we do have standards," he said. "We are not fly-by-night ruffians. We merely want to pursue our objectives with security. We have no reason to kill you."

"That wasn't the way it looked when your black mistress raided my dojo!"

"An object lesson, no more. She spared your life deliberately."

"And in the hospital—"

"They were underlings, not party to our higher decision. With a man like you in charge of such operations, such errors will not occur."

It was possible, I realized. They did stand in need of better leadership. Miko was an excellent talker, but his ship-alert system stunk; he was an incomplete leader. But he was intelligent enough to recognize his own limitations. Probably their really competent people were spread thinly.

I gave it one more try. "Ilunga told me you would kill me."

"Ilunga is a woman," he said, almost contemptuously. "You humbled her. It is quite possible that she hopes *you* will kill *me,* as she aspires to my position."

Answer enough. And they did have me covered. I would have to gamble. Gamble that I could beat him, and that the demons would keep their word.

"One other thing," I said. "I didn't come here just to go away again. I need to know the source of the drug."

Now he hesitated, which was a good sign. A liar would have agreed readily. "Few demons and no straights can know that place," he said finally. "If I told you, they would cut off our supply, and we would all die."

"*You* don't offer much of a bargain, then," I said. "If I lose, you'll tell me, because I'll be an addict, a demon. If I win, I deserve the information. You have to be prepared to gamble yourself."

"No. My gamble is in fighting you. This is sacred."

I laughed. "You are demons! Creatures of hell, bound to a hell-drug! How can anything be sacred to you?"

But he was serious. "Kali would know. And punish. I can offer you your life, no more. If we cannot agree on terms, I shall be forced to kill you now." And he raised his arm in a gesture to the rifleman.

Kali. Who was that? It was a clue, perhaps sufficient. He seemed to have spoken the name unawares. And they *could* kill me.

"All right," I said. It was a hell of a gamble, because the last thing I wanted to do was to take a sniff of Kill-13. But I had to chance it.

"This way," Miko said.

We were on a kind of catwalk overlooking a tremendous interior room. In fact, it was the cavernous hold of the tanker, converted to human use. The walls were painted red, and the broad floor was carpeted. One end was set up like a dojo, with training equipment and even hangings of bright silk and pictures on the wall. It was a lush residence, but the reek of oil was omnipresent.

The rifleman remained on the catwalk, covering me, while Miko, the other demons, and I climbed iron rungs set into the wall, to the bottom of the hold.

I certainly was not going to make any quick break out of this one, even if I were prepared to break my word.

Miko signaled, and the rifleman lowered his weapon. Not that that made much difference now. The wounded demons formed themselves into a semicircle on the floor. Miko approached carefully, barehanded. He knew one of the barehanded martial arts, obviously, probably kung-fu. His kung-fu uniform meant nothing; all demons called themselves members of the Kung-Fu Temple, even karatekas like Ilunga.

We made formal bows, then closed.

Miko leaped straight into the air, his lameness disappearing. He emitted a terrible *kiai* yell and made an awful face. *"Saaaa!"*

If he thought to frighten me, he was a fool. I was an old hand at this. I too leaped high and let fly a worse yell. *"Yaaaa!"* And I made a face I wish I could have seen.

God, he was fast! He flipped across the deck, his bare feet flashing toward my head.

I jumped away, blocking with my forearms. I had also removed my shoes. I tried to make a counter kick at his inverted face, but he was already changing position. His eyes blazed orange as his head avoided my blow.

Then he was on his feet, and his fist scored on my shoulder, rocking me back. I countered with an uppercut to his nose: an inverted fist, *uraken*. His forward inertia prevented him from getting out of the way in time, and I drew blood. It was a neat shot, and must have looked impressive, but I knew it was sheer luck, and only a minor injury. One tries many motions, not expecting them to work, and sometimes they do.

He didn't seem to be in pain—largesse of the drug again—but he was aware of the dripping blood. He must have assumed that my reflexes were faster than they were; actually I was relying on my many years of conditioning, making automatic responses that were faster than any thought-out ones could be. I had to, because of his incredible speed. So he made a mistake in judgment, deciding that he could not defeat me fairly after all.

He pulled back, reached into his kimono, and brought forth two blades. They were *sais*—long sharp knives with projecting tines, to catch opposing blades. Each one was like a Neptune's trident, but with the center prong twice as long as the other two. The main blade was about a foot long. In short, a wicked instrument, one that could stand up to a sword.

I had no sword. Barehanded, I had no chance against this weapon; even if I managed to get hold of one *sai*, the other would get me. He obviously knew how to use it. With his speed, he would cut me apart in moments. So I ran.

"Coward!" he yelled gleefully. "You have nowhere to go! I'll pin you to the wall!"

Easy talk, from the armed to the unarmed. But I had a surprise of my own to unveil. "Bless you, Chiyako!" I thought I drew out my *tonfas*, clashing them together so that they emitted their peculiar clacking sound, loud in this chamber. There was a murmur of surprise from the demons.

They chuckled when they saw my crude looking weapons. Certainly the *tonfa* was as unlikely an instrument as any; it had no blade, little mass, and was only a foot and a half long. But it did have its points, as Chiyako had demonstrated, and it was ideal against a blade. I hoped Miko knew no more about the *tonfa* than the other demons did.

Miko thrust one of his *sais* at me. The twelve-inch blade sliced toward my gut, but I moved one *tonfa* to intercept it, rather like a Ping Pong paddle catching the ball. The point stuck momentarily in the wood before he jerked it back.

I did not take the offense at once. My weapon was defensive in nature, not suited to fancy ploys. At least, not by one who was less than expert in its use, as I was. I wanted to test the skill of my opponent in this new circumstance. I could not afford overconfidence.

That skill was not long in the proving. The demon danced about, his blades flashing in and out in a blinding display. He twirled the *sais*, and he seemed to float in the air, jumping and somersaulting with the amazing reflexes of the drug. I tried to keep my gaze on the weapons, but this quickly made me dizzy. That may have been part of his strategy. At this rate, I would soon make a mistake, either blocking a feint, or failing to block a genuine thrust. The demon might not know much about the *tonfa*, but he did know how to bewilder an opponent.

I had to be more aggressive. Time would play into his hands, not mine. I whirled my *tonfas* around their short handles, making feints of my own. He wasn't fooled; his blades flicked in and out, nicking me in the arms, the legs. Both the edge and the point of the *sai* were dangerous. I suspected that the main reason my wounds were not worse was that he wanted to defeat me without injuring me too badly for me to survive a dose of Kill-13.

Still, I managed to strike him several times about the body, and these blows had to hurt, like wooden boxing gloves. The *sais* were specially designed to fight swords, but I did not carry a sword. The trident was almost useless against the squat *tonfa*. He was always moving, so I could not score cleanly, but just as he was making me bleed, from a dozen shallow cuts in my arms and upper body, so my blows with the wood were bruising him. I was sure I had scored several strikes that would have knocked out the average man, as the *tonfa* is as solid as a policeman's billy-club.

But this was no average man. Welts were rising on his muscular upper arms, and a nasty bump was rising on his forehead, and no doubt worse bruises were hidden by the uniform, but he was a demon, and he took no notice of them.

He thrust at my neck, and this time I gambled. Instead of intercepting it with the flat of my board, I struck upward at his hand. Too late and I could receive a fatal cut; too early and he would have time to counter my move, perhaps disarming me. But I timed it right.

The edge of the *tonfa* caught his hand, hard. The *sai* went flying away. He was half disarmed.

But with the other blade he caught my exposed hand, slicing it across the back. I dropped the *tonfa*; I only hoped the tendons leading to my fingers had not been severed. My gamble had gained me nothing, after all; now I, too, was half-armed. And one *sai* could do a hell of a lot more damage than one *tonfa* could stop.

I backed away. I had to stop the bleeding. I concentrated, and felt the force of *ki* going to that hand, strengthening it, shutting off the flow. I had learned the power of *ki* from a venerable Japanese warrior, an expert in Aikido. Hiroshi was his name, and he was able to do extraordinary things, utilizing this hidden power. With me it was intermittent; only in moments of extreme stress or need could I draw on it. If I lost this fight, I might try to use the *ki* to combat the effect of Kill-13 on my system. But how much better to win!

Miko gambled too. Confident of victory, he leaped at me and struck downward with his remaining *sai*. I caught it on my other *tonfa*, the blade between the board and the handle, holding it there momentarily. Now, with no second blade to guard against, I struck him with my wounded hand on the *sai*-arm. I used the "knife-hand" blow, the side of my hand held stiff. Blood was streaming down my arm, despite my *ki* effort, but my force was undiminished. I made contact at the middle of his forearm—and the *ki* made my hand so strong that his arm snapped like a twig.

Now he was unarmed, victim of his rash attack. But I was not fool enough to relinquish the initiative. As he hunched over, I followed through with a descending elbow strike, *hiji oroshi-uchi*, that hit him in the upper middle back, right between the shoulders on the spine. His spine snapped. He went into a terrible muscle spasm, his whole body contorting.

Miko fell, and I think now he felt pain, for he was dying. "Kali!" he cried, a hideous scream, and that was all. The drug had left him no physical reserves for recovery.

I turned to face the other demons, alert for treachery. But they made no move. "It was a fair fight," I said. "I did not go for a weapon until after he did."

I walked boldly to the ladder and climbed the rungs, conscious of the rifleman's red eyes upon me. My nerves screamed at me to hurry up, but I knew that if I showed fear or even undue haste, I could take a bullet in the back. I could not stop the cold beads of sweat forming on my forehead, running down my neck, and I left blood on every second rung, but I kept the pace steady.

At last I made the catwalk. I walked to the stairs leading up and out, and I thought I heard a click, as of a rifle bolt being pulled back.

I launched myself up the stairs, across the deck, and over the rail into the darkness beyond the ship. Yet another fear came to me then: suppose that I struck unseen debris floating on the water, knocking myself out and drowning?

I hit the cold water, not cleanly, but safely. I let myself go under, swimming with the current. I waited till the river had carried me some distance downstream before I struck for shore. I just didn't want to give the demon marksman any additional chance to change his mind.

There was no pursuit. For what it was worth, the demons had honored their pact with me.

CHAPTER 11

BLACK MISTRESS

"Kali," Kobi Chija said musingly. "I know of no man by that name. It is not Chinese or Japanese.

"I don't either," I said. "But it is all we have to go on." I paused. "Kali—is it possible that Kali is a woman?"

"Possible, certainly, but still not Oriental. Unless—" He looked up, startled. "Kali—the black goddess!"

"Goddess?" Now I was startled. "He did speak of sacrilege. Or sacredness. It could be some idol they worship. *Is* there such a god?"

He fetched a book. "Yes! Not American, not Chinese. Indian, I believe. The Goddess of Death."

"Indian! That fits! The Mayas—"

He smiled. "The *real* Indians. Hindu." He found his place in the book, a text on mythology. "See, here it is. Kali is a terrifying demon of Hindu mythology. She has black skin, four arms, three eyes-and an insatiable lust for destruction."

"Sounds like Kill-Thirteen, all right," I said. "They must have adopted her as their symbol. Maybe they made the same mistake I did, thinking Indian had to be American. Let me see that book."

So I learned about the black goddess Kali: she wore red armor—the color of fresh blood?—and a necklace of human skulls about the throat. Her black scepter ended in another skull. She held daggers in her hands. Her consort was Yama, God of Death. Among her devotees were the Thuggees, the notorious strangler assassins of India.

It was fascinating, but unhelpful as hell. Obviously there was no real goddess, except perhaps as a statue, an idol. No one we could trace down to question about the source of Kill-13.

"Dead end," I said in disgust.

Kobi shrugged. "Who can say? Perhaps an avenue will appear, though the way seems blocked at the moment."

No point in pursuing that right now. I turned to a better subject. "How is Chiyako doing? I wish she'd let me visit her."

"She returns this afternoon," he said, smiling. "She is embarrassed about her appearance."

"She has no need to be!" I exclaimed.

"Perhaps the issue is unusually sensitive. She has been trying to determine her own feelings." He glanced at me quizzically, and I realized that I had been asked a question.

"I guess you know that I love her."

He did not remark on my American bluntness, but answered it with a certain directness of his own. I suppose my manners were something of a trial to him. "I had suspected that *you* did not."

"Not love her? I—"

"Not *know.*"

Close enough. "I never found the right girl before. That is, well, this is awkward. There has been a lot of emotional history to untangle. Cambodia, you know."

He nodded. He knew.

"Is she—are you free to tell me whether—"

"She awaits your decision. She has not been spoken for."

Good news! Yet— "If I may ask—an attractive girl like her—why not?"

"We follow the Chinese custom."

Volumes were spoken in those words. I knew little about it,

except that Chinese custom embraced arranged marriages and extremely intricate protocol. Chiyako had not married because her father had not yet made that decision for her. Yet undoubtedly he would not oppose a marriage she genuinely wanted. His attitude would be a sure guide to hers.

"I don't really know your ways," I said, feeling shaky. "How does one—" I faltered again. Suddenly it seemed ludicrous, this notion that a strict Chinese father would permit his daughter to marry a white man.

"One's father pays a call," Kobi said.

Then the answer was not an absolute no. If I would follow the forms, he would decide, in due course. But: "Suppose one's father is dead?"

"Then the ranking male of the family." He saw my frown. I could hardly start bringing in distant relatives, who would have no grasp of the situation, and might even have racial prejudices. I did not want the word miscegenation to be bandied about. "Or a patriarchal friend, conversant with the forms."

I brightened. Hiroshi, the Aikido sensei. He would do it. And he had international stature.

Then I had another ugly thought. Caucasians were not the only ones with prejudices. "Suppose one's friend is Japanese?"

Kobi's brows raised. "Japanese?" Bad feeling was notorious between the Chinese and the Japanese. But after a moment he shrugged with mock resignation. "One must be tolerant, even of Japanese."

I knew it was going to be all right. Hiroshi and Kobi would hit it off famously, and out of that dialogue could very well come a matrimonial contract.

For Chiyako was the girl I wanted to marry. It was not that I had known her long—all of a week!—but that she was part of Shaolin, true to its philosophies. The life I might have had in the monastery would be fulfilled in her. The fact that she was a young, talented, beautiful girl was an incidental bonus; the time would come when she was old, yet love would endure. That was the distinction between Chiyako and all other girls.

Somehow, by what devious internal process I could not fathom, that triggered a realization. "Kali. She's like Ilunga!"

"An exaggeration," he murmured. "At heart she is an intelligent, sensitive girl. Even now, she has much to offer. Had she been fairly treated—"

"Sure, but there's a family resemblance," I exclaimed. "Black, female, savage, destructive."

He shook his head sadly. "If that is the way you see her."

I was curious. "How do *you* see her?"

"I suspect she is as much a woman as my daughter, as loyal to her principles. As worthy of respect."

"But what principles!" I said. "Kali principles."

"It does seem more than coincidence. Perhaps Ilunga knows more than she has said."

I dreaded another encounter with the black mistress. But there seemed to be no alternative, if I was to pursue my mission. "I'll have another talk with her," I said. And felt an odd relief.

"Will you wait here until my daughter comes home? I shall bring her this afternoon."

I was sorely tempted, but that reminded me of other important business. "I have a letter to write," I said. A letter to Hiroshi, in far Japan. "Would it be all right if I visited her later in the evening?"

"A letter," he murmured, comprehending. Yet somehow it seemed as though he were disappointed. I was reminded once more of the head monk as he bid me farewell, so long ago in Cambodia. Then Kobi smiled, accepting this temporary parting gracefully. "As you will. Perhaps you should also talk to Ilunga at this time, so that you have full information."

So I had done the right thing, resisting the short-range pleasure in favor of duty and the long-range commitment.

It was a terrible mistake.

*

This time I caught Ilunga in her apartment. I had spent the afternoon on the letter, destroying draft after draft until I had it right. I asked Hiroshi to speak for me and to try to arrange a marriage contract. I had mailed it air, special delivery, on my way here. So it was evening, and I hoped this would not take long. I wanted to see Chiyako again.

As I mounted the grimy stairs of the decrepit building, I felt an impending gloom. No one should have to live this way.

The locks were off, so I knew she was in. I knocked and stood back, ready for anything. I was wearing corduroy pants, a black pullover, and special hard pointed shoes with little pieces of iron in the heels. My *nunchaku* was tucked out of sight; I had brought it to use on the multitudes of semi-vicious roaming dogs in the neighborhood. And as insurance, just in case Ilunga happened to have some of her demon goon squad around. I did not want to fight, but if I had to . . .

Her door opened. Ilunga stood illuminated by soft light. She wore a black rubber dress that clung to her figure, showing it off to extreme advantage. I could hardly tell where the material ended and her dark skin began; it was as if she were strikingly nude. Her hair was down, brushed and oiled so that it shone, and I smelled her perfume.

She laughed, recognizing me. "Is that how you dress to visit a lady?"

What the hell did she think this was, a date? "I want to know about Kali," I said bluntly. "I don't want trouble."

"The two are synonymous," she said. "Kali equals trouble. Come in."

"This is no social visit."

She laughed again, seeming to be completely at ease. "What did you do so badly the last time that you are afraid of me?"

What was in her mind? Disgruntled, I entered, alert for any trap.

Her apartment was lovely. It was such a contrast to the run-down building that I blinked, literally. The walls were painted in restful pastels, the floor was richly carpeted, and classical music played softly in stereo. Authentic African sculpture rested on sills and tables, and African spears were mounted on one wall. Elsewhere were modern abstract paintings, signed originals.

It wasn't fakery. The entire apartment was too well put together; it had a unity that could come only from complete conformance to the cultured whim of one person.

Ilunga had shown me another image of herself. Not the maiden, not the bitch, not the lonely beauty, but the artistic, intelligent, mature woman.

"So Miko did not kill you," she said, seeming unsurprised. "Have an hors d'oeuvre." She wasn't fooling: a small black walnut table had canapes, anchovies, ham rolls with cream cheese inside, olives stuffed with almonds, and assorted nuts.

"He hardly tried," I said. I took a cracker with meat and cheese spread, but declined a cocktail. I was feeling increasingly out of place. "He wanted to convert me."

Her eyes widened momentarily. "That would have solved all problems." She reclined half-supine on the couch, a distractingly handsome woman. Her lips were ruby red, and her fingernails matched. Only her broken nose spoiled the effect, and it really was not too obvious in this light. I suspected she was almost blind; demons needed bright light. That was the price she paid for her vanity; she could not have beauty and vision together. It was hard to believe how vicious she could be. But I steeled myself to believe it.

"Sorry to disappoint you," I said dryly. "I killed him, instead."

"I know. I have assumed his place in the network."

"So soon! That's some efficiency!"

"The drug has to be dispensed on schedule, or all hell breaks loose."

"I can imagine. But how did you know whom to contact? I thought these things were highly classified."

"I am one of the favored. As you might be, if you joined us."

"I'm no facsimile of Kali," I said.

It was as though I had struck her. "How do you know of that?"

"Miko told me about your black goddess. The resemblance was apparent. It figures that you have quite a future in this outfit. But I'm different. I'm male and white and straight."

"My future could be yours."

"Don't try your park-wiles on me! The drug kills that sort of thing."

"It kills only what is ugly in man."

"His sex?"

"There is more to you than sex."

I didn't like this. She was beginning to make sense. "I hope so. I'm getting married soon."

She reacted, but I was uncertain how to interpret it. She had tried to mark me, in our park encounter, as though she were jealous, but she didn't seem jealous now. Sad, perhaps. "To the Chinese girl? I think not."

"Why not?"

With no other forewarning she sprung the trap. "Because she is in our power."

She might as well have kicked me in the unguarded groin again. It did not occur to me to disbelieve her, at first. Kill-13 seemed to act as a truth-drug, along with all its other attributes; no demon had lied to me yet, that I knew of. "How?"

"The taxi the old man took, bringing her home. The demons ambushed it at a red light."

"I would have heard about it!"

"How? No one knows yet that they are gone,"

"Kobi would have fought."

"Against a gun held by a demon?"

So the demons had resorted to guns for this venture. "Yes, to protect his daughter."

"Then he is dead."

I remembered Kobi's seeming disappointment when I declined

to accompany him to the hospital. Had he had a premonition? "Let me use your phone."

She gestured to it. There was no trace of gloating in her manner; she seemed sorry for me.

But even before I called, I knew the demon net was pulling in tight. They had outmaneuvered me. They must have started planning this caper the moment I beat Miko, or even before. Why hadn't I anticipated their counter-moves? Why hadn't I stayed to bring Chiyako home from the hospital myself? This could not have happened then.

"Do not blame yourself," Ilunga said as I dialed. "Demons have watched you for several days. We know when to strike. You could not have avoided this."

I didn't reply. I had seen little evidence that the local demons were clever enough to pull off so neat a play. Perhaps there was a national or world organization whose finesse was greater. Still, it was questionable.

How had they known about my involvement with Chiyako? There had never been anything obvious about our relationship; I had been circumspect. Not because I cared what the demons thought, but because I valued the acquaintance too highly to make a spectacle of it. Naturally I visited Kobi's house often; he and I were working together against the demons. They would have had no reason to suspect my involvement with his daughter. So I had taken her out one afternoon; this was the polite thing to do for the child of an honored *sifu*. The demons would naturally minimize the relationship, failing to appreciate the sexual attraction because of their own weakness in that department. Chiyako had been in the hospital several days, and I had not even gone to visit her. How could the demons know it was at her own request? While she sorted out her feelings for me, and I did the same for her. No, there was no certain evidence.

Someone must have told the demons that the surest way to put pressure on me was to put pressure on Chiyako. And the demons had acted immediately.

Who had betrayed Chiyako? Who had known me well enough, and also had had contact with the demons? Almost no one.

I realized that the phone had been ringing at the other end for some time, with no answer. Neither Kobi nor Chiyako were at home. Yet there was nowhere else they would be at this hour, on this day.

Except with the demons.

I put down the receiver, looking at Ilunga. "You knew about me and Chiyako." I said. "You wanted to compete with her, one way or another." A terrible rage was building in me. "You just made me an offer to take her place. As you took the place of the demon you sent me to kill, Miko. You betrayed her. Kali's way." I drew out my *nunchaku*.

"Do not flatter yourself," she said coolly, putting her bare feet upon the couch. Her long thighs showed. "I lost a battle to you, not the war. I'll never take up with a honky bastard."

The *nunchaku* moved in my hand as if of its own volition. I was expert in no weapon, but this was the one I handled best. I felt its awful power, an extension of my awful emotion. "Then what did you mean, just now, 'My future could be yours'? It sounded like a proposition."

She closed her eyes, not deigning to notice my ready weapon. "The Kill-Thirteen cult will expand enormously. There is room at the top. Especially for competence. I hate you for what you are, but I hate all men, including the sexless demons. You would make an excellent demon leader. Together we could move up, into fantastic power. Take your Chinese girl with you, I don't care about that. Only swear that you will never betray my interests, and take a sniff with me. When I am really a goddess, you can be a god. We don't have to like each other."

"So you had Chiyako kidnapped, so that I would help you take over the cult," I said. It was a grandiose plan, but quite possibly workable. The cult, by my own observations as well as hers, was short on effective leadership. Only the compelling power of the drug itself held it together. I could do a better job of organizing Kill-13 distribution than the present pushers; I knew that without any special conceit. And I could outfight the present demons, even when they were armed and high on the drug. I had proved that the hard way. So Ilunga's notion made sense.

Except that I had no hankering for that sort of power. I could not be corrupted from my mission. My Shaolin commitment was eternal, and I could expiate my blunders of the past only by expunging this devastating drug from the world.

I balanced on my foot, on the verge of an attack that would mark a new phase in my war against the demons. I knew it was useless to bargain with them for Chiyako's release, or that of her father, if he was alive. They would either kill her or addict her the moment I made my move. But I *could* kill demons, starting with the black mistress herself.

"I did not betray her," Ilunga said.

I paused, knowing that violence was folly, seeking some way out of it, some way to recoup. I felt like a rat in a trap. "Who, then?"

"Amalita Pedro."

It had to be true. Amalita had known, and was insanely jealous. She had the means and the motive to destroy Chiyako, and had done it. Why hadn't I realized that before?

"You are not thinking well," Ilunga observed. "You would do better with the drug. Isn't that obvious?"

It *was* obvious. I was reeling from emotional body blows. My fevered reasoning was a patchwork full of holes. Whatever I decided right now was bound to be a mistake. But I would never take the drug.

I lowered the *nunchaku*. "What do you recommend?" I asked. One part of me was appalled that I should seek her advice; she was the enemy!

"Go after her," she said. "Immediately, before they contact you. Strike fast and hard."

"I don't know where she is." Now I sounded querulous.

"Neither do I. But I can guess."

I shook my head, trying to clear it. "You're helping me? Turning traitor to your own organization?"

"I was not inducted voluntarily. My purposes are my own."

I remembered Kobi's description; how Ilunga had been tricked into her first sniff, not realizing she would be addicted. So she had made the best bargain she could, and formed a fighting arm of the demons, working with men she hated. Now she wanted to bring me in on the same basis. "Still—"

"Of course if I help you to recover her—" she began.

"No!" I cried. "No bargaining!" Yet I was bargaining. Somehow she had fought me and overcome me in this verbal struggle. Just as I had overcome her physically, before. It was now apparent that I had won little if anything by that encounter; her strategies were more comprehensive than mine. However I might protest, I had to listen to her, for Chiyako's life was now at stake.

"All right. No bargaining," she agreed. "I will tell you the source."

"You know the source of Kill-Thirteen?" I demanded incredulously.

"A Mayan temple in the jungle of Honduras. That is all I know, and I learned it only this afternoon, with the assumption of my new position in the hierarchy."

"Why on earth should you tell me this?"

"Female illogic."

Fat chance! She was either trying to send me into another trap, or to enlist my loyalty to her interests. "If the demon leaders learn you have told an outsider—"

"I think you will keep my secret. We have a common purpose, when you choose to recognize it."

Yes, she still hoped to convert me. Perhaps that was the only way she could expiate her failure to mutilate or kill me. Still, I had to follow up this lead; it was the only one I had.

Yet I was not satisfied just to walk out of Ilunga's apartment. "You knew I was coming," I said. "You set this up for me."

"This is the way I live," she said. "The heightened perception

Kill-Thirteen gives me enables me to appreciate fine things, and now I have the money and leisure to indulge my tastes for material and aesthetic things. I find that is not sufficient, however."

"You eat hors d'oeuvres every night?"

"No. That much was for you."

"How did you know I was coming, when I didn't know myself?"

"I—hoped."

"I thought you hated me. That you wanted me dead."

"That is true, and untrue. You told me I would change, if I ever went half-way to know a decent man. I have gone half-way."

This was becoming uncomfortable. I was fishing for negative answers and not getting them. She had evidently done some serious thinking in the past few hours. "You said you'd never take up with a honky."

"Not openly." She smiled with resignation. "I have an image to maintain."

"I don't understand you."

"I don't understand myself. Go to your Chinese girl."

"What do you figure my chances of recovering her are?"

"One in a hundred, if you're lucky. Your way. My way, a hundred to one your favor."

That was the way I figured it too. Take a sniff, join the demons, and Chiyako would very soon be back with me. Throw away my mission, desert Shaolin, for the sake of a Shaolin girl. Paradox. "I need a drink."

"I thought you didn't drink."

"Not openly. Image." But it wasn't funny. The whole project seemed hopeless. I loved Chiyako, but that love could kill her. Either way I chose. Better for her if I had never known her. Just as it had been with the head monk.

"You know that one sniff would bring her back," Ilunga said. "But you won't take it."

"You wouldn't understand."

"Try me." She made a little gesture with her hand. "I know

something about having a mission, about being alone. I never met a man before who put his principles first. I could respect a man like that, and I'd be disappointed if he took the easy way out."

She was right. There was a parallel in our situations. Kobi had been right too; Ilunga was no simple criminal but a woman with many redeeming qualities, once her framework was understood.

I kneeled beside her on the couch, and she stroked my hair. I let the *nunchaku* drop to the floor.

"As I said," she murmured as her hands moved on down my body with consummate skill, "we don't have to like each other. Just a little respect."

Somehow I did not regard what followed as a violation of my commitment to Chiyako. My effort of the following days would proceed regardless. Ilunga's life would continue as before, and she would still hate men. We were ships of hostile nations passing in neutral territory, exchanging amenities on a guarded basis. There was no commitment on either side beyond that.

It was still one hell of an experience.

*

It was with a certain trepidation that I went to Nicaragua to see Vicente Pedro. He had to know what his wife Amalita had been up to. But I had to have his help. All I could do was tell the truth, the whole truth, and stand for the consequence. If he didn't kill me, he would help me.

I had, of course, checked Kobi's home. It was empty. The two had left the hospital in a taxi; that taxi had driven off. And never arrived at its destination. The driver was gone too; his family was distraught. The demon goon squads were not ones to quibble about killing innocent people. The taxi was found in an alley, blood-stained and bullet-ridden. Ilunga had told the truth, but I believed her when she said she had not been involved in that particular deal. She never touched a gun, and neither did her trainees.

Pedro's vast estate was near the Honduras border, and his com-

prehensive enterprises reached well beyond it. Given the hint—
Kill-13 in a Mayan temple—he would know how to follow it up.
I hoped.

I had saved his life, in the snowy wilds of Japan's Hokkaido
Island. I had carried him down the snow-covered mountain, back
to civilization, where modern medicine had helped him recover.
He was duly grateful. But he was also extremely jealous. In fact, he
was very like his wife in that respect. The matter with Amalita
might or might not balance out.

The only way to get to his estate, or to anywhere in Nicaragua, was by way of the capital city, Managua. I phoned ahead, of
course, and received an impersonal acknowledgment from one of
Pedro's *secretarios:* a private aircraft would pick me up in Managua.

My plane stopped at Bluefields, Nicaragua, unscheduled, but
there was a storm ahead. The city is on the Atlantic, a fishing
center and port. Most of the population was black. There was one
paved street, five hundred meters long; the rest was mud, and
more mud. It rained incessantly.

I understood that this was one of the major cities of the Atlantic coast. I stayed in, feeling miserable.

Next day we made it to Managua. I remembered it from my
prior visit, over a year ago. A hilly city rising from the lake on its
north. This was December. No snow, of course, but it was the
rainy season. The equator was only a few hundred miles to the
south. A warm Christmas was only two weeks away, and decorations were everywhere. There were garlands, a few Christmas trees,
some Santa Clauses. But many figures of the three wise kings, *Los
Reyes Magos,* bringing toys to children in Latin America. Booths
were in the streets, on the sidewalks, selling toys and food. There
were many drunks abroad.

I stayed the night at the Plaza Lido Hotel, downtown. Restless, I went out to wander the cobblestone streets in my shirt sleeves,
amazed by the winter warmth despite the latitude. Only a day ago
I had trekked through snow.

The rain had let up, for how long, I could not be certain.

Many natives were out now; the population of the city seemed to be mostly Indian, about five-feet five-inches tall. I towered above the crowd.

I bore south at first, uphill, stretching my legs. There were parties in the private homes, fiestas; I saw them going on in the open houses. People were dancing to wild Latin music—rhumbas, zapateos, mambos—I couldn't tell one from the other. But I wished I could join in.

I passed through a marketplace, still open this evening. There was much good food, meat, fish, and so on, but it was covered with flies. Much of it was alive; I saw chickens and pigs. The smell was so strong I felt like retching. And there were crows, as there had been in Chinatown.

Then I worked my way on around the Presidential Palace—such a contrast to the market—and back north a mile or so, to the water. I moved along the Malecon, past a small beach on Lake Managua, looking at the water to see if I could spot one of its unique fresh-water sharks. Of course I couldn't; it was dark now, and I was not inclined to go for a swim. I went down a set of steps, around Ruben Dario Park, and encountered a small carnival. People were dancing there, more Latin dancing I didn't understand but enjoyed watching. Those women sure knew how to move in those dresses.

A nine-year-old boy offered me a shoeshine. I had some native money, but didn't know the going rate for such services. He thought I was haggling, and in the end he did it for the equivalent of two American cents, and seemed well satisfied.

I saw many beggars. Some were blind, or claimed to be, and some were merely old. Women as well as men. Some sold lottery tickets. Some sold newspapers; I would have bought one, if I had been able to read Spanish. In this foreign city, I felt awfully ignorant.

There were many handsome buildings, some tall new sky-scrapers. But also many old buildings of stucco or even mudwall, and red tile roofing. The streets were narrow, and the drivers crazy. The carnival seemed the safest place to be.

I rode a small ferris wheel, getting a boyish thrill. Then a girl joined me, and made an offer that needed no translation. I wasn't interested, but if I had been, the smell would have cured it. She hadn't taken a bath for a month.

But even that sort of girl reminded me of Chiyako. I was unable to enjoy any of this anymore. I went soberly back to my hotel room, only two blocks south, and spent a restless night. There was no TV to distract me, not even in Spanish.

The phone woke me. "Huh?" I answered groggily, noticing the bandage on my hand was loose. Fortunately that *sai* cut had not been serious.

"Pedro here," the familiar voice said. "Do you not remember where you are supposed to be?"

"You're *here?*" I asked, still bemused. "In Managua?"

"Well, I am not in Japan, Senor! Do you think I would let an underling pick up my friend?"

So he didn't know about Amalita! "Pedro, there's something—"

"Tell me in the airplane!" he said jovially, and hung up. Tell him what: Kill-13, or Amalita? In the plane, where one false move would crack us up?

There was no help for it. We looped over the city, appraising the flat tops of its numerous downtown stores, its parks and statues, its many-columned capitol building, the stately Presidential Palace that I had viewed from the ground. In front of the baseball stadium I could see the big statue of Somoza. And near the carnival, the big plaza in front of the cathedral. Then out across the lake.

I glanced at Pedro. He looked tanner and fitter than he had a year ago. Once he had been wheelchair-ridden; now he stood and walked powerfully. He had gained about twenty pounds of muscle, and grown a big black mustache.

I took a deep breath. "Pedro, I have two pieces of news, and you may not like either one."

"The drug and my wife," he said.

I didn't try to conceal my dismay. "You know?"

"Jason, I am a wealthy man. I can afford to know. But I have a confession."

"*You* have a confession!"

"Amalita was never mine. I bought her with my money. I kept her secluded, but I was a cripple, and she was passionate. When you came, it might have been any man, but it was you. At least she had good taste. You at least were honest; you did not know her status. In my anger I misjudged you. For that I am sorry; I apologize."

"There was another time," I said grimly. "Save your apologies."

"Let me finish, amigo! After I could walk, I married her, but still she was not mine. The baby—"

"The baby," I echoed sickly.

"was mine. Did you think I would not have that verified? The blood tests exonerated you, Mr. Striker."

"I'm glad!" I said with feeling. "Still—"

"Still she was not mine. She wanted your type of body, not mine. Only my wealth she wanted from me. I was shamed; I thought of having her put away."

That meant death or a mental institution. He wasn't fooling. These Latin magnates played hard ball.

"But I gave her leeway, still hoping. A caged tigress is no cat at all. Jason, she is a beautiful woman."

"Yes," I agreed. He, too, looked for more than surface qualities. What he meant was that Amalita was fiery, ruthless and cunning, like himself, and young and pretty. A sleek tigress. The proper internal and external mate for him.

"You sent her back to me broken in body, wounded in spirit. There is no hate in the world, Jason, like that she feels for you now. When you struck her, you knocked out of her those illusions, all those notions that her type could ever make it with your type.

When *I* strike her, she understands, and it makes no difference. But you—you meant it. You tamed that animal."

"Not quite," I said bitterly.

He smiled expansively, and did a little swerve with the plane that made my stomach jump. *"Now* she is mine. In spirit as well as word. And I thank you. Any other man who beat up my wife, I would kill." He paused. "But just to be sure, I will help you to recover your Chinese girl."

"Thank you," I said, somewhat inanely. "Amalita said you were sick."

"So I was," he agreed. "Sick with despair and fury. Over her. She thought I had become impotent, but it was her attitude, not my body, that did it. That is changed now."

A load was off my conscience. "What do you know about Kill-Thirteen?"

"No more than you. I have dabbled." He paused delicately. He had more than dabbled; he must have made millions in assorted illicit enterprises, drugs included. "But never in that particular commodity. Because I have not been able to make contact. They will not deal with anyone who is not an addict."

"Well, my information is that their source is in an old Mayan temple, somewhere in the Honduras jungle."

"Aha!" he exclaimed, his eyes lighting. "I have connections in that country. Perhaps I shall take over that lucrative trade after all."

"I wouldn't," I said. "One sniff and you're addicted. You'd be taking a hell of a chance." And I certainly didn't want a commercial genius like him running the demon show.

He pondered. "A single dose addicts?"

"So it is reported. And it is gaseous. So someone might pipe it into your room, or just open a cupful in your face. A demon assassin, maybe. They take their cult seriously."

He nodded. "Then I would be marked. My associates would note my red eyes. Business would suffer. You are right. It is too dangerous to play with. Better to remain with the conventional drugs." He sighed. "All right, Jason—we shall burn their depot."

"Uh-uh," I said, relieved. "That could pollute the whole neighborhood with addictive smoke. Better to bury it."

"What is there to addict, there in the jungle? Burning is certain, and it will be far too diffuse to have much effect. Certainly we must burn their fields, and destroy their equipment. And their formula."

"Yes!" Then I thought of something else. "Amalita—is she at your estate?"

"I am not so trusting, Jason," he said, laughing. "She would kill you or seduce you, perhaps both, simultaneously. I have hidden her away for the duration, elsewhere."

That was good to know.

CHAPTER 12

PYRAMID

We rode jeeps along small dirt roads to the Honduras border: Pedro, I, and twenty armed men. We crossed the broad boundary river, the *Coco,* and proceeded on foot into the prairie and swamp of the *Mosquita* section of the country. The going was rough, advancing into jungle terrain. Quite a contrast to the dry, pinewoods hills and short grasses of Pedro's region. It reminded me unhappily of Cambodia and my adventures there, before being rescued by the monks. I hoped there were not leeches. But to my grief there were. Plus plenty of black-green giant horseflies with considerable sting, and clouds of *jejenes,* somewhat like no-see-ems, crawling up the nostrils and other orifices. And at night, mosquitoes. Praise God for Pedro's repellent.

We had guns but were under orders not to shoot, lest our quarry be alerted. There were wild animals: tapirs, monkeys, deer, snakes of all kinds, a few jaguars. Many multicolored birds: parrots, hummingbirds, vultures, hawks, falcons and ducks and other waterbirds in the rivers. But we stuck to our "C" and "K" rations and our white cheese, salted ham, dried salt codfish and Spanish hard crackers. Even cans of sardines and Vienna sausages. And such wild fruit as we came across, avocados, juicy mangos, guavas, papayas, bananas, plantains, sour oranges, and something called *pitayas* on vines. We did not go hungry.

Pedro located a couple of Indian guides, and they questioned the villagers in the vicinity.

Just like that, success.

The locals knew about the demon operation; nobody had inquired before. The Indians didn't like the foreigners, who refused to mix or hire or share any profits, and had strange orange eyes, like creatures of hell. The natives were afraid the army would intervene, making the innocent villagers suffer. Such things had happened in the past.

Yes, the Indians would help us by pointing the way and giving information. Especially since Pedro was reasonably generous with money. They had personal reasons, too. It seemed that a demon had come across an Indian hunting party, and beaten the hell out of them, just for practice or sport. When the Indians gathered in the town to get up their courage to attack the demons, the demons had attacked instead and routed them, killing several. So the Indians hated the demons, but were deathly afraid of them.

No, they would not go near the Mayan city itself. That was taboo, and besides, it was well guarded by the demons.

So the black mistress's information had been valid, and soon we might have word of the real black goddess. Ilunga really had helped me. Yet it made little sense, because if we destroyed the Kill-13 source, Ilunga herself would be deprived. There would be no demon empire for her to scale. So I knew there was a vital missing element, some side to this I had not been shown.

We trekked for three days. It was not that we had far to go, it was that progress through the intensifying jungle was slow. We did not even dare chop away obstructing growth, because the sound of the machete could give away our presence. Surprise was of the essence.

We arrived. The city itself was so overgrown as to be nothing; it would take a team of archaeologists years to expose its secrets. But the temple was a massive structure whose gaunt stone terraces rose right out of the tangle and into the sky. The thing looked as huge as the Great Pyramid of Egypt, and there was a certain family resemblance.

Nearby were fields of growing plants. Poppy bushes with their yellow flowers; slightly larger coca plants, for their harvest of leaves and sap; and, in dark sheds, the sinister mushrooms.

Our Indian informants had told us there were fifty demons in the city. Few were evident here; no doubt they had exaggerated. Still, we had to be careful. These demons had modern firearms. Anything premature, and they would gun us down wholesale from the cover of their emplacements.

We observed the complex from hiding, using powerful binoculars. Apparently they were overconfident and careless, taking inadequate precautions against the possibility of just such a foray as ours. Did they think that cowing the local Indians was all that needed to be done?

"It has to be within that pyramid, the secret of the drug," Pedro said. "The sheds are merely for storage and packing."

"That's some edifice," I said. "How did the Maya build all that, without motors or even the wheel?" Rhetorical question. They must have worked hard.

"Classic period," Pedro murmured, still gazing. "Beautiful."

"Classic?"

"The ancient Maya rose to greatness in the south, here," he explained. "They had a calendar more accurate than any other devised by man; they had mathematical knowledge never recovered. For perhaps a thousand years they flourished, then suddenly their cities closed down and they moved out to other places, the Yucatan, Mexico, leaving only these peasant farmers. No one knows why. It is a great mystery, but what structures they left behind!"

"Maybe Kill-Thirteen wiped out their civilization," I suggested, half facetiously.

"More likely soil depletion," he said. "More likely yet, rebellions of the lower classes."

We continued to watch as the afternoon advanced. The temple-pyramid was huge, perhaps 150 feet high, formed in great terraces, each layer smaller than the one below. Near the bottom the jungle overgrew the stonework, but it rose above with only slightly-daunted splendor. A massive staircase led up one face of it to the top. There were bare standing columns projecting near the base, evidently the ruins of collapsed palaces.

We could see the demons going in and out of one of the smaller buildings near the pyramid. Evidently they had renovated it for their purposes, and made it into a barracks. We counted twenty entering as dusk came. Naturally they were not active in the dark, because of their poor night vision, and they would hardly illuminate the area and attract attention to themselves. They deployed two sentinels; then all was silent.

"Living quarters in the building, laboratory in the pyramid," Pedro said. "Eliminate the building, and the rest will be simple."

I hoped so, but I didn't trust it. "Suppose Chiyako is in there?"

"With all those men? Hardly! They'd isolate her, for security."

"Demons aren't much for sex," I said. "But they would kill her, if—"

"Very well, we shall look first," he said, humoring me.

We moved in at night, naturally. We wore night-sight goggles and carried infrared projectors: the demons would not be able to see this light.

We were not dealing with timid people, and I knew that a mistake could cost Chiyako her life. Still, Pedro's method was uncomfortably direct.

He crept up on one sentinel, jumped to cover the man's mouth with one hand, and plunged a knife into his kidney region. But I couldn't protest; I had my own sentinel to subdue. I went rapidly into a *hadaka jime,* a naked strangle, my forearm around his throat and my shoulder against his head so he could not cry out. I intended to ease up as soon as he was unconscious; he could be tied and gagged.

But there was a third guard. He rose from the brush silently, a sword gleaming. Clever; he must have been set to watch the sentinels. He was of the conservative demon school, not deigning to use a gun. Therefore especially dangerous.

I had to act, or I was done. I threw myself to the ground. I still had my strangle on the other demon. His neck snapped instantly. But the advancing sentinel didn't care; he stepped by the body, concentrating on me. I knew he would not miss his thrust.

Then a thrown *shuriken,* a star-shaped blade, caught him in the throat, and he dropped. Pedro had acted, again, with good aim.

We inspected the building. The demons were grouped about one of their sniff-cups, waiting to renew their fits. It seemed that a tight rein was kept on the drug, even here. A number of them were, by the signs, beginning to suffer from withdrawal pangs.

It was all one room inside, without even a bathroom. There was no place to hide a prisoner. Chiyako was not there.

"You see?" Pedro whispered. "These are peons. Slaves to the drug. But make no mistake; they will fight like fiends to protect their source."

I nodded. "They seem to be all here."

"All except maybe a priest or two. We will never have a better chance."

"You're right," I said, still not liking it.

He brought forth a phosphorus grenade, primed it, and flung it in through the window. Then we ran for it as the explosion rocked the old stone building.

Some few demons emerged through the door; Pedro's men gunned them down mercilessly. Again I felt a qualm, and again I reminded myself of the unjustified killing the demons had done themselves. My karate students . . .

"Fire the poppy fields," Pedro ordered. "Burn the warehouses." Two of his men went out with thermite grenades.

The rest of us closed in on the pyramid. But starlike lights fell from the sky, swinging from little parachutes and giving off brilliant illumination. We were met with a hail of bullets, dropping our men with uncanny accuracy. Pedro and I hit the ground together and scrambled for cover behind a low stone barricade.

"A .30 caliber machine gun, air-cooled," Pedro muttered. "And magnesium flares. I should have known."

"We pulled a boner, all right," I agreed. We had underestimated the strength of the enemy, and alerted the demons by our first attack.

We waited, pinned down by that gun. The blaze went up in the fields and warehouse, sending smoke toward us. Another mistake: the fields were upwind from the pyramid, so that we got the odor. And now we were silhouetted against that light, so that the demons could see us even better.

Pedro's men were battle hardened. I wondered how he had recruited this elite little army. They kept up a steady fire from cover, seeking out the demon troops. But as the smoke passed over them, something happened. They jumped up from their, cover, screaming like crazy men. Then they charged up the steps of the pyramid, heaving grenades.

"The fools!" Pedro cried. "I gave no order!"

"The smoke!" I said, catching a whiff myself. "It must be dilute Kill-Thirteen. They're intoxicated with it!"

We put handkerchiefs to our faces as filters. "And the damned demons wouldn't be affected," Pedro said, his voice muffled. "They're already on it. What a blundering idiot I am! You warned me about burning it."

"There must have been a hell of a lot more drug in the warehouse than we figured," I said.

Now a new danger developed. Demons on the surrounding roofs of the old city and in the trees, with automatic rifles. They gunned down Pedro's men from the back and sides, leaving the dead sprawled all along the steep steps.

The wind shifted slightly, bearing the poisonous smoke away, but the damage had been done, compounded by our miscalculations. "We eliminated only the field workers," I exclaimed, such a

brilliant strategist by hindsight. "There must be just as many soldiers, and now most of ours are gone."

"Bad situation," Pedro agreed. "But I always come prepared."
He led the way with a rapid crawl back to our supplies. He brought
forth a *kyudo* bow.

Actually, *kyudo* is not so much a weapon as an art, a philosophy, "The Way of the Bow and Arrow," sometimes called Zen
Archery. Practice is similar to that of the Shaolin weapons. The
point is not to excel in marksmanship or win contests, but to cul-
tivate proper grace and manner and serenity. Thus *kyudo* is a way
of life, with the archer's ability to become one with all things,
reflected by how close his arrow comes to the target.

I doubted that Pedro possessed the true *kyudo* spirit. But I
kept my mouth shut. Upon occasion, a weapon is used for actual
fighting.

For me he produced a set of metal tiger's claws, *shukos*, and a
kusarigama, the chained sickle. "You know what we have to do
now," he said soberly.

"But my weapon is the *nunchaku*," I protested. "I'm not too
skilled in this."

"Necessity is an excellent teacher."

True. I hefted the *kusarigama*. The sickle was a curved, sharp
blade, with a perpendicular wooden handle, much like the, tool
for harvesting, from which it derived. Set in the wood was a metal
handhold. The chain was anchored to the corner of the L, and
extended for some six feet, terminating in a steel ball about an
inch and a half in diameter.

I had practiced with this weapon at the monastery a little. I
was not expert, but I could use it if I had to, and it was a hell of a
dangerous device. It was not intended for subduing foes; it was for
cutting them to pieces.

Pedro set himself up behind suitable cover, and took careful
aim with his long bow at the nearest rooftop demon. He let fly.
Nothing happened.

"Now I have the range," he said, undismayed. He aimed another arrow. This time the automatic rifle clattered to the ground.

"Silent, effective," Pedro said with satisfaction. "No noise, no flash. They cannot tell where I am. One by one, I shall bring them all down." He was actually enjoying this.

"But you can't reach the emplacement on top of the pyramid," I said.

"You know how to climb?"

"If I don't, I'll soon learn!" I said grimly. I put on the tiger's claws, fitting the metal bands over my hands so that the sharp curved spikes projected from my palms.

"I will lob some arrows up there, to occupy their attention," he said.

I did not use the stairs, of course. I crawled to the side of the pyramid and put my hands against the base of the first terrace. I was able to reach its surface; the claws dug into the old stone and anchored me as I swung my legs up. From a distance the individual terraces looked small, but from here each was like a cliff.

Now if only no demon were watching this flank. There was a moon, but I was in its shadow. And Pedro was giving the demon snipers reason to look out for themselves. They could not know that only two of us were now making the attack.

Had they killed Chiyako already, or were they holding her hostage against the unexpected? The latter; I *had* to believe that. And *I* was the unexpected.

Tier by tier, I climbed. Four levels up, the pyramid narrowed, and there was a broad platform. This was even worse, because here the moonlight shone. I had to run through it, gambling that I would not be observed and picked off in that moment. But I made it to the inner wall of the next tier.

But this was twice the height of the others. I could not get my fingers over the edge; I had to scale the sheer wall. Unless I wanted to go around to the steps.

Ha! Pedro just might have picked off all the snipers by now, but I was hardly going to risk my life on that assumption. And anyway, the machine gun nest at the top still had command of that section.

There was a crash to the front. Pedro had picked off another sniper, but how many more were there?

I felt along the wall. My fingers slid over irregularities; the whole face of it was covered with pictures and inscriptions. What an archaeological treasure was here, wasted on modern drug addicts. I remembered reading somewhere that the Mayan decorations were not art at all, but science, with every symbol carrying specific meaning. I was becoming more ready to believe that the drug *could* have originated here, a thousand or two thousand years ago.

But those inscriptions helped me get a grip. I dug my claws into the stone, wincing for more than archaeological reason as large flakes crumbled and fell noisily to the terrace. I braced my feet against the artistic contours of the ancients, and climbed.

The stone cracked off, and I fell back. Now I was glad for that broad platform, because without it I would have tumbled over the edge and bounced down the other tiers to the ground. Then it would have required no sniper's bullet to finish me.

I tried again, and made it up a good yard or so before the stone betrayed me again. This time I landed on my feet, almost silently. But I knew this could not go on long. My arms, already tired from the climb up the lower terraces, were suffering. The moon was getting higher, diminishing my shadow. And the longer I took, the more likely I was to be discovered.

Then the image of Chiyako reappeared in my mind, and I tried once more, and climbed to the next ledge.

There was a small stone enclosure at the top, the remnant of the Mayan pinnacle, a temple or observatory. Inside that was the .30 caliber machine gun, its barrel poking out to cover the long steep staircase.

I crossed to the back of the structure and climbed to its roof. Then I braced myself on the ledge just above the snout of the machine gun. My first job was to put that out of commission.

My luck had held for a long time, allowing me to get all the way up here, but now it reversed. As I braced to leap, the stone gave way. I tumbled ignominiously down—on top of five suddenly-alert demons.

I rolled aside, feeling pain in the hip from my fall, and flung the sickle at the head of the man directly behind the machine gun. The blade thrust into the top of his bent head, killing him instantly. But now it was caught. I should have used the ball first; my reflexes were wrong for this weapon.

I hauled on the chain, using the leverage to pull myself to my feet. As I drew close to the dead man, a demon recovered his feet and charged me with a machete. I blocked his downward swing with my forearm, and with my other hand gripped his loose-fitting khaki shirt. I did a *tomoe-nage,* putting my foot in his stomach as I fell on my back, and threw him over the edge and down the side of the pyramid.

Still there were three, and my weapon remained entangled in the skull of its victim. This would never have happened with the nunchaku. All three came at me, two with knives and one drawing a pistol.

This was a common weakness among the demons: they attacked without fear and without proper organization. It was another break for me. Had the gunman stayed back to take careful aim while the other two engaged me, I would have been finished.

I swung the reverse end of the chain. The ball missed the first, smashed the nose of the second, and slammed into the ear of the third, the gunman. Then I put my foot on the head of the demon behind the machine gun and wrenched out my blade in time to parry the thrust of the unhurt demon. I caught his knife in the crook of my sickle, whipped the ball at his ear, and as he ducked, my rising knee caught him under the chin. His reflexes had been fast, but my planning had foiled him.

I looked anxiously around for Chiyako, but she was not here. I charged outside, waving to Pedro somewhere in the dark below, searching for some other place where the girl might be prisoner. But there was nothing.

A bullet zinged by my ear. I dropped to the stone; not all the snipers were gone yet!

A man came out of the enclosure. It was the demon with the smashed nose. I had forgotten that these people felt no pain; I had to knock them out or completely disable them before they would quit.

He saw me and grabbed for the machine gun. Now I had to move. I launched myself at him as the muzzle swung around. But as I rose, the unseen sniper below fired again, forcing me down.

I hurled the *kusarigama*, but it clattered against the machine gun harmlessly. There was nothing else to do; I had to risk the sniper. Maybe Pedro would bring him down before he got me.

I scrambled for the machine gun, and got my hand on the barrel, shoving it aside as it fired. I felt the heat of the passing bullets and the displacement of air they made. The barrel heated, burning my hand. Then I grappled with the smash-nosed demon.

His face was a mask of blood, black in this poor light, but he was high on Kill-13, and his strength was awful. I tried to take him down with a judo throw, but I was tired from my climb and the fight, while he had the power of insane concentration. He pushed me back across the roof toward the dark edge.

It would have been impossible for the sniper below to pick me out; the two of us were too close together, moving about too rapidly. A bullet could strike either of us, or both. But the sniper was a demon; he did not care about losses, so long as he got me. He fired, and kept on firing, the bullets chipping away at the stone structure behind us. Some were tracers; they looked like a fireworks display as they bounced off the stone and sailed high in the air.

This was an impossible situation. But it gave me an idea. I hugged my opponent to me and waltzed him around to the side of the structure, out of the sniper's line of fire. Now I had only one enemy to deal with.

He caught my leg and boosted me over the edge. I scrambled wildly as I felt myself falling, and one hand caught the rim.

I was still wearing the *shukos!* Those claws must have. been gouging the demon cruelly, yet it had made no difference. My hand scraped along the stone, the claw digging in, and I broke my descent.

He thought he had me. His demon overconfidence was a liability. It took him a moment to realize that I was still clinging there. Then he stamped at my hands, but I was already swinging back up, away from the gulf. I caught at his foot, trying to topple him over, but he was still too fast and too strong for me. He fell on top of me, his knees striking my chest crushingly.

I squirmed away. This demon was simply too tough; I could not, in my present condition, overcome him. So I got up and ran.

Right to the machine gun, where my *kusarigama lay.* I snatched it up and kept running, the demon hot after me. Another sniper's bullet spanged into the stone. Why hadn't Pedro neutralized that one yet? I ducked around to the other side of the structure, but the bullets still came, and so did the demon.

One more corner, out of the reach of the sniper, and now I was at the rear of the pyramid. And it was a sheer drop off of over a hundred feet. I didn't know whether it had been built that way, or damaged in back, but there was hardly room to stand.

The demon skidded around the corner. Unawed by the height, he dived at me, as if seeking to hurl us both off the edge.

I swung the sickle with all my remaining strength. The blade sliced into his neck and through it, and the point dug into the stone. Something flew through the air and struck my chest.

It was his head. The thing bounced gruesomely on the stone, then rolled over the edge and dropped out of sight.

I slumped weakly beside the decapitated body, glad I could not see it clearly. I had won—*but where was Chiyako?*

CHAPTER 13

EARTHQUAKE

We cleaned out the pyramid, losing two of our remaining four men in the process. Some demons were almost dead, not from our action, but from the debilitating end-stages of the addiction. Blind and emaciated, they nevertheless fought, ambushing us from crannies. This horrified me for another reason: they could not have been addicted for more than a couple of years, yet had progressed to this stage. What a price a demon paid for his habit.

There were a number of internal passages, and chambers where sundry items were stored: poppy seeds, coca leaves, marijuana leaves, hashish blocks, dried mushrooms and peyote buttons, together with assorted chemicals and steroid-like drugs. There really *did* seem to be thirteen major ingredients.

In the deepest room was a laboratory, modern in most respects, powered by a generator. This showed one reason the demons must have set up a dummy company to import materials; such equipment could not be purchased locally. No doubt they had floated supplies up the Coco River and hand-carried them here. Thus they had avoided contacts in the Honduras, so that there would be little evidence of their location or purpose.

The laboratory was overlooked by a huge figure of the four-armed goddess Kali. The black cast-iron statue was set up in such a way that humans or animals could be sacrificed and their blood channeled into the Kill-13 equipment.

"The secret ingredient," Pedro said wisely. "Sacrifice. There must be a chemical, an enzyme, a catalyst, that modifies the other ingredients and unites them into a stable and tremendously potent drug."

"Kali will punish," I said, echoing Miko's words. "The old demons go to make substance for the new."

"There are no written records," he said. "We shall never know the exact formula, or the proper processing of the blood, unless we find a living demon. One who knows."

"None will talk," I said. "We've been through that. Only the leaders have real information, and they are too smart to yield anything."

He looked at the Mayan hieroglyphs decorating the walls of the room. "I wonder if it is written here?"

I shrugged. "The same thought passed through my mind. But you told me that no one could read Mayan."

"Partly true. They are working on it, and many symbols have been deciphered. Perhaps some enterprising scholar—"

"Discovered the ancient secret," I finished. "No, it does not make sense. Why would he have brought in a Hindu god for a Mayan temple? That's no scholar. Ignorant men must have put this together, after stumbling on the formula by blind luck."

"Perhaps it was a scholar from India, demented."

I looked at him, and he shrugged, embarrassed. "No doubt you are correct," he said.

"Pedro, you aren't planning to research that formula yourself?" I said, alarmed by his attitude.

He shook his head regretfully. "I admit to having considered it. But these demons, they live two, maybe three years, then go to the pot to make new drug. Perhaps only the careless ones go so soon, the ones that overindulge. But the end is plain. It is simply too dangerous. One slip, and I am on the greased channel to the black goddess."

"Then let's break up this infernal laboratory and get out of here! One grenade should do it."

Pedro shook his head. "A popular misconception, for those not familiar with explosives. A grenade is a man-killing weapon. It hurls pieces of shrapnel around; not good for material damage, except for delicate things like radio equipment."

"Oh," I said, embarrassed. "They could replace the glass tubes and things."

"Yes. So we want to collapse the whole passage. I have a pack full of explosives, bars of C-3 strung on detonator cord. Twenty of those properly placed and the job will be adequate. Shame to do it to this palace, though."

"More shame to have the demon cult regenerate within it."

He nodded sadly. I wasn't certain whether his regret was for the waste of good archaeological prospects, or for the lost millions that control of Kill-13 might have made.

We got the C-3. I looked at the blocks of explosive nervously. I was sure it would not go off prematurely, for Pedro would not have gambled that way. But: "Suppose some, of it doesn't go off? You have only one detonator."

"When one block goes, it all goes," he said with certainty.

It was arranged: a delayed explosion, to give us time to get clear of the pyramid. When it went off, the whole edifice settled a little, filling in the network of passages. There would be no more Kill-13 from here.

But in all the pyramid, and in all the cleared buildings of the city, there was no sign of Chiyako. Or of any woman. She wasn't here, and seemed never to have been.

Pedro well understood my concern. "It was only your black woman's guess that she was here," he pointed out. "These things happen. But the search is not over. They must have depots, supply routes, supervisory personnel. Somewhere in that chain she remains. We have only to discover where."

"With no leads?" I demanded bitterly. "They don't make written records, they don't talk, they only fight to the death. We may have destroyed Kill-Thirteen, but they will have the last laugh."

"There are written records," he said.

"I don't mean the Mayan writing!"

"Written in Spanish."

Suddenly he had my full attention. "Where?"

"In Managua. It is the only route out of this region, if they want large, fast shipment."

"Why not a Honduran city?" I asked, brightening. I had pretty much worked it out for myself, but was hungry for confirmation.

"I would have heard of it, and I have heard nothing. Now that I have seen their enterprise, I know how they do it. When they set up here, the Salvador-Honduras war was raging. Not the time for making contacts there. And Honduras is backward and corrupt at best. So it was down the river to the sea, down the coast to Bluefields, then across to—"

"Blueflelds! You' mean I was right where the demons were?"

"No doubt. But only in Managua have the orange-eyes been seen. They use commercial flights for their packages. There will be official records, bills of lading, names, addresses. Someone has to pay, to sign the customs declarations, even false ones."

"Pedro, you're a genius!" I exclaimed. "Why didn't you mention this before?"

"We were not going in that direction before," he pointed out. "We sought the source, not the terminus." He glanced about the ruined city once more. "If only the drug were not so dangerous," he sighed.

*

Pedro dropped me off at Managua and departed with alacrity for other business. I had no doubt that business was Amalita. But he loaned me one of his clerks, who had been told nothing about my mission but who was conversant with the city and its govern-

ment. After a good, sorely needed night's rest, we would com-
mence the quiet search for demon records.

It was now the very height of the Christmas season. The festivities had intensified. The city seemed to be one big fiesta. There
was music and dancing and drinking everywhere, and the churches
were busy. In five days the Christ would be born again. I wished I
were home, but I had little desire to celebrate in any way until I
recovered Chiyako.

The mills of officialdom grind slowly. I did not realize that the
secret to success was money: frequent greasing of palms. Because
of the language barrier, Pedro's clerk did not know of my ignorance. He must have assumed that I was too poor or honest to play
it the Latin way, and I dare say that was correct. Still, it was frus-
trating, this inexplicable delay. We worked for two days before
finally approaching access to the records we needed.

We visited the Customs Building at the airport, the Telephone
Company, and at the end learned that the records. I needed were
kept in the *Camara de Comercio,* Chamber of Commerce. That
was an office building in the middle of the downtown area. We
finally got hold of the right official and the right file. I saw the
name on it: *Kan-Sen.* But the official paused, giving me a last
opportunity to proffer some lubricating cash—and I still didn't
catch on.

"Sorry, Senor," he said then. "Official hours are over today."
He closed the file.

"But—"

"Come back tomorrow. Or after the holidays."

That was when I realized that he wanted money. Extra money
from me, just for doing the job the state paid him to do. Furious,
I refused. I would come back tomorrow. If need be, I would camp
all day in his office.

Pedro's clerk shook his head as we left. "This is as far as I can
take you, Senor Striker," he said regretfully in his halting English.
"Now you know where the information is."

"Right!" I told him wrathfully. "Go on home. I'll take it from here, my own way."

Grateful for the release, he departed. I dare say he was out of town within the hour. I could hardly blame him; my attitude must have seemed the height of folly to him.

So I went back to my room and turned in, early.

"Bah! Humbug!" I muttered as I ground into sleep.

*

I woke with alarm. The whole room was shaking. Items were falling off the dresser, and the bed itself was dancing on the floor. Then the glass of the window shattered. I felt seasick; my sense of balance seemed to be shot.

I had been dreaming some weird thing about the Ghost of Christmas Past, Scrooge and all that. Was I really having a visitation by the ghost, because of my surly refusal to be generous with graft for the poor local officials?

My head cleared. Good God! I thought. The demons must have bombed the building!

But there was no smoke, no flame. I scrambled into my trousers as the room swayed drunkenly, tossing me back on the bed. I didn't know what was happening, but I knew I had to get out of here. I was on the third floor!

Plaster fell like hail as I staggered down the hall. People were crowding toward the elevator, as bemused as I. Many were in nightclothes; this was some time in the night. Exactly what hour was impossible to tell; I had lost my watch. I didn't trust the elevator; I ran for the stairs, putting out my hands to brace myself against the walls as I went.

Somewhere in that mad lunge downward, I stumbled over something. There were people crowded all along the stairs, but I noticed this anyway. It was a child, a small girl, huddled on one step. *"Terremoto!"* she cried. "Earth quake!"

Managua was in the throes of an earthquake—a bad one!

A worse shudder came. The stairs twisted and creaked, and

cracks appeared in the wall. People screamed and fell down the stairs. Without thinking, I picked up the girl—she weighed about fifty pounds—and hurdled the unsafe-looking steps and dashed on.

"*Mamita! Sueltame!*" she cried. I paid no heed. I had never before felt such claustrophobia. The entire weight of the building seemed about to crash on my head.

I made it to the ground level and sprinted out the front door. The moment I was free of it, I realized my selfishness. There were dozens of people trapped in the hotel, many of whom would die if not helped. I set down the child and started to go back in.

There was a huge awful groaning and grinding sound in the ground, as though hell itself were opening up. And the building collapsed.

I watched it fall, slowly because of its size, or perhaps my awareness was heightened. The lower blocks crumbled, and the roof caved in on itself. In a moment a cloud of dust obscured everything, forcing me and the other escapees to retreat, coughing. Meanwhile, the ground was moving in waves; people were swept off their feet, but I kept vertical, thanks to my physical training.

As the air cleared, we saw that the collapse had been only partial. The main walls still stood. But there was no telling what carnage was inside. Probably the little girl's parents had been killed, and I would have to take care of her until some foster-home could be found. What a burden!

I looked around, but the child was gone. In this crowd it was impossible to locate her; she might be lost or dead or with friends. So much for my effort to help a stranger. I was disappointed. My burden had been removed before I had time to appreciate it.

The neighboring buildings were no better off. Rubble littered the street, and water bubbled from broken mains. Electric wires crackled with short-circuits. Now the fires were starting; a thickening pall of smoke showed on the near horizon. Police appeared in longsleeve blue shirts and high black boots, shaken like the rest of us, ordering us to get out of the city immediately. Christmas decorations crunched under their feet as they moved on.

There was nothing I wanted more than to get out, but there were two problems. First, I had no transportation; nobody did. I didn't relish hoofing it through an earthquake; a building might fall on me. Second, I hadn't finished my research. I had to locate the demon supply route. Where was Kan-Sen?

Nothing I could do here except to add to the confusion. I proceeded toward the Chamber of Commerce office building, a few blocks to the east. But progress was slow, because I was not a machine, I was a human being, and there was intolerable misery all around me. I heard the screams of a woman, coming from a caved-in building, and I had to help. But she was crying words in Spanish; I wished I could comprehend it. After some inevitable confusion, I saw that several women were trapped behind a fallen lintel. They were choking on dust, but weren't seriously hurt. I heaved on the beam and managed to clear enough of a passage for them to file out.

The girls were scantily clad, some in no more than panties and bras, others in torn skirts. They were Indian or part-Indian with black hair, either long or short, and garishly painted faces. I assumed they had been caught asleep, with no time to dress, but why the eye-shadow, heavy rouge, and red-painted mouths?

One in a slip approached me, saying something. I presumed she was thanking me. "Glad to help," I said.

Strange that all of these women should be so young and shapely.

She tried to kiss me, but I pulled back involuntarily. That was more thanks than I wanted. Then she reached into the top of her slip and took out one breast, putting it in my hand. Novice that I am, I never had that happen to me before, and I was startled. I drew back again.

Then she made a gesture to her crotch, spreading her legs, and at last I caught on. She was offering me sex, as thanks for saving them. In fact, these were prostitutes.

Embarrassed, I shook my head. "No thanks, no thanks!" And

I backed away so hastily I tripped over a brick. In a moment they were lost in the melee and the night and noise.

I went on, winding through the carnage, appalled at the mischief a few minutes of earth-vibration could do. The entire face of this beautiful, festive city had changed, instantly, and I knew it would never be restored. I could not even guess at the loss of life. Thousands, surely.

What had these people done, that such holocaust should be visited upon them in the hour of their merriment? There was so much misery that nothing I could do could make any apparent dent on it. All so pointless . . .

I passed a liquor store, the odor of burst bottles strong in the air. There were looters there, searching out the intact bottles. "Hey!" I yelled, knowing that looting was illegal, anywhere. As if there were not enough misery already, without these bastards aggravating it.

The nearest looter jumped, startled. He was a hulking, mean-looking brute, half drunk. Then, seeing me unarmed, he snatched up a broken bottle and charged me, yelling obscenities: *"Gringo! Saramambiche! Yankee!"*

I was in no mood to play. I had been glad to help the women, for they were in the same fix as the rest of us. I had no brief for liquor or liquor stores. But looters were the scum of the earth, preying on the helpless, the disaster-struck. And I was reminded vividly of the last bottle-attack I had seen, in which Chiyako had been mutilated in the breast. It was as though this stranger were a demon, repeating that act—as well he might, if I gave him the chance.

I turned sidewise, avoiding his rush, and seized his wrist, pulling him forward. At the same time I gave him an upper-elbow strike *hiji jodan-ate* just under the armpit in the upper ribs. Several broke. Then I took his bottle out of his hand and smashed him in the face with it. I didn't even look at the result.

I strode into the store. "Get out of here!" I bawled, waving the bloody bottle.

They needed no translation. They understood me well enough. They got out. I knew they'd be back, like creeping rats, the moment I left, but still there was some passing satisfaction in it. This was a tangible action against a tangible evil. There was a lot of violence in my soul right now, and looters were a legitimate target for it.

Finally I got to the Chamber of Commerce building, as the bleak dawn was breaking. Now, technically, I was a looter myself, but I wasn't taking anything of possible value to anyone else. All I wanted was information.

"Kan-Sen," I muttered, over and over. "Kan-Sen, Kan-Sen, Kan-Sen."

For hours I poked through that abandoned, ruined building, searching for the proper room, the proper file. Everything was changed; I could not be sure exactly which chamber I needed. I was afraid the papers would be burned, but I was in luck: no fire here. Yet. Still, the documents were in Spanish, making it tedious for me to check them out.

All about me, the disaster of Managua proceeded. The magnificent Central Bank of Nicaragua, a fifteen-story complex, survived the quake intact, a building so well constructed that even this shaking could not bring it down.

So what happened? Looters set it afire. The firemen, lacking proper equipment, with the water mains broken, had to watch it for three days while the fire crept downward. Story by story, the blaze lit by men destroyed what nature had not. Looters!

I camped right at the building I was in, raiding the candy machines for food, and the soft drink machines for liquid. When they ran out, I went farther afield. There was a small abandoned restaurant across the street, the *Colonial,* with plenty of canned food and bottles of "El Colonial." I had to drink it; there was nothing else. It hardly contributed to my equilibrium.

Several nations seemed to be airlifting in supplies, providing clean water but no food, because the government wanted to force the refugees out of the dangerous city. It made sense, because the people stubbornly refused to vacate. There was no future for them here, but they stayed so long as there was anything at all to eat. I did the same.

The police were shooting the looters on sight. Martial law had been declared, as well as a dusk-to-dawn curfew. But there were few police and more and more looters. I watched from hiding as the National Guard caught three looters in a nearby furniture store, lined them against the wall, and shot them all. I knew I couldn't remain much longer; one side or the other would get to me.

I was still at it on Christmas day. The sound of gunshots was constant in the background, as National Guard troops waged war against the small army of looters. Every time the action came near, I had to duck out of sight.

Now the odor of decaying bodies hung heavy in the air. As the heat of the day approached, the stench of putrefaction became so strong I had to tie a handkerchief soaked in cologne over my face. At times I also smelled the sweetish aroma of burning human flesh. Hordes of black flies appeared, insect looters. I saw a pack of dogs worrying the flesh of a dead man, and vultures almost too gorged to fly. At night the area was lit by the fires of the burning buildings.

Then more ominous sounds commenced. Boom! Boom!— blasting! The government was setting charges to demolish the remaining buildings, so that they would not be a menace anymore. And another sound: big guns. I recognized them from my military days. Were they also using artillery to speed the process?

Bad news. I would hear the demolitions experts at work before they blew up this building, so I could get out in time. But if they dropped a shell on it instead, from a distant gun . . .

Feverishly now, I worked on the remaining files. Kan-Sen, Kan-Sen—where *was* that name? Still it eluded me.

Steadily the explosions came nearer, as the heart of the city was razed. Surely they wouldn't blast *this* building without rescuing these files.

I was still at work when the government troops, sweeping methodically through the downtown section to clean out all remaining survivors, discovered me. I was too exhausted to fight or run, which may have been just as well, for they were well-armed and tense. No doubt they had been attacked from ambush several times already. "I'm American," I said as they surrounded me.

"American!" their officer said in English. "What are you doing here? Spying for military secrets? You work with the CIA?"

"I was in a hotel," I said. Then, in a wild flash of inspiration: "I am looking for a friend. A woman."

He frowned, not sympathetic to the appetites of Americans. "If she is in this building, she must be dead now."

"No, no! She is in another country. At the house of——of Kan-Sen."

"Kansan?" he asked, perplexed.

"*Kan-Sen.* His address is in the records, but I can't read them. I was inquiring the day before the quake."

He looked at me as if I were crazy, and that was a reasonable suspicion, in the circumstance. Who but an addled Yankee would spend three days poking in the ruins looking for a forgotten address, while the city was destroyed around him? "You do not know where your friend lives?"

"He's not my——" But I stopped. "No. I need his address."

He shrugged, deciding I was harmless. "If I give you that address, will you depart the city quietly?"

"Quietly as a moth," I promised.

So he humored the crazy American, not wanting international trouble on top of the natural disaster. He checked a master card file, drew out a card, and gave it to me. "I hope he can help you get resettled," he said. "So many are ruined now, homeless——"

"Yes, yes, thank you!" I cried with broken gratitude as I saw the name *Kan-Sen* on the card, and an address. "Now I have no problem!"

He looked as if he doubted that statement, but he kept silent, merely shaking his head.

And in that manner I left the desolate city of Managua, accepting a ride out in a Mercedes-Benz police car, and resumed my quest. It was a marvelous Christmas.

CHAPTER 14

KAN-SEN

I had anticipated a country estate, complete with guards at the gate. There was, as I had seen, a lot of money in the hands of the more powerful demons, and they liked nice living. But Kan-Sen's address turned out to be in the industrial heart of a great city. Giant storehouses loomed over the narrow streets, and railroad tracks ran past interminable loading platforms.

I looked again at the file card obtained from ruined Managua. There was no mistake: the spot indicated was a monstrous, block-long, deserted warehouse. The few small windows were painted over; obscene graffiti covered the bricks. *Fu yo!* said the chipped wall I was facing at the moment, reminding me of the hieroglyphs of the Mayan pyramid. "Fu yo too," I told it. And smiled: suppose, once the scholars finally deciphered the Mayan script, a similar message would be revealed? An ancient obscenity inscribed for posterity?

I walked entirely around the block, finding no obvious entrance. All the doors were closed, blocked, and padlocked. There was a decrepit iron fire escape up one side, but I didn't trust it. Either it was unsafe, or booby-trapped, or led to no entrance.

Had I come all this way for nothing? Or was someone trying

to fake me out? There could be something hidden inside this grim building.

But if there were, it was surely demon-guarded. I had to find a discreet private entrance. If they caught me and recognized me as the destroyer of their source-plantation, I would disappear forever. And so would Chiyako.

I might even now be under observation. I walked away, emulating an indifferent sightseer, and retired to a diner for a snack. Night was the time to pursue my quest further.

My meal was bleak, and not just because of the cheap food. I knew in my heart that my search was futile, that the demons had planted false records all along their supply route: an elementary precaution. This could be a decoy, or merely a way-station, not the delivery point. The Kill-13 packages could continue on the train to the real depot, where they would be surreptitiously unloaded. That might be anywhere in the city, or in another city. But this was my only lead, and I had to follow it through.

At night I surveyed the manhole covers in the streets near the building, judging their patterns. The sewer serving this block should run *this* way, so, and pass under the building somewhere along *here*.

I pulled up a cover and climbed down the grimy ladder into the stinking hole. Once I had the lid back on, I turned on my waterproof flashlight. It had a red filter to mute the glare, coincidentally ideal for use against demons. I would have liked knee-high wading boots and rubberized coveralls too, but had had no opportunity to get such things. Might as well wish for a gas mask while I was at it.

I sloshed along the huge pipe, glad that the weather in this region happened to be dry right now, so that there was minimum sewer flow. Still, the liquid was ankle-deep to knee-deep, and the odor was nauseous. Floating and submerged things brushed softly by my legs—fecal matter, sanitary pads and other sodden refuse. One larger object got hung up on my shin; when I disengaged it with my hand it turned out to be a dead cat. Huge roaches walked the walls, and rats scurried. At least it wasn't so cold down here; it was January above, but the sewer had its own climate.

I have a fair directional sense, and the right-angle joints of the sewer system made it easy. Even so, I began to feel claustrophobic, afraid I'd get lost. What a fate, to wander forever in this nether network, eating garbage!

The pipe narrowed, forcing me to hunch over, and now the sides were covered with slimy black fungus. The dim light of occasional manholes was a blessing, as was the slightly fresher air in their vicinity.

Then I stepped into a hidden hole in the bottom of the crumbling pipe, and took a bellyflop into the gook. I swallowed some before I recovered my feet, and now the miasma was on me and *in* me. Yuch!

I counted paces as I hunched along, until I was sure I was under the building. Somewhere there should be a kitchen or machine-washing area, and there would be an access there. I found it, mounted a series of slippery iron rungs, and squeezed through.

I was inside the cavernous cellar. I found a dirty sponge and mopped off as much of the stench as I could. My clothes were unsalvageable; if I wore them I would signal my presence as far as anyone's nose would reach. So I stripped and left them just inside the sewer. The demons had weak eyes, strong ears, and I just did not know about smell. Anyway, this was no occasion for personal modesty.

I left my flash with the clothing. Naked, I set about my explorations. I already knew one thing, from the flow of fluids through the sewer and the heat of the room: this building was occupied.

I stole up the stairs and cracked open the cellar door. And paused in amazement.

I faced a lush garden. The moon shone brightly down, and stars twinkled overhead. Palm fronds waved in the gentle breeze, and semi-tropical vegetation grew thickly.

But surely this huge central courtyard was not open to the sky! The city smog made most of the lesser stars invisible, and tonight was overcast, while here the Milky Way itself was evident. And this was mid-winter; there was snow on the roofs. No place for palms!

It had to be internal. A closed-in garden, a greenhouse, supplemented by daylight sunlamps. Probably the night sky was a projection on the ceiling. A veritable planetarium.

The demons had excellent taste. But why? This was expensive and artistic. Why build it and maintain it, and hide it away in a bleak facade of a building?

I remembered how lovely Ilunga's apartment was, in the center of a slum, and how handsome the inner furnishings of Miko's ship-depot were. This followed a certain pattern.

Then I saw the huge black statue of the goddess Kali, and I understood. This was Demon Heaven, paid for by all those twenty-dollar-a-sniff habits. Good demons would be rewarded by visitation rights, and perhaps honorably wounded ones came here to die in comfort. Bad demons would go to the pyramid, to the arms of Kali for punishment.

So my search was almost complete. This *was* the prime nexus of the worldwide demon network, hidden so cleverly. There must be a private entrance tunnel, leading from some other building. Perhaps there was a secret panel in a railroad bathroom.

This, surely, was where Chiyako would be held. But it was also fraught with peril for me. There would probably be a small army of demons here.

I stepped through the door and ran quietly for the cover of the tall plants. But I was careless; I had forgotten the most obvious estate defense. For this *was* an estate, hidden inside a building.

Two dogs appeared, black Doberman Pinschers, their noses lifted to catch my scent. Silently they charged me, jaws gaping. I timed my attack, and delivered a downward blow with the side of my hand to the bridge of the first dog's nose, probably killing it. But the second was upon me, rearing on its hind legs to bite me. I stiffened the fingers of both hands and stabbed them into the sides of its throat. This dog was no demon; the pain put him away.

But this fast action had been noisy. Necessarily so; you can't reason with an animal, or gesture it to silence as you might a man. Now the demons would be alert. I had to find a hiding place, fast.

I ran across the court, trying to get as far away from the fallen dogs as possible. The demons would come there first. I made it to the edge of the garden, where a lighted corridor led away.

As I entered that passage, my body tripped an electronic eyebeam. An alarm sounded. My second mistake, compounding my problems. I was just not cut out to be a sleuth. But I ran on.

Suddenly there was a hissing. Gas jetted from vents in the ceiling, flooding the hall. I tried to hold my breath, but the stuff tingled on my skin, numbing it. It was some kind of nerve poison that could act through the skin. Not Kill-13, fortunately.

Then the floor was coming up at me. I never even felt it strike.

I didn't think I was unconscious long, for they were just tying me as I pulled out of it. I was still too weak to resist, but I tensed my muscles as the rope tightened about my wrists and ankles, so that there would be some slack when I relaxed. I didn't know what they planned to do with me, but at least I was alive.

They left me, bound hand and foot on the floor. I struggled to free myself, but there was not enough slack. And soon they returned.

"Set our guest on a chair," a voice said. They picked me up and put me on a chair, my bound wrists falling behind the backrest. It was comfortable enough.

The demon who faced me was Eurasian, half Chinese, half European by the look of him, and about fifty years old. His skin was faintly yellowish. He was stocky, not too tall, and bald. He wore rimless glasses that did not conceal the color of his eyes, the deepest orange I had yet seen. He wore rings on his fingers, and a gold chain about his muscular neck holding a black jade figure of Kali: her eyes were red rubies. Overall, he was dressed in a blue velvet kimono, embroidered with gold cloth. And simple sandals on his callused feet.

I knew this was Kan-Sen, the master of the demon empire.

"Mr. Striker, you have caused me much mischief," he said.

"You started it," I replied shortly.

He shrugged, not deigning to argue technicalities with a prisoner. The motion showed the power of his body; this was one finely conditioned man. "It seems we were betrayed. No straight should have been able to locate this place, unless someone within the organization helped him. The lapse is not fatal, despite the loss of our production site, as I have reserves of approximately a billion dollars worth of Kill-Thirteen. This will tide us over until a new supply farm is in operation. But obviously we must verify the source of the leak and deal with it, before proceeding."

So they thought someone had simply told me about all their locations. Small credit given for my difficult research. But let them go on a search for the mythical traitor.

"It will be easiest for all parties concerned if you simply tell us how you located our ship, our farm, and our capital," Kan-Sen said.

Uh-oh. Ilunga, the black mistress, had told me of the ship, and given me the hint about Honduras. She was the one Kan-Sen wanted.

Naturally I was not about to tell him.

"Bring the girl," Kan-Sen snapped. "First douse him; he smells." A demon dumped a bucket of cold water over my head. No harm done, as I was naked and the room was warm. But it did remind me of my state. A naked man is psychologically vulnerable.

They brought Chiyako, and I felt more vulnerable yet. She was dressed in a slit black skirt, and a straight jacket. Her hair was mussed, but she did not appear to have been mistreated. And she had a gag on her mouth. No, not exactly a gag, a bit, like that of a horse, to prevent her from biting. No doubt she had given the demons quite a bad time.

"Understand, Striker, that *you* will not be released," Kan-Sen said. "You are too dangerous. But we have no real quarrel with your fiancee. Tell us what we want to know, and she will go free."

Oh, God! They were offering to exchange Chiyako for Ilunga, and how could I refuse? The demons had dealt roughly but honestly with me before; I could probably trust them in this.

But if I made that deal, the demons would be able to recoup with the certainty that no one would betray them again. All my efforts would have been for nothing.

I did not hold any particular brief for Ilunga; I regarded us about even now. The black mistress had hurt me and helped me, and understood me in her fashion; I had done the same for her. Certainly I would never sacrifice Chiyako to protect Ilunga. Yet if that protection meant sowing the seed of destruction in the demon empire after I was dead . . .

"Your alternatives are three," Kan-Sen said. "First, you can refuse to cooperate entirely. In that case, the girl dies." Here he gave Chiyako a little shake, to make his meaning quite plain, "And you will be subject to torture until we gain the information. Second, you can assist us in this matter. Then she will be freed, and you will die cleanly. Third, you can agree to join us as a demon. Then your girl will remain, taking the drug also."

"*Yo!*" Chiyako cried around the bit. The thing prevented her from getting her tongue up to form *N*.

"And the two of you will work as a team for us, rebuilding what you have destroyed."

"For the whole two years the drug lets us live!" I said sourly.

"Not so! You can live twenty years at least, if you take care of yourself. Simply a matter of resting thoroughly between sniffs, not taking more than the minimum drug, eating well so that the bodily resources are not depleted. Vitamin A supplements to protect the eyes; magnesium, testosterone, and so on. It is not an arduous program, and the drug has substantial rewards to offer. Particularly when your supply is assured."

I looked at Chiyako, and knew that I could not sacrifice her, though the world came to an end. But anything I did would be useless, unless she agreed. What use to save my life and hers, if she walked out of my life forever? As well she might.

"She must decide," I said.

Kan-Sen removed Chiyako's bit. I saw the sores at the corners of her mouth where it had chafed, and I felt a mindless rage I dared not show. "You can see that we have neither drugged her nor harmed her in any way," he said. "We have only restrained her and held her for your benefit, though we scarcely expected you to come here." Then, to Chiyako: "Speak, fair woman. You have heard the bargain."

She spoke in Chinese. It sounded like "*Tunia macarinambo.*"

"In English," Kan-Sen said. His voice was even, but obviously he had exerted some willpower. He was half-Chinese, and must have understood the words, and it must have been a doozy of an insult.

"Kill us both," Chiyako said.

Kan-Sen gestured sadly. "Now that would profit us nothing. Surely you understand that my approach is positive. I want you with us, not wasted in death."

She made no further answer. Her eyes were fixed on mine, but I could not read what was in them. I had the eerie feeling that whatever came to pass, she would prove to be stronger than I, despite her seeming frailty.

"Perhaps you do not properly appreciate the consequence of that choice," Kan-Sen continued after a moment. "Your deaths will not be pleasant ones. In the interest of fairness, I shall make a small demonstration."

Suspecting what was coming, I threw myself off the chair, straining to snap my bonds. But the demon guards were ready for me. Two of them hoisted me up and held me in place on the chair, while a third brought out a small device. It was a board with a steel loop on top, tightened by a screw on the side. There were straps to fasten something to the board.

"This is a thumbscrew," Kan-Sen said. "When the pain is sufficient, you will scream. Shall we see how strong your willpower is?"

They applied the device to my left thumb, behind my back. I

felt the straps being fastened to hold my hand in place. Then they tightened the screw. The band constricted.

I tried to hold out, but the pain became appalling. I had never known that so much agony could come from so small a portion of the body. The sensation became worse and worse, lancing up my arm and through my skull. My thumb felt as if it were about to burst. It seemed as though blood were squirting out, bone splintering. Something snapped, and I thought it was the bone. The sensation was intolerable.

I could not help myself. I screamed.

Immediately it stopped. The demons removed the thumbscrew, allowing me to catch my breath. Slowly the pain diminished.

"Do you really want to die under such duress?" Kan-Sen asked me solicitously.

"A thumbscrew won't kill him," Chiyako said. She was tough, all right; if this little demonstration had been intended to make her weaken, it had failed miserably.

"We have other instruments," Kan-Sen said. "In fact I rather pride myself on my collection. It has become a hobby of mine, you see, since demons feel very little pain. At what stage does pain return, as the fit wears off? I have made a study, but I shall not bore you with the details. I assure you it is possible to die, and very slowly."

"I'll take your word," I said. The fact is, I do not much like pain. He spoke with a certain scientific detachment that assured me that he had no need to bluff or bluster.

"More important," Kan-Sen continued, "do you really want to watch her die similarly?"

"Her!" I cried involuntarily. I had not appreciated that she, too, would be tortured. But of course she would. And while I was forced to watch; that was SOP.

"I might point out that such measures would be largely ineffective against demons, while the fit is on," Kan-Sen said. "This is often a disadvantage, as we wound ourselves unnecessarily and take unreasonable risks, but it does represent a fine immunity to such persuasions. Naturally there will be Kill-Thirteen available for each of you during the interrogation; if you wish to eliminate the pain by taking a voluntary sniff, we certainly shall not deny you."

Chiyako said something more in Chinese. He merely looked at her. "Such pretty little thumbs."

I tried to speak, but the very crowding of obscenities choked me.

"I shall leave you two alone for a while, to discuss the matter," Kan-Sen said. "Perhaps you will reconsider. It is not an ungenerous offer I have made."

He and his demons departed, closing the door behind them. I noticed the latch as it closed, because it *was a* latch, not a knob. A projecting bit of metal. I was sure someone would be standing behind it, listening to our conversation, but I didn't care. It was enough for the moment just to be with her. Even bound as she was, and as I was.

"Do not surrender," Chiyako said. "There is another way."

"I love you," I said. "I could never stand to see you tortured."

"They killed my father," she said. "I could never join them, or assist them in any way."

"I arranged to have an elder speak for me, to ask for your hand in marriage."

She paused, and I saw a sparkle in her eyes. Was it joy, or grief? "It would have been arranged," she said. "My father told me." She leaned over with some difficulty, restrained by the tight straitjacket, and kissed me on the mouth.

"I can't join them, and I can't let you be tortured," I said. "I'll have to tell them who their traitor is."

"But they will rebuild!" she exclaimed. "It will be as before! Worse, for they have grandiose plans."

"I think I know who their man is," I said. "They'll eliminate him anyway, and rebuild anyway. It is all they can do. They just want confirmation." It wasn't even a man they wanted, but I hoped to sow further doubt in the minds of the eavesdroppers, until the moment I told them directly. If some chance to escape occurred before then . . .

"You will not have to see me tortured," she said.

"Then you agree?" I hardly believed this, though I had already decided.

"I love you, Jason," she said, standing back. Then her leg came up in a sudden, beautiful roundhouse kick, aimed for my head.

Instinctively I threw myself aside. Her foot smacked into my ear, a glancing blow that still sent me reeling with a ringing in my skull. I crashed to the floor, but she was over me, her shoulders swinging forward for balance, her foot lifting for a head stomp. I could not help admiring the flash of her calf and inner thigh as that foot came down to crush my skull. I remembered the first time I had seen that leg, during the fight with demons outside Kobi's dojo. Meanwhile my reflexes carried on. I squirmed aside, and rolled into her other leg, bringing her down on top of me.

Then the room was filled with demons. They hauled her off me. "Oh, Jason!" Chiyako cried with sorrow and exasperation. "You spoiled it!"

I could only stare at her from the floor. Had she gone crazy?

Kan-Sen was there. "A very nice move," he said. "Extremely pretty! She tried to kill you, so you could neither talk nor watch her die. Fortunately you resisted."

I had not realized. Chiyako had figured it out, a way out of the impasse. She had tried to tell me, and must have thought I under-stood—and I had voided it.

I would never have another chance at so lovely a demise: to be kicked to death by my fiancee's beautiful limbs.

"Do not tell them!" Chiyako cried as the demons bore her away. She did not know that it was another woman, the black mistress, that she was protecting.

"I think you need a bit more time to consider," Kan-Sen said. "A spirited girl like that—she is worth saving, isn't she? You would not want to die, knowing what would be the consequence to her.

Therefore you protected yourself, knowing that such misery is so easily avoided. I congratulate you."

I sat silent, too discouraged to reply. He was, quite possibly, right. How could I know my own motives?

He threw a robe over my shoulders and left with his demon entourage. At least I was not naked anymore. But now I had new food for thought. Surely he had overheard our conversation, and already knew that I was ready to talk. Why hadn't he simply demanded the information on the spot, perhaps threatening Chiyako directly?

Because he didn't really want it? Was his threat to Chiyako a bluff? His real intent might be to convert me, or both of us, and all the rest was mere window dressing. He had been remarkably tolerant of our resistance.

If he converted us, we would tell him the identity of his traitor anyway, and help him greatly in his effort to restore and expand the demon empire. He would make every effort to change our minds, and avoid killing either of us as long as possible.

My counter-betrayal of Ilunga would merely symbolize my conversion. If I went that far, why not farther? Stage by stage, he would guide me into the fold.

I saw all this, and was appalled by it, but the threat to Chiyako was forcing me to consider the alternatives most seriously. How would the demons use her, before she died?

The door opened. This time Ilunga was with the demons. I suppressed a start of surprise. "Do you know this man?" Kan-Sen asked her, indicating me.

"I recognize him. I raided his dojo." She seemed to be at ease, a good actress.

"We hope to convert him to our cause," Kan-Sen said. "We might even bargain with him, to spare the traitor in our midst, if only he joined us. Perhaps you should talk to him."

"I would rather kill him," she said.

"An interesting observation. Were you aware that his fiancee, Chiyako, just made the attempt?"

Ilunga looked at me, surprised. *"She* tried to kill him? She loves him!"

Kan-Sen nodded. "She loves him. An intriguing parallel, is it not?"

"No parallel at all!" Ilunga snapped.

No parallel? Kan-Sen was entirely too smart!

"A woman in love will do anything for her man," Kan-Sen said. "She might even provide him with forbidden information at great peril to herself. Perhaps the Chinese girl did that."

"Perhaps," Ilunga agreed. We all knew that it was not the Chinese girl he really meant.

Now Kan-Sen had made me yet another subtle offer: Ilunga. He had suggested that she loved me—and she had been unable to deny it. He understood her motive better than I had. Why else had she helped me, knowing the terrible consequences she faced? Not for power; she could have had that with far more certainty by killing me. She could have sent me into an ambush.

"I rather think *you* might persuade him," Kan-Sen said to her. "To encourage you, I shall hold your quota of the drug, pending your success."

There it was: the steel beneath the velvet. The one way to torture a demon was to take him off Kill-13. And Kan-Sen would even suspend vengeance on Ilunga, in exchange for my conversion. He was pulling out all the stops, and giving her a powerful motive to cooperate.

Too quick a revelation would have spoiled his larger design. He wanted it to happen in the right manner. That way he would have three good demons——Ilunga, Chiyako and me—instead of three corpses. And we all would know who called the tune.

In fact, Kan-Sen was something of an artist. I had to admire his style.

Ilunga made a snort of disgust and walked out. She was not going to play the game of attempting to kill me, knowing now that was futile. And any dialogue we might have would only give her away.

Kan-Sen let her go. He had made his point. "She will return, I think, to reason with you," he said to me, as though we were two generals planning strategy. "In due course. Meanwhile, we shall keep your fiancee safe."

Yes, he would play one girl off against the other, magnifying the potential jealousies he had so aptly brought out. And play me against both.

He was just too clever; his plan was too well orchestrated. Sooner or later one of the three of us would break, and that would put further pressure on the others. Already I was doubtful about the wisdom of holding out, if my conversion saved Chiyako.

I was left alone once more.

Dammit, if this went on much longer, I would capitulate. The girls were tough, both of them; neither would yield. I was the weak point. I had to get free, to fight. Action was my way, not silent sweating.

I worked my way off the chair again, lay on the floor, and forced my wrists down over my feet. The contortion was extremely difficult, impossible for most people, but I had had many years of training, and I was desperate. The robe got in my way and I heaved it off. I got my feet through at last, and now my hands were in front of me.

My left thumb was a sight. The flesh was purple and the nail was half torn off. That little demonstration with the thumbscrew . . .

I hopped to the door and got my wrists up against the sharp door latch. I rubbed the rope violently across it, fraying the fibers. But I could not get full play.

I brought the rope to my face. Now I could work on the bonds with my teeth.

Still it was hard work. The cords were nylon: almost impossible to chew through. I tugged, trying to loosen the knot, but this was not a simple matter with the teeth. The job was interminable, especially since I expected to be interrupted at any moment. If I were being spied on visually, too bad for me.

Unless Kan-Sen actually wanted me to go free. Could this be

another part of his plan? He could have had me bound more securely.

No! It was paranoid to think that everything I did was part of
his design. He was simply overconfident. He must have been concentrating so hard on his conversion-scripting that he had overlooked the obvious. He had given me time to consider the alternatives alone, and forgotten that I might attempt the alternative of
escape. Maybe he was taking a catnap, in preparation for the long
haul.

Maybe he was with Chiyako. After all, he was part Chinese,
and she was an extremely attractive Chinese girl. He obviously
admired integrity and fighting spirit and martial arts ability, and
he took testosterone to prevent the drug from unsexing him.

Ferociously I ripped at the cord, as though it were Kan-Sen's
neck in my teeth. I tasted blood on my lip, but now I was making
progress.

Somewhat to my surprise, I made it. The cord fell away from
my hands, and it did not take long to untie my feet. I donned the
robe and jammed the bit of rope into a pocket. It might serve as a
garrote.

I peeked out the door-—it was not even locked!—and discovered to my surprise that I was in a small, isolated building in the
middle of the garden. Furthermore, it was daylight. I must have
been unconscious for many hours. Well, I knew better than to
trust unduly the innate sense of time, when drugs were involved. I
had thought I had been out only seconds.

It must be true, then, what Miko had told me about Kill-13:
it had to be voluntary, or it could be fatal. Otherwise they could
have given me a sniff of the vapor while I was out. Was that what
had happened to Pedro's men, when the drug-laden smoke caught
them at the base of the pyramid-—involuntary addiction?

Well, the garden was exactly where I wanted to be. No dogs to
sniff me out, unless they had more in reserve, and plenty of hiding
places. I could reconnoiter at my leisure, picking off demons one
by one. If I could only find where Chiyako was being held.

This time I would be more careful about electronic eyes, too. But I had no time to waste, because soon someone would check on me, and then the chase would be on again. I had to get a better weapon.

But I was already in trouble. There was a demon in the garden, a demon holding a leash, and the leash was on a huge cat. A leopard. And the animal had already picked up my scent.

The cat lunged toward me, though I was hidden in the brush, and the man ran after, hanging on. Then I saw the feline's eyes. They were almost blood red. The leopard was high on Kill-13!

I knew I was done for. I just might overcome the cat, or the man, but not both. Not without a long-distance weapon. Especially since the cat would have uncanny reflexes and viciousness, and the demon man had a gun in his hand.

Then another figure appeared. I thought it was another demon, and it was, but not a regular one. It was Ilunga.

She intercepted the pair just as the demon touched the collar-fastening and loosed the leopard. The cat leaped forward, making a cry very like the human demon kill-screech, and the demon raised his gun.

The black mistress threw a knife. Her aim was true; it struck the man in the center of the chest and he fell dead, pierced through the heart.

But the leopard, at first after me, now pounced on this closer prey. Ilunga raised her bare hands to fend it off, but its flying weight bore her back and to the ground. I heard something hit—something like a head striking a rock—and saw her lying still. The leopard started to maul her, but I jumped on it from behind and closed its muzzle with one hand. With the other I tried a stranglehold on its furry throat, while my legs fastened around its body in a scissors hold. I applied desperate pressure, twisting its head, and in a moment the animal's neck broke.

I let it drop. I meant to check the black mistress, who had so gallantly come to my rescue, but now other demons were present.

I dived for the fallen demon, reaching for the gun he had carried. But two demons jumped me. One grabbed my arm, wrestling the gun away, while the other held a capsule under my nose and popped it with his thumb and forefinger.

A thin vapor came out and spread in a little cloud. I tried to hold my breath, but distracted as I was by the fight I reacted too late. I had already taken a good sniff of it.

The stuff passed into my nose with an immediate exhilarating effect. I thought at first it was another sleep-gas— but it was not putting me down, it was pepping me up. Phenomenally! Suddenly I felt three times as strong as ever before. At the same time, the garden took on a lovely orange cast, and the foliage darkened toward black, as though the light had changed. As though I had donned orange sun-glasses.

Orange . . .

Then I realized. I had just had my first sniff of Kill-13.

CHAPTER 15

KALI

About twenty demons faced me, bearing assorted knives. A sight to haunt an ordinary person—but I was hardly ordinary. I was extraordinary. In fact, I was phenomenal. Invincible! Irresistible!

I elbowed the demon behind me, striking with incredible power. He caved in. I caught him with my left hand and hurled him into the one still hanging onto my right. I reached out and caught their two greasy mops of hair, one in each hand. Their heads came together like two eggs. In a moment I dropped the messy shells, letting the yolks spill out on the turf.

I stooped to the corpse with the knife in it—Ilunga's knife—and twitched out the beautifully red edge. Now I was armed, not that I needed it, and could kill rapidly. Fortunately there were plenty of subjects to practice on.

The two bits of cord from my hands and feet were weighting my pocket. I threw them away. Then I cast off the robe, too, as its slight encumbrance annoyed my superior perception and finely-tuned balance.

Like lambs to the slaughter they came. But already the demons were changing, as the glorious drug spread through my system. They were not men, they were sub-men, goblins. Dwarfs with runty torsos and swelled beads. Trolls. Fit to be trampled, skewered, and tossed carelessly aside.

While I—I was magnificent. Godlike. I felt no pain, no doubt. I knew myself to be the ultimate.

The goblins were stupid. They actually tried to attack me. *Me!* The first came at me with a knife, a fat-edged sword-like Chinese blade. I had a fine eye for weaponry, the best eye. His weapon was better than mine, longer, cleaner, so I tossed mine aside and took his. I simply blocked his descending arm, caught the wrist, turned rapidly outward and broke it. The knife dropped obligingly into my waiting hand. My coordination was fantastic! I then delivered a knee to his atrophied testicles, turned, and slashed the belly of the next goblin. Beautiful! I could do this all day!

Actually, they weren't goblins anymore. They were animal-headed men. No matter. I jumped, cut, rolled on the ground, leaped up and down, huge long bounds, like those seen in martial arts motion pictures, except that mine were genuine, avoiding the many enemies that got in each other's way. All the time I slashed with my sword, and hit with my arms and legs, reveling in the feel of flesh parting and bones crunching.

I picked a poignard from a dead demon-animal, and used it artistically in my left hand. A wolf-head charged me, long jaw slavering; I skewered him. A panther-head came next, and I made a puncture in his low forehead with my poignard that emerged from the back of his head.

A buzzard-head sailed in, buttressed by a melee of snakes and toads, surrounding me. I jumped high, way over their heads, needing no trampoline; made a somersault in air, vaulted over the buzzard and defeathered him from the rear. I caved in the temple of a rhinoceros head with the ball on the poignard's pommel; his nose-horn plowed into the dirt.

But there were more and more of them, an inhuman sea. There appeared to be scratches on me, though I felt no pain. Even rats can overwhelm a man, if they attack in sufficient number with sufficient tenacity.

I analyzed the situation as I fought. My mind was sharp. I was able to think with marvelous logic. These might be vermin attacking me, but they were very swift, armed vermin. Sheer luck and mass would give them an advantage. It was not that I feared dying, but retreat was for the moment the intelligent course.

Except that there was nowhere to retreat. I was in the midst of the ant-hill, with biting ants on every side. I could not protect my flank. No matter how fiercely I beat back the ones in front, more were always at my rear, with their stingers.

Now they were fish, piranha, and I was a shark. Still they were nibbling at me from all sides. It was only a matter of time, and not much time. It was ironic that one so glorious should fall to a horde of such inferiors, but there seemed to be no escape.

Then something remarkable happened. The Goddess Kali came to my rescue! Shining black, her four arms bearing twin swords, she waded into the fray. One sword was a Japanese *katana,* the other a wavy Malayan *kriss.* Kali's eyes were a blazing scarlet, literally. Twin beams of red light projected from her eyes. Long tusks curved downward from her grotesque upper jaw. Foam drooled from her mouth where the tusks parted the lips. She had long, curved, black claws on hands and feet. Her naked torso carried quadruple breasts that swung pendulously from side to side as she fought. Goddess of death, indeed!

She sliced off the hands and arms of several monsters before they realized what was happening. Blue and green blood spurted where she struck, making little fountains. True to her legend, she drank of the blood she shed.

Now the enemy had to battle on two fronts. I reviewed my strategy accordingly, my awesome intelligence assessing the new situation instantly. I renewed my attack, bringing my sword-knife down on the head of the nearest creature. He had the visage of a baboon, with a blue snout and a painted posterior. His skull split asunder like a ripe watermelon. The delicate pink fruit and white seeds were laid open to view. I was tempted to taste of them my-self, but had no time. I grabbed his bamboo spear and spitted the next, a bird-head, my point emerging from his back. He was a skewered chicken. Glory! Gory! Glory!

Meanwhile Kali worked on the others. The demons should have been terrified at the sight of their goddess punishing them, but instead they foolishly fought. One struck at her with a hatchet; she severed his head, then caught the flying hatchet from the air and buried it in the forehead of another. Her progress was marked by severed objects sailing high—hands, noses, eyeballs, ears, tes-ticles.

There had been about twenty demons at the start of the battle. Now there were ten. These regrouped, four concentrating on me, six facing the black goddess. All were well-armed. I realized that though the odds had changed, the fight was not over. Excellent!

I did find it mildly annoying that I should be rated as the lesser antagonist. By rights *I* should have had the six, she the four. Well, one had to make concessions to the vanity of a goddess.

Somehow I slipped. There was iridescent blood all over the ground, making the footing treacherous, but I was disgusted at myself for the lapse. I was impregnable; how could I allow any-thing to interfere with my balance, my dignity? The four animals closed in, their great teeth grinding against each other in anticipa-tion. Maybe they thought that if they consumed my flesh, it would give them my grandeur. I rolled to avoid them, sending the blood up in a scintillating spray. The light passing through it made rain-bows. They could not score on me!

But that gave me an idea. I scooped my free hand through the pooled gore, and swept it up into their faces. Splash! Splash! They were blinded by hot blood! But soon it ran low. I would have to kill some more, to renew the supply. I grappled within the nearest corpse, ripping out intestines, hurling them into the snouts of my enemies. More fun!

Kali started throwing knives. Like lightning bolts they flew, clean and bright and deadly, striking demons on chests, arms, legs and heads. She was a veritable arsenal, her four arms moving in rapid rotation, one drawing while another hurled. Absolutely beautiful!

The demons fell, five, seven, eight. Hey, no fair—the goddess had taken out a couple of *mine!*

Somehow the last two put up more resistance. But at last I drew my blade across the femoral artery in the thigh of the last one, and watched the red fluid pump out while I held him down. As he drained, he died, and I was tired.

I looked about. Kali was gone. Only her statue remained in the garden, blood-spattered but triumphant. She had earned her rest. All about us both were slain demons, their wounds gruesome in the bright sunlight. The corpse I had disemboweled was hardly recognizable as human. The green foliage of the garden was quiet.

I was fatigued. I tried to stand, and could hardly make it. What had happened to my omnipotence?

Suddenly I knew: the fit had worn off. I had been given one good sniff of Kill-13 and immediately proceeded to strenuous activity. This had burned off the fit far more rapidly than usual, and now I was entering the throes of withdrawal. I had minor wounds all over my body; I had lost blood. I had expended resources beyond any normal limit.

My power of the fit would now be replaced by an equivalent weakness, as high went to low. I had tapped reserves that should have been sacrosanct. All I wanted to do now was collapse and sleep.

I heard something. Dully I looked up—and saw Kan-Sen. He was holding Chiyako, still in her straitjacket and with her feet closely hobbled. She was helpless. The bit was back in her mouth, the straps tied behind to her bound hands, pulling her head back cruelly to expose her neck. She looked disheveled and miserable.

"What a demon you have made!" Kan-Sen said. "I would never have believed it, but I see that alone you have slain my entire complement. I am so glad you have joined us!"

"You may have dosed me, but I'm not with you," I said tiredly.

"And I didn't overcome your minions alone. Kali helped me."

His eyes flicked to the statue. *"Kali* helped you? My friend, you suffered royal visions indeed. That sometimes happens during the first fit."

Perhaps he was right. It was ridiculous to think that a statue could have come to life, and the living Kali had vanished as my fit expired. Still, how could I have killed all twenty demons, alone? Some were beheaded, others dismembered or disemboweled.

"Well, I'm over the fit now," I said.

"You can never be truly over it," he said. "One dose is addictive."

"Or so you would like me to believe," I said.

"Your true nature comes out, and yours is violent, my friend. See how you have killed! You are a demon at heart, a killer; you revel in bloodshed."

I lacked the strength to argue with him. I certainly didn't revel in that gore now.

"Join me, and you will have all the drug you crave. My store-room is full. You *do* crave it, don't you?"

I craved it. "Go to hell," I said. He would not be talking with me like this if he really believed I was addicted.

"I cannot take time to reason with you, unfortunately," he said. "I have contacts to make, supplies to deliver—and you have depleted my immediately available personnel. Join me, or this girl dies!" He drew forth a knife and brought it to Chiyako's throat. Bound as she was, she could not resist him.

So it had come at last to the naked choice, all finesse aside. Her life for my cooperation. He had lied about the one-shot addiction, and about the fatality of an involuntary dose, but sure as hell I would succumb if I yielded now.

I knew he would do it. I had to give in.

"Never!" Chiyako cried around the bit, trying to hobble away from him. "We both shall die first!" Or attempted words to that effect.

My mouth was open, for I had been about to agree reluctantly to Kan-Sen's terms. But when Chiyako spoke, my hand went automatically to my knife. I had to protect her!

I had no knife. I had dropped it somewhere in my tiredness as the last demon died. In any event, I was too weak to attack, while Kan-Sen remained fresh. I had no hope of defeating him in combat—unless I took another sniff of Kill-13. Which was the same as joining him. So I had lost, and knew it.

But he mistook my move. "No one defies me twice!" he cried. Slowly he brought Chiyako to him, and slowly he forced the blade toward her throat.

"No!" I cried, lurching up. I meant "No—don't kill her; I will join you!" But again he misunderstood.

"Then she dies." And carefully he slit her throat.

In shock I stood there, watching the blood of my love pour out, staining the strait jacket, coursing down her dress to the ground. Her head turned, her eyes caught mine for a fleeting instant—an instant of unutterable love and pain—and then she fell.

My horror turned to rage. Adrenalin poured into my system, reviving it. Had he spared Chiyako, I would have had no power to resist him, though he slew me, but now some deeply buried reservoir was tapped. Suddenly I had the hysterical strength to do what had to be done.

I charged Kan-Sen. But he was ready for me, the bloody knife flipping back over his shoulder, then downward, through the air in an expert throw. It struck me in the shoulder, penetrating deeply.

But I was not to be stopped. I plucked it out with one hand and moved in to stab him with it.

He was high on Kill-13; his reflexes were faster than mine. His hand shot out and clubbed mine, sending the knife flying away.

I bulled into him like a punch-drunk boxer, but he was already diving for the knife. We fell together, on top of Chiyako's warm body. My eye met her eye again, inches away, but hers was blind. In that moment of my distraction, Kan-Sen came up with the knife. He stood, hauling me up with him.

I grabbed his wrist to stop his thrust, while with my other

hand I tried to hit or strangle him. But my shoulder wound got in the way; my arm simply would not respond properly. He bore me back, bringing the knife down.

My feet were blocked by Chiyako's body. I stepped over her, feeling her blood on my bare feet. I dug my toes into the earth, bracing against Kan-Sen.

We hovered there above her, weaving back and forth, but the advantage was his. I had to step back, and back again, while that wicked blade inched closer. He stepped over the body, his heel almost striking her nose.

Then his foot landed in the pool of blood that had gushed from Chiyako's throat. It coated the flat leather sole, and he slipped. His arm came down in an automatic effort to regain balance. I augmented that motion with a shove, and as we fell, once more over Chiyako, his knife was caught between us, the blade pointed inward.

My weight landed on him, shoving the knife down. I could not see the action, but he gave a sharp cry and went limp.

So Kan-Sen expired, victim of his own knife, and the blood of the girl he had murdered. Now his blood mingled with hers.

I kneeled beside Chiyako, hoping for a miracle, but she was long beyond recovery. Numbly fighting off the returning fatigue, I set about the rest of my task. I took matches from Kan-Sen's pocket and set fire to the dry leaves on the ground under the small forest. But they failed to burn well.

I staggered through the empty complex until I found a work area, and gasoline. I spread it methodically as far as it would go, over floor and wall. I lit it and moved back into the garden.

My love would have a fitting pyre. I trusted the fumes from the incinerated Kill-13 would be diffuse enough not to cause undue commotion in the city. It was still night; I discovered that in the course of my search for inflammables. Kan-Sen had simply changed night into day by turning on the artificial sun in the garden. So maybe few citizens would be exposed before it dissipated into the other smog.

How would I live without Chiyako?

No way. The mission for which the Shaolin monks had set me up, sacrificing themselves in the process, had been accomplished, with the help of this last kung-fu loss. Chiyako had been sent to me to see that I did my job, not to make me happy. Let it be sealed over again, until time made the truth tolerable.

Meanwhile, I would remain here. It was possible that my extraordinary activity had burned out the initial sniff of Kill-13 so completely that I could survive withdrawal. Perhaps my *ki* would help me too. Kan-Sen had obviously feared I was not fully hooked. An involuntary sniff followed by severe exertion, and the drug's weakness was exposed.

So I could probably throw it off. But to what point? I had destroyed Kill-13, but the drug had destroyed me too. My remaining strength was exhausted, my last reserves were gone, my love was dead.

I sank down between the twin fires I had set, waiting for the end. As the awful heat and light closed in, consuming the heart of the demon empire, I pondered. I was at peace, but my thoughts continued. ·

Everything had fallen into place except one thing: the animation of the goddess Kali.

It could have been part of my vision, as Kan-Sen had claimed. But I had not, even in my vision, slain twenty demons. Their bodies on the turf were wrong, for one thing; the pattern of the carnage suggested two fronts, not one.

But neither could a metal statue have come to life—and if it had, it would not have fought on my side. Kali was goddess of the demons, not the straights.

There was only one explanation. Ilunga had entered the fray, and I had seen her as the black goddess. I had left her unconscious, after the leopard fight. Obviously she had revived, for the body was no longer there.

Yet why had she helped me, against her own kind? And why had she vanished the moment the job was done? She hated me, she said. I was out to destroy the demon cult, and she was an addict. She would probably die in the agonies of an impossible withdrawal.

So Kan-Sen must have been right. Ilunga had a thing for me, however she might deny it. After being labeled as a traitor she had no certain future with the demons. So she had helped me.

Could she have had the foresight to raid the Kill-13 supplies while I was facing Kan-Sen? In that case she was gone-—and I could not begrudge her that escape. Obviously she was not about to go on a demon-conversion binge that would only exhaust her own supply of the drug.

So it was neatly ended. I sat by Chiyako, holding her head in my lap and her hand in my hand. I was bleeding from a hundred cuts, but it didn't matter. I felt the cleansing heat of the encircling fire. Perhaps this way was best. If Chiyako had killed me before, they would have tortured her to death, then executed Ilunga and rebuilt the Kill-13 factory in the Honduras or elsewhere. This way the job was really done, for the leadership and knowledge were gone.

A shape came toward me. It hauled me away from my dead love, away from the fires, and I was too weak to resist.

"No, Kali!" I gasped. "I am not one of your demons."

"White master, you're going to *live!*" Ilunga said as she heaved me up over her shoulder with demon strength. Her tone indicated that the words she meant were "Honky bastard"; strange that she should not say them directly.

And so the black mistress had the most exquisite vengeance of all. She saved my life.

Printed in the United States
6918